MW00462109

CRAIG KEFFELER

ASESINA

Black Rose Writing | Texas

©2020 by Craig Keffeler
All rights reserved. No part of this book may be reproduced, stored in a
retrieval system or transmitted in any form or by any means without the
prior written permission of the publishers, except by a reviewer who may
quote brief passages in a review to be printed in a newspaper, magazine or
journal.

The author grants the final approval for this literary material.

First printing

This is a work of fiction. Names, characters, businesses, places, events, and
incidents are either the products of the author's imagination or used in a
fictitious manner. Any resemblance to actual persons, living or dead, or
actual events is purely coincidental.

ISBN: 978-1-68433-484-1
PUBLISHED BY BLACK ROSE WRITING
www.blackrosewriting.com

Printed in the United States of America
Suggested Retail Price (SRP) $19.95

Asesina is printed in Garamond

*As a planet-friendly publisher, Black Rose Writing does its best to eliminate
unnecessary waste to reduce paper usage and energy costs, while never compromising
the reading experience. As a result, the final word count vs. page count may not meet
common expectations.

For Joy-bug

Asesina (a-seh-**see**-nah): female assassin

ASESINA

PART ONE

CHAPTER ONE

Staring at the empty doublewide trailer, a rather sweet-looking Mickey Gilley with a wraparound deck and a wicked Aztec-themed racing stripe, Angel reached into the waistband of her oversized coveralls, pulled out a .40-caliber handgun and eased back the slide.

The gun, a Glock 23, weighed exactly thirty-one ounces, had a beavertail backstrap grip, a thirteen-round mag, and felt comfortable in her hand. Not too light, not too heavy. Clutching it a bit tighter, she lifted her head above a stack of laminated doors and shielded her eyes from the late afternoon sun, which had started its slow descent across the Franklin Mountains.

For the better part of an hour she had been crisscrossing one abandoned housing site after another using the half-light of dusk to navigate her way through Ciudad Juárez's latest country club development. Luckily this stretch of *la frontera* near the Panamericana Highway was a popular dumping ground for everything from doorless Frigidaires to busted stereo speakers, so nobody thought twice about the stolen Chevy Monza she'd deep-sixed a few kilometers back.

Thirty meters in front of her a two-way radio crackled, a sharp buzz followed by a sustained trill. It was the second callback in the last five minutes.

"Pick it up, fellas," she murmured. "We don't need visitors."

But neither of the two bull-necked security guards bothered to move. The oldest seemed perfectly content propping his feet up on the neoprene covered steering wheel of a customized silver and black Yamaha Adventurer golf cart, his bored partner lounging beside him bouncing a lime green range ball off the dashboard like a petulant child.

Both men were huge, their strength discernible in their overdeveloped pectorals and in the stubby formation of their massive thighs and calves. What was missing was any sense of professionalism. Having parked their tricked-out Yamaha under an imported Cypress tree, a pair of vintage Mendoza HM-3 submachine guns tossed in the back like a couple of unused toys, neither seemed interested in securing tonight's perimeter.

Which was all Angel needed to see.

Ducking behind the doors, she chambered a nickel-plated hollow point and zipped the Glock into her leg pocket. The radio squawked again, this time the buzz lasting a few seconds longer.

Swearing loudly, the older guard snatched it from the cup holder, hollering, "God damn pinche cabrónes! Call in, call in, call in . . . why the fuck can't they just leave us alone?"

"Not happenin', Vato," said the younger one, still mindlessly bouncing the range ball off the dash. "It's AMLO's new *federales*. They're in charge of tonight's protection. Got a big VIP coming in."

"Really, who?—that bastard Corral?"

"No, I saw the governor on Tu Canal. He's at a polo match in Monterrey."

"Trump? Is it fuckin' Trump? Please tell me it's Trump." The older one was animated now, sitting up straight in his vinyl seat. "Maybe he's coming over to finally make us pay for the wall?"

"Yeah, and maybe he's bringing Ivanka with him? The two of you could hook up and make a *looove* child." The younger guard made a lewd pumping action with his hips and both men howled like coyotes, bumping fists.

Still huddled behind the doors, Angel let out a breath of disgust, reached into the right rear pocket of her coveralls, removed a pair of powder-free nitrile exam gloves, and flexed all ten fingers into the black latex. They fit snugly. Next, she buttoned the coveralls up to her chin, adjusted her rubber shoe covers, then cautiously slipped under a tangle of rebar and hustled north behind a row of cholla. Having mapped the area from memory, she knew that nothing had changed since her previous reconnaissance. Fifty-one partially finished villas spread across six hectares of virgin desert, every structure covered in a patina of grit. Near the skeletal clubhouse, a drainage culvert emptied into a sandy arroyo running just inside a slat metal fence topped with concertina wire. This was her backup route, her ace in the hole so to speak.

Hopefully it wouldn't come to that.

Easing behind a beige pony wall, she marked the time on her gold Rolex wristwatch: 5:20. She had exactly forty minutes to breach the perimeter, more than enough. Relaxing her head and shoulders, she placed two fingers in the hollow between her windpipe and the large muscle and felt for a pulse. Fifty-six beats per minute.

"Too fast," she hissed, "way too fast." Her heart was pounding so hard she could feel it against her ribs. "Get your shit together, girl."

Months of work had gone into making tonight's hit possible. The *jefe* who'd authorized the contract was a cartel comandante who had poured thousands of dollars into bribing, among others, the Chihuahua State Police, the Army's Region XI Headquarters in Torreón, and the Ministerial Federal Police. So this job had to come off perfectly. That much had been made crystal clear to her.

Discreetly, she lifted her head above the wall.

For a second time the sun caught her squarely in the eyes, forcing her to blink. Straight ahead a row of lemon colored foreclosure signs stretched in a tight S-curve along the tract's only paved road, ankle-high knotweeds budding in the asphalt cracks. Halfway up the road, a lane of hard-packed gravel curled into a graded laydown area dead-ending near a VIP viewing deck. The blistered deck overlooked an apron of screwbean mesquite, several large ant hills sprouting beneath their splayed canopies. The guards had parked their cart to the left of the laydown area, maintaining a perfect sight line to the trailer.

Centering her weight on the balls of her feet, Angel scanned the tract without moving her head. On the opposite side of the trailer another dry creek bed circumvented the south end of the subdivision, meandering past a flatbed truck mounted on cinder blocks, its engine missing. Next to the flatbed, a barn-sized Silverado pickup and an off-white EcoSport SUV had been padlocked inside a foursquare chain-link fence. Sliding back down the wall, she settled onto her haunches, her sacrum giving its usual twitch. Feeling edgy, she unzipped the right front pocket of her coveralls and removed a small wad of pink Kleenex, holding it gingerly in her left hand.

It felt light, delicate, like a gift.

Carefully, she peeled back the layers one by one and a tiny capsule tumbled into her palm. It was a pheenie, Phenobarbital, a little something to take the edge off. For as long as she could remember, barbs and meth had been her weakness, her kryptonite. It had been that way ever since East Mesa Juvy in San Diego.

Something rustled in the branches above her head. Angel froze. An Inca Dove broke across the tree line, barely skimming the branches. She nervously fingered the outline of the Glock, timing her breaths, tuning out the wind. But there was only silence. No voices, no radio callbacks, only thousands of sparkling dust motes floating across the scrub, coloring the sky a speckled pink.

Beneath a pencil-thin Candelilla, a black-tailed jackrabbit nestled in a clump of horehound, its long ears pinned back, its sunken eyes trying to figure out what this interloper was up to. To the hare's right, a loose dirt trail flanked by barrel cactus and choked with creosote inched its way past newly-dug bedrock. Stretching her neck, Angel sniffed the air. It smelled fresh and organic and earthy like sage. A grateful smile etched its way across her lips, her mind churning through memories, the flashbacks converging from all directions. They were stark and eternal visions; a fusion of vast openness and mournful beauty that didn't fit neatly into a social media post. But it was another time, another place, so she buried them, and with a slight motion broke the capsule in two, snorting heavily.

What seemed like a few seconds was actually over two minutes.

She was still leaning against the half-wall, eyes wide, staring at the sky. A mass of cottony clouds strayed across the horizon, the opaque sun running a blurred line along the sierra. Lightheaded, she lifted herself onto her toes and listened to the passing chirp of a round-tailed squirrel, savored the sweet scent of Daisy Fleabanes wafting over the horehound like perfume.

Any moment now.

Her breathing grew faster, dappled light warming her face.

Any frickin' moment—

Tucking her calves beneath her thighs, she settled into a Vajrasana pose, her eyes resting on a knot of stringy Ocotillos that stretched high into the cobalt blue sky like giant sentinels, the soft luster of the setting sun washing over their bright red flowers. Seconds pooled, forming a minute. Her head lolled backwards and she raked in another deep breath. Suddenly everything grew quiet, the wind silent. Relaxing her chest and shoulders, exhaling deep from the diaphragm, she gained her center, muttering, *"Dios bendiga,"* God Bless.

A soothing rush of phenos flushed through her veins like a whisper of cool air.

Having seen enough, the jackrabbit rocketed into a patch of brittlebush, vanishing like an illusion. A covey of blue quail scurried across a rocky outcrop. Angel's eyes widened, drawn to the birds' surefooted grace. "Okay," she sighed, pushing herself onto her hands and toes. "Let's do this."

Duck-footing along the pony wall, she paused at a stone planter filled with rocky dirt and the dried remains of dead petunias and risked another glimpse over the wall.

Both guards were snoring, mouths agape, heads sagging to one side. No surprise there. Even though she could barely see them, she knew the type: lazy, poorly trained, too much time on their hands, not enough supervision, like 'roided-up latchkey kids. She, on the other hand, was an entirely different animal. Nicknamed the *Libero*, a fútbol term for sweeper, because she was good at taking out the trash, Angel was a hitter, an *asesina*, a professional killer.

Sneaking one final glance over the stucco, an icy clearness in her eyes, she dropped to all fours, pressed both hands flat to the ground, toes firmly under her, and began propelling herself in one long fluid motion. First the hands then the right leg followed by the left, moving with the smooth angular cant of a cat. The pony wall was over fifty meters long, but her progress was whispery, hushed, like cutting a hole in the wind.

Within a minute she had cleared her first marker, a rotund carrot colored cement mixer called a Giant Bomb, and was picking her way through rows of tacky cement nymphs, their mortared bases chiseled from their foundations when the workers tried to salvage something for scrap. On her left, a cluster of broomlike cholla concealed her slender frame from long-range surveillance. To her right, the beige stucco wall shielded her from the guards. A few more meters and she stopped, kneeling beside a bosomy mermaid, listening for voices.

Both guards were awake now, bitching loudly about the Bravos de Juárez, the local fútbol club that couldn't buy a win lately. From the older one came a deep, resonant belch that was audible for over thirty meters. "*Muchas gracias*," Angel uttered, little more than a murmur. She now had their exact location and could narrow her approach.

Angling away from the wall, she dropped down into a branching track that veered wide of the trailer, skirting a dried-out wooden fence topped with twists of barbed wire. Counting her steps, she cleared a slight rise and followed the rutted track to the mouth of a drainage ditch, pausing as the voices grew louder, the meatfaced older guard complaining loudly about his wife who wouldn't quit bitching about his mota smoking.

"Dump her fat ass," was the vacuous response from his fuckwit partner, who had gone back to lobbing the range ball against the dash, its constant thumping like a metronome inside Angel's head.

She slipped under a snag of bailing wire, scrambled into a cut ditch, and trailed it until it opened onto the arroyo. Taking quick inventory—there was a litter of coyotes sheltering under a half-shrub of cat's claw—she circled wide of the spiky acacia and accelerated down a gentle slope into a sandy creek bed, her progress cut off by a woven field fence. Someone had hung a huge sign on top of a corroded steel post: NO PASAR! No Trespassing. Checking for motion sensors, Angel squeezed between a gap in the fence and hunkered down near the rear of the gatehouse to test the outer gate.

It didn't budge. Inching forward, she lifted the gate's swing latch and with a slight ferrous scuff wiggled the door handle, trying to shake the metal paw off its catch.

Four days earlier, before the protection details had cleared the perimeter, she had snuck in and unscrewed the locking assembly, filing down both ends of the U-bolt. The trick was to keep the latch intact with the paw loose enough so it would slip off with the proper jiggle. After several tries it worked and she ghosted past the unmanned guard station, stopping just short of the interior gate, a Venetian-style monstrosity so beloved by Ciudad Juárez's one-percenters.

Normally the gate would have been powered by a 48-volt lithium battery, but the automatic opening system had been disconnected, replaced by a six-meter drop bar with a heavy-duty shackle lock. Angel removed a deep-cut steel pick from her coveralls, popped the lock, and wormed her way through the wrought iron bars, her rubber-covered feet barely touching the silica-like sand used for heavy construction. She cleared the gate, sidestepping a pile of empty paint cans, and nearly missed her second marker, a newly laid flagstone path hidden behind a slender yucca.

Imported from Tucson, the buckskin colored stones curled north through a weed-strewn rock garden, bending a few degrees uphill towards a wood-framed gazebo. Near the opening of the gazebo a cement power trowel had been tipped on its side, a clump of pigweed stems wedged between its float blades. Scrambling next to the trowel, Angel knelt beside it and checked her pulse.

Forty-nine beats per minute. *Better.*

Back on her fingers and feet, she traced the flagstones up a slight rise to a gravel parking lot shaped like an Aztec sun shield. For some unknown reason someone had painted a cheesy sundial in the middle of the lot, making it look like some trippy landing pad. At the top of the rise she slipped between the collapsible bollards and headed straight down a footpath towards a shag-headed palm planted at the base of the trailer's all-aluminum stairway.

This was the sales office and the gateway to your dreams.

The trailer's new owner, a dodgy bank out of Ascensión, had acquired the club's remaining undeveloped lots in a rigged foreclosure sale, promising to jump-start the cash-strapped project with fresh funds. But like all corporate promises, it had the half-life of a mouse fart because Angel was staring at a state-of-the-art dome security camera hanging lifelessly from its oxidized mounts, ventilated by several wayward .22 rounds.

God bless the imbéciles, she mused. *They make life so much easier.*

But at this point she had a decision to make. Either loop wide of the trailer and avoid the *idiotas* altogether or head straight for the swamp cooler where she'd hidden her stash. Through the palm fronds she could see the two overgrown baboons tossing back shots of mezcal.

Right . . . the swamp cooler it is.

That would be a mistake.

Keeping low, she traced a one-lane cart path around the back of the trailer until it emerged at the fringe of a desiccated putting green. She checked for alarms as she counted out thirty steps, searching for a narrow cut that diverted southeast then tacked back towards the swamp cooler. Sparing only a fleeting glance—the older guard was swearing about his kids—she spotted a clearing three meters to the left and scrambled down the cut. Twenty meters from the trailer her eyes strayed to a scarred tract of desert chewed up by bulldozers. Everything suddenly felt weak, an icy chill trickling down her spine. An intense fury began to well up inside her, and for a split second her eyes stayed glued to the desecrated desert, a bitter hatred striking a pick through her heart. As she scuffled past a heap of two-by-fours, her attention still fused to a pile of uprooted rainbow cacti, her right heel brushed against a flat, rubberized pressure pad buried in a patch of Mexican Hat.

She stopped dead in her tracks.

The pad clicked twice, arming itself.

Later, the events of the next few seconds would pass through her mind with the clarity of a slow motion video, but right now all she could do was pray.

The pad clicked again.

And I thought God was a Chicana . . .

The wireless alarm went off like a school bell inside her head. Seconds later a shot whizzed past her ear. Another pounded the sand next to her, sending up a spray of silica.

"That was quick," she breathed, standing motionless.

Then her reflexes kicked in. Moving like a gazelle, she leapt over a busted header and propelled herself up the cut and past the shag-headed palm, her arms and legs pumping rhythmically. As she sprinted across the parking lot, to anyone watching she was a shadow. Human or animal? Near the flagstone path another round clipped the gazebo behind her, sending her bailing out of the rock garden, diving headfirst under a sprawling Whitethorn Acacia, pain pinching at the back of her neck, lungs punishing her.

She cursed herself: *a hardware store sensor . . . a cheap hardware store sensor!*

Head up, she crept forward, flattening her body under the Acacia's lace-like leaves.

Near the VIP viewing deck the guards' angry voices heightened. They had abandoned their cart and were circling the trailer. Angel couldn't see them, but their swearing carried well enough as they cussed and yelled at the spiny cactus and low scrub tearing at their legs and arms.

Her eyes swept the grounds, homing in on the drainage culvert. It would be dicey, but if she could keep the trailer between her and the guards, it might work.

She raised herself onto her toes. *Go!*

Crashing through the undergrowth, she careened towards the back gate, tracers stitching the branches above her head. She was barely through the wrought iron bars, skidding along the arroyo, her body hugging the lip of the bank, when she spotted the opening to the culvert and bolted inside.

Slugs ripped over the top of the arroyo as she frog-marched down the metal tube and popped out on the opposite end. *Which way now?* From a distance, flashlights pinwheeled across the brush, rounds smacking the culvert behind her, the guards shooting at motion. She felt a glimmer of irritation. Choking back her anger, she forced herself to concentrate. A bullet sent up a wisp of dust beside her. Unzipping her leg pocket, she felt for the Glock. The grip slid smoothly into her palm. Shifting her weight, readying herself, she brought the pistol up when the shooting abruptly stopped.

The guards had paused to reload. Probably to refortify with mezcal, too, she figured.

An idea suddenly flickered through her mind.

She crawled forward under a coil of barbed wire, then snaked her way through the chaparral. She was furrowing under a huge Soaptree yucca when the shooting started up again, this time both men using submachine guns. Angel heaved herself onto her forearms, stretching her torso lengthwise beneath the yucca's spiky green leaves. She lifted the Glock and rested her right index finger on the trigger guard, relaxed but ready. Then the rounds started echoing from a different direction.

Where the hell are they?

Angel swallowed a breath, her heart pounding so hard she could feel it in her temples. Voices drifted over the pony wall, low at first, then louder. She propped herself onto her elbows and sighted down the adjustable Trijicon. The two guards had spread out, circling the trailer, widening their angle as they approached the front gate. They weren't drunk, but getting there; the younger one periodically sprayed the brush with his HM-3 while his partner stumbled through the cacti, swearing bitterly. Angel could take them both out, but that would only bring more *federales*, and right now it was a simple alarm breach.

Another round thudded in the thicket behind her. Flashes from the Yamaha's headlamps spiraled over her head. The cart was outfitted with off-road hog lights, range about sixty meters. Catching a glimpse of the younger guard tromping towards the main gate, pouring clip after clip into the chamiza outside the wall, she realized she couldn't approach from the front of the trailer. She had hoped they'd slough it off as a nuisance, a thief—neither of these two muscleheads had the energy to chase down every trespasser who tripped the *federales'* bullshit alarms—but so far they had responded appropriately.

Be patient, she reminded herself. *Keep it together.*

A dim ray of light slithered through the sagging palm fronds fluttering above the front door of the sales office. Just below the vinyl screen door sat a beige 380-volt Xikoo swamp cooler. A few meters to the left of the cooler was a busted section of plywood skirting. During her recon four days earlier, Angel had pried loose several planks from the trailer's cross-hatched panel and stashed a gray Louis

Vuitton messenger bag between leftover batts of fiberglass insulation. The Vuitton contained a prop she needed for tonight's job, one that couldn't be hiked through the desert.

A spray of bullets shattered her reverie. *Good, they're getting pissed.*

The guards had parked the Yamaha next to the rock garden, and from the shadows the hog lights gave them a wide view to the front of the trailer. Angel stirred: *Time to get around these pendejos.* Grabbing a handful of pebbles, she cupped them in her right hand and tossed the stones towards the rear of the Mickey Gilley. When the guards pivoted, she broke from behind the yucca and cleared the half-wall, darting to the opposite side of the trailer and scrambling behind a pallet of cracked Saltillo tiles.

The older guard mounted the rickety aluminum stairs, shining a four-cell Maglite into the trailer's Agave Room. It was empty. Grumbling like a crotchety bear, he marched back down the stairs and plopped into the seat next to his partner. They argued for a few minutes before deciding to let it go. Nobody wanted to deal with the *policía*, not tonight, especially with the *federales* running the show. The younger guard released the foot brake and steered the cart over the flagstone path, cutting across the putting green before pulling up next to the blaring alarm. Like an angry primate, he leapt out of the Yamaha and waddled over to the alarm. Lifting his left boot, he nudged the noisy pad with the steel-toed tip.

The alarm wouldn't stop blaring. Having heard enough, he raised his boot and smashed the pad with his heel. The early evening went quiet. For the first time in what seemed like an eternity, Angel could feel herself breathe.

The younger guard tromped back to the cart, jumped behind the steering wheel, and pushed the Yamaha into a lazy U-turn, heading northeast towards another empty subdivision. As the cart accelerated, Angel saw the cratered-faced older guard turn in his seat, holding a submachine gun in his right hand. He calmly flipped the HM-3 to "bush rake."

Angel's eyes widened. *Oh shit—*

But before she could finish, she'd dropped face-first into the caked dirt, landing hard as bullets splintered the yucca above her head. The older guard swept the prickly scrub in one long motion, howling at the top of his lungs. *"Manos arriba!* Hands up!"

Every nerve in Angel's body was on fire. Swallowing back the urge to vomit, she raised the Glock, index finger tapping lightly on the trigger guard, and sighted down the front post and rear ring.

Where did they go?

Then she heard a deep belly roar of laughter from behind the Mickey Gilley as the tricked-out Yamaha made a wide figure eight and spun off in a cloud of dust, the older guard still firing wildly into the brush. Out of the corner of her eye, she saw a terrified coyote hightail it into the drainage culvert and disappear. "*Gracias a Dios,*" she whispered, Thank God.

Apparently, they'd found their intruder.

CHAPTER TWO

Neurosurgeon Ernest L. Girard was ignoring the texts from his physician assistant. There were ten minutes left on his break and he wasn't about to waste them on some hyped-up, adrenaline-junkie ER doc who couldn't handle a simple vertebrae compression. Besides, Dr. Ernie, as he was affectionately known at the Crystal Horseshoe, had more pressing things on his mind.

Or should we say his lap.

Stoked on an eight ball of ketamine and wallowing in that euphoric rush of invincibility that comes from being one of the top spine surgeons in Beverly Hills, Girard was busy stuffing C-notes into the candy colored g-string of Moniqué, a topless bubble dancer who was piston-grinding her shapely ass into his crotch. The only thing screwing up this god-like glow was the smartphone. It wouldn't stop chirping. That's because Girard was on trauma call at Santa Monica Memorial Hospital to the tune of five grand a day plus billings—the going rate for high-end neurosurgeons—and, not wanting to be bothered by these incessant texts, had triaged his phone answering duties to the practice's PA.

Needless to say, that wasn't working out too well.

Now having to vet their neurotrauma calls through a non-physician, Memorial's top-notch ER team was understandably furious. But Girard's group was the legendary Hurston Neurological Institute, and having generated over $130 million in hospital revenue last year, nobody from administration would be calling to chastise him any time soon. And that's how Dr. Ernie's thirty minutes of T&A should've ended, if it hadn't been for some hellacious bad luck.

But unfortunately the exact instant the wondrous Moniqué finished her lap dance and sashayed back to the Horseshoe's mirrored Lucite stage, Girard's beleaguered PA responded to an all-hands-on-deck Code Black, courtesy of a two-car T-boning at Wilshire and Lincoln.

Also at that exact same moment, one of Girard's post-operative patients, Roberto Martinez, presented at Hurston's Bel Air office with complications from a sacral laminectomy that Girard had botched three weeks earlier when he was stoned. Normally this type of screw-up would've been handled by the group's PA, but he was nowhere to be found since he was knee-deep in head trauma and spinal cord injuries. So while the well endowed Moniqué bent temptingly at the waist, a mind-rattling techno-punk pulsating from the club's new Eminence sound system, Dr. Ernie's hard-pressed PA fired off one final SOS.

Like all the others it would go unanswered.

Livid that his on-call neurosurgeon wouldn't respond, Memorial's emergency chief had to reroute his intracranial bleed patient to the county trauma unit, transfer a lumbar spine fracture to another hospital, and immobilize a Grade 4 whiplash until a more reliable "back guy" could be found. Nobody would see Roberto Martinez, who left irate after waiting for over three hours in Hurston's mostly empty office and had to hunt down an out-of-network neurosurgeon, who took one look at his leaking shunt and immediately scheduled corrective surgery. He also suggested Martinez hire a malpractice lawyer.

As for Dr. Ernie, with the noisy Horseshoe crowd ratcheting up its feverish appreciation, the winsome Moniqué turned one last time towards her favorite patron and seductively extended her long right leg, slowly rotating a four-inch, diamond-studded stiletto heel. When Girard gave her the thumbs up, she brought the heel down hard on a fuchsia prop ball, bursting it like a party balloon.

Little did Dr. Ernie know, it was the sound of his life collapsing.

CHAPTER THREE

Angel was still flat on her face, Glock out, hoping the guards didn't decide to return.

Satisfied they were gone, she pulled herself up, searched the grounds, then hustled over to the busted panel in the center of the Mickey Gilley's plywood skirt. She shoved her right arm through a gap in the broken planks and fished around for several seconds.

A smooth leather strap slid easily between her fingers, and she gave it a slight tug.

Out came a charcoal-colored Louis Vuitton Marius messenger bag.

She quickly inspected its zippers, making sure nothing had been disturbed, then hitched the bag over her left shoulder and backtracked down the flagstone path.

The early evening wind had calmed, the temperature falling a few degrees. With no sign of the guards, she hopped over the pony wall and headed southeast, following a gravel service road that connected the empty subdivisions. She figured she had about fifteen minutes to reach the golf course. Working from memory, she dropped down into a dry arroyo and cut through a patch of brittlebush, pausing as a migrating yellowthroat broke from a nearby cholla, its tiny wings soaring above the bright red flowers blooming from the tips of the Ocotillo.

"A good omen," she murmured, lengthening her stride, the soft buzz of hummingbirds floating alongside her. She had cleared an outcrop of sandy boulders and clambered up a slight ridge, drinking in the sights and sounds of the scrub, when her nose caught the sour stench of jet fuel. Veering left, she traced a thin footpath atop a swell in the desert and halted near the crest.

Beyond the ridge the terrain flattened, exposing a long grid of L-shaped stakes planted at an angle to reflect the sun. The shiny metal stakes had been aligned to mark which tracts of desert were to be bulldozed into Spanish-style subdivisions and an eighteen-hole golf course. Phase One of the *Club de Campo Nueva Aurora*, the New Dawn Country Club, had been built with a heavy influx of laundered drug money, but the current recession had claimed the second and third phases, leaving the back side a bit underdeveloped.

That would be her way in.

Opening her stride, she skirted a large red ant hill and was about to hurdle an agave plant when her peripheral vision caught something flickering in a clump of Giant Sacaton. Swerving off the path, she scrambled next to a white sweet sage, its tiny hairs tickling her cheeks. Thirty meters south a handful of 200-liter drums had been dumped in a shallow pit, the word *Aviación* stenciled in black across their lids. This is interesting, she thought. Never one to let an opportunity go to waste, the Cártel del Noreste had repurposed the L-stakes into runway markers for its Cessna and Beechcraft turboprops hauling fentanyl out of Nicaragua. But it seemed their efforts had drawn the attention of the Mexican Army's Special Forces and its patrón, the U.S Drug Enforcement Administration.

Crouching lower, Angel spotted a set of tire grooves running past the agave plant. She traced an index finger along the thick indentations, recognizing the tread pattern, a modified SandCat armored vehicle. A few meters to her right, several more impressions had been etched in the sand. They looked fresh, probably left within the hour.

"*Hola, federales,*" she whispered, crossing an X through the grooves with a sage branch. "Let's see what you have in store for us tonight."

Steering wide of the L-stakes, she crisscrossed another dry creek bed and pushed her way through a stubborn thicket of Manzanita, carving up the distance. She located the tallest of the shrubs. It was among its pink upside-down, urn-shaped flowers that she spotted her third marker: a cairn of smooth river rocks piled high next to a well-used riding trail. Slightly east of the rocks lay a steel-pipe cattle guard, and behind it a row of green and orange anti-vehicle barriers dropped four days earlier. Hunkered beside one of the barriers, a pair of coal-black eyes as dark as a moonless night stared at her; the kangaroo rat sat upright on its haunches, gnawing impassively on a flour-colored mesquite bean, completely oblivious to the threat only a few centimeters from its hind legs. But Angel had seen it, even recognized the model: a top-of-the-line Coon Slayer III, a steel-jawed leghold trap. Her body stiffened, heartbeat firing up again. The trap was triggered by a pan tension device that released a five and three-eighths-inch steel jaw. She had seen firsthand what these legholds could do to livestock, much less smaller animals.

Her pulse was dialing in loud and clear now. She sucked in a deep breath, exhaling through her nostrils, raging in silence. A woman of few passions, she had a deep affinity for animals, especially those of her native Chihuahuan Desert. A fondness she didn't share for humans. She took several more cleansing breaths, trying to tamp down the bile, then padded forward a few meters, pulling a cotton handkerchief from her back pocket and wiping her face.

Remotely, she felt heartache; more immediately, fury. Rotating her left wrist, she checked her watch. There was time. Now whether it was smart or not was an entirely different matter.

"To hell with it," she whispered, glaring at the leghold, failing to douse her anger. She lifted her head and shoulders, her eyes scouring the scrub searching for something—anything—that was long and strong. But this close to Juárez the lowland desert had been stripped bare, leaving only empty hectares of dense sandpaper bush and blue Palo Verde. Squinting harder, she was about to give up when she caught a glimpse of something shining near a pinyon tree. *There*. Buried under a coil of barbed wire, nearly covered by tumbleweeds, was a scattering of steel fence posts.

Without thinking, she abandoned any semblance of training and flew down the trail, bounding through the Manzanita until it opened onto a pasture of tanglehead grass, crickets skittering in all directions.

Tearing through the underbrush, kicking aside tumbleweeds, Angel scrambled to the nearest windblown post and dropped to all fours. Suddenly, a thin shadow crossed overhead, followed by the steady thrum of copter blades. As it grew louder she frantically combed the area for cover, but she was too far out in the open. There was too much ground between the pasture and the creek bed. If someone was glassing on her, the helicopter could triangulate her position and that would be it.

Squatting lower, she unzipped her thigh pocket and pulled out the Glock. The direction of the wind shifted. A cool breeze touched the back of her neck. Any second now, she thought, willing herself to be calm. The helicopter rotors lifted, throbbing in deep, pulsating bass. She tapped her finger on the trigger guard, throat dry, eyes hunting. After a few heartbeats the thudding began to dissipate. The copter turned northwest, arcing high and wide over the desert floor, dropping behind a ridge, too far away to spot her. After what seemed like an eternity it circled back towards the river, then disappeared. Angel stayed motionless, letting a few minutes pass, listening, waiting.

The desert was silent. All she could hear was the soft flutter of wind shimmying the tanglehead. She zipped the Glock back into her pocket, scuttled forward a few meters, and gripped the steel T-post. With a loud grunt, she jerked it free from a snarl of barbed wire.

The kangaroo rat watched indifferently as she retraced her steps, holding the post in her right hand, nimbly avoiding a patch of prickly pear cactus. She threaded her way through the Manzanita and halted in front of the Slayer, standing as still as a Buddha. With the last splash of sunlight dipping below the mountains, she wondered: what kind of monster sets a leghold as a security measure? It was only then that she realized how alive the evening was about to become, not with the familiar sounds and smells of the desert, but with every tactic and countermeasure the *federales* could muster to protect one of their own. She was thinking about that when the memory of the *whop-whop-whop* of copter rotors sent a searing tightness through her chest.

The helo grew louder, its searchlights prowling along the riverbed, its beam playing off the steep banks. It was like nothing she'd ever seen or heard before. Only nine years old, Angel was racing through a maze of corrugated tin shacks, the stench of urine and feces burning in her nostrils. The two-bladed helicopter hovered directly above her, its searchlights fanning across the underbrush.

"Run, Niña, run!" her mother had screamed, her shrill voice pitching high with fear. But the helicopter didn't land; its beams stalked the flapping tin roofs. Off the footpath, Angel stumbled onto soft dirt, her mother still hollering. She felt her throat tighten, her lungs about to burst. She could barely breathe as the helo poured warning fire above a row of shacks, scattering the squatters. Why don't they land? Why won't el ejército land?

The campesino guiding them shouted and the group cannoned down a ravine, skidding past a snarl of tangled scrub. That was when she heard it, the crackle and pop of small arms fire, and dogs. Packs of search dogs howled savagely as she leapt across the muddy bank, sliding feet-first under a swirl of cable wires before tumbling down into a weed-strewn gully. She was the first to see the tunnel covered by a faded Coca-Cola sign.

With unimaginable joy she furrowed under the battered sign and plunged into the tunnel, never once looking back. The corroded pipe surfaced near a busy 7-Eleven in Nogales, a silver Greyhound bus waiting. Sitting beside her mother, clutching her trembling hand, for the first time in days she felt safe as they rode the bus all the way to the ocean. That next morning she got her first glimpse of San Diego and its sparse mesas that blended so unsparingly into the country she'd left behind. This was her new home, her paradise.

Or so she'd been told.

A gust of wind brought her back.

Whispering a prayer for the animals, she lifted the steel post high above her head and slammed it into the trigger device, snapping the jaws shut.

A rangy jackrabbit dashed across the wash and with four easy strides cleared a dip in the gully, scampering through clumps of saltbush. Near the river, the air-cav turned northwest towards the setting sun, the rugged Franklins a mosaic of otherworldly colors. But somewhere near the Santa Fe Bridge, the distant pitch of rotors reversed itself and turned back, Angel's heart sinking. The helo was a Bell JetRanger tasked out of the Air Force's 5th Air Group in Chihuahua City. She knew this because a rival cartel had tipped off army intelligence about tonight's hit, the Cártel del Noreste receiving a heads-up from one of its *estacas*, its cells, embedded inside the Third Brigade.

Listening to the unmistakable drone of the JetRanger, she crouched low as a swirling breeze ruffled the branches in a nearby acacia. The next few minutes seemed like forever. She tossed the post into the brush and eased her way around a patch of lechuguilla, hugging the lip of the riding trail. The cool, arid dusk was alive with scents, mostly creosote and sage—both familiar to her. Fifty meters ahead a breeze-block shell of a security booth sat empty. She ignored the graffiti-sprayed Members Only sign, looped wide of the traffic barrier, mindful of the booth's CCTV, and peeled off towards a sparsely-used hiker's path. "Groomed," the country club brochure had promised, but the sun-baked gypcrust was little more than a single-lane trail hemmed in by rows of newly planted chinaberry trees. She located her next marker, a mangy cottonwood, its upper bough twisted in the shape of a Z, then counted out twenty steps and halted.

The air had grown still, the soft wash of helicopter blades prowling along the Juárez side of the Rio Grande. The two-bladed JetRanger sliced through the thin clouds like a giant scythe; the early evening solitude was broken only by the chirping call of a warbler. Sweeping aside a mound of broken branches beneath the cottonwood, she took a frantic minute to find her opening—a thin clearing sheared between glistening coils of concertina wire—then squeezed her way through and emerged at the lip of a fitness trail, crouching beside another lechuguilla plant. A wave of light from the helicopter suddenly bled over her position. She wormed her way deeper beneath the cottonwood as the JetRanger widened its search pattern, bathing the golf course in precise arcing motions.

Through a snarl of concertina wire she could see a wide swath of Bermuda grass: the *Nueva's* eighteenth fairway, its man-made creek curling downhill, bisecting a pair of kidney-shaped sand traps before flowing languidly past a Saguaro garden into an algae-filled recycling pond. Running alongside the creek was a gravel sweep used by the club's Honduran groundskeepers to carry heavy-duty oil field hoses that siphoned untreated water into 300-gallon tanks mounted on rented gooseneck trailers. Blasts of the non-potable water were sprayed each evening on the thirsty fairways in a clear violation of the local ban on lawn watering. The gravel sweep caught her eye because it climbed straight into the *Nueva's* pro shop, its parking lot partially shielded by a ledge stone wall.

The JetRanger banked smoothly over the horse stables, its search lights wheeling across the corrals. Angel broke from under the cottonwood's gnarled branches and climbed the fitness path halfway up the hill towards a footbridge that would carry her over the man-made creek. The howling from nearby dogs let her know that the canine team had finished its patrol above the recycling pond. Whoever had timed the search had unwittingly done her a favor. Now she knew the pro shop was clear. Feeling a rush of adrenaline, she sailed across the bridge, keeping the JetRanger's distant beam in her peripheral view, covering the remaining sixty meters in a matter of seconds. Her plan was to connect off the pro shop to the main entryway using one of the many cart paths that emptied onto the club grounds. But radio chatter off the driving range was too close, so she abandoned the gravel sweep, keeping the empty gooseneck trailer between her and the radios, scuttled up a footpath onto the asphalt parking lot and hunkered next to an empty golf cart.

Another customized Yamaha Adventurer.

She let a few seconds pass. This was the tense part. As the chatter dissipated, she slid to the rear of the golf cart and knelt beside an empty golf club rack, her eyes tracking a motorized spotlight across the *Nueva's* cobblestone courtyard. In the distance, a layer of smog formed a milky shroud over Our Lady of Guadalupe in downtown Juárez, the early evening dusk giving the cathedral a soft, chalky glow. The only sounds Angel could hear were the sharp trill of a thrasher and the mating clicks of cicadas. From a nearby row of lacquered plant boxes, newly planted Guzmanias perfumed the warm night air. All along the cart path the groundskeepers had cultivated rows of white lilies and heirloom roses, their beauty peeling back like miniature masterpieces. The roving spotlight settled on a colonnade of white brick arches and reclaimed stone columns, the *Nueva's* front entrance, its ornate gates swung open. Angel saw a row of armored-plated limousines idling in the courtyard: Escalades, BMWs, Range Rovers, even a squat-nosed Hummer. But her target wouldn't be riding in any of them. Her briefers had assured her the judge's protection detail would be using a different entrance.

A nimbus of dope smoke tickled her nostrils.

Beyond the thick hedge, a sleek, well-dressed couple passed in front of the Yamaha, the man conversing in a language Angel didn't recognize. Kneeling beside the cart's side-view mirror, she took a moment to inspect her reflection, relieved to see her makeup had held.

Normally an attractive woman, tonight she'd taken the precaution of tinting her caramel colored skin a pallid tan and rinse-dying her jet-black hair a silvery charcoal. Under the oversized coveralls, she was wearing a tuxedo-style Armani jumpsuit cropped above the ankles with jeweled T-strap sandals encased in her thin rubber booties. Tucked inside the Vuitton bag was a spray bottle of Chanel and a pair of opal stud earrings.

Another high-intensity beam swept the front of the pro shop. Angel ducked.

Atop the *Nueva's* roof garden, voices drifted across the manicured grounds like a lively intermezzo—the playful, easy banter that only the rich seemed to have mastered. For 100,000 pesos each, Juárez's elite were congregating to press the flesh with tonight's featured speaker: a highly telegenic federal judge who was rumored to be a close personal friend of El Presidenté and, if one could believe *La Prensa*, the anointed frontrunner to become the next Governor of Chihuahua.

Unfortunately, the judge had also seen fit to put himself on the payroll of three different drug cartels and, equally stupid, had been skimming from each, laundering his take through a remote German bank in the port city of Lübeck. But sadly for the judge, Nordost-Industriebank was proving to be not obscure enough, having endured two cybersecurity breaches, the latest accessing the judge's transactional history and hawking it to a Slovenian broker, who'd parceled the data to a banking client in Berlin, a competitor of Nordost.

Doubly unfortunate for his Honor, the bank's auditor had uncovered an old Bital routing number out of Matamoros and immediately notified his chairman, who passed the discovery on to one of his off-the-books financiers: the *comandante* of the Cártel del Noreste.

Thus the need for Angel's visit.

Keeping her head low, she inched her way down a row of Yamahas past numbers 12, 11, and 10, halting beside number 9. The cart, emerald green like all the others, had been washed and buffed to a perfect sheen. Stashed beneath its front seat cushion was a converted nine-millimeter Uzi submachine gun modified from semi-automatic to full auto and every bit as illegal in Mexico as the Sig-Sauer P226 tucked in the mesh pocket beside it.

Both guns would stay in the cart. They were her fall back. But that wasn't going to happen. She had planned this job meticulously, priding herself on knowing every detail, from the precise coverage ranges of the *Nueva's* security cameras to its members' names, their schedules, habits, and countless other personal nuances one gleans from surveilling a guarded club sixteen hours a day.

To gun her way out would be a personal humiliation and most likely a deadly one.

Leaning against the Yamaha's back fender, she lifted her Glock from its zippered pocket and set it on the studded floor mat. She pulled off her coveralls and plastic shoe covers and stuffed them in a green trash receptacle, then retrieved the Glock, wiped it clean with the cotton handkerchief, and shoved it under a lacquered plant box. Next came the ultra-thin nitrile exam gloves, which she balled into a tight wad and crammed under the Yamaha's front seat cushion.

Stepping back, she inspected her work. It wasn't perfect, but it would have to do.

Smoothing her jumpsuit, she oriented herself to the voices wafting from the roof garden. To her right, a crushed limestone walkway came off a cart path at a shallow angle, curving left to avoid a white cantera stone fountain before swinging back to the right again and emptying into the main entry oval. From the oval, a paved lane led through the rose gardens into tonight's registration area.

Whispering a prayer for luck, she pulled back her shoulders and stepped gingerly onto the walkway, wiping a stray curl from her eyes. *Speed, but not haste,* she reminded herself.

For the *asesina* who loved animals, it was time to go to work.

CHAPTER FOUR

Dear Fellow Healers—greetings and salutations.

By now you've heard of my terrible fight with an insidious disease and I would like to update you on my prognosis as well as on some exciting new changes in my career.

Until last January my life was truly blessed, highlighted by recognition for my work in kyphoplasty at the national AMA Conference in Chicago along with being named chairman of one of California's new Investigative Review Committees—doing my part for single-payer reform, as one might say. However, over the spring I began noticing changes about myself. I was questioning certain decisions I had made, not the least being my marriage to Heather, my deteriorating relationship with my partners, and whether to "out" myself as an alcoholic.

Unable to cope or to share my anxieties with anyone, I began to ratchet up the drinking and started frequenting topless clubs along Sunset Boulevard. At first my "visits" were limited to weekends and off-call evenings but soon escalated to binge partying, regardless of my trauma call status. My mother and father tried to intervene without success. My practice partners were surprisingly sympathetic. But despite numerous attempts at peer counseling, I chose to brood, isolate myself, and seek solace from an old friend, Johnnie Walker.

This past September, I spent two weeks in Maui indulging my disease; hung over during the day, cruising at night, until I was scared witless by a false-positive STD test.

Returning home to Beverly Hills, I hit rock bottom in the operating room at Santa Monica Memorial, where I began abusing a substance called Sevoflurane, a vapor anesthetic used to keep my patients unconscious. Why I chose this drug I'll never know, but one whiff and all I could think about was getting high 24/7, until I blacked out in the Champagne Room at Areolas.

Not willing to admit my problem, backsliding into denial, I blatantly lied, telling my friends I was under stress, sleeping poorly, and not having sex. On the last day of my binge, I stole a bottle of Sevoflurane from the fifth floor pharmacy cage at Memorial and was found unconscious in the staff lounge by the evening supervisor.

This led to my board-mandated admission to a rehab clinic in Palm Springs called The Flatirons, which specializes in treating physicians with multiple addictions. Admittedly, at first I thought these sessions were beneath me, a waste of my time; but after weeks of intensive therapy I began to hear what those around me were saying and, more importantly, accepted Jesus Christ as my personal savior.

With His blessing, I was discharged to a recovery-based program designed specifically for doctors with substance abuse problems. I am now living a clean and sober life—praise Jesus—and while being an addict doesn't absolve me of what I did, it does explain a lot of my feelings and urges. Today, I'm back at Hurston Neurological seeing patients and the only thing I ask for is your forgiveness—plus any referrals you might have. After all, I'm still in private practice and we all have bills to pay. God bless you and may Jesus Christ be with you always.

Ernest L. Girard, M.D., F.A.C.S

P.S. I prefer seeing your state employees and cash-paying patients only. Reimbursement rates for the new GavinAid eligibles are embarrassingly low, and I'm trying to wean my practice off these types of patients.

Attorney MaryAnn Taylor twisted her stiff neck from side to side, feeling a sharp spasm in her right shoulder blade. She tried sitting up straight and breathing through the pain, but none of it worked, so she reached into her carryall and fished around for a bottle of Advil.

"Perfect," she muttered, realizing she'd left the ibuprofen in her SUV. "Three more cases and I'll be doing them drug-free."

Slender, with hazel eyes, nut-brown skin, and a slightly upturned nose, Taylor was part-time counsel for the state of California's Investigative Review Committee, Region Nine, and it looked like today's meeting would be running into overtime.

As she gently rotated her head from side to side, she heard a nasally snort behind her and turned to catch *LA Vibe* political writer, Andrew Crowder, reading over her shoulder. She could smell Doritos on his breath.

"Looks yummy," he purred. "Personal letter from the big guy—are we sharing?"

Taylor hurriedly shoved the letter into her carryall, arching an eyebrow. "I'm thinking *no* on that one," she said. "Besides, I don't recall privileged communications as being part of our deal."

"Funny. Because I was wondering exactly what our deal is, *girlfriend.* So far you haven't given me shit."

This time she turned completely around, keeping her eyes flat, tamping down a slow burn. Only an old college classmate could talk to her that way, but there were limits, and Crowder had tested them all. He was researching a story on California's new single-payer system, what was euphemistically called GavinAid, and Taylor had agreed to let him tag along, thinking the publicity might do her practice some good. But after seven days with randy Andy, she was beginning to see the error of her ways. Having reconnected with Crowder three weeks earlier, she had hoped his frat boy ways were a thing of the past, but his caveman persona still persisted and the picture wasn't pretty.

Forty-three years old, five-foot-six, paunchy with intense brown eyes, Crowder had bounced around every daily in the Southland, blogging a bit, churning out a tolerable screenplay, anonymously of course (he'd made her read it), but remained a rarity among today's journalists: a tough, noisy, in-your-face Angeleno with an absolute fearlessness when it came to investigative reporting. Because he had already notched a high-profile exposé on unlicensed plastic surgeons, his editor thought fifteen thousand words on the nuances of GavinAid would be right up his alley.

During his first term in office, President Donald J. Trump and his fellow Republicans had gone out of their way to neuter Obamacare, but in the process had outraged countless Americans whose medical premiums were now triple what they used to be. Firmly at the top of that list were millions of irate Californians. Leveraging that anger, and working with huge majorities in both the State House and the Senate, California Governor Gavin Newsom had shepherded through America's first single-payer healthcare system (the only exemption being state of California employees), but in the process had tacked on a cost control hammer never seen before in modern medicine.

By statute, if certain expense targets weren't met after GavinAid's first year of existence, the California Health Regulatory Board would be activated with the authority to set hospital charges and monitor patient utilization for the millions enrolled in *Golden State Plus*. But as so often happens with major healthcare reform, once the bright lights of policy initiatives began to fade, the darkness of day-to-day implementation reared its ugly head.

In an inaugural year that made the original Obamacare rollout look seamless, countless IT snafus, incomplete member rosters, and drastic overuse of medical services resulted in thousands of provider claims that were denied, then underpaid, then expunged. This tsunami of bureaucratic ineptitude triggered hundreds of millions in cost overruns, and after months of endless patient complaints and poll numbers lower than Death Valley, the governor finally activated the Health Regulatory Board and its twenty-two statewide investigative review committees.

This only further aggravated California's Medicare and Medicaid beneficiaries, who challenged the constitutionality of GavinAid in *McCarthy v. Newsom*. But in a highly controversial decision, the U.S. Supreme Court ruled 5-4 that the state did have the authority to implement its new single-payer system *and* shanghai all federally-covered enrollees into GavinAid, placing the care of millions of Californians under the watchful eyes of the board's investigative review committees. Needless to say that decision didn't sit very well. Aping Sarah Palin, critics tagged the review committees as death panels, and they were viewed as an anathema by 92 percent of Californians surveyed by YouGov.

Region Nine, Taylor's committee, had the second largest caseload in the state and was the committee Crowder had chosen to profile.

"Excuse me, Ms. Taylor. Do you have time to sign last week's transcripts? They're ready when you are." The eager voice belonged to a young court reporter wearing large raspberry colored eyeglasses and sitting beside an ancient stenotype machine. She was surrounded by a rolling Zuca backpack, a digital recorder with backup stenomask, and three accordion files packed with last week's case transcripts. "I'd really like to close these out before we leave tonight."

Crowder lifted his unshaven face. "Whoa, back off, four eyes. Me and the counselor are working on something hot. Pulitzer Prize-winning shit. So take a number and wait, *capiche*?"

Stunned, the court reporter drew back slightly, her eyes drawn to Crowder's nose ring. It looked infected. "Wow . . . like what's your problem? I'm just trying to get these files done."

"Whatever," snorted Crowder. "Just wait your turn, alright?"

"No . . . it's not alright. And who put you in charge anyway? You look homeless."

"And what would you know about the homeless, snowflake?"

The stenographer paused. "That most of them look like you."

Crowder's mouth stretched into a wide, greasy smile showcasing a row of nicotine-stained teeth. "My, my, aren't we the feisty little enchorita? Say, how about a drinkie-poo later on? We can get cozy, just you and me, rattle around a bit—"

The stenographer's face turned pale, as if she might want to vomit. "Not in your wettest dreams, jagoff. Just keep paying for it."

"Oh, baby bird, don't be such a hater. Come on, let me buy you a drink. We can ruffle a few sheets. Wake up the neighbors."

Taylor peeled off her rimless bifocals and rubbed the bridge of her nose. It was a nervous habit she'd developed as a child. "Shut up, Andrew. Shut up *right now.*"

"What? What'd I do?" Crowder looked dumbfounded, leaning back in his chair, arms out. Taylor glared at him, then turned to the galled court reporter. "Don't pay any attention to him. His parole officer should be here any minute. I'm sorry, but I forgot your name."

"Monica. Monica Richmond."

"Certainly, Monica, I'd be glad to sign your files right after this next case. I was also thinking that if this session drags on any longer we're gonna have to order out for dinner."

"Eww . . . and watch maggot-teeth eat? Don't make me gag." Richmond gave Crowder a disgusted look. "I'd rather stick a pen in my ear."

"Stop, I'm blushing," he sniped.

Taylor spun around, but this time Crowder raised both hands in surrender. "What's wrong with you?" she hissed under her breath. "You can't talk to staff like that. Ever hear of sexual harassment? #MeToo?"

"Ever hear of *independent contractor*? My dirtbag editor likes to remind me of my peon-like status every time we text. So save me the lecture. Besides, I'm judgment-proof."

"And how does that work?"

Crowder grinned, intertwining his fingers behind his head, leaning further back in his saddle-colored chair. "I don't own any assets. They'll never collect a dime."

She looked at him incredulous. "It's hard to believe we went to the same college together."

"Just your good luck . . . God, I wonder which mid-level bureaucrat signed off on this architectural monstrosity. Doesn't it give you the creeps?"

The new beige-hued C. George Deukmejian, Jr. Building was designed like a fat, squatty layer cake with painted concrete walls, zigzagged wood ceiling, and what looked like an acre of earth tone carpet. There were no windows except for a single row of glass strips that had been purposely covered with grainy film so that no one could see in or out, which only added to the 'Duke's' conspiracy mythos. From the rear of the conference room a handful of bleary-eyed staffers shuffled through two mammoth cast-iron doors, sucking on energy drinks or shade-grown coffee, returning from their breaks. Mostly millennials, well-educated, the vanguard of medical reform, or so Taylor had assured him, Crowder was counting on these junior hirelings to be the real deal and not some careerist wannabes trying to pad their résumés. Despite their rocky start, the new investigative review committees hadn't proven to be the double-barreled disasters their critics had predicted. Built on cost control and daily utilization monitoring, the committees were functioning exactly the way they were supposed to, and despite the need for journalistic impartiality, Crowder believed they were the only hope to rein in the millions in cost overruns that were threatening GavinAid, especially with national Republicans and their drive-by pundits circling like vultures ready to pick apart single-payer.

Bored, he leaned in close to Taylor's left ear, the scent of his Hai Karate causing her eyes to water. "Remind me again why all these bureaucrats have real jobs and you're only part-time?"

Taylor's shoulders slumped. Feeling another twinge of regret for agreeing to this ill-advised arrangement, she put on a fake smile and remembered to talk in quotes. "Given the complex challenges of reviewing denied medical care, the staff is responsible for preparing, reviewing, and advising the committee on all clinical aspects related to each appellant's case. To date we've heard two thousand, three hundred and fifty-two formal appeals—"

"Yeah, yeah, I get it. The staffers do all the heavy lifting, but what about you? The state of California couldn't afford a full-time lawyer?"

"No, I'm sure they would've loved to. But it was a compromise between the Centers for Medicare and Medicaid Services in D.C. and Governor Newsom, so that GavinAid could get its federal waiver. As part of that compromise—and you know all this—the new investigative review committees were required to hire lawyers from the private sector rather than use civil service attorneys. Senate Republicans didn't like the idea of deep state government lawyers arguing against patient appeals, so they demanded that private-citizen attorneys represent the state of California on all care denials. Sort of a checks and balances type of thing. I'm one of nine part-timers assigned to this committee. We get paid by the appeal, no union, no benefits, and we split the caseload evenly, all very Reaganesque. The money's not great, but the work's pretty cool."

Crowder watched the staff shuffle to their designated seats. "I still can't get my arms around Governor Gav pulling the trigger on all of this. That took a pair of *cojones*."

"Not really. Under GavinAid it was either that or let single-payer go down the tubes. Remember how the hospitals ran that Just Say No to Cuts campaign with the Band-Aids, and the docs threatened to walk if the state reduced their fees. I don't see how the gov had much of a choice."

"Yeah, but the physicians got exactly what they wanted when he suspended the Medical Practice Act and allowed outside companies to buy into their practices. And from a political standpoint there was no reason to mobilize the review committees; he could've stalled for a few more months. Chief Justice Roberts called them human abattoirs in his dissent."

Taylor smiled sweetly. "The Chief Justice would now, wouldn't he? But the governor signed GavinAid and it's his baby, so when the cost targets imploded there wasn't much room to maneuver." Opening her flapover briefcase, she removed a laptop computer and several brown file folders and placed them neatly across a rustic pine table marked Counsel's Area. After six months as part-time counsel, Taylor was finally getting the hang of the job, and to her surprise genuinely enjoyed it. For the first time in her life she actually felt like she was doing something important, something worthwhile. And while she loved private practice, these committee meetings had become sort of therapy for the soul.

As the conference room began to refill, her eyes drifted to an elongated table fronting three Naugahyde chairs reserved for members of the California Investigative Review Committee, Region Nine, presided over by Dr. Ernest L.

Girard, neurosurgeon-to-the-glitterati and Taylor's wayward client. To say theirs was a complicated relationship was being generous.

Obligated to be impartial, Taylor's job was to insure that all state guidelines were followed, but Girard was a senior partner with Hurston Neurological Institute, her firm's largest client, and the person most responsible for her getting this gig. Not that she had any illusions about his kindness. It was an act of pure self-preservation, given that many of his practice transgressions often slopped over into committee business. As the staffers took their seats, she smiled to herself, recalling a recent case where the state's UR nurses had rejected payment on three of Girard's simultaneous surgeries, each performed at different hospitals and all clocked in at the exact same time. Girard was listed as the primary surgeon on all three and had barely avoided a billing fraud rap.

"I hear your boy's sort of an *el grandé dicko*," whispered Crowder. "Motor never stops running, bit of a temper, drugs and booze; a real shitbird according to those who know him."

Taylor didn't bite. She was getting used to his gonzo tactics. "Dr. Ernie Girard is one of California's most esteemed neurosurgeons," she offered blandly. "He graduated from the Yale School of Medicine, completed his surgical residency at UCLA, and was fellowship-trained at the Mayo Clinic in Rochester. He's also a founding partner in the world-renowned Hurston Neurological Institute and board certified in both spine *and* neurological surgery. The man's considered a civic treasure."

"Nice looking, too," added Crowder, "real Marlboro Man. You spankin' any of that?"

This time Taylor tilted her head to the ceiling, a headache working its way behind her right ear. "You really are a disgusting pig, you know that, don't you?"

"Thanks, I get that a lot. But could you throw me a bone? Anything, *por favor*, I'm dying back here."

"Off the record?"

Warily, Crowder turned off the recorder on his smartphone. "*No más.*"

"And only if you'll shut up for the next two hours."

"Oooo . . . tough love. Careful, Stormy, you're giving me a boner."

Taylor recoiled at the thought, goosebumps shivering up and down her forearms.

Gossiping about Ernie Girard was a mistake and she knew it, but she trusted Crowder—God knows why—he was a professional after all, and representing the overbearing, misogynistic Dr. Ernie could suck the life out of anybody. So call it repressed anger, passive-aggressive retribution, or a combination of both, she honestly believed that talking about it might help. At least that was how she was rationalizing it. But there was a line, and she knew she was skidding awfully close to it.

"Tell you what," said Crowder. "I'll start with what I've heard and you can just nod if anything sounds kosher, fair enough?"

Taylor's conscience was screaming, "Shut the hell up!" but her discipline had wilted like a desert lily in the summer heat, sped up by the fact that Girard was a card-carrying deplorable. So she detached herself insofar as that was possible from her firm's most billable client and simply nodded.

"Attagirl," said Crowder. "Hold on a sec." He tapped several commands into his cell phone. "Okay, here's what I've got: Dr. Ernest L. Girard, Dr. Ernie to those who know and love him. Gifted, chauvinistic, loves to hear the sound of his own voice; we're talking industrial-sized ego and stubborn, pathologically stubborn. The man's never been wrong in his life." Taylor gazed at her suede flats, nodding. Crowder continued. "Volatile, sarcastic, a serial divorcé with gambling debts up to his eyeballs and arrogant enough to think that all hospital executives and journalists are something you scrape off the soles of your Bruno Magli wingtips . . . and pharmacological problems. I've heard rock, ketamine, bales of weed."

"I'm not touching that one."

Crowder gently rubbed the gold stud in his right nostril. "Fair enough, we can come back to that later. Say, who's the pasty-faced white bread standing next to him? Dude looks like a young Karl Rove."

Taylor glanced over to the committee table, the muscles round her jaw clenching. "Harold Chase, licensed physical therapist, manages a chain of walk-in PT clinics in Brentwood and Culver City."

"And?" Crowder asked.

"And what?"

"Come on, Ms. Dullard, we're off the record, loosen up a bit."

She gnawed on the tip of her Bic, her eyes burning a hole through Chase, her face reddening like a ripe strawberry.

Forty-six years old, Hal to his friends, Chase was straddling his overstuffed Naugahyde chair, laughing violently, his fleshy chin shaking like a giant paint blender. He had thin, blow-away ginger hair and a jowly face that at the moment was fixed on Girard, who was regaling a pair of female staffers with his latest exploits as a volunteer SWAT field surgeon with the Los Angeles Police Department. The animated Dr. Ernie appeared to be pantomiming a police German shepherd gaining ground on a terrified crack addict, his teeth snapping ridiculously, mimicking the dog's mauling of the drug dealer's leg.

"Trust me, he's not worth your time," said Taylor. "The man's a total dweeb." But her eyes stayed frozen on the pudgy therapist, whose owlish face had contorted into a wide bug-eyed look, a scum of toothpaste smeared across the corner of his mouth. "Just leave it at that."

Crowder studied her face for a second. "Don't tell me you and Turd Blossom Jr. got biblical together?"

Taylor spun on him, livid. "I said let it go!"

"Okay, okay, no *problemo*, don't go all postal on me. You and white bread used to do the mambo. I get it. Nobody's judging, but geez Louise."

Taylor's breath stopped. "One more word out of you and we're done. Do you hear me?"

"Wow, Old Harold really got under your skin."

This time she stood and leaned in close, eyes flaring. "Did you hear what I said?"

Crowder flinched. "Whoa, like chill, ISIS-girl. No more Harold questions, I got it."

Taylor nodded, dropping heavily into her chair, regaining her composure. "Sorry. But you're such a pain in the ass and it makes me so tired."

"And you scare the shit out of me, so we're even. Tell me about the other she-member of our little troika. The woman looks like she's ready to take someone out."

Studiously trying to ignore her two male colleagues, a stern, dignified woman with pixie-short hair, a harsh wrinkled face marked by deep stress lines, and dark green eyes that gazed straight ahead, was neatly arranging a medical file on the conference table before taking her seat. Unlike her male colleagues, she wore a tense, agitated expression, suggesting she was ready to get on with it.

"Juanita Reno, former Vice President of Government Relations for the California Nurses Association," answered Taylor. "She's often called upon to babysit the boys when they're misbehaving. Looks like she'll be busy tonight."

"Quite a crew. How does one get the gig? State application, campaign donation, oral sex?"

Taylor gave him a sour look. "How long have you been working City Hall?"

"Too long."

"Then you know the drill, everything's political payback. Reno was nominated by the CNA. Chase got named because his ex-wife is chief of staff for the California Secretary of State, and Girard gave generously to the former mayor of Los Angeles before he got termed-out. He also did the mayor's microdiscectomy a few years back."

"I'm guessing that rules me out?"

"What, cynics and scribes need not apply?"

"I thought they were the same thing."

Below the committee's table, the "courtroom" formed a perfect square with a sleek folding panel behind a second trestle table carved from the same reclaimed wood as the maple ceiling. A brushed aluminum sign hanging from the table marked it as the Applicant's Area and there were two podiums in the center for expert witnesses and eight rows of padded folding chairs for the gallery. Given that it was rush hour on the freeways, the conference room was less than a third full.

"Who's the stud-muffin over at the applicant's table?" Crowder asked eagerly. "He seems quite the crowd pleaser."

Taylor's eyes drifted to her left. "Jerry Anson, attorney. He's got the next case."

Crowder gave her an expectant look. "And what's the 4-1-1 on him?"

"Still off the record?"

"Christ, this is like pulling teeth. Since when did you become such a hardass?"

"Is that a *yes*?" He nodded, so she continued. "Jerry Anson: transplanted Texan, very bright, smooth as silk in the box. A flaming Bernista, but he's got skills. He's the guy I'd hire if I was ever on the other side of that table." Anson was soothing his worried-looking client: seventy-two-year-old Esther Robinson, a large woman, not obese but someone who moved slowly, stiffly, having endured chronic back pain for the last six years.

Robinson's request for spine surgery had been denied by three different state utilization review nurses, but not one to shrink from a fight, Esther had appealed her denial and hired Anson at the suggestion of one of her doctors. Sitting beside her, wearing his favorite oversized Dodgers jersey and blue Nike trainers, was her grandson, Marcus.

Catching their glances, Anson flashed Taylor a cryptic smirk before unbuttoning his tailored suit jacket and taking a seat next to Esther Robinson. Handsome in an outdoorsy sort of way, Anson had hauled fracking sand during his undergraduate days, and his tanned face, tightly cropped beard and carob colored eyes made him popular eye candy around the Duke.

"Tasty . . . very tasty," slurred Crowder, a raging bisexual who appeared to be joining the fan club. "I'm thinking me and Brokeback are gonna be besties. Tell me more."

"I didn't know you were one of the chosen."

"Variety is the spice of life. Besides, you don't know everything about me."

"Thank God for small miracles."

"Cute. Just tell me about Bronco Billy."

"Undergrad from SMU in Dallas, moved to Escondido and spent three years at California Western School of Law in San Diego before passing the bar exam on his first try. Like I said, the man's got game. He's rumored to be knocking on the door of a partnership at Todorov, Kerry & Brown in Century City. He's also the go-to lawyer for anyone whose medical care has been denied by—"

"Ooohhh! Ooohhh, I got this one—*Gavin's Angels*. Can you believe it? That's what Fox News is calling them, Gavin's Angels. Damn, I wished I'd thought that one up."

"But you didn't, and while Fox News has its own take, we prefer to call them utilization review nurses, and they're employed by the California Department of Health Care Services. Try not to forget that."

"Right. Any of 'em hanging around?"

"Do you want to hear more about Anson or not?"

"Yeah sure . . . go ahead." But Crowder's eyes roamed the conference room as if he was searching for female mud wrestlers.

Taylor's voice dropped a few decibels. "Anson began his career prepping malpractice cases at Todorov before stumbling into this lucrative gold mine. His first case fell into his lap after a fellow associate experienced a psychotic breakdown in Todorov's Wilshire office. Rumor has it, the partners downloaded the associate's entire medical appeals file to Jerry's laptop while the poor guy was being hauled off to rehab. That was ten months ago."

"And our boy's been running with it ever since?"

"Like Orenthal in a crowded airport. The man has billed out over a million bucks in the last six months according to the paralegals. Under GavinAid, once a denial-of-care order has been issued, the patient's only recourse is to appeal before an Investigative Review Committee like this one—"

"—which tends to be a tad one-sided given the overwhelming resources of the state of California," countered Crowder.

"Which is your opinion, or should I say bias?"

"So the patients have to hire young Anson if they ever want to see a dime of medical care?"

"His going rate is seven hundred fifty dollars an hour."

"Sweet." Crowder's eyes homed in on Anson who was busy calming his anxious client.

And Esther Robinson needed calming. Fidgety, nervous, gnawing on a ragged cuticle, Anson gently placed his right hand on top of hers and held it there for a few seconds. The gesture seemed to work. Her shoulders relaxed. A warm smile creased her lips. A former dietary aide, Robinson had worked thirty-eight years for the Gleneagle Nursing Home in Carson before retiring on a medical disability. And despite the grumblings from his managing partner, Anson had taken her case pro bono because he liked the way she kicked sand in the bureaucrats' faces. But he also knew her requested spine procedure fell in that clinical gray area between surgery and therapy and that DHCS had all the analytical firepower. Despite his calm demeanor, Anson was sure this was going to be a tough, uphill slog. Nodding towards the chairman, his heartbeat quickening like it always did before battle, Anson winked at Taylor, hoping to get a rise out of her, before assuring Esther Robinson that "everything was going to be fine," with a lot more confidence than he felt.

CHAPTER FIVE

"This Investigative Review Committee for the State of California Health Regulatory Board, Region Nine, Los Angeles, has reconvened. Please restate your names for the record." Chairman Ernie Girard lifted his head, locating the two lawyers.

"MaryAnn Taylor, Committee's counsel."

"Jerry Anson, on behalf of applicant Esther Robinson, and I would like to reiterate for the record that given the ongoing legal challenges to the California Health Regulatory Board, we refuse to recognize the jurisdiction of this committee—"

"Yes, yes, thank you, Jerry," said Girard, cutting him off. "We're all quite aware that single-payer hasn't lived up to all of our hopes and dreams, but neither have the Angels, Kevin Spacey, or Cabo San Lucas. So get over it, son. The rest of us have."

Anson's fists knotted beneath the table. "Thank you, Doctor, and while I appreciate the wisdom, given the current number of administrative challenges to the board's jurisdiction, and the authority of its investigative review committees, any decision rendered by this death panel could eventually be found null and void. Therefore, I would like to state for—"

This time Girard flicked a piece of stripper glitter off his collar before interrupting. "The U.S. Supreme Court's not good enough for you, Jerry? Nine judges with robes in D.C., remember them? They ruled, you lost, so quit jerking us around with these ridiculous motions. As for your objection, it is duly noted, and accept my congratulations on getting the term 'death panel' into this afternoon's transcript. I'm sure we'll be reading about it in tomorrow's *Times*."

Anson stood, eyes glued to Girard. "Objection, condescending and—"

"Sit *down* or I'll have you physically removed. Ms. Taylor, if you please."

Taylor looked at both men warily before opening her legal file. The committee staffers would be following along on their laptop computers but MaryAnn preferred to work from hard copy, old school. It kept her sharp. "Next applicant is Esther Robinson, Van Nuys. Ms. Robinson is appealing her denial-of-care order for a requested spine fusion procedure, having been diagnosed with lumbar degenerative disc disease. The committee's case management nurses have reviewed her care plan and rejected surgery as a first option, recommending instead a regimen of physical therapy and pain management injections. The applicant's medical records are in front of you."

"Thank you. Now it's your turn, Jerry. Enlighten us."

This time Anson stood slowly, buttoning his suit, trying to gauge how belligerent he could be without expert witnesses. "Ms. Robinson is the seventy-two-year-old guardian of her only grandson, Marcus, who is with us here today." Anson smiled warmly at the youngster. "She has endured several years of excruciating back pain and remains an excellent candidate for spine fusion surgery. We're only asking—"

"Yes, thank you," Girard again cut him off. "It's all right here in her medical records, counselor." He turned to the applicant. "Mrs. Robinson."

Esther Robinson raised her right hand. "Yes, Doctor."

"How intense is your pain, ma'am?"

"Night and day, sir. I've tried everything but nothing seems to work."

"Everything, Mrs. Robinson?"

"Yes, sir. I've done my exercises, lost weight, taken all my meds. I've done everything the medical people told me to do."

"Does that include bringing your grandson here today as some kind of prop for sympathy, ma'am?"

Anson shot up. "Objection! You're badgering the applicant."

"Oh, for chrissakes, Jerry, can we lose all the up and down crap, it's giving me a headache." Girard was nursing a mild hangover from the tequila shooters at the Crystal Horseshoe. Fortunately, his next urine sample wasn't due for another two weeks. "Mrs. Robinson, help us out here. Are you in so much pain that you're willing to let Mr. Anson pimp out your grandson for sympathy?"

"*Are you kidding me?*—pimp out her grandson?"

"Is there a question in there, Jerry?" Girard inquired.

Anson stared directly at Taylor. "I'm guessing you're okay with all of this?"

Embarrassed, Taylor bit her lip and began idly rearranging legal files. Three rows behind her Andrew Crowder could hardly contain himself, tapping on his iPad like a meth-crazed marmoset.

Anson stepped slowly around the applicant's table and hovered a few feet from Taylor. "Legally speaking, you're fine with this . . . it all works for you?"

"What's your point, Jerry?" Taylor asked.

"Verbal waterboarding an applicant, that's my point!"

"Verbal waterboarding," snorted Girard, "that's priceless. What's next, trigger-warnings, safe spaces?" But Taylor kept her eyes glued to the legal briefs. Mortified by Girard's behavior, she pinched the bridge of her nose, refusing to look up at Anson. Or Girard for that matter, recalling something about the gift that keeps on giving.

"Nothing?" pressed Anson. "This death panel isn't going to recognize even the most basic of legal rights?"

"That's twice on the death panel plug," Girard chimed-in. "Good to see you've brought your A-game. Three's a trifecta. I hear you win a MAGA hoodie."

"No, Your Honor," Esther Robinson answered forcefully.

Girard looked at her, confused. "No what, ma'am?"

"No, sir, I didn't bring my boy here to make you feel sorry for me. I'm in pain and that's the God's truth. My Marcus is all I have. I couldn't find a babysitter for him."

"Then you wouldn't mind if I asked him a few questions?"

"*Again*, he's a minor . . . anybody out there listening?" Anson threw up both arms in a bit of theatrics, briefly contemplating tossing his Mont Blanc pen, but that seemed a bit over the top.

For her part, MaryAnn Taylor remained deathly silent, rubbing her forehead, silently praying that someone would pull the fire alarm.

"No, that's fine, sir," Esther Robinson said confidently. "He's a good boy . . . got a mind of his own."

Girard grinned smugly at Anson. "See, now that wasn't so hard was it, Jerry? You gotta learn to relax, counselor. Try some yoga, a few restorative poses each morning. It'll calm your nerves." Girard turned to the boy. "What's your name, son?"

"Marcus Allen Robinson, after Grandma's favorite football player."

"Your grandma has good taste. How old are you, Marcus?"

"Eight . . . nine in three months."

"What do you want to be when you grow up? An athlete, a teacher, an architect?"

"Nope."

"Fireman, police officer? Maybe even a doctor like me?"

"No, sir, I want to be a reality TV star like Trump."

The entire room broke up laughing, while Anson nodded knowingly at Girard. "I rescind my objection. He's all yours, *Doctor.*"

Girard smiled wanly. "Order please," he sniffed, contrite. "I guess I deserved that." He had a hard time showing a sense of humor when the joke was on him. "Marcus, when you're at home, does your grandma have back problems? Is she in a lot of pain?"

Marcus looked affectionately towards his grandmother. "Grandma don't move real well," he said earnestly. "She tries, but after a few minutes all she can do is lay on the couch. So I wash the dishes, clean up some. I can make my own bed."

"Congratulations. Does your grandma get out much?" Girard asked.

"Grandma can't go to church, so we watch the Trinity network on TV and sometimes NFL football. I like Jared Goff, he's cool. I also like watching the Dodgers in the summer. They're pretty cool, too. And because Grandma can't get out, I don't go to regular school with the other kids. She teaches me at home."

"Thank you, Marcus." Girard looked at the other two committee members. "I think I've heard enough. Anyone else?" The room was quiet, compliant. "Then I believe we're ready to rule."

"If the committee pleases," interrupted Taylor, "the applicant's medical records are in front of you. The staff has gone to a great deal of effort researching clinical outcomes on spine fusion surgery for overweight women in their seventies, which have proven to be quite poor by CERC—"

"Excuse me," Girard jumped in. "Remind me again who CERC is?"

"The Clinical Evidence Review Commission," Taylor replied evenly.

"And do we know where they get their data?"

There was no answer, so Girard lifted his right index finger and ran it slowly along the crack of his butt then pretended to sniff it. Anson's eyes widened, while

Crowder applauded loudly. Taylor dropped into her seat, giving Girard a pinched, sour look.

"As always, Doctor, we stand in awe," she offered acidly.

"As you should, but with regard to this appeal, the Review Committee is going to uphold the denial-of-care order—"

"*What?*" Anson was out of his chair again.

"Oh, for the love of God, Jerry, *sit the hell down!*" There was silence while Anson begrudgingly complied. Girard continued. "We're upholding the denial-of-care order for spine fusion surgery, but I am going to authorize payment for Mrs. Robinson to participate in a clinical trial for the latest minimally invasive disc replacement procedure. I believe there are several trials being conducted in the Los Angeles area. I've also heard they're using a more advanced lateral approach these days along with improved implants, less blood loss, not nearly as messy."

"Not nearly as messy," repeated Anson. "Is that a clinical term, Doctor?"

"Young man, let's leave the sarcasm at the door next time." Girard turned to Esther Robinson. "Mrs. Robinson, I believe one of these new surgical trials should do the trick for your pain. So get yourself enrolled and let's see how things go from there. Sound good?"

Anson slumped deeper into his chair, glaring at Girard in bewilderment. "And how is she supposed to *find* one of these clinical trials?'

"Well, as our vice president is fond of saying, the Lord works in mysterious ways." Girard winked at Esther Robinson. "Next case, Ms. Taylor."

CHAPTER SIX

"Good evening, ladies." Angel had managed to maneuver next to a pair of elegant women wearing strapless evening gowns. "Correct me if I'm wrong, but I'm detecting a hint of tuberose and tiaré. May I ask what you're wearing?"

Turning, the older of the two arched a perfectly-shaped eyebrow, feigning a breach in decorum. "Givenchy," she politely replied. "But then I'm guessing you already knew that."

The woman was gracefully chic, almost sylphlike in her demeanor, her subtle tranquility suggesting a bored familiarity with these types of charity events. Unconsciously, she touched her left earring, a Sutra, sizing Angel up. The *asesina* eased in closer, whispering, "I think you might be giving me too much credit," with a hint of tease in her voice. "Sometimes a girl just gets lucky."

The woman's dark green eyes sparkled like gems. "Somehow I doubt that, señorita."

Angel smiled at the compliment, extending her right hand. "Maria Fernanda Perez, just Maria to my friends. I apologize for intruding, but I was hoping to join you while our hosts sort us out. Some of our male guests seem to be prowling like wolves tonight." The woman chuckled, taking a sip of Cristal before turning towards her younger companion, who barely lifted her shoulders as if to say, "Why not?"

Angel liked what she saw. The older woman was slender, but not emaciated, with her silky brunette hair twisted into a low chignon. Her heels were Valentino, her bracelet Cartier, and an opera-length strand of cultured pearls hung tastefully around her neck. The younger woman was equally haute, wearing a stunning diamond necklace with matching teardrop earrings, her long braided hair colored a trendy marsala. It felt like they'd arrived together. Whether as mother and daughter, or something else, didn't concern Angel. She just needed the pair for the next fifteen minutes or so.

"And will Mr. Perez be joining us tonight?" asked the younger woman playfully.

"I'm afraid not," answered Angel. "We divorced over eight years ago and his new wife might frown upon a reunion . . . his loss, though."

The younger woman looked pleased. "Then it looks as if we'll be a threesome. How very European."

That brought a smile to the older woman's face, her eyes having settled agreeably on Angel's tailored figure. "I'm Yesenia Torrez, and this is my escort, Chela, who is usually much better behaved."

Yesenia extended her left hand. It was soft and smooth and devoid of a wedding ring. Angel held onto it an instant too long, adding pleasantly, "It's a pleasure to meet both of you."

This time Yesenia shifted her right hand on top of Angel's and left it there. She was wearing only light makeup, any traces of age artfully concealed by a talented stylist. "Likewise, Señorita Perez."

"Maria, please."

She smiled again. "It is a pleasure to meet you, *Maria*.

Angel felt a rush of satisfaction—*the pieces coming together*. She was guessing the older woman to be in her late forties, maybe early fifties, strikingly beautiful and perfect for tonight's needs.Impishly, Angel offered both women her arms, escorting them down a long curving path of terra-cotta pavers that bent east before emptying into an outdoor patio bar poled in the middle of the *Nueva Aurora's* croquet lawn. To the north, the shimmering lights of El Paso sparkled like tiny fireflies. Angel accepted a glass of champagne, pretending to admire the carved lintels adorning an ocher-colored limestone arch, but her eyes homed in on the three armed security guards stationed under the bar's canopy of white orchids and pink rhododendrons, each carrying a Heckler & Koch G36 folding assault rifle and coordinating their positions through wireless "bonephones."

Her surveillance was abruptly interrupted by Chela, who'd sidled next to her. "And how do you know Judge Ramirez?" the younger woman inquired.

Angel pivoted, attentive. "I'm a senior partner with a patent law firm in Chihuahua City. I'm afraid the good judge has pegged me as an easy target for tonight's fundraiser."

Soft lights flickered on-and-off throughout the grounds indicating the silent auction was about to begin.

"Speaking of which," Angel added charmingly, "duty calls. May I?"

Again she offered Yesenia Torrez her free arm. Catching Chela's amused smirk out of the corner of her eye, she was momentarily surprised when Yesenia hesitated.

"And your partners . . . were they pegged as easy targets, too?" Yesenia probed.

"Yes, but sadly they had to beg off—pressing legal matters. But they did give me the company credit card, and some might question the wisdom of *that* decision."

Taking a final sip of Cristal, Yesenia Torrez tilted her head to the right before accepting Angel's arm. They strolled leisurely behind an exotically attractive woman with tightly curled auburn hair and what looked like natural blonde highlights that caught the faint glow of the portable lights. Boisterous voices cascaded off the club's rooftop terrace; the party seemed to be in full swing. From her earlier recon, Angel knew the guests would be mingling around a black onyx fountain spurting crisscrossing streams of French champagne and encircled by several spectacular arrangements of white gardenias and burgundy Neoregelias. Opposite the fountain were twenty linen-covered tables, each with a breathtaking view of the X-shaped *La Equis* monument and crammed with silver lamé bags full of Baccarat flutes and Lalique figurines, all nestled around centerpieces of purple butterfly orchids shipped in from Beijing.

Five days earlier, impersonating a floral designer, Angel had gained access to the roof terrace and immediately ruled out a sniper shot due to the clever placement of sixteen potted hibiscus in two-meter-high vases encasing the entire rooftop area. The vases had been aligned to shield tonight's guests from the prying lenses of the paparazzi hovering outside the *Nueva Aurora's* gates, but the vases hadn't necessarily bothered her, improvisation being the mother's milk of her profession; she simply recast her plan choosing a more personal approach. Tonight's contract would be honored the old-fashioned way, face-to-face.

The three of them joined a cluster of arriving guests meandering through long rows of manicured gardens filled with budding roses and pink carnations. The main security checkpoint came into view under a halo of temporary Klieg lamps. As they approached, Angel acknowledged the first of several security guards, allowing her eyes to adjust to the bright carbon-arc lighting. She couldn't help but notice the man's long sloping forehead and brutishly-thick chest, which made her realize how unprepared the *federales* were for someone like her. Someone who wasn't a trigger-happy narco-gangbanger or deranged terrorist willing to immolate herself, but a spot-and-stalk killer trained in planning and countersurveillance. She was escorting both women towards a khaki awning dotted with dozens of glossy sponsor decals, when Yesenia lightly squeezed her forearm. "Last chance to bail," she warned. "Be careful or you might get stuck with us for the evening."

A thrill shot through Angel's body. "Such an onerous task, surrounded by two beautiful women," she said. "I expect to see myself on the front page of the *Sociales* section in tomorrow's *El Diario,* and I don't know what'll bother my partners more: male envy or sexual fantasies." Yesenia tightened her grip, and the three of them followed a group of party-goers zigzagging their way through a red velvet rope line leading to the registration tent.

The front of the tent was open on two of its four sides, with chilled bottles of Krug anchoring both ends of a linen-covered table and a trio of security guards checking guests through. As she stood nonchalantly, Angel's eyes made a complete counterclockwise circuit, inventorying everything, prepping her contingencies. Against the back wall sat a fireproof metal cabinet, a portable generator humming beside it. Leaning against the 6500-watt generator were four FX-05 assault rifles, *Xiuhcoatls,* "fire snakes." A ceremonial guard on loan from the elite Estado Mayor, the presidential bodyguard, was smoothly directing traffic from the front of the queue, welcoming each guest in his courteous baritone, and she counted five more uniformed guards, each wearing radio earpieces and politely assisting invitees along the rope line. Yesenia whispered something clever in her left ear, allowing Angel to pivot away from the only rotating surveillance camera. That was when she heard it, low at first then louder, requiring all her effort not to break into a wide grin.

The bouncy *narcocorrido* was Mario Quintero's *Mis Tres Animales,* serenading from an ancient transistor radio somewhere outside the tent. As Yesenia kept talking, Angel's mind became lost in the music, reminiscing about her mother and father and a spare wooden shanty balanced on cinder blocks in a sprawling, decrepit colonia. There were other memories, too, warm and pleasant: the charred smell of homemade cabrito tacos simmering on charcoal grilles; the muddled chatter of Spanglish; old men drinking Carta Blanca and smoking their foul cigarellos; the dusk glimmering off the coffee-colored Rio Grande as the stars twinkled above the horizon.

Some things never change, she thought, brushing back a smile. Despite its lavish trappings, its A-list attendees and flashy paparazzi, beyond the sculpted walls of the *Nueva Aurora*, stray dogs still barked, barefooted children still played fútbol in weed-strewn parks, and the street vendors still hawked their *milagros* and T-shirts to tourists along *Avenida 16 de Septiembre*.

Only in the battering crush of so many could one find such complete anonymity.

It was something she was counting on.

Suddenly it was their turn. Closely following the two women, Angel stepped forward, chest tightening—the moment of truth. But it turned out to be anticlimactic. A tall, lanky guard with a helpful face and nervous eyes cupped a hand over his earpiece, trying to hear above the din. The young man looked rattled. The line of dignitaries snaking out of the tent wasn't moving fast enough and he was catching hell for it. Mistakenly assuming the three of them would be joining their husbands, he held Angel's false passport under a black light, and when no warnings popped up, waved them through.

Relieved, Angel led the two women through a three-meter-high metal detector and stopped at the base of a paved walkway to accept a flute of Krug from a circulating waiter. She turned to Yesenia Torrez, patting her messenger bag. "I'm afraid you'll have to excuse me. I must drop off these Cohibas in the club humidor. There's an after-party poker game, and a lawyer without her cigars could get disbarred."

"A woman smoking cigars . . . and playing poker?" asked Chela, somewhat surprised.

"Especially a woman," responded Angel, "*especially* a woman."

Chela nodded, despite the disappointment in her eyes. "Perhaps we'll see you upstairs at the reception?" she asked hopefully.

"Only if you'll promise not to outbid me."

Chela brushed a stray tendril of hair from her face. "No promises, Ms. Perez—"

"—Maria, please. How soon they forget."

"I'll look forward to seeing you at dinner." Chela raised a flute of champagne and gazed into the refraction of the crystal, a lovely open smile lifting her lips.

Seductively, she turned, and Angel watched the two women get swallowed up by a steady stream of arriving guests. Standing perfectly still, feeling one up on the world, she allowed herself a brief moment of triumph. *She'd beaten their external security. She was halfway home.* She hiked the charcoal-gray messenger bag over her left shoulder and twisted her stiff neck from side-to-side until it popped. *Let's see what the federales have laid on for us tonight?*

She accepted the guard's sloppiness as an omen of good fortune—she was superstitious that way—and swiftly assessed the security inside the well-lit compound, searching for any changes in routine or heightened levels of awareness. There were none. Luck was with her.

Moving swiftly, she bypassed a massive outdoor fire pit and slipped behind a wall of mesquite trees, neatly avoiding a laser tripwire, only to discover a partially-lit servant's path running parallel to the main walkway. She was about to set foot on the path when her instincts told her to stop.

Something gleamed in the rosebushes.

Leaning down to fiddle with a strap on her sandals, she spotted a necklet of fiber optics dangling from a basket of red heirloom roses. It was a microwave motion sensor: German-made, self-calibrating, twenty-gigahertz, draped around the roses to look like a decorative light.

Duly warned, she made a more detailed sweep of the grounds and realized that someone *was* actually paying attention. Ten meters in front of her a pair of closed-circuit television cameras had been mounted on mesh wire at both ends of the badminton court. Beneath the cameras, several pressure-sensitive ground plates had been dug alongside a stretch of temporary fence that separated the club's conference center from its golf course. The top of the fence had been reinforced with concertina wire. Recalling the cardinal rule of vanity that first impressions were often the most deceiving, Angel realized that whoever had installed this package meant business.

On cue, an unmarked utility vehicle with two whip antennas eased to a halt in front of her.

"Good evening, señora," the driver said in a precise, clipped manner, shining his headlamps in Angel's face. "You're a long way from the party."

Cupping both eyes, Angel squinted through the beams and saw a squared-off chin, intense brown eyes, a soldier's physique. The insignia on his left shoulder identified him as part of a small but effective VIP protection detail pulled together by the assistant attorney general.

This was something new, she thought, raising an eyebrow.

I'm afraid I'm terribly lost," she replied sheepishly. "Could you point me towards the main reception area? I'm supposed to meet my escort there."

Using his modified HM-3 submachine gun, the guard motioned towards the club's opulent main lobby, its copper-trimmed doors rising grandly into an elaborate portico. "That way . . . and señora, stay on the main path."

Angel nodded. "I certainly will." She made her way past the badminton court onto a winding half-lit cobblestone walkway. Feeling naked without her Glock, she approached the cavernous lobby behind a gaggle of septuagenarians sipping aged Cinco Tragos, each being warmly greeted by an obsequious attendant standing behind a carved oak desk. The attendant bowed slightly as Angel approached. "And how are we this evening, señora?"

"Quite well, thank you," said Angel, missing Yesenia's "senorita" moniker. "It's a beautiful night for an event."

"Will you be joining us for cocktails on the roof terrace?"

"No, just dinner tonight."

"Very good. Unfortunately, due to security precautions, I'll have to check your bag before you enter the dining area."

"Of course," she said, opening the messenger bag. "But as you can see, it's just a box of Cohibas that I'll need to drop off in your humidor. It will just take a minute."

"Certainly, señora." The attendant bowed, closing the bag. He remained there as Angel strolled in the opposite direction of the grand dining hall, past an expensive collection of antique furniture. High above her was a box-beam ceiling; below, a heart pine floor mopped to a low sheen. Several airbrushed paintings of past Mexican presidents had been mounted on both sides of the paneled hallway. At the opposite end was a lavishly-designed lounge filled with deep cowhide armchairs, a washed blue chandelier, and fleur-de-lis embossed wallpaper. Several meters to her right, at the back of the bar, was a delivery entrance where a tiny Chontal woman, her raven hair held back by a rhinestone headband, pushed a tall metallic food cart through the kitchen's double doors, rolling it directly towards Angel.

"The gods are with us tonight," she murmured.

Timing her move perfectly, Angel began walking lockstep with the cart, shielding her body from the lobby attendant. As the cart approached a silver damascene door fronting the women's spa, she took a quick look over her shoulder, then slipped unseen into the changing room.

The bright vanity lights forced her to pause at a marble sink to let her eyes adjust. From the reflection in the mirror, she counted six cream colored stalls, each with galvanized pewter hooks on the doors. To her right, a row of full-length mirrors led to a Swedish steam sauna. To her left, a line of custom-made hardwood lockers were filled with designer toiletries. Directly above her, she heard guests making their way to the roof garden, their steps echoing loudly off the Travertine tile. Confident that she was alone, Angel turned and entered the fourth stall from the spa door, bolted it shut and placed the Vuitton bag on top of the toilet lid. Reaching behind the tank, she removed a white plastic shopping bag that had been taped to the back of the toilet and tore it open. Inside was a thin sheet of dark polyethylene, a quart-sized Handy Bag, a sealed envelope wrapped around a tin of black boot polish, a flathead screwdriver, and a Number 10 Bard-Parker scalpel. She removed each and spread them across the lid of the toilet.

The Handy Bag had been reinforced with gray duct tape and packed with eight wafers of shaped C-4 explosives, just like her handlers said it would be. After taking a few seconds to inspect the items, Angel unwound the rubber band holding the linen envelope wrapped around the tin of boot polish and tore the envelope open, shaking out a pale blue Post-it note. Scribbled on it were the license plate number, make, and model of the vintage pickup truck her target would be driving.

Angel memorized the information, then ripped the note into tiny shreds and flushed them down the toilet. She checked her Rolex—the silent auction had fifteen minutes to go—and shoved the rest of the items into the messenger bag, placed the cigars on top, then meticulously wiped down the stall.

She propped the door open with her foot—the changing area was empty. With the Vuitton bag in her right hand, she retraced her steps out the spa door and waited. The noisy lounge was filling with bored donors in search of something stronger than champagne. Angel kept her eyes pinned to the attendant, waiting for him to turn his back. The metallic food cart was nowhere to be seen. The tiny woman who'd been pushing it was probably upstairs serving hors d'oeuvres. With her left hip pressed against the wall, Angel listened to the steady stream of refugees parked at the bar beneath a mammoth portrait of Andrés Manuel López Obrador. When the attendant finally turned to greet an arriving couple, Angel slipped into the hallway, carefully rotated her face away from the surveillance camera, and without looking back, strolled quietly past the gallery of presidents and out the delivery door.

By 7:00, the *Nueva Aurora* was swarming with dozens of well-dressed dinner guests eager to gorge themselves on *Lobster Veracruzana* or *Filet a la Plancha* and hear the latest policy initiatives from one of Chihuahua's most conservative federal judges. With the judge safely locked inside, the protection teams had switched their primary focus to the main buildings, leaving the local cops to patrol the perimeter. Nobody was paying attention to a stylishly-dressed woman scouring the lot for a 2007 Ford F-250 pickup with vintage powder-blue Chihuahua plates. The judge had a soft spot for old trucks; he thought they made him look like a man of the people. Nor did anyone notice the fifty-two seconds it took for the same woman to jimmy the lock on the passenger side with a screwdriver—it wasn't until model year 2008 that passive anti-theft computer chips had been embedded in the keys of Ford's F-250s—and slip undetected into the back seat of the truck.

Pressing her left hand flush against the rear door panel, Angel wormed her way back-and-forth across the cab and squeezed directly behind the driver's seat. Keeping both palms flat on her thighs, elbows tight to her body, she settled into a cross-legged position on the floor and took several deep breaths, emptying her lungs, then refilling them. She did this ten times, saturating her blood with oxygen. As her body started to unknot, she closed her eyes and began to visualize what was going to happen next. Part of her was preparing for the kill, the other part picturing her escape, which emphasized hiding in plain sight. She was going to ride the F-250 straight out the *Nueva Aurora's* front gate.

Feeling energized, she removed the scalpel from the Vuitton and unsheathed its stainless-steel blade, gripping the green plastic handle in her right hand. Working off the reflections from the parking lot LEDs, she unfolded the flat sheet of polyethylene, cut a hole in its center and pushed her head through, letting the plastic drape over her shoulders like a poncho. That done, she curled deeper into the cab, flattening her spine against the door panel, sitting tight.

The cramped back seat was damp and musty and filled with the usual detritus of a judge's life: dog-eared legal files, a chipped iPad, last week's copy of *El Financiero*. Angel shoved it all to one side, keeping her shoulders low, mindful of the overhead lights. Checking her watch, she figured the guests would be seated by now, her target in the center of the dais enjoying the limelight.

The parking lot lamps flickered. The club's exterior doors were now locked for security purposes. Any late arrivals would be seated in the lounge until the appetizer course was finished.

Feeling at ease, she applied two fingers to her carotid artery. Her heartbeat had tapered to forty-eight beats per minute. Perfect. Tucking her head between her knees, the distant chatter of portable mics clicking like cicadas, she let out a soft breath and found her center.

"Almost time," she whispered.

Luck was with her now.

•   •   •

Three hours later, Angel's eyes opened. She was still huddled on the grimy floor mat.

Lifting her head, the parking lot was nearly empty, the night sky surprisingly clear, stars twinkling over the city. She tried to identify the Milky Way, but the LEDs were too bright, so she curled back down behind the driver's seat and let her mind journey in and out of wakefulness, seeking fear then banishing it. When she reached calm, she exhaled. While the security guards handling the judge's protection were good, she was better.

Soon her entire body began to tingle, adrenaline coursing through her veins like a hit of speed. She reached into the Vuitton bag, flicked open the tin of shoe polish, and began rubbing black beeswax over every centimeter of exposed skin except a tiny red angel wearing a sombrero tattooed onto her right triceps. Feeling a sudden chill, she took the scalpel blade and ran the flat edge along the tattoo. It felt smooth, soothing. Raising herself, she punctured the overhead interior lamp with the scalpel's plastic handle, catching the shards in her free hand and tossing them into the Vuitton bag. Next, she removed her white gold Rolex watch and slipped it into her pants pocket. Her internal clock said it was time. She settled deeper into the back seat, shifting slightly so she could see the judge's reflection when he opened the driver's-side door.

Gravel rasped outside. A shadow crossed the windshield as voices circled the pickup. The judge's bodyguards breezed around the F-250, giving it a cursory glance before hustling off to their chase vehicle.

Too lackadaisical, thought Angel, and immediately chastised herself. Underestimating one's enemy was a fool's mistake. Pressing her spine tighter against the door panel, she repositioned her knees and exhaled deep from the belly. Another shadow darkened the driver's-side window. The door lock opened, and the back of the judge's head slid behind the steering wheel.

Inhaling, holding her breath, Angel knew she was nearly invisible beneath the black plastic.

She maintained her crouch, praying there'd be no other passengers—she badly wanted to avoid collateral damage—as the judge settled into his seat. He flicked on the car radio, tuning the volume low. Nobody else entered the cab. The jurist touched a number on his cell phone, told his protection team he was heading home, then twisted the ignition. The V8 engine roared to life. It took a few seconds to navigate the mostly-empty lot, the judge slowing to roll down his window and wave to the guards manning the front gate.

Clearing the country club grounds, the F-250 accelerated through the quiet neighborhoods. Angel lifted her pelvis, touching the tip of the scalpel with her left index finger, noting the street signs as they flew by. They were heading due east.

This is good, very good, she told herself.

Every time the pickup hit a speed bump, she pressed her weight into both feet, easing up another centimeter onto her toes. She kept her elbows tucked against her body for balance, her eyes glued to the back of the judge's head. In a heartbeat they were under an overpass and Angel knew exactly where they were going. *Contingency number one . . . perfect.*

For this option, the cartel had arranged for the judge's chase car to be stopped along Boulevard Zaragoza east of the highway, leaving the F-250 unprotected for several minutes. As the lamps from the cement overpass whisked by, the pickup began to slow, passing a shuttered *tortillería.* Four heavily-armed soldiers stood leaning against a camouflaged SDN Humvee, a portable street sign flashing *Control de Tráfico* on the right side of the boulevard.

The F-250 crawled to a stop near the flashing sign, and a slender officer stepped forward, raising his left hand. The judge rolled down his window, and a flashlight shone in his face. After a second or two, he was waved through, but the chase car a few meters back was ordered to stop, its occupants told to get out.

The judge's cell phone buzzed. "What now?" Irritated, he listened to the response. "No, I'm almost home. Catch up at the villa. You can finish your shift outside the gates." The judge disconnected and tossed the smartphone onto the seat beside him. He pressed the accelerator and the F-250 left the chase car behind. Angel exhaled. *They make it so easy.*

She let a couple minutes pass, hovering motionless. They turned left on Rafael Terrazas Cienfuegos. Angel lifted from her deep squat, reached around the headrest, and pressed the scalpel blade against the judge's throat.

"Jesus . . . shit, what the—?" The F-250 swerved right, striking the curb.

"Easy," commanded Angel. "Straighten it out and keep both hands on the wheel, eyes straight ahead. Do anything stupid and I'll open an artery." The judge's knuckles turned white as he gripped the steering wheel tighter. Angel counted the blocks as they kept driving. She was searching for a corrugated tin shed with a Sol Beer sign painted on one side.

Light from the street lamps reflected off the windshield as the pickup gained speed. The judge's breathing was rapid now, his eyes frantically darting to and from the rearview mirror.

Nobody was there, the chase vehicle still stuck at the checkpoint.

"I have money . . . cash, American dollars. It's in my—"

"Shut up," ordered Angel. On her right, a tattered Sol Beer ad painted on the side of a ramshackle shed passed by. "Take the next left," she instructed. The F-250 drove thirty more meters then made a slow left hand turn onto a pitch-dark side street, its headlights catching a pack of stray dogs tearing into a trash bag. "Pull up behind the white Fusion and keep your seat belt fastened."

The judge eased the pickup behind a dingy off-white sedan. The Fusion's left rear panel had been spray-painted with the word "Morena" in bright red. "Turn off the headlights," said Angel.

"How much? How much are they paying you? I'll double it . . . triple it." The judge was pleading now. "I've got cash . . . thousands of U.S. dollars, more than enough. Just talk to me."

"Is the cash nearby?"

The judge's neck twisted slightly. "No, but I can get it. I just have to make a few calls."

"Fair enough. It's just past nine o'clock in the morning in Germany—the banks should be open by now. How fast can you wire the cash you stole from the *comandante*?"

For a split second there was a look of pure terror in the rearview mirror as the judge realized he'd been caught. Like a caged animal he lunged for the door, but Angel whipped her left forearm around his head and pressed the blade against the left side of the jurist's throat just below the chin.

As she pulled laterally across the skin, a steady application of pressure opened the carotids.

The judge's eyes rolled back as both hands reached for his throat, blood spilling between his fingers and down into his lap. He bled out within seconds.

Angel wiped the blade on the judge's sleeve and crawled into the front seat.

The pickup was still idling. Like a contortionist, she maneuvered the driver's seat all the way back and deftly straddled the judge's body, using torn pages from the *El Financiero* to wipe an opening in the blood spatter across the windshield. She shifted the F-250 into Drive and the pickup crawled down the street and back onto Cienfuegos. Angel steered it towards the dilapidated shed with the Sol Beer sign. She parked the vehicle, climbed out, and scanned the barred windows all around her.

At this hour the neighborhood was quiet, everyone in bed. She opened the door on the passenger's side of the pickup, reached across the back seat, grabbed the Vuitton bag, unzipped it, and removed the Handy Bag full of C-4 plastiqué. She peeled off several crystal-white tabs with detonator sticks attached. Using the scalpel, she cut a slender opening under the floor carpet on the passenger's side of the pickup and tucked the leftover C-4 beneath the carpet, covering the opening as best she could. She had no illusions about the explosives being found. That was expected—the murder had to look like a botched terrorist act. But eventually word would get out that the judge's throat had been cut and that was fine, too. The *comandante* wanted everyone to know what happened to those who stole from him. As if anyone needed a refresher.

Angel closed the passenger door and began dropping detonators around the shed. Moving unseen, her back against the building, she used a cross step to circle the shed, her body blending easily into the shadows. As she set the explosives, sirens blared in the distance. Almost done, she thought. When detonated, the slender tabs of C-4 would destroy a good deal of the shed, but not enough to singe the flats of marijuana inside. The plastiqué in the pickup wouldn't react. Their detonators were set on different frequencies.

When she'd hiked the few blocks back to the Fusion, she retrieved the entry remote adhesed to the front bumper and opened the driver's side door. Before climbing in, she pulled off the plastic poncho and tossed the blood-covered polyethylene beside an abandoned BarcaLounger for the dogs to rip into. Settling into the driver's seat, she leaned forward, searching for the electronic detonator tucked beneath the front passenger seat. She snatched it and placed it in the seat beside her.

The sedan started on the second try. Breathing deep, Angel drove past the shed, catching a glimmer of razor wire flickering from the roof. It reminded her of her escape into Nogales as a child. Reaching for the detonator, she counted to three and pressed Activate.

The Sol Beer sign sparked brightly, lighting up the evening sky behind her.

So far so good, but the evening wasn't done yet.

PART TWO

CHAPTER SEVEN

At forty-five miles an hour the black BMW 650i barely made the sweeping two-lane curve, its concave rims kicking up a pinwheel of sparks along the curb. If it hadn't been for the vehicle's automatic driveline tamping down the overcorrection, the sedan would've jumped the sidewalk, calling even more attention to itself.

Dieter Eberstein watched the BMW downshift, gunning its 445-horsepower engine.

"Beautiful," he mumbled, barely hiding his disgust. "Next time why not just fire off an M-80. It would be less conspicuous."

Eberstein turned to see if anyone was watching, but there was only a smattering of pedestrians loitering near the Pavilion. A light drizzle, unusual for Los Angeles, dampened the checkered tablecloth at the outdoor café where he was sitting. Restless, he pulled a cheap burner phone from the inside pocket of his sport coat and checked its display for messages.

Thankfully, there were none. His meeting was still on.

Sliding forward in his seat as he sipped his espresso, he scanned the parked cars along the sidewalk, keeping intermittent surveillance on the customers who came and went. In front of the café's patio, three nearby boulevards emptied into a slender greenbelt. Two of the streets ran parallel to a popular walking path, the other dead-ended in front of a Rite Aid drugstore. There were also a skate park, a concrete band shell, and several joggers dressed in burgundy-and-black Adidas gear circling the greenbelt at a brisk clip. Eberstein gave one of the more attractive runners a short courtesy nod.

"Will that be all, sir?" The waiter's voice startled him.

"No . . . actually yes, yes, thank you," Eberstein stumbled. "It was excellent."

The waiter nodded, collected the bone china cup and saucer, and threaded his way through a row of empty tables, hurrying to get out of the wet mist. Eberstein's eyes followed him searching for signs of alarm. But the disinterested waiter ducked through a glass-paneled double door and never once looked back.

You're getting paranoid, Eberstein lamented. A thick, stultifying mist hung like a wayward cloud over the cramped townhomes. But one didn't survive six years as a seven-figure C-suite executive without a healthy dose of mistrust. Paranoia was simply part of the job.

His burner phone rang. A quick, shrill chirp, repeated twice over. There was only one person who knew the number, so Eberstein let it chirp. Straightening his shoulders, inching further forward in his seat, he flattened his elbows on the arm caps of his chair and eased both hands beneath the table, keeping his eyes glued to the boulevard.

A traffic horn sounded as he touched the laminated wood grip of the Sig-Sauer P220 nestled between his thighs. With a smooth practiced motion, he racked the slide to chamber a round, then tucked the Sig-Sauer into the waistband of his worsted wool slacks. He'd bought the unlicensed handgun at an outdoor flea market in Primm, Nevada, its serial numbers filed off and swabbed with acid, its grip refitted. At the dealer's suggestion, Eberstein had purchased a box of hollow points from a neighboring vendor, then taken the afternoon off to sharpen his skills at a shooting range along South Figueroa near the LA Coliseum.

He checked his wristwatch, a ruthenium-plated Nomos Tangente purchased for cash on Rodeo Drive. A small gift to himself he'd splurged on. Having grown up in a Soviet-era apartment block in the Pankow neighborhood of Berlin, Eberstein loved everything about LA: the women, the weather, the constant action. Draining the last of his espresso, he tossed a few dollars onto the table as an aqua-colored sanitation truck crawled to a halt in front of him, its mechanical arm reaching for an oversized recycle bin. Eberstein's phone chirped again. This time he picked up.

"*Parken*," he snapped then broke off the call.

Slipping the burner into his sport coat, he exited through a squeaky half-gate, looking both ways before crossing the busy street. There was one final chirp. He checked the display and grunted to himself before dropping the phone on the wet asphalt and smashing it with the heel of his loafer. Retrieving the larger pieces, he tossed them into a huge bin.

All along the street shoppers lingered as boutique windows backlit by powerful track lighting came alive with promise. Standing under a colorful overhang, Eberstein carefully searched his reflection in a jeweler's large picture window, hunting for a familiar face or misplaced gaze behind him. Spotting none, he turned left and walked quickly down a quiet side street into the skate park, moving with the hurried speed of an old buddy running late for a breakfast meeting with a friend.

Near the greenbelt, Luca Manser finally spotted an empty parking space and violently spun the BMW's steering wheel like the Formula One driver he'd once dreamed of being. As the 650i fishtailed over the gutter, easing into a designated handicap parking space, Eberstein's eyes followed its progress. "A handicapped space? A *goddamn* handicapped parking space. Are you out of your mind, Luca?"

Fortunately, foot traffic was light. The only offended spectator was a fit, young cyclist in a Lotto Belisol jersey watching the 650i pull into the handicapped space without the proper disabled placard. The cyclist came to a halt near the BMW's right rear tire, intent on straightening things out. But he had barely laid down his CrossRip when the heavy-set Manser exploded from the driver's-side door and stormed around the front of the sedan, glowering at the rider like an irate bear.

Suddenly realizing his overzealousness, the well-meaning cyclist quickly remounted his touring bike and began pedaling furiously in the opposite direction, looking over his shoulder every few seconds as he pulled away.

A wise decision, thought Eberstein. His boss, Luca Manser, president and CEO of Deutsche Ärzte International, DAI, was the classic caricature of an old-school Bavarian: stout, meaty, with fleshy red jowls, and a mane of silvery ash-blonde hair that touched the shoulders of his loud Eurasian beaver coat. Locking the sedan door with his remote, he flashed another disgusted look at the retreating cyclist then windmilled his matching fur hat at Eberstein, his cerulean blue eyes vanishing behind a series of staccato blinks.

"Dieter! Good God, it is you. Come here, let me have a look." Manser squared to face him, studying his CFO's sunken gray eyes. The pair sized each other up as only familiar colleagues could. Having just turned forty-six, the willowy Eberstein stood medium height, bald, with strong cheekbones, flat forehead, and a sharp Saxon jawline. Otherwise, he was completely nondescript, except for the vacant dove-gray eyes that reminded Manser of a predator. It was something that had bothered him ever since he'd hired the brilliant, taciturn analyst away from Siemens years ago.

Still searching Eberstein's face, Manser's smile tightened. "I can see crow's feet around your eyes, Dieter-boy. Doing a bit of worrying, eh? That's never good for my bank account."

The early morning sun made a brief appearance before slipping behind a shroud of bruised clouds. Having collected its refuse, the garbage truck roared down the opposite street, the men giving it time to pass. "It's good to be outside," was all Eberstein could think of saying, extending his hand. But Manser gave it a long, dry look, took a step forward, and wrapped his CFO in a huge bear hug. "The office would've been much more comfortable," wheezed Eberstein, turning sideways so his boss couldn't feel the Sig-Sauer. "But one can never get enough fresh air."

"Special business deserves the proper setting," said Manser, releasing his grip. "Let's walk, this way."

They strolled north through a crowded neighborhood, the CEO lighting up an unfiltered Camel, blowing a wreath of smoke away from Eberstein's face. "Good Germans never forget the rain, my friend. Too much California can thin one's blood."

"Yes, warm balmy weather can be quite the nightmare," said Eberstein, his words coated in sarcasm as he tightened his full-length overcoat. Deutsche Ärzte's hospital acquisitions in Texas, California, and Nevada had acclimated him to more agreeable climates, far from the wet clouds and suffocating rigidity of the corporate headquarters in Stuttgart.

There wasn't a day in Germany he didn't miss the States.

The men crossed to a small playground, taking an oblique direction away from the busy park, sauntering easily, enjoying the walk. They wandered down a long narrow street past several boxy two-story stucco "dingbat" duplexes with their tuck-under parking. Once reviled, these weatherworn dingbats had been repainted and were now considered fashionably chic. This was old LA, seemingly untouched by progress, its flat tar roofs and slender columns hiding an irony of immense proportion, an enigma of the Second World War, a mockery of what might've been.

Something that could've survived only during the presidency of Donald J. Trump.

Eighty meters into the alley, the two men queued outside a recessed ticket booth, waiting on a pimply-faced teenager sitting behind an old-fashioned cash register guarded by bulletproof glass. Her pale blue eyes were buried in her smartphone. "Twenty-five bucks each," she mumbled without looking up.

Eberstein paid cash for both of them, not wanting to leave a paper trail, and they entered a shabby squared-off anteroom, the overpowering tang of disinfectant causing Eberstein's eyes to water. A metal security door in the middle of the room was propped open by a pair of unused stanchions. The door led to an oak-paneled hallway that emptied into a dingy neo-classical meeting room serving as the center of a small museum. Muted light streamed in from a row of stained-glass windows high above the exhibits. Cold and dank and smelling of urine, the museum had been commissioned in 2016 by the German American Scientific Society and housed the abbreviated history of the Third Reich's failed attempt to produce an atomic weapon.

Treading reverently, Eberstein couldn't help but feel its impenetrable darkness. It made his skin crawl. All around him dozens of crude diagrams, wooden models, and the biographies of scientists who had labored under Adolf Hitler's grotesque nightmare were scattered, some in glass cases, others out in the open on tables. Wooden benches resembling church pews had been carved into the room's heavily lacquered walls, and several crude initials, plus a Star of David, had been scratched into the rough brick. Keeping his overcoat on, Eberstein watched Manser clasp both hands behind his back and fastidiously tour the pathetic exhibits where the official retrospective began in 1944 ahead of the Allied takeover. "The business in Juárez was concluded to our mutual friends' satisfaction?" he asked, his nose inches from a glass display describing the Nazi's earliest attempts at cold fusion.

"Yes, our Mexican partners send their regards," said Eberstein. "Obviously, they weren't too happy with Judge Ramirez's creative banking practices."

"Or the fact that he was stealing from them . . . getting rid of him sent a message. I assume their wire transfers arrived in the usual offshore accounts?"

"Arm's-length, everything untraceable."

"Let's hope so," warned Manser, his huge hands engulfing a hard clay model of an atom.

Eberstein fidgeted; he hated being second-guessed. "Right. And what other options did we have? The acquisition of Hurston Neurological doesn't get done without the cartel's money. Besides, somebody had to throw a bag around this mess. We're running out of time."

Almost at once he regretted sounding pushy. Manser hated that kind of thing. He considered it disrespectful. Arching an eyebrow, still holding the clay model, his boss turned slowly towards him. "Relax, Dieter. I'm sure the good Doctor has everything under control.

"*Relax?*" Eberstein's voice pitched an octave too high. "Relax? Your greedy fucking Dr. Girard is a walking disaster. His malpractice lawsuits, his drug habits, his doctor-lawyer scam. He could be a federal witness for God's sakes!"

Manser turned the model over in his hands, his mouth stretching into a tiny sneer. "I see. So now he's *my* greedy Dr. Girard? I thought we were in this together?"

"Don't twist my words, you know what I mean. Girard's so far off the reservation, he's almost—"

"Yes, but the man impresses me," said Manser, cutting him off. "Such vigor and energy, and such a complete whoredog. Who would've thought a middle-aged neurosurgeon with such insatiable tastes for drugs and prostitutes could screw up a $73 million deal to buy out his group. Amazing, truly amazing."

"I'm glad you're so easily amused."

"Christ, Dieter, since when did you become such a pussy? The cartel is happy. Texting them Ramirez's banking records was a chit well used. It keeps our investment relationship intact and, as you pointed out, we need their cash. In fact, given last quarter's financials, I'd say we'd be broke without them. Our liquidity has somehow vanished. By the way, where did the cartel get their information on our wayward doctor? Quite impressive for a bunch of cocaine savages."

Eberstein cringed, his eyes flicking about the empty museum, anxiety radiating off him like a beacon. "Could you say that a little louder," he muttered caustically, his head on a swivel. "I don't think the microphones quite got all of it, especially that part about the cocaine."

Having survived ten years in DAI's cutthroat culture, rising from budget analyst to assistant controller to CFO, Eberstein had developed a healthy fixation for privacy.

"So now you're my security expert?" There was a hint of amusement in Manser's voice. He put down the clay atom and surveyed the empty room. "But you didn't answer me. The cartel— how did they get their information about our illustrious Dr. Girard? It was way too detailed for local talent."

"Those cocaine savages, as you so politely put it, run a two-billion-dollar enterprise with sources throughout Central and South America. They tapped their contact inside the Costa Rican Department of Intelligence and Security, who accessed Datum, a secure database. That provided them with a detailed history of Girard's trips to and from Juárez. Then they traced his credit cards to the Hotel Lucerna, where they used photo surveillance to monitor his cash drops at several different branches of BanCrédito."

"Money laundering?"

"His share from the malpractice settlements skimmed with his lawyer buddies here in LA."

Manser nodded approvingly, mildly impressed with the cartel's sophistication, as well as with Girard's acumen. He felt no such warmth for his fellow Germans who had migrated to southern California for the weather and loathed this pitiful "museum" with its stained walls and scuffed flooring and morbid exhibits that only reminded them of a past they were trying hard to forget. Manser's attention drifted back to a composite photo of Germany's elite research scientists, his voice betraying the hatred he felt for their failure to create a nuclear weapon.

"Look at these men, these disgusting cretins who betrayed the German people so utterly—the *Intellektuellen*." For a moment he looked like he was going to spit, but instead he redirected his gaze to several black-and-white photographs of Nazi leaders, many of them defaced. "Hitler, Bormann, Goring. Some say heroic warriors, but history has judged them to be monsters. But these scientists," Manser thrust a thick finger at a different composite photo, "these *Juden*, who were either too cowardly or too traitorous to save The Reich. And what did they do instead?— abandoned our beloved Fatherland to the degenerate Slavs and drug-addled Americans who raped and pillaged our country like animals. Tell me, Dieter, what do you believe in?" Eberstein didn't bother answering. He was studying the museum's static surveillance cameras, relieved to see they were several generations out of date. "Anything other than the almighty dollar or your next Ferrari . . . or last night's hooker?" Manser was baiting him, but Eberstein refused to bite, focusing instead on the security cameras.

"Ancient history, Luca. The war ended seventy-five years ago. Nobody cares but you and the skinhead freaks you hang out with. You're lucky this place hasn't been shuttered."

Manser grunted, standing perfectly still as he inspected a cheap wooden model of the bomb. Unable to relax, Eberstein discreetly slid a hand into his overcoat pocket, removed a slim three-ounce T-10 Bug Detector, and flipped the On switch. His boss eyed him with amused disdain as Eberstein let out a noticeable sigh of relief when the detection alarm didn't react.

"Sometimes great leaders must do horrific things," Manser continued. He loved to lecture, his tone laced with superiority. "There is no moral high ground, my friend. When you jump into bed with savages, count on spending the rest of your life looking over your shoulder." Manser adored this hideous claptrap, making a point to visit at least once a month. A year earlier, when the museum was running low on cash, a mysterious donation of three million dollars had magically appeared. But he helped in other ways, too. His lawyers, hidden behind a labyrinth of front companies, defended the museum's right to exist as an act of freedom of speech, using their contacts within the current administration and threats of legal action to keep the museum off any hate group lists.

"So let's quit pretending our hands are clean," preached Manser. "Once the cartels get their hooks into you, there's no turning back. They wire us funds. We pay them back with usurious interest rates. We let our banker friend ID a judge who's stealing from them; they reciprocate with surveillance on Dr. Girard. One hand washes the other . . . until it doesn't."

Eberstein gently massaged the inside pocket of his overcoat, tracing the outline of an engraved pewter flask his late father had given him for his twenty-first birthday.

Fighting off the sudden urge to take a nip of his beloved Doornkaat Schnapps, the only thing he'd missed during his months in the States, he squirreled his hands deeper into his pockets and pivoted to face his boss. "The Hurston acquisition should go much smoother now," he said, trying to sound more confident than he felt. "Once the deal closes, we'll use Hurston's pension funds to refinance our debt on the new rehab hospital in Reno. We'll then resell Hurston and Reno along with our Fresno and El Paso facilities to Regent for over $900 million. That should clear us about $250 million in cash, and it gets better."

Manser put down the wooden model, paying attention for the first time. "I'm listening."

"The Inglewood National Bank is holding all of Hurston's debt, almost $61 million. The bank went belly-up last month and was raided by the FDIC, who will manage it until a new owner can be found. Their first order of business will be to clean up the balance sheet by repackaging Hurston's loans with the bank's other toxic assets and selling the combined debt for about twenty cents on the dollar."

Manser stopped in his tracks. "You're sure of this?" His azure eyes were glistening.

"I bribed one of their loan officers."

"So once we've acquired Hurston," Manser said, thinking out loud, "we stop making payments on its loans then renegotiate with the FDIC to buy back the debt at about twenty-three cents on the dollar *before* they can repackage the loans as part of some discounted portfolio they'll sell to some predatory hedge fund."

"It's the American way," said Eberstein. "Trump, Trump, Trump. We trim over $45 million in debt, refinance at a lower rate, *and* dramatically increase Hurston's market value."

"And that will be enough to cover the subprime mess from Obersalzberg?"

"*For fuck's sakes, Luca!*" Eberstein's face suddenly turned red, his eyes darting around the room like a hunted animal. "Are you out of your mind? The FBI monitors everything, especially in a dump like this. Never mention that fiasco in public again unless you want to wake up tomorrow with your face plastered all over social media with that filthy neo-Nazi trash you hang out with!"

Embarrassed, Manser waved a hand in surrender. Not used to being chastised, he stared silently at the painted cement floor, then let out a long disagreeable sigh, wanting to say something but deciding not to. Neither man spoke for a few moments as their moods became increasingly tense, the silence thick. "We could've lost the whole company . . . everything," whispered Eberstein, like someone reliving a near death experience. "Your glorious Berchtesgaden project nearly wiped us out. Are you listening to me?"

Seething, Manser folded both hands in front of him, intertwining his fingers, palms up, thumbs out. It was a nervous habit he had developed as a child when he became irritated. "Talk to me again like that and I'll shove that gun you're carrying right up your bony ass." When he twisted his neck, his ridiculous fur hat dipped below his forehead. "And quit your goddamn whining. Berchtesgaden is done, buried. Hitler's bunker is gone. Just get the damn deal done."

Shuttered and returned to the German government in September 1995, the General Walker, the former U.S. military hotel that overlooked Hitler's underground bunker system near Berchtesgaden, had sat empty for years until Manser's group purchased it using one of DAI's offshore subsidiaries, hoping to convert it into an exclusive orthopedic hospital for its wealthy alt-right European patients. But renovations stalled under local zoning protests, and Deutsche Ärzte was forced to switch strategies, choosing to invest heavily in thirteen new medical office buildings in Berlin and Hamburg, piling up millions in corporate debt. But the timing was off. Europe's economy had stalled under the weight of another continent-wide recession, and the company was forced to dump its entire stake in the General Walker, but only after its auditors ordered a complete write-down on its books. It was Eberstein who had come up with the idea of acquiring and flipping cash-heavy U.S. hospitals and physician practices like Hurston Neurological to pay back the $250 million in private equity loans that DAI had taken out to cover the write-down.

"We need to get this deal done, *soon*," Manser murmured. "We miss our next loan payment and we'll have to explain to the Board—"

"—how we funded the write-down in the first place?" Eberstein finished his thought.

"And I doubt they'll look kindly on borrowing millions from a Mexican drug cartel."

Eberstein rubbed the back of his neck, his mind absorbing the implications. But it was too late for recriminations—too many laws had been broken, too much blood had been spilled. Tired of his CEO's second-guessing, he edged closer to Manser and whispered, "Exactly what else would you have me do? Apologize for saving your company? Say I'm sorry for keeping you out of prison, which is exactly where you'd be if it hadn't been for the cartel. So trust me, Luca, the Board is the least of our problems."

"Is that why you have that gun stuffed in your pants like some two-bit gangbanger?"

Eberstein's face reddened, his hands shifting instinctively towards his waistband, his whole body feeling gutted. "And you avoided my question," he countered quickly. "Tell me what we could have done differently. Our Mexican colleagues are happy; the Hurston deal is back on track; and the Board doesn't know shit. So just let me do my job and I'll get you your goddamn money."

Manser's eyes bulged, his hands shaking slightly. "You're never done with these animals, you're never out. Did you know their hitter, Angel, is a woman? I'm telling you, these people are clever, and ruthless. They'll do anything."

"Then let's make sure our involvement stays untraceable."

Manser nodded. There was nothing left to say. Gazing down at his diamond wristwatch, he suddenly realized how quickly the morning had disappeared. He was eager to get out of the museum. Facing Eberstein, he asked, "And exactly where are we with *my* Dr. Girard? Are his fellow neurosurgeons on board?"

"There are a few holdouts, but he's working on it. The surgeons will vote on the sale at their next partners' meeting."

"You're sure of this?"

"As positive as I—"

"Get sure." Manser said, his voice simmering. "We can't tolerate any more delays. Between raiding Hurston's pension fund and renegotiating the practice's debt, we'll finally have enough cash to get ourselves out of this mess."

What little warmth there'd been between the two had evaporated. Eyeing Manser, Eberstein remembered when he had once admired this aging visionary who had built Deutsche Ärzte from a small hospital holding company into one of Germany's largest international conglomerates. Now he was betting his life's work on a group of Los Angeles neurosurgeons. It was insane.

"Get it under control, Dieter." Manser's intensity caused his breath to come in short, ragged bursts. Turning towards a dusty portrait of Hitler, he put a huge arm around his CFO's shoulder. "Otherwise, we could both end up like him."

CHAPTER EIGHT

"There you are . . . come here."

Reaching down, Angel scooped up a grey-and-white shorthair cat with the mackerel markings of a tabby. As she held him in the crook of her arm, the cat purred like an outboard motor.

Angel stroked the top of his head. "Who's hungry?"

One final murmur and the tabby arched its back and slid to the floor. With great pomp, he set his tail at a jaunty angle and led Angel to a porcelain food dish, gazing up expectantly.

This was Duque, one of the few living things on earth she loved completely. She had found him in a vacant lot beneath a waterlogged La-Z-Boy barely breathing, his two littermates already dead. She had been mapping side streets as potential contingency options in case her condominium was ever breached, when she'd heard the kitten's tiny squeal. The La-Z-Boy had been dumped next to a vacant two-story townhome with grenade-proof slits for windows. Angel could barely lift the soaked recliner but had managed to balance it precariously on her thighs before reaching beneath the springs and pulling out the tiny cat. Hissing, the injured kitten had glared back insolently, eyes like polished obsidian stone. Angel let him sniff all ten fingers, then wrapped him in a woolen scarf and carried him home to her third-floor condo, bottle feeding him for a week until he could eat on his own.

Eventually she named him Duque because even at that precious age the tabby was showing signs of an attitude. That was almost two years ago, and their relationship had evolved since then, Duque redefining the word aloof. Joining him was his comrade-in-arms, who came gliding out from behind a window curtain at the sound of the popping tuna can. Long and athletic, with soft pumpkin-colored markings that resembled a toy tiger, Cheché, a mixed-breed toyger, flopped over on the hardwood floor like an exhausted diva, caressing Angel's foot with her nose. Cheché used to belong to a neighborhood teenager, a bookish thirteen-year-old whose parents had divorced, with the cat becoming a casualty when the girl and her mother were forced to move back to their family home in Janos. The evening before she was to leave, the tearful child had rung Angel's doorbell and stood there shaking, presenting a blasé Cheché for adoption. No words had been spoken, but each understood the cat's predicament, and Angel had accepted the eighteen-month-old with the black mascara eyes, remembering the heartfelt relief in the child's eyes.

Wearing a red Sparta Prague jersey and stretch blue jeans, she finished scooping albacore tuna into two small bowls, then grabbed a cold bottle of grapefruit Joya from her stainless-steel Sub-Zero and rubbed the cool glass against her cheek.

Outside the kitchen window, the dark rain clouds that had smothered the city's cramped rooflines had given way to a radiant sunshine-filled day. She scrolled through her smartphone, relieved to see that there were no new texts or alerts. It had been almost twelve hours since the Ramirez job and she had gotten out clean. The judge's security teams had been slow to react when Ramirez had failed to show up at his villa, giving Angel enough time to ditch the Fusion near the Mercado, toss her Vuitton bag into a liquor store Dumpster, and join a group of late night partiers as they strolled across the pedestrian bridge into El Paso. On the Texas side, she had cleared U.S. Customs using the same passport presented at the fundraiser and hailed a Border Cab to drop her off in the city's historic Duranguito neighborhood.

From there she had found her way to West Overland Avenue, stopping for a bowl of spicy menudo and pig's feet and a sweet Mexican coffee at an all-night cafeteria next to a padlocked *carnicería*. Sustained, she spent the next two hours doubling back to make sure no one was tailing her before checking into a newly-refurbished Victorian that had been converted into a boutique hotel near San Jacinto Plaza.

With her clothes still on, she had slept for three hours, awakened at dawn, and hiked back to a huge parking lot on the U.S. side of the Stanton Bridge, where she purchased an oversized UTEP sweatshirt that covered most of her designer jumpsuit and a pair of wraparound sunglasses from an early rising souvenir vendor. She used the rest of her dollars to buy a ticket on a twelve-seat cross-border minibus carrying U.S maquiladora managers into Juárez.

The drive had lasted only twenty minutes since most of the traffic was going the other way. She jumped off at the Hotel Santa Fe and handed the sunglasses to a street kid selling Chiclets.

Strolling southeast through downtown Juárez, monitoring reflections in the shop windows, she loitered past several small colorful stores, but her only stop was to buy a sugary *concha* at a crowded *puesto*, where she sat watching foot traffic for thirty minutes until she was convinced nobody was following her. Then she hailed a local cab that dropped her six blocks from her condo near the *Parroquia de la Resurrección del Señor*. Once inside the church, she spent a few minutes lighting a candle in the nave before sneaking out through a hidden door near the sanctuary, then weaving her way through several vacant alleys, passing the spot where Duque had been found, before mounting a construction roll-off container parked next to the Hercules fence that surrounded her gated complex. After carefully scanning the grounds, she lifted herself over the wire and onto a planter box near the waterfall pool. It was a short scamper up the backstairs to her condo.

She'd unlocked both deadbolts and stood in the entryway, feeling that cozy, familiar sense of belonging. This was the only place she had ever owned. Having purchased it through a Nogales lawyer using one of the three Panamanian shell companies the cartel had taught her to set up, she'd also used the same procedure, only with a different shell corporation, to sign a one-year lease on a modest two-bedroom apartment in the Eastwood Heights area of El Paso. No one knew of either property. Not even the cartel. They were her bolt holes, her margin for error.

•   •   •

A sliver of sun peeked through the window, its delicate light warm and pleasant, filling Angel's stylish kitchen with a sense of contentment. The outside air was crisp and clear, the rain having washed the city clean.

She ran a hand through her black hair after rinsing out the tinted dye, then sorted through a stack of mail before opening a window beside the convection oven to let cool air fill the room. It felt good to get back to her daily routine.

After her release five years ago from the Central California Women's Facility in Chowchilla, she had migrated to Mexicali, and with the help of an old cellmate, hired on as a *sicario* for the Los Zetas, one of Mexico's most notorious crime groups. Founded by ex-commandos from the Mexican Army's elite *Grupo Aeromóvil de Fuerzas Especiales* (GAFE), the Zetas had a near mythical reputation for training and ten months into her *obligación*, Angel was handed her first assignment: a DEA snitch working out of the Miraflores district of Lima. His body was later found in a Dumpster along Avenida La Encalada near the U.S. Embassy, the narc's throat cut.

Soon, her reputation grew. The work became steady, lucrative. In the ever-shifting world of the *narcotraficantes*, she became known as a sure thing, dependable. Based out of the Campestre District in Juárez, most of her jobs were high-level snatch-and-grabs, *levantons*, rival kidnappings. But sometimes the assignments were bigger, political. Last night was the latter.

And her plan had worked to perfection.

In her mind it was always about predictability—a same certainty to police procedures. Once the judge's body had been found, the *federales* would respond in their typical time-honored way by rousting the usual street criminals, and when that proved fruitless they'd begin to work backwards, scrutinizing every ID from the fundraiser. Eventually her passport would kick out and her photograph would be forwarded to the appropriate state and federal agencies inside Mexico, along with the U.S. Department of State, the FBI, the U.S. Department of Homeland Security, the El Paso Police Department, and the Texas Highway Patrol.

Once the Americans got involved, the competency level would pick up dramatically. Facial recognition software from the pedestrian bridge would time/date her late-night arrival into El Paso, and the FBI would eventually find the Border cab driver who dropped her off in Duranguito. They would also hunt down the table worker at the cafeteria and the front desk clerk at the Victorian hotel, and soon they would have a description of an ordinary-looking woman in her late thirties who'd paid her bill in cash, which was not unusual in that particular barrio of low-slung brick-and-stucco tenements where families without proper legal status often paid in cash.

But the hotel maid wouldn't be much help, and neither would swabbing the room. Angel had kept an extra pair of exam gloves and had slept in the room's slipper clawfoot tub, painstakingly wiping down everything before checking out. A BOLO would be issued, but after a few weeks the case would drift to the bottom of law enforcement priorities, especially when the Zetas released rumors through their tame social media bloggers that the late Judge Ramirez had been skimming from the cartels.

Predictability.

Duque finished his tuna and squirreled his way into Angel's lap, demanding love.

Carefully picking cat hairs off her jersey, Angel settled the "King" atop her thighs and reached for a second smartphone on the side table, tapping in a four-digit security code. She began scrolling through her encrypted email. The location finder on the phone had been electronically blocked and rerouted through a cyber grid in Zagreb. From there it would be dumped into a massive data center in Dubai, ultimately flaming out at a server farm in Xi'an. Abruptly, the handsome face of a clean-cut Afro-Latino popped onto her screen. It was the beginning of a file marked "high priority." The text described a young man who had just finished a very successful counterinsurgency op out of Chihuahua City, an assignment sanctioned by the U.S. Army Special Operations Command without the knowledge or permission of the Mexican government.

"Naughty, naughty," Angel murmured. "Why can't we all just get along?"

The fit, young operative reported to a nearly nonexistent intelligence arm buried deep in the U.S. Department of Defense's Joint Task Force North stationed at Fort Bliss in El Paso, and by the looks of things the officer was quite adept at his tradecraft. Over a period of five weeks he had tracked dozens of fentanyl shipments flown out of Cuauhtémoc into different airstrips along the U.S. border. His job was to pass on drop sites and delivery times to U.S. Immigration and Customs Enforcement (ICE) officers in El Paso and Brownsville, who'd interdicted with a great deal of well-orchestrated publicity. As Angel read on, she began to admire the Zeta's intelligence-gathering capabilities. It was an astute investment to have penetrated such an obscure covert team stashed in the sprawling military bureaucracy at Fort Bliss, one that opened up countless avenues of evasion.

Then abruptly, she stopped reading, scrolled back, and reread several pages.

"Interesting," she murmured, draining the last of the Joya. Apparently her young Spec Ops warrior wasn't so perfect after all.

Earlier that month, while infiltrating at Anapra near Juárez, the officer had recklessly used one of his covert legends to enter illegally, off-the-books, not realizing his presence would be flagged by a local agent of the *Instituto Nacional de*

Migración, a bureaucracy compromised by the cartels. The surprising thing was, according to the file, that the young operator didn't seem to care. He was part of a new breed of Spec Ops hunters who weren't particularly bothered by what the brass thought about their personal lives. Besides, according to cartel sources, it was party time; the officer had worked six months undercover and needed to unwind. Plus, with three deep-cover assignments already under his belt, he had grown comfortable working the streets of Juárez and Chihuahua City, confident in his ability to move seamlessly among his cartel and police informants, unaware that he'd been made four months earlier. All this and his assignment as the U.S. Army's liaison to the Defense Intelligence Agency's ultra-secret listening post atop El Paso's Franklin Mountain, the Zetas knew.

Wickedly impressive, Angel acknowledged as she memorized every detail before taking a break to brew an espresso. Outside the wind had picked up, the clouds massing again, blooming to the west. Stroking Duque, she listened to the whistling sound of her steam-driven Barista machine, waiting for her cup to fill. She opened another window over the kitchen nook. The Barista finished, and she took the warm stoneware mug to this favorite spot overlooking a small half-block park. Below she heard the comforting noises of the neighborhood. The melodic trill of an iPhone meant the oldest Pena girl in 2H was home early for lunch. Next door, their windows partially cracked, the Guzmans were laughing loudly, enjoying their favorite telenovela, the TV volume set on high.

From the streets came the wail of police sirens accompanied by the steady blare of car horns. Dogs barked. Engines backfired. The cathedral bells from *Resurrección* echoed deep timpani; it was her very own operetta, a feast for the ears. Savoring the last few notes of the bells, Angel reran her only voice message over in her mind, its hatred and intensity searing into her brain.

"Face-to-face, Ángel," the *jefe* had ordered, his anger palpable. "I want you to look him in the eyes and let him know who did this to him." They were her final instructions from a cartel kingpin who had grown tired of a bunch of wet-behind-the-ear DEA agents confiscating his opioids. But it was not the agents he was after or even the handsome special forces operative who was running the interdiction—they would be dealt with later—but instead a competing cartel boss who had ratted out his drug shipments to the DEA.

But it was never that simple to kill a *comandante*, especially one with government protection. It required a great deal of planning and research.

Taking another deep breath, Angel closed all three windows to block out the noise, sipped her Italian roast, and nestled into a leather armchair. Both cats were asleep. Cheché had curled into her bed beside the chair, Duque in a spot near the window. Reaching down, Angel lightly stroked Cheché, who purred contently. Feeling left out, Duque climbed down from the window, clawed his way up Angel's pant leg, and curled into her arm.

Realizing she was about to get feline help whether she wanted it or not, Angel picked up Cheché and maneuvered both cats into her lap, then began reading.

It would take over four and a half hours, studying reams of intelligence, including every actionable detail of the targeted kingpin's upcoming schedule. But by page 267, the makings of a plan began to formulate in her mind. Buried in the *comandante's* travel schedule was an opportunity outside of Mexico, one far away from the cartel leader's heavily-guarded compound in Acapulco.

Angel stroked both cats softly. Cheché purred. Duque snored quietly.

It looked like a Caribbean trip was in order.

CHAPTER NINE

Forcing another Sudafed through a wrinkled square of foil, Senior Investigator Blas Mondragon popped the decongestant into his mouth, tipped his head back, and swallowed. His allergies were acting up. A parched wind gusting through the rambling stuccos that lined the muddy Rio Grande River had dragged in enough mold and pollen to swell his sinuses like a ripe melon.

He locked the front door of his Volkswagen Bora and snatched his Styrofoam cup of *cafecito* off the blistered roof. A tiny spider-vein crack had metastasized in the passenger-side window and he groaned inwardly, running his hand along the glass. The Bora had been his late grandmother's, a candy-red 2009 four-door sedan with rust stains deep enough that the paint was starting to peel. It had a laundry list of maintenance problems, and a cracked windshield would be at the very bottom. But as he touched its warm hood and eyed one of the Bora's many dents, a wave of nostalgia flooded over him. His late grandmother, Lucía, had been a saint; in his eyes she could do no wrong. Having raised him since age nine, she was the only person in the world who had truly understood him, and for that he was forever grateful.

"*Dios te bendiga,*" may God bless you, he murmured.

Mondragon tossed an American quarter to a scrawny *parquero* to make sure his tires were there when he got back and headed towards a line of yellow-and-black crime-scene tape that circled a team of police officers and technicians. Grandma Lucía had always liked the fact that he was a cop, that he was doing something positive with his life. He was thinking about that as he watched a pair of forensic technicians processing a smoldering hut, a giant Sol beer can spray-painted on one of its sides. The hut was little more than a corrugated tin shed dropped on a concrete slab, its nail holes leaking rust. It had been used for sheltering dope, which this afternoon included four huge stacks of compressed *mota*. Every so often a police cadet would pull a flattened bale off the top and toss it into the rear of an armored *Policía* JLTV, a Joint Light Tactical Vehicle, which had been requisitioned to haul evidence to an army holding site near the Cordova Bridge. From there it was anyone's guess where the reefer went.

Mondragon blew his nose into a light blue cotton handkerchief embroidered with tiny Ocicats, a gift from his lieutenant's daughter. Turning his back on the crime scene to clear his mind, he scanned the colorful gang graffiti that seemed to be everywhere. The block itself was deathly quiet. Most of its residents had the good sense to realize a murder investigation was about to roll over them and had scrambled inside. He knew canvassing would be a waste of time; nobody would talk to the *policía*. The investigation would depend entirely on the physical evidence.

Not an easy task.

Since leaving his precinct in downtown Juárez and driving past the squalid slums dotting the Rio Grande, Mondragon felt as if he'd fallen off the edge of the world into an inferno of poverty. Every window had bars or was cemented shut. Every roof was topped with broken shards of glass, every building guarded by packs of feral dogs. Off the streets, the alleys were filled with debris, the homes covered in peeling stucco, the ledges coiled with razor wire.

Mondragon wiped his rheumy eyes. The stench was like an assault on his senses, the smell of piss and industrial trash wafting over the potholed streets like an open sewer. A bright ray of sunshine filtered through the rooftop concertina wire, causing him to squint. But like a camera, his mind began to register everything. It was a gift, his eyes absorbing all that he saw. Every water-stained mattress and charcoal stove and defaced billboard; each bolted door and barred window and stripped-down vehicle. But the entire scene broke his heart because it hadn't always been like this.

These same cratered sun-baked streets had once been home to scores of hard-working neighbors who'd ridden company buses to and from the thriving *maquiladoras*, assembling the plasma TVs and frostless refrigerators and cheap brake sets that Mexico's northern neighbors so badly craved. It had been a neighborhood full of families looking out for one another. Children playing fútbol in the streets, grizzled old men parking themselves on tattered lawn chairs, flipping cards and arguing Las Chivas or Cruz Azul. But today these same homes sagged under the weight of enough makeshift shrines and anti-grenade screens to remind Mondragon that he lived in one of the most dangerous cities in the world. Drug-trafficking will do that.

He crushed the Styrofoam coffee cup under a square-toed Tony Lama boot and genuflected twice, then approached a stone-green Ford F-250 pickup parked in the center of the crime scene. The victim, federal judge Jesus Ramirez, was still pinned beneath the driver's-side safety belt, his throat cut lengthwise below the chin, his tailored Canali jacket and designer slacks soaked through-and-through. Mondragon covered his face with the handkerchief. Something foul and chemical was causing his nose to run. Kneeling, he looked beneath the F-250. Stagnant blood had pooled under the front axle, its sulfuric scent causing Mondragon's nostrils to curl. He pulled on a pair of latex gloves and slipped under the tape, waiting patiently outside the restricted internal area: a tight five-by-five-meter square cordoned off by red tape. As he watched three investigators from the Secretariat of Security and Civilian Protection, the SSPC, stamp their feet to stay warm, not realizing—or caring—that they were contaminating the crime scene, he noted that none of the SSPC officers were actually collecting evidence, just hindering the techs who were trying to do their jobs. To make matters worse, Mondragon caught a whiff of something metallic, slightly astringent: meth.

As he side-straddled the red tape, he saw a bottle of Tonayan, a cheap sugar cane liquor, being passed around by the SSPC officers. Kneeling again, he caught a tiny reflection beneath the pickup's right front tire. He checked to see if anyone was looking, then inched a few steps closer to the pickup and crouched beside the tire. Someone had tried to hide a bent spoon and a slender length of foil. He scooped up both and slipped them into the pocket of his well-worn bomber jacket, then drew away from the pickup's bumper. The stench was so nauseating his eyes were watering like a busted faucet.

This was worse than bad, he reckoned. Not just the meth and sloppy police work, but the fact that the SSPC, normally tasked with administering public safety rather than actual hands-on field work, was supervising the crime scene. By protocol, the investigating agency should've been the *Policía Estatal*, the state police, but if the SSPC was on site it was because Los Pinos, Mexico's White House, was making certain their people were on top of this.

Mondragon cleared his throat. "Good afternoon, gentlemen," he said guardedly. "How can I help you?" All three investigators turned coolly, just slight movements, a shifting of shoulders and tightening of faces. Each looked at Mondragon as if he was something they'd scrape off their shoes.

Two of the three were in their mid-thirties. One was completely bald with bloodshot eyes and folds of fat pouring over his belt. The other was tall and sinewy with close-cropped hair, dark eyes, and a hawk-like face. Probably ex-military, figured Mondragon. The third was the oldest and shortest of the trio and was holding the half-empty bottle of Tonayan. Mondragon guessed he was at least sixty-five and surprisingly uncomfortable working a crime scene. There was something broken about the way the three men interacted, like they'd been thrown together at the last minute. If they were from Mexico City, they didn't look it. The two younger cops were dressed in off-the-rack suits probably purchased at a big box store somewhere along the highway. The older man wore a cheap sport coat, but had added a Gucci silk tie and gold cufflinks, and his salt-and-pepper hair had been perfectly groomed. Compared to him, the younger two looked like *patánes*, peasants. Someone had hastily patched this crew together to make sure that none of the evidence was lost to the locals.

Mondragon cleared his throat a second time. "Excuse me, excuse me, gentlemen? My name is Blas Mondragon. I'm in charge of this investigation. Could I see some ID, please?"

One of the younger officers, the tall, fit one, studied Mondragon's face. Stepping away from the pickup, he prowled forward with a belittling sneer. "Tell you what, Marquez."

"Mondragon," Blas corrected.

"Whatever, let's not waste each other's time. Nobody gives a shit if you think you're in charge. We both know this case is way above your pay grade. So take a step back and stay out of our way. Got that?"

Mondragon didn't respond, letting the insult pass, his eyes canvassing the scene. It didn't take long for the officer to get fidgety and glare him down like a Doberman.

Probably using, Mondragon thought. Proceed with caution. "As I said, my name is Blas Mondragon and I'm—"

"Are you fucking deaf!" snapped the tall one. "Did you hear a word I said?"

Mondragon felt a migraine building behind his ears. The officer moved a few centimeters closer, pushing right up to the investigator's face. "Just fucking leave," he hissed, his nose inches from Mondragon's. "I don't want to see your worthless hide around this crime scene until we're done. Got that, *Mar-quez*?"

The other two SSPC officers shook their heads, chuckling. Both were leaning against the F-250 pickup. The tall one loosened his cheap woolen jacket, giving Mondragon a peek at the Beretta semi-automatic holstered under his right armpit. Tracking Mondragon's eyes, he stood perfectly still, grinning like a fool, his front teeth stained rot-brown, his maniacal eyes bloodshot.

Definitely using, Mondragon thought. Head down, he shuffled over to the older SSPC officer, who hurriedly swigged the Tonayan. Mondragon could smell his Cocoa Pacifica cologne, and noted that the man's dark curls were not just styled but colored too. A pampered federal bureaucrat used to working the gilded halls of Los Pinos in Chapultepec, probably not too thrilled about being assigned to the hinterlands with these two drug-addled mutts.

"They answer to you?" Mondragon asked confidingly.

The older man shrugged, covering his mouth with his left hand, a Movado wristwatch peeking out from under the monogrammed cuff. The suit might be cheap, but the dress shirt was tailored, the cufflinks 24-carat gold. "SSPC?" Mondragon ventured.

A raised eyebrow, then more silence.

"S2?" Mondragon pressed. "Presidential Guard . . . *Estado Mayor*?"

But the older man wasn't budging. His lips hid a knowing smirk. Mondragon was fishing, and he knew it. When the taller officer saw them talking, he slammed his fist on the hood of the pickup, cussing violently. Shoving past a technician, nearly knocking her down, he covered the distance between himself and Mondragon in a few long strides and again pressed his face to within centimeters of the investigator's nose. "Listen, dickhead, maybe you didn't comprehend. If I need anything, I'll whistle, like a dog."

All three SSP men laughed as Mondragon's fists balled up tight at his sides. The man's halitosis was stomach-turning. Still nose-to-nose, Mondragon whispered, "If you don't get off my crime scene in thirty seconds I'm going to text your badge numbers—if you've actually got any—and a photo of your faces to the state homicide team and the governor's office. Then you can pull rank and explain what you're doing working *their* crime scene."

Mondragon lifted a cellular phone from his jacket. All three officers stiffened, the tall one trembling with rage. Not used to being challenged, his fingers inched towards the Beretta, but he thought twice and instead ran his tongue along his stained teeth. He nodded towards his bald partner, who snatched the bottle of Tonayan from the older officer and traipsed over to Mondragon. The tall one motioned towards Mondragon's feet, and the bald officer poured a couple ounces of liquor on Mondragon's Tony Lamas.

"You feelin' me now, *picaflor*," the tall one said, standing shoulder-to-shoulder with his bald partner.

Mondragon swallowed dryly. He tilted his head back, his face taking on a hard look, and loosened the leather hair tie holding his long ponytail in place. He let a few more nerve-wracking seconds pass as he watched the tall officer's jaw clench tight and his eyes fill with hatred.

"Fucking *puta* faggot," the officer spat.

Explosively, Mondragon slammed his forehead into the man's nose, fracturing his nasal ridge. The sinewy officer dropped like a fallen tree. Instinctively, his bald partner reached for his own Beretta, but the muzzle of a Heckler & Koch MP7 submachine gun was already pressed lightly against the back of his shaved skull. "I don't know about you fellas, but I could sure use a shot of Tonayan right about now." Dressed in black Puma gear and wearing a full-face balaclava, the Special Forces sergeant stroked the bald SSPC officer's left ear with the barrel of the MP7. "How about we put down the hardware and you assholes vacate the crime scene like my partner asked. That's unless you wanna end up like our vic over there? It's your choice, *compadres*."

Mondragon's heart dropped in his chest; his legs felt like water. He had been on the crime scene less than ten minutes and it had already devolved into an interdepartmental shit storm.

But the Special Forces sergeant had an air about him, and as Mondragon glanced his way, he saw a tiny grin peeking through the fleece balaclava.

"To hell with it," muttered the tall officer, regaining his feet, holding his bleeding nose. "You two fucks want this, it's all yours." The bald officer holstered his Beretta, and both men picked up their gear and stomped off. The older man watched sedately, nodding his respect to Mondragon before following his partners under the red tape. A few meters outside the restricted area, the tall cop, still holding his bleeding nose, abruptly spun and made a long slitting motion across his throat towards Mondragon.

"Nice to see you're making new friends," said Sergeant Hector Vasquez, lowering the MP7 to his side, a nine-millimeter Sphinx SDP strapped on his opposite hip. He pulled off the balaclava. "Although I don't think the two of you are gonna be Facebook buddies."

Mondragon blew his nose into his handkerchief, sounding like a wounded mallard, then fished out a pack of Marlboro Reds from his jacket pocket and tossed it to Vasquez.

"About time you got here," said Mondragon. "I was beginning to think I'd have to process this whole scene by myself."

"You're welcome," replied Vasquez.

Mondragon waved him off, his eyes settling on a handful of rail-thin *escuchas*, watchers, standing just beyond the crime scene tape using their cell phones to take photos of the *peritos*, the white-shirted investigative specialists from Chihuahua's Juárez-based Crime Analysis and Forensics unit. For the past four hours, the *peritos* had been dropping tent-shaped index cards next to blast evidence scattered around the scorched hut. The hut had been one of Juárez's countless *narcomaquilas*, local packaging operations used for distributing weed and crystal meth. Someone had torched it to make a point.

"Hector, would you mind wandering over there and using that considerable charm of yours to collect those cell phones. I'd prefer the *escuchas* not be making a documentary of our work for the cartels."

"And?" Vasquez asked with a raised eyebrow.

"And what? Would you like a handwritten note?"

"And '*thank you* for saving my sneezing, limp-dick ass' would be nice."

"Yes, thank you for all of that. But I had the situation under control."

Vasquez smirked. "Yeah, it looked like it. That wasn't my partner about to get his butt kicked. But hey, what do I know?" A look passed between the two, the ebb and flow of an old partnership. Both men were survivors in the Juárez bureau of SEIDO, (*Subprocuraduría Especializada en Investigación de Delincuencia Organizada*), the Assistant Attorney General's Office for the Investigation of Organized Crime. They had paired up nine years ago and were mocked as the *Supercívicos* around the office. Mondragon nodded towards the *escuchas*.

"The smartphones while we're young."

"Speak for yourself."

Mondragon, his weathered face lined with wrinkles as deep as wheat furrows, looked offended. "What? That's not fair. I quit smoking a month ago. What more do you want from me?—Pilates? Mindful Movement, CrossFit . . . gawwwd—"

"None of that would hurt, partner. You look like a starving campesino."

Rail-thin and rangy like a ranch hand, Mondragon had long skinny legs, ropey shoulders and forearms, and a gray-speckled ponytail that made him look like an aging hippie. His tanned skin lay creased across his face, but the stubble on his chin sang of coolness rather than apathy. But no one would ever accuse him of being a fitness aficionado, and besides, it wasn't his physique that mattered. A cop for thirty-two years, the last twelve with SEIDO, he had a reputation for keen intellect, along with a dogged passion for the facts. But he was also painfully introspective, more academician than detective, and blessed with a strong sense of right and wrong. Add to that a streak of arrogance that made him one of the most belligerent if not infuriating investigators in all of northern Mexico, and you had an officer viewed by many as an anachronism, a throwback. An old-school cop who did his job professionally and treated every victim with respect, but who also stubbornly refused to accept the realities of today's narco-violence, which meant tolerating Chihuahua's endemic corruption. But Blas Mondragon hadn't been raised that way.

He'd grown up in Mexicali and lost his mother to breast cancer at the age of nine; his father drank too much and got behind on his payments to a local *prestamista*, a loan shark, eventually skipping town to become a roustabout on an oil rig near Tampico. That left Mondragon's grandmother to raise him, a job she had done brilliantly.

Her first order of business had been to pull him out of the public *escuela* system and home-school him straight through high school. That helped him earn a scholarship to New Mexico State University, where he discovered a talent for criminal justice, graduating magna cum laude and joining Mexico's Federal District Police as an investigative trainee in Tijuana. But his grandmother had also taught him to think for himself and, more importantly, to be himself. It was during his sophomore year at Las Cruces that he finally accepted what he'd known since age sixteen.

That he was a gay man.

As Vasquez ambled towards the *escuchas*, Mondragon shouted, "Hector, wait a minute. We need to talk."

Vasquez's shoulders dropped. "What, more of your friends on their way?"

Mondragon met his eyes, his tone serious. "Sort of . . . two hours ago I got a call on a secure SAT line from the deputy head of security for the Presidential General Staff in Mexico City. He was calling on behalf of the chief of staff, who decided to skip over Blanco and Herrera and put me in charge of the Ramirez case. Certain facts about the judge's murder had already reached the presidenté, and he made the decision to fly in an investigative team from S2. Until then, I'm responsible for the crime scene."

Suddenly Vasquez became deathly quiet. His eyes glued to his partner's. "This is a joke, right? This is you being funny?"

"No, I'm sorry," said Mondragon. "The deputy called me at the office. As of now, I'm in charge of this investigation. I got you reassigned so we could work it together."

This time Vasquez went completely silent. His partner's words had hit him like a slap in the face. Arching his head upward, he gazed at a pale blue sky full of cement dust. A thin shadow thrown off a stone wall darkened his face. "And you said yes?"

"If I hadn't, it would've been assigned to one of those *pendejos* we just chased off."

"So you took it, no stalling, no dodging, nothing. Did you call the lieutenant?"

Mondragon shook his head no. "I'll do that later. Right now, I just want to clear this case. It's important to me. The judge was—"

"Unbelievable, *un-fucking-believable*! Do you have any idea how screwed we are?"

"Like I said, I want to do this. I want to show—"

"Show them what? That we got three major cases that are gonna get stalled because another corrupt politico gets iced? Does Mexico City know we were on Ramirez's backup team?"

"They thought it would be useful to have someone familiar with the judge's routine, said it would help prioritize suspects."

"And you believed that shit?"

"They said they wanted me."

Vasquez flicked his cigarette to the ground and walked towards the *escuchas*. "Alright ladies, you know the drill. Give 'em up, let's go, right now."

Not surprisingly there was little movement among the dark, mournful faces with their sunken cheeks. Several *escuchas* pocketed their cell phones and drifted to the opposite side of the crime scene. Mondragon followed a few steps behind his partner, letting the man's anger run its course. When he finally caught up, he put a hand on Vasquez's shoulder. His partner stopped, turning.

"We're nothing but scapegoats," said Vasquez, his voice barely a whisper. "But you already know that, don't you?"

"There's a reason they put me in charge."

Vasquez smiled thinly as he tapped out another Marlboro. "Yeah, because you're the perfect fall guy. We get good results and Mexico City looks very progressive, very American, putting their trust in a gay cop. We don't catch this killer and they have somebody to pin it on, somebody who's *expendable*."

"I like to think we're better than that."

With the MP7 resting on his left shoulder, Vasquez flicked a match against his thumbnail and cupped a flame to another cigarette. He was in no hurry to chase the *escuchas*, knowing full well the moment he took another step towards them they'd scatter like quail. Instead, he took a long drag on the Marlboro, his fingers trembling. It had been a stressful morning and was about to get worse.

"You're just a token, Blas, that's all. Don't get me wrong, you're a great cop, one of the best. That's why they called you in. But this is nothing more than a political opportunity for these jackals. Never let a crisis go to waste. If we solve it, great; if we don't, no problem. How can you trust a gay cop anyway?" Vasquez exhaled slowly and took another deep pull on his cigarette, then grounded the butt into the soft dirt, his eyes drifting away. "Politically speaking, they're covered and that's all they care about."

For a moment, Mondragon didn't say a word, giving his partner some room. "Are you going to be okay with this?"

Vasquez, who was trying to rub the fatigue out of his eyes, looked at him incredulously. "Sure. Why the hell wouldn't I be? We've got a dead federal judge, no witnesses, and my partner's getting leveraged because he's the only cop in Juárez with the balls to come out. What kind of stupid fucking question is that? *We were on backup duty at the club*! You know how many calls I've gotten already? Christ, the fucking Governor cut his vacation short in Monterrey. So, *no*, partner, I'm not okay with this!"

Mondragon's mouth tightened; his throat was dry, the Sudafed kicking in. For a few seconds there was strained silence. "The balls to come out . . . is that you being ironic?" he asked.

Vasquez gazed at his boots for an instant before both men's shoulders started shaking with laughter. Mondragon went first. "I'm sorry I didn't call you earlier. I needed time to gather my thoughts. But now that you're here, I'd like you to look at the crime scene. Tell me what you see."

Standing side-by-side, the *peritos* scrambling around the F-250, Vasquez studied the pickup, and after a couple minutes spoke evenly. "The truck was abandoned a few meters from a torched *narcomaquila*, its driver dead from a severed carotid artery. The wounds are clean; he probably bled out quickly. There are bloodstains running down his chest and abdomen, pooling on the floor mat and beneath the vehicle. No signs of torture or a struggle. Killer must've surprised him. Find any weapon?"

"None," answered Mondragon.

"Of course not." Vasquez's eyes blinked furiously, an irregularity Mondragon put down to nerves. "It's probably at the bottom of the river by now."

Mondragon looked hard at his partner. For the past six months the two had been assigned backup duty to Ramirez's protection detail, the Assistant AG's office having credible intelligence of several cartel threats. Two nights earlier, security teams at the *Nueva Aurora* had escorted Ramirez to his pickup around midnight. The judge had then waved them off, saying he was headed straight home and the chase car would be enough.

Seeing Vasquez's hand shaking, Mondragon reached over and put his own on top of it, gently squeezing.

The *Nueva*'s surveillance cameras had caught the F-250 leaving the main entrance at 00:12. Later, the chase car had been stopped at a traffic checkpoint on Boulevard Zaragoza and delayed for twenty minutes. When Ramirez hadn't shown up at his villa, the entire protection detail was called in, and thirty-six hours later the pickup was IDed with Ramirez inside. His throat cut. The chase car was nowhere to be found. In a few days, the bodies of the security officers would probably be discovered at the bottom of an empty well.

Mondragon and Vasquez watched a pair of *peritos* open the driver's-side door of the F-250 and unhook the safety belt, then carefully lift the body out and place it on an old-fashioned stretcher. With doubt written all over his face, Vasquez watched the stretcher roll past, while Mondragon kept his eyes frozen on the corpse, studying it with forensic detail. Slowly, like pieces of a puzzle, the fragments would begin collecting in his mind, knitting together the similarities. It's what his lieutenant liked to call his detached voyeurism—the ability to see what others missed, only in vivid, intense detail. Vasquez finally broke the silence. "This isn't working, bro. We've got squat, less than squat. A dead judge, no apparent damage to the pickup, and I doubt any witnesses will be coming forward."

Mondragon sucked in a gulp of dry air. "Fair enough. Follow me."

He navigated his way past the evidence cards, the caffeine working its magic. They ducked under the red restriction tape and stopped a few meters short of the F-250's headlights.

Fortunately, the media hadn't got wind of the assassination yet, but Mondragon had no illusions about how long that would last. "Eyeball it again," he ordered Vasquez. "This time look harder. What are we missing?"

His partner straightened, working a kink out in his neck. "Like I said, no weapon."

"Correct. What else?"

Vasquez concentrated, but couldn't see anything amiss. Frustrated, he turned both palms up. "I got nothing."

"Blood," Mondragon replied. "If he had bled out here there would've been a great deal more blood underneath the carriage. But look—" he shined a penlight beneath the vehicle, then into the interior. "Not enough blood."

"Our vic was killed someplace else and driven here, but why?"

"Hold that thought."

Mondragon wandered to the rear of the pickup and inspected the tailgate.

Vasquez's ear mic buzzed. "They've found another deader near La Central. Dispatch thinks they're connected. They want us over there in thirty minutes."

"Tell Dispatch we'll get there when we get there," said Mondragon. He wasn't about to be rushed and sincerely doubted the deaths were connected. The judge's murder was a one-off, done professionally, no witnesses, which wasn't going to make their job any easier. He popped another Sudafed and, feeling restless, quietly drew away from the pickup and wandered towards a gaggle of Selena Gomez wannabes near the hazard tape. Dressed in ragged designer jeans and tight-fitting leather jackets, probably on their way home from school, they were squealing come-ons to the blue-uniformed cadets who were unloading the compressed bales of marijuana into the sand-colored JLTV. Mondragon gave the girls a wide berth, approaching the teetering shed from the opposite side of the crime scene. Stacked high inside, the dope had been machine-pressed into square bricks the size of briefcases then vacuum-packed in clear plastic and bound with metal security tape, the same type of tape used by immigration officers working for the *Secretaría de Gobernación*, the agency responsible for guarding the bridges connecting Juárez and El Paso.

Mondragon flashed his penlight along one of the metallic bands and started scribbling serial numbers, thinking it was a testament to the cartel's reputation that none of the bricks had been touched. Halfway through the bands, he heard a distant clipping noise like a riding lawnmower and stepped out of the shed, looking up.

A twin-engine Black Hawk helicopter roared southeast, dipping low, its weapons locked on. Normally, it would be hunting drug traffickers operating out of the Anapra and Chihuahuita colonias on the outskirts of Juárez, but politics were the new priority. The helo plunged hawk-like towards an array of shiny metal roofs skimming the Rio Grande. Mondragon felt a knot tightening in his stomach. Earlier, a young trainee in border security had texted him that an Army UH-60 Black Hawk was scheduled to touch down at the *Aeropuerto de Ciudad Juárez* at approximately five o'clock. The Black Hawk had been assigned to transport a special investigative team from S2, the intelligence arm of the Secretariat of National Defense. S2's senior officers were loyal to the new presidenté, who obviously wasn't going to depend on the assistant attorney general or any other law enforcement agency to solve the murder of his friend.

Feeling a cold sweat working its way down the small of his back, Mondragon turned to Vasquez. "That helicopter is hauling an S2 team. It'll probably put down near the old Plaza del Toros. We've got about forty-five minutes until they get here."

The men watched as the winking lights off the UH-60's tail drifted further south, cutting across the valley, shimmering like a dragonfly in the hazy dusk. "Maybe," said Vasquez, "but I can guarantee you that Black Hawk will be home before nightfall. No one wants to be the first helo shot down by a cartel RPG . . . wouldn't look good on the service record."

"At least they wouldn't have to deal with S2."

"Good point," admitted Vasquez as the Black Hawk sliced through the scattered clouds.

The two started back towards the F-250, leaving the cadets to unload the bricks of marijuana. Lost in thought, Mondragon felt a raw wind shimmy his long ponytail. "The approach of winter hidden in the slightest breeze," he quoted softly.

"Poetry, really? We're up to our knees in shit and you're reciting poetry."

"It clears the mind, opens the soul . . . gives one context."

"Wonderful. I'm sure S2 will appreciate what a renaissance man you've become."

"Give it a try, that's all I'm asking. It'll help awaken your senses, stimulate creativity."

"Thanks. But since partnering with you, people already think I'm gay."

"It's an exclusive club, very high standards."

"Apparently, but Dispatch isn't impressed. They're calling again. They want a preliminary report ASAP and they're not asking nicely." Striding towards the crowd, his eyes riveted on the *escuchas*, Vasquez abruptly stopped. "Oh, and I almost forgot. The *peritos* found this behind the driver's seat under the floor mat." He was holding a tiny sterling silver charm about the size of a dime and shaped like an angel. "Mean anything to you?" He tossed the charm to Mondragon, who caught it with his right hand and turned it over in his gloved fingers, hoping the *peritos* had dusted it for prints. Even beneath the latex, he massaged the smooth silver like it was something familiar.

But as he rubbed it, seemingly for ideas, the only thing he could feel was the embarrassment and grief welling up inside. It had been the toughest case in his life.

And he'd screwed it up royally.

CHAPTER TEN

Dr. Ernie Girard hurried down a sterile-white hallway, peeling off his latex surgical gloves, and tossed them into a green trash hamper. Beside him, thirty-six-year-old surgical assist nurse, Amy Lin, was doing her best to keep up.

Lin had luminous blue-green eyes and shoulder-length brunette hair that had been tied back into a bun for surgery. The bun had since come undone and now hung loose, softening the contours of her face. She'd been assisting Girard for less than a month and had a serious sort of intelligence about her. "So that's the latest minimally invasive technique?" she asked, slightly winded. "I've never scrubbed-in on one before."

"Smaller incision, minimal disruption of tissue, less scarring, plus the new device is a lot more flexible than the previous model," answered Girard, not breaking stride. "We've seen a significant reduction in readmissions, lower infection rates, and shorter hospital stays. The insurance companies are wetting themselves."

"Congrats. Keep it up and the 'ol big whack' will go the way of the flip phone."

"And lose those hefty insurance payments we get for all our complicated spine surgeries? Don't make me wash your mouth out with soap."

A knowing look passed between them. "By the way, how did Ms. Robinson get on your surgery schedule? You're booked solid for weeks."

"I had a cancellation," Girard said evasively.

"You mean you bumped a GavinAid patient, probably an old Medi-Cal eligible, right?"

"The poor and ignorant will always be with us. Besides, this woman is important to me."

"Now that *is* something different," she teased.

Girard gave her an icy look. "Ms. Robinson was getting screwed over by the state's UR nurses—"

"You mean Gavin's Angels?"

"Congratulations, you've been watching too much Fox News. It'll make you go blind. And yes, the UR nurses ruled out fusion surgery, so I had to improvise. Ms. Robinson was deemed an excellent candidate for our clinical trial."

"Sounds like a rationalization to me."

"Thank you, Dr. Freud. I'll do penance in another lifetime. What's amazing is that it took so long for someone to upgrade the new implant. Once it gets through final FDA approval, Cytogenic is going to make a killing. I've been buying its stock on the margin for the last six months."

"Don't they call that insider trading?"

"Hardly, my broker assures me I'm clean. But he would now, wouldn't he? The martini-swilling dipstick is probably buying on his own account, too. Amy, I'm sorry, but there's somebody I have to see. How about lunch . . . thirty minutes?"

Lin stopped, smiling impishly, and ran her fingers through her long satiny hair. Girard slowed. "What," he groused.

"Lunch would be fine, but I was thinking about something a little more substantial. I'm off in an hour and my feet are killing me. Know where a girl might get a good massage?"

Spinning abruptly, Girard reversed his stride and stood face-to-face with her, brimming with horniness. "As a matter of fact, I know someone who's pretty good with his hands. Say the Oceana, my suite, in an hour and a half?"

"The Oceana? So it is true, the latest Mrs. Girard's kicked you to the curb? That didn't take long."

Deflated, Girard snorted like a wounded bull and pivoted away leaving her to hustle after him.

The two glided past a row of metallic-gray lockers. Girard halted in front of a dented one and spun the combination lock, opening it on the second try. He reached in and removed a gaudy ruby-red plastic shopping bag. "The soon-to-be-ex-Mrs. Girard and her attorney served me two weeks ago, and completely undeserved I might add. Still, the whole thing is gonna cost me a frickin' fortune. I'll be working like a dog just to eat."

"Poor Ernie, four wives in the last twenty years, you're oh-for-the-century."

"My very own 'leave no lawyer behind program.' See you in an hour and a half. Call me from the lobby."

"It's a date. What should I bring, Jack Daniel's? Or are you on the wagon again?"

"Very funny. JD will be fine."

"Great, I'll stop at Ralphs." She eased in tight, running an index finger down his V-neck scrub top. "And let's not forget the Viagra, cowboy. I don't want anybody wilting on me."

This time Girard's eyes flitted from her nose to her waist and everything in between, mentally marking the spots on her wrists where he was going to tie the restraints. "Lin," he breathed, whispering in her ear. "Why would I need Viagra? I'll be with you."

She searched his eyes, a devious smile creasing her face. "Tell me, Ernie, whatever happened to your last surgical assist nurse?"

"Oh, her?" he answered with an innocent face. "She got boring, but then she's nothing compared to you." And with that he gave her a quick peck on the cheek and loped off down the busy hallway. It was 11:30 in the morning, and as he plunged through the crowded recovery room, working his way across the pastel-colored visitors waiting area with its polished-concrete floors and tinted skylights, several worried-looking families gazed up, hoping to hear something.

Girard deftly avoided them, scanning the waiting area until he found the person he was after.

Marcus Robinson was sitting on a two-toned mid-century modern couch next to Jerry Anson. Both were engrossed in an ESPN segment running on a billboard-size flat-screen television. Marcus leaped up immediately when he spotted Girard. "Yo, yo, Doc, what's happenin'?" The youngster giggled at his silly effort at slang.

"Yo, yo?" Girard repeated loudly. "Where the hell did that come from?"

Several waiting guests turned when they heard the doctor's inappropriate tone with the child.

"I just started public school," Marcus declared proudly. "Grandma said it was time. How's she doing?"

"She's going to be fine. Someone will be down soon to take you upstairs, but she'll need to stay in the hospital tonight. She should be ready to go home by late tomorrow afternoon."

Anson stood. Both he and Marcus were beaming. "Beastly, Doc, you're like clutch, dog." The youngster bumped fists with Girard.

"Thank you, son, but you call me Doc or dog one more time and I'm gonna smack you upside the head. Here. I don't know what got into me but I bought this for you." Girard reached into the red shopping bag and tossed him a black "The Apprentice" hoodie. "I doubt it'll fit."

The soon-to-be nine-year-old beamed as he stretched the hoodie over his head. "Yo, Dr. G., check it out, I look sweet."

"You look like a snot-nosed kid," replied Girard. "And by the way, that's the closest you'll ever get to a reality TV show, so focus that tiny little attention span of yours on taking good care of your grandmother. And try to get some decent grades in school."

"Natch, Doc, whatever you say. Hey, I got a question for you."

Girard turned impatiently. "What is it, son?"

"Before her surgery, Grandma said you're a better man than you pretend to be."

But Girard had spotted an eager process server snaking his way across the waiting room, aiming directly towards him. From the skylight, he could see that familiar look of legal trouble.

"Sorry, dog," the doctor said distractedly, eyeing the door to the staff lounge. "That must've been the anesthesia talking."

CHAPTER ELEVEN

The neon bumper sticker plastered to the metal filing cabinet read "Ethics Are Never Elastic." It had been crossed through with a Magic Marker, and over the years countless smart alecks had tried to scrape it off. But the sticker—like its owner—was still firmly in place.

The brightly-lit basement office could best be described as retro-cluttered. Low-ceilinged and windowless, with four gunmetal grey cabinets propped against beige walls. A scarred rosewood coffee table had been abandoned in the center of the room, flanked by several well-stuffed Pendaflex folders. To the left of the coffee table sat a large Statesman desk that was almost completely covered by an outdated laptop computer, an inkjet printer, and the office's pièce de résistance: a state-of-the-art, front-loading, electronic drop safe for daily cash deposits.

What was missing was any semblance of a personal touch. There were no wall hangings, diplomas, or any family mementos of any kind. It was a place of business, serious business, and even though the Department for Audit and Compliance occupied the lower end of the Hurston Neurological food chain, its director, Rory Armstead, enjoyed a near mythical reputation for knowing exactly where all the bones were buried. Still, he was surprised to see Dr. Ernie Girard standing in his doorway. "Look what the cat dragged in. Chiefy, how's it hangin'? You slummin' or did you just miss me?"

Girard flicked an imaginary piece of lint from his scrub top. "Eleven forty-five, Rory. Had enough time to skim this morning's till?"

"Man's gotta eat. What brings you down here?"

"Just making sure my favorite bean counter isn't stealing too much of my petty cash."

"Sorry, yesterday's deposits have already gone to the bank. Your bookie'll have to wait until tomorrow. But it's about time you graced us with your presence. Got any idea how hard it is to run this place all by my lonesome?" An unlit cigar bounced playfully between Armstead's lips as he spoke.

"No, but I imagine I'm gonna have to sit and listen to you whine about it."

"Damn straight. Grab a seat." Armstead gestured to a vintage 1990's side chair covered with computer printouts. "First, mazel tov. You fellas really outdid yourselves on this one—we're getting bought out by one big-ass German company. Nicely done."

Girard set the printouts on the floor and settled into the armless chair. "Thank you, Rory, that's quite a compliment coming from a felon like you, but before we talk about that, am I interrupting anything? Finished with your morning nap?"

"You done maiming patients upstairs?"

Girard grinned. "Touché."

"I can always find time for you, Ernie."

Black, forty-six years young, with a Mensa-level mind and rapid-fire cadence, Rory Armstead also had a sly, irreverent sense of humor, which was uncommon for a financial analyst. But it was common knowledge that he ran Hurston's financial shop like a drill sergeant, showing little patience for fools. Still gumming his wet cigar, he leaned back in his chair, his eyes roaming his Pendaflex files, making sure nothing was peeking out. Girard had a reputation for eyeballing documents.

"Now what can I do you for, Ernie? You usually don't make house calls unless you wanna complain about expenses or you need an advance."

"Now that's a bit harsh." Girard frowned, setting another file on the floor. "How's that lovely wife of yours?"

"Please, you couldn't come up with her name if God came down to help you. Besides, you got that silly asswipe grin on your face like you're getting a bonus."

"Michelle," Girard answered brightly. "She's a physical therapist, if I'm remembering correctly? And your son's a junior at Stanford."

Armstead looked genuinely surprised and even more skeptical. "My apologies," he said deferentially. "They're both doing fine and thanks for asking. Now how can I help you?"

Girard smiled broadly, pleased with himself. "A man can't just come down here and have a cup of joe with his favorite director, shoot the breeze a little? Maybe take a look through those file cabinets of yours. By the way who has the keys to those bad boys?"

"Sorry, that's a company secret."

"I'm a senior partner, so that makes those cabinets mine."

"No can do, Chiefy, those big nasties are my job security. At least until the kid gets through Palo Alto. And don't be thinking about sneaking in later—I got the room wired."

Girard shifted uncomfortably. He could never tell when Armstead was jerking him around. But he caught an impish smirk on the accountant's thin face and realized he'd been punked.

"Cute, Rory. Does it take an effort to be a dick or does that come naturally?"

"It's a gift."

"Then how about some coffee? If you're going to make fun of me the least you can do is pour me some of that filthy Folgers you're always bragging about."

"My pleasure . . . cream or sugar?"

"Black."

Armstead got up, poured two cups of coffee and handed one to Girard. "There you go, Chiefy, none of that small-batch single-estate swill down here. Folgers, strong and black . . . good enough for my old man, good enough for me. Besides you're gonna need a little jolt once you see this month's balloon payments."

"Balloon payments? Now that sounds pretty grim. I'm not so sure I want to hear about that."

"Right, I forgot. We're pretending we're not up to our gonads in debt."

"And how are we supposed to know any differently? You keep telling us what a cash cow Hurston is—all that loot we're raking in—and you being the financial wizard, we naturally assume you know what you're talking about. Or are you full of crap like all the other CPAs who've taken our money?"

Armstead stretched his neck in mild annoyance, leaning backwards in his chair. "You know damn well the practice is printing money or *was* until y'all bought them worthless outpatient diagnostic centers. Never figured the UR nurses would drag their feet on authorizing our GavinAid scans, did you?" Girard grinned, sitting up straighter in his chair. "But we could've weathered that," Armstead continued. "We could have dodged that projectile turd, but then the state employees' third-party administrator started disallowing our scans, and what few out-of-state carriers we had dropped us like a hot brick. So yeah, we're a bit tapped out. But now that there's a buyout in the wind, things are looking up. It's all good, right?"

Girard sat stone-faced. "What buyout?"

"Right, let me unzip so you can get a better grip."

"Nobody said anything about a buyout. We're just blowin' kisses at each other."

"That's not all you're blowing. I know it's supposed to be all hush-hush, but when was the last time you fellas ever kept a secret. We're being bought out by Deutsche Ärzte International, a bunch of tight-assed German mofos."

Girard didn't say a word. He didn't have to. He sipped his scalding hot brew then dropped his voice a decibel, his manner becoming serious. "High marks, Rory. I won't bother asking which of my colleagues is running at the mouth, but I do need to know if you're up for this. Have you ever done a major acquisition before?"

Armstead chewed his lower lip, trying to figure out where all this was headed. "How much you taking home on this deal, Ernie—personally?"

"And why would that be any of your business?"

"Inquiring minds want to know." Armstead laid his gnawed cigar on an old-fashioned facsimile machine and handed his Los Angeles Kings coffee mug to Girard, who dutifully refilled it from an ancient Mr. Coffee that wheezed and percolated like an old furnace. The Folgers smelled strong and musty, reminding Girard of his grandmother.

"Why don't you let me worry about how much I'm making. I just need to know if you're up for this. And I want to know how this thing goes sideways."

"It's that important to you?"

"As the kids would say, *D'oh!* I've got a battalion of creditors crawling up my ass, so *yes*, I definitely need this deal to get done . . . and quickly."

Armstead sipped his coffee, letting silence fill the gaps. There was a tightness to his lips, tiny age lines working the corners of both eyes. Despite the give-and-take, and the fact that he genuinely liked Girard, he didn't trust him as far as he could spit. Most neurosurgeons who floated through Hurston either pretended not to care about the business end or tried to micromanage him. But Girard was different. He had a touch of street in him, all swagger and nerve ends, and the man definitely knew his way around the money side of the practice. Plus he appreciated what Rory brought to the table. But he was also a walking time bomb when it came to his own finances, which according to the latest rumors included six-figure markers at four different casinos on the Vegas Strip, along with a $1.5 million debt to a Macau triad.

"Despite GavinAid—and maybe because of it—physician groups like ours are still one crazy-assed bird," Armstead stated, running a hand along the front of the drop safe, trying to work through how much he could tell Girard. Speaking deliberately, keeping his voice low and modulated, he leaned forward in his chair. "Our financials look all nice and tidy, but they ain't nothing like a hospital's. Upstairs in the clinic we work off of straight dinero, scrilla, cash-money—very few accruals. If we're lucky—and that's if we're very lucky—we receive payment about forty-five days after we treat our patients, and that's only if GavinAid doesn't slow things down any more than it's already doing. On the plus side, we've done a good job of keeping our operating expenses low and playing nice with the referring docs. When this place is humming, it's pure Obama."

Girard frowned. "Pure Obama?"

"In the black, Ernie, in the black."

"Very clever. Now tell me how this deal goes south."

"There are three things we preach. First," Armstead held up a bony finger, "show up on time for clinic; second, answer the phones; and third, collect all the money we're owed. If we do those three simple things each and every day we're golden."

"Yes, yes, we appreciate the down-home wisdom, but where's the problem?"

"The problem is *listening*. It ain't something you fellas excel at. Gather a bunch of self-absorbed workaholics with God complexes—not a single one of you with any real listening skills—you get my point. Y'all figured it was much savvier to buy overpriced diagnostic centers using subprime loans leveraged with half-empty medical office buildings. So now we're so highly levered that when the commercial real estate market slackens just a titch . . . shit city."

Girard opened both palms, lifting his lip in a sort of smarmy pout. "Fair enough, professor, but let's be optimistic: new money, German conglomerate, medical tourism that bypasses GavinAid, all very trendy. Is this gonna happen or not?"

"I don't see why not. DAI is a decent-sized multinational based out of Stuttgart. It's growing—" Armstead propped his feet up on the desk, "—but like all greedy foreigners they're trying to buy a piece of Uncle Sam's healthcare pie before Trump gets tossed. They call it reverse medical tourism, and the krauts are good at it. They recently bought three hospitals in Reno, El Paso, and Pasadena before deciding to acquire our humble little physician practice. If I had to guess, I'd say they're planning on hustling Hurston to their wealthy eurotrash patients, and then arranging junkets so they can fly out to LA and enjoy a few days on Rodeo Drive before going under the knife. It's solid strategy. DAI gets paid cash. Don't have to sit around for months hoping their elective surgeries get approved by whatever government-run system they're stuck with."

"Medical tourist junkets?" Girard sniffed scornfully, like a man who'd just eaten a bad taquito. "That's where all this is headed? My life reduced to schlepping bad-backed Nazis around Universal Studios?"

Armstead tried to keep a straight face. "Ironic, isn't it? Or maybe it's karma's biting you in the butt."

Girard shook his head. "Have you always been such a smart-ass?"

"It's important to have a skill."

"Let's hope you bring more than that to the party."

Armstead leaned forward and put his cup down, clasping both hands. "Listen to me, Ernie. If you're serious, it'll go down like this: Before the deal gets approved, I'll be handling the internal due diligence on behalf of Hurston. That means finalizing last year's financial statements, noting any outliers. If we've got problems, I'll find them. If there are no problems, I'll pass the statements on to DAI's auditors. Since this is a private placement, once we've handed our books over to DAI's outside CPAs, they'll perform random audit checks, and I'll bet my car their accountants don't find a damn thing."

"Isn't that their job, to vet the numbers? Come on, Rory, you're good but not that good."

Armstead shrugged. "Their auditors will pocket over $1.5 mil to clear our books, and the M&A brokers are looking at another six to seven million on a deal like this. Nobody's gonna make waves."

"M&A?" Girard looked confused.

"Mergers and acquisitions. The rest of the loot will be divvied up by Hurston's merry band of brothers. Y'all be raking in about $66 million. That's a lot of scratch, Chiefy, so nobody's gonna be sounding any alarms. DAI needs this deal to clean up its balance sheet and we need the cash to get out from under these shitty diagnostic centers you geniuses bought. There ain't gonna be no red flags."

"How do you know so much about the deal already? Nobody's announced anything."

"Like I said, your partners can't keep their mouths shut and the CPA's share and the M&A fees are standard industry numbers."

"So all we have to do is to make sure the financials pass."

"Sorry, big dog, if the numbers don't work, I ain't clearing them. I'm not going to jail for you or any other partner, and you gotta be cool with that." Armstead could feel Girard's eyes slice right through him. The accountant wiped a drop of coffee from his lips and chewed the inside of his cheek. Despite the glib back-and-forth, Girard chaired Hurston's executive committee and could make life miserable for Armstead if he wanted to.

"Fair enough," Girard relented, "but Rory, we need to have an understanding. I will be your first and only call if there's a problem. I don't care what the fuck-up is—an under-accrued account, bogus expense receipt, whatever—you call me *first*. Understand?"

Armstead paused, his face creased. "Agreed. But you'll be carrying the weight after that, and I'll need a memo to that effect."

"You'll have it by the end of the day, and one more thing—do us all a big favor and save the quick-witted shit for the interns. These are Germans we're holding hands with, the world's tightest a-holes. Play nice, okay?"

"Just call me Mr. Congeniality."

"Christ," Girard muttered.

Armstead flashed him a mangy smile, then leaned back in his chair, opening both arms towards the reams of financial statements scattered around his office. "Where should I start, Chiefy? What do you think the krauts are gonna want first?"

Girard motioned towards the file cabinets. "I'd start by re-auditing last year's income statement and balance sheet. Check all the numbers, including our cash reserves set aside for excessive malpractice claims. I've got four med/mal cases outstanding, and we've reached the coverage limits on our current policy. We could be looking at another five to seven million in possible exposure, and technically speaking, the practice's partners are on the hook for it."

"*Damn*, Ernie, anything else?"

"Oh grow the hell up. Since when did you become such a dickless wonder?"

"Right after I got married. Any other helpful hints?"

Girard thought about it for a second. "Yeah, how's your German, *Herr* Rory? *Sprechen Sie Deutsch?*"

CHAPTER TWELVE

It was nearly a year ago, something straight out of a nightmare. Mondragon was sitting in an ER jammed with aftermarket hospital equipment, the jarring pitch of a Philips IntelliVue monitor rattling around in his brain, when a trauma nurse approached.

"Senor Mondragon?"she asked.

He straightened in his metal folding chair. "Yes, that's me."

"We've stabilized the patient. She could wake up any minute or it could be a couple of hours. We can text you when she does." The nurse was being kind but she also looked tired. Still, it wasn't what he'd wanted to hear.

The digital clock above a pharmacy cart blinked 1:35 in the morning. He had been sitting there for over two hours, investigating what looked like a cartel hit gone bad. Three dead, one wounded, the wounded woman was strapped to a gurney behind a flimsy lavender-colored curtain a few meters away. There was a slight rustling noise. Alert, Mondragon tossed his Styrofoam coffee cup into a blood-stained trash can, sidestepped the nurse, and pulled back the curtain.

The bay was tiny, barely large enough to accommodate the IntelliVue, a pair of tandem IV poles, a rolling trauma stretcher, and a mobile CT scanner. The suspect's wrists and ankles had been strapped to the sides of the stretcher with rawhide cuffs, what aides called four-pointing. As she lifted her bruised face, her deep-set eyes gazed at Mondragon with a blank curiousness. He saw a gaunt thirtysomething with sallow cheeks and a thin, underfed physique. A cotton coverlet slid off her right forearm revealing a tiny red angel wearing a sombrero tattooed into her triceps.

"Can you hear me?"Mondragon asked, noting that each of the suspect's fingertips had been burnt to a smooth mass of purplish scar tissue. No answer. The woman's face didn't move; her eyes bored a hole through the water-stained ceiling tiles. There was a stillness about her that was

unnerving. Quietly, Mondragon pulled up a chair. "I need you to listen to me. You've been taken to a hospital and you're lucky to be alive. Whatever plan you had laid on yesterday is gone. You're not leaving this place unless you start talking, and it can be either to me or to an Army interrogator. It's your choice."

The suspect's eyes flickered back and forth across the cramped bay, assessing everything. Mondragon's concentration was broken by the piercing screams of a young woman in labor two bays over. The suspect stayed silent, faceless, as if anonymity was her best course of safety. She coughed, gargling roughly. The nurse leaned over to wipe a smear of blood from her lips, and a ripple of streetlight bled through the barred windows.For the sixth time the suspect's forearms tightened as she tested the leather cuffs, the bulging veins and thin capillaries in her neck pushing themselves up like an addict's.Painfully, she raised herself. Mondragon felt a chill as she studied him, weighing what she saw before shutting her eyes and dropping her head back down. Mondragon asked again, "Did you understand what I just said? I need an answer this time."

But the suspect's eyes simply froze, her irises as pale as window glass. The face itself was both scornful and disbelieving, like somebody already on the run.

Surrounded by the sickly-sweet smell of diesel fumes mixed with the more pungent aroma of open sewage, Blas Mondragon held the silver charm close to his penlight, examining it one last time before dropping it into a cellophane bag and zipping the bag into his jacket pocket.

"Evidence," he said flatly.

Hector Vasquez tapped out another Marlboro. "Wonderful. I'll call Dispatch. Let 'em know we'll have this one cleared in about an hour. They can call the lieutenant who'll text the assistant attorney general, who will surely notify our illustrious presidenté. Maybe we'll get a medal."

Mondragon scrubbed a hand through his hair. "Sarcasm and drugs, our two growth industries."

"Are you going to tell me about the silver charm or do we get to play twenty questions?"

The *peritos* who weren't handling Judge Ramirez's body finished their collections and gathered their gear, making their way to their vehicles.

"I just want to be sure, that's all." Mondragon deflected. "Check my files. Go over the case notes before I say anything more."

Vasquez's eyebrows arched like roller coasters, both fists tightening. Taking a step closer to his partner, he gave Mondragon a scornful look. "Blas, how long have we worked together?"

"Long enough."

"Long enough for you to trust me?"

Mondragon nodded.

"Right here, right now, we've got the entire brass chasing their tails, looking like fools. S2 is gonna want answers, so if you got anything, anything at all, now would be a good time." Vasquez inhaled to cover his anger. He started to walk away, then abruptly turned. "If they could've gotten somebody here sooner, we'd both be riding desks. So if you've got anything, *anything at all—*"

A team of *peritos* slid the steel-topped gurney with the judge's body zipped into a canvas bag into the back of a white coroner's van. The rear door slammed shut as the boxy vehicle ground its gears, inching past a wedge of onlookers, its flat roof silhouetted against the distant lights of hope dotting the El Paso skyline. Neither man spoke. Both knew their time was running out.

Mondragon waited, his mind in overdrive. The suspect was frothing up tiny specks of dried saliva, all the while testing the cuffs around her wrists and ankles.

"They're for your own safety," Mondragon lied, effortlessly and without self-consciousness. For a moment their eyes locked. The suspect's lips twisted into a knowing smirk, until a trill from the IntelliVue broke their concentrations.

The nurse frowned. "What now?"

Sliding around the stretcher, she reset the IntelliVue and adjusted the pulse oximeter. She rechecked the suspect's vital signs—relieved to see the digital waves dancing within their prescribed ranges—then started a peripheral IV line to get an infusion pump going. Mondragon snuck a peek through the curtains at the half-moon nurses' station, his attention drawn to a young round-faced aide with loop earrings the size of Christmas ornaments. The aide was harmonizing with her iPod, her head bobbing to the music.

Mondragon walked over to her, clearing his throat. "Excuse me. Excuse me, miss." The aide dragged a hand across her cheek before casually lifting her head, her long brunette hair spilling effortlessly down her shoulders. Irritated, she pointed to her iPod. "I'm gonna need whatever clothes this woman came in with, including all of her possessions."

The aide assumed a flat, puzzled look. "I don't know where they keep that stuff, but I'll ask around. Hey, are you a cop? What did she do?"

Mondragon didn't bother answering. Instead he returned to the bay, his attention wandering to the IntelliVue's touchscreen. "She's improving," the nurse said hopefully, reading his mind. She held the suspect's right wrist. Mondragon noticed that the suspect's long fingers had engulfed the nurse's hand. His former lieutenant would've said they were surgeon's fingers, or if he could've seen the puckered scars on the woman's stomach and shoulders, a felon's.

"Is there anyone we should call—husband, family, boyfriend . . . girlfriend?" Mondragon was getting impatient. "I need to ask a few questions, and I wish you'd trust me. We both know you're better off talking to me rather than to the Army. Attempted assassinations are being handled by S2 these days. I'm afraid Los Pinos doesn't trust the locals anymore, too much money changing hands. So it's either me or the Army, and I can guarantee they will torture you."

The suspect's head turned, her eyes narrowing. For the first time the emptiness had vanished, replaced by something Mondragon hadn't seen before, a strange twisting motion of her lips. Mondragon's thoughts were interrupted by another shrill beep. One of the IV bags was running low. As the nurse stepped past him, reaching around the pole to start a new one, he suddenly realized what he'd just seen.

It was the beginning of a smile.

Mondragon was the first to break the silence. "Alright, Hector, it's our turn. Let's speak for the dead. You take the engine and chassis. I'll process the cab. *Cadete*," Mondragon hollered at one of the trainees, a squat, muscular youngster. "Make sure no one steps inside this tape, *comprende?*"

The cadet nodded as Vasquez popped the hood on the F-250 while Mondragon wedged his wiry frame over the driver's seat, avoiding the dried blood as his bony knees knocked against the leather-covered steering wheel. He squatted on the passenger floor mat, closed both eyes, and relaxed his neck and shoulders, putting his mind inside that of a killer's.

The judge's throat had been cut. The weapon had been razor sharp, possibly a hunting knife. The bloodstains on the windshield were still well preserved, less than a couple millimeters wide and beginning to skeletonize, which wasn't unusual given the early morning temperatures. What *was* unusual was a lack of arterial spray in a portion of the back seat, which was not consistent with the angle of entry from the cut. The entire cab should have been covered with blood. Instead, a large section of the back seat was pristine. Either wiped clean or never been stained in the first place?

Mondragon slid out of the F-250 and shut the door behind him, then circled the pickup. "It was a botched cartel execution a year ago near the PRONAF," he confessed to Vasquez. "You were out of town in Delicias with the in-laws. Three dead. The suspect T-boned an SUV while trying to get away. The hitter was a woman. She was taken to a hospital by ambulance. I caught the call. She gave me nothing, but the silver charm is her calling card, her signature."

"You mean like in the movies, like on Netflix?"

Mondragon gave his partner an irritated look. "All I'm saying is that I saw the same design in a hospital ER: a tattoo, on the killer's right triceps. Two nights ago, when she left us the charm, she was taking credit for the judge's murder, taunting us. How else does one break into the commando of assassins unless you're a cop or connected, or in our case—word of mouth?"

A strained hush followed while both men kept working. Finally, Vasquez turned to Mondragon, snarling, "That's it? That's all you got? A tattoo that looked like the silver charm we just recovered, in a hospital emergency room? That's your big breakthrough?"

"Not similar, identical. It's her. I can feel it."

"*Jesus Christ,* Blas! It's a wonder you can get out of bed in the morning! Where do you dream up this shit, huh? Not once in your life can this just be a simple cartel murder. Lord knows we've had thousands of them, but *noooo* . . . his Majesty has to be different, his cases so complicated, so intriguing. You're gonna get us both screwed if you keep talking like this. S2 isn't gonna tolerate your bullshit, not on this case." But when he looked back at Mondragon, he saw something that surprised him: a flash of temper, even rage, completely unexpected considering the man's usual quiet demeanor.

"It's her," was all Mondragon said, his voice cold and sharp, like a sheet of ice. He was staring at his hands, fists clenching and unclenching. "The PRONAF hit was botched. Our woman was the only survivor. I figured her to be a low-level operative, maybe a lookout, or someone who handled the safe house, who knows? But she had this tattoo on her triceps, an angel, exactly like the charm in the pickup."

"You get a name? Something we can work with?"

This time it was Mondragon who shifted uncomfortably, his eyes gazing downward. "No," he said distantly. "The hitter got away."

"And how did she manage that?"

There wasn't any glass in the emergency room windows, stolen long ago, replaced by rusted ornamental bars, thinly slatted light sifting between the crosspieces. Mondragon heard water dripping from a busted gutter. Tired, he stayed awake by concentrating on the nurse's name tag: Reina, no last name. Apparently that was all one was entitled to. He watched her dress the suspect's bandaged head. She brushed one of the leads off the suspect's neck, her smooth hands identical to his grandmother's, firm but soft. Her scent rosemary water and sage. Catching him staring, she smiled politely. There's a certain kind of empathy that caregivers understand, a temptation to kindness that inevitably leads to hope. Mondragon was thinking about that when an ear-splitting din from an arrhythmia monitor in the bay next door shook him from his reverie.

The suspect sensed an opportunity. Her eyes snapped wide. Waiting for Mondragon and the nurse to turn their backs, she dug her heels deep into the soiled linens, arching her back like a gymnast, locking both wrists for leverage. Then she started twisting her left hand back-and-forth, dragging it through the padded cuff, stretching the ligaments in her thumb. As she pulled it through the softened leather she'd been working on, she reached over and untied her right wrist and both ankles, then palmed a pair of Iris scissors from the laceration tray, shielding it against her right wrist. When the nurse turned, the suspect grabbed her by the lab coat collar and pressed the scissors against her throat.

Mondragon heard her scream and tried to shove his way past the IntelliVue, but his feet got tangled up in the IV pole, and he lurched forward, clumsily slamming against the monitor. As he reached for his Glock, a powerful kick caught him squarely in the groin.

Grunting, he doubled over in pain, grabbing for the IV pole. A second kick landed to the side of his head, dazing him. His hands slid down the stainless steel pole as he fell to the floor, the cool linoleum reaching up and pressing against his left cheek. Shrill voices swirled around him. He tried to open his mouth but all he could feel was the room spinning. Someone shouted, but not at him. There was another terrifying scream, then a sudden blast of pain went off like a firecracker inside his skull. The curtains parted as he tried to climb to his feet. He grabbed the rails on the stretcher, his knees buckling, and crumpled to the floor, staring at the faded pattern on the linoleum. When he finally rolled over, the suspect was standing directly above him. A shadow passed, and Mondragon could feel her presence detached from the chaos like the touch of death itself. A crushing blow split his nose, and the last thing he remembered was the stained ceiling tiles and Reina's paralyzing screams as the suspect dragged her out.

Off the Franklins, the late afternoon sun set slowly, radiantly, in half-darkness, an iridescent dusk lit by the neon warmth of the massive Border Parking sign. Blas Mondragon pulled an old-fashion Dictaphone from his jacket and clicked Record.

"No evidence of bullet holes, windshield is still intact. Blood castoff remains viable. I traced the spatter angles to the area of convergence and there's a perfect pattern arc across the driver's side windshield, droplets two-to-three millimeters wide and grouped tightly. It appears the killer tried to wipe it clean so she could see out the window, which is consistent with our suspicion that the murder was committed at a different location. We know this because of a lack of blood pooling beneath the pickup." He removed a ball of twine from a canvas rucksack—more tattered gym bag held together by duct tape and several faded New Mexico State Arizona Bowl decals—and began stringing spatter angles inside the cab. When he'd finished, he lifted an iPhone from the rucksack and photographed the dimensions of each angle, which he would later scan into a software program he had developed and was rightfully proud of. Hector Vasquez lit his fifth cigarette.

"The string's a nice touch, we flyin' a kite?"

"Goniometry," Mondragon explained. "It's a concept used by physical therapists to measure range of motion. By tracing the cast-off patterns, I can measure the directional angles that will help determine the point of entry and path of the blade. I simply tie off the string, record the various diagonal patterns, then download the photos to my iPad. The software should give us a good idea of the spatter angles from the cast-off."

"Very elegant," said Vasquez facetiously, "but isn't that what the techies get paid for?"

"Would you like to wait around a few weeks for the results?"

"Good point. But just so I'm up to speed on everything, so far all we've got is a girl's charm, a woman hitter who knocked you on your butt in a hospital ER, kite string, and gonorrhea or whatever you're calling it?"

Noting the tone in his partner's voice, Mondragon raised an eyebrow, letting Vasquez's sarcasm cool a bit. His friend was beginning to feel the pressure of the case, mistakenly letting his impatience morph into irritation. "He was murdered somewhere else, then driven here," Mondragon said calmly. "I need to re-create the scene exactly as the killer did it."

"I'm pretty sure we're talking about cartel talent . . . maybe gangs."

"Doubtful about the gangs; the job was too well planned. That would rule out the Aztecas."

"What about Los Mexicles? It's their turf."

"The murder was too detailed. And forget about the other *pandillas*, they don't have the creativity." Mondragon tilted his hand sideways mimicking a handgun. "Drive-bys usually suffice, lots of spent shell casings, a few hand-painted *narcomantas* claiming responsibility. No, I'm afraid our killer went to way too much trouble on this one. Quite meticulous . . . cut the judge's throat someplace else then drove him here and left the body in the pickup. Then she torched the *narcomaquila* to make a secondary point or to cover her real motive. That part I'm not sure of."

"Sounds good enough for me. Let's file our report with the coroner, write it up as a possible cartel hit—well thought out, but still a cartel hit—and brief S2 when they get here. I'm sure they'll like your long-lost tattoo story, it's very original. I bet they love that kind of shit."

"Thanks," Mondragon said curtly, tiptoeing around a busted Fanta Limón bottle. Using his penlight, he flashed the beam on the passenger's-side door lock. "Hector, take a look. The lock's been jimmied."

Vasquez gnashed his molars, his voice sharpening. "Don't do this, Blas."

"Do what?"

"Do I have to get the crayons out and draw you a picture? Overanalyze another murder, get sideways with the lieutenant on some cockamamie story about a killer who ditched you in a hospital . . . argue with S2 when they get here, which I know you're gonna do. Any of that ring a bell?"

Mondragon waved a hand, keeping both eyes pinned to the back seat of the F-250, concentrating on the area behind the driver's side. Careful not to disturb anything, he squeezed knees-first into the rear of the cab. "Don't stop, please, I'm all ears," he said.

Directly behind the driver's seat, Blas found a pair of dusty footprints and several legal files, along with a wrinkled newspaper, *El Financiero*, with blood stains on a few crinkled pages.

He shoved them to one side. "This is where she waited," Mondragon said, his voice barely a whisper, his body tingling. *Okay, slow it down*, he told himself. *Start at the beginning.* This was how it had to go, what he had to do—put his mind into that of a killer's, to think like a trained *asesina*, letting the evidence form and reform in his consciousness like a jigsaw.

The lock, simple enough, no one would notice the door being jacked. The killer then squeezed her torso behind the driver's seat and waited for her victim. With what?—a knife, I'd assume— but what kind of blade, and how sharp and what about impact spatter? Mondragon's head ached. He felt a rush of heat, his face turning red. Something wasn't adding up.

The killer would've been covered with blood.

He gazed back at Vasquez, who was still lecturing on the wisdom of mailing it in.

Too many questions, Mondragon realized. He needed more time. Something he didn't have.

Edging back into the front seat, he put both hands on the steering wheel as a familiar frustration began to gnaw at the back of his mind. The killer knew exactly what she was doing, covering her tracks at every step. Mondragon rotated his wrist and checked his watch. Roughly forty-one hours since the security team had escorted the judge to his pickup. His skin went cold, as if it had been doused. Time was slipping away.

". . . A simple drug execution, gangs, cartels, gangs working for cartels. Blas? Hey, did you hear a word I said?"

Mondragon gave his partner a quizzical look. "What about the bricks of dope?"

"Killer torches the *narcomaquila*, leaves behind the bud to let us know that she's a player—that this wasn't about drugs. She's also warning off our snitches."

"Sounds about right."

"Wonderful. Then do us all a big favor and finish processing the scene so we can hand this over to S2." Vasquez put his palms in the small of his back and stretched, turning his attention to the smoldering hut. "Hey, you . . . yeah you, get away from that door! *Vámonos!*" He was shouting at a young mother cradling a baby in her left arm, who was testing the padlocks on the *narcomaquila* with her free hand. Earlier she had been taking photos. "Damn *puta madres*, you'd think they'd run out of cell minutes by now."

"They're recording everything for the cartels," Mondragon offered, noting how aged each of the teenagers looked. "Don't be surprised if we have visitors soon, and I'm not talking about S2."

Mondragon eased out of the pickup and stood near the front of the hood, arms folded. Having finished with the interior, his eagerness tempered by past disappointments, he waited for Vasquez to finish inspecting the exterior. "Spare tire, jack, both gone, probably stolen," his partner said. "Everything else looks to be in order." But Mondragon wasn't listening. His attention was still pinned on the cab. The scene felt strange, like he was missing something. He opened the passenger's-side door and checked the glove compartment. Empty. Running a hand under and around the seat and dashboard, he found nothing. Picking up the rubberized floor mat, he noticed that the carpet had been loosened along the edge and peeled back the customized rug.

Bingo.

"Hector, come here." Mondragon was dangling a small Handy Bag. Inside were flat wafers of putty. "C-4 if I'm not mistaken?"

"*Fuckin' A*, man, be careful with that!" Vasquez almost tripped stumbling back to the F-250. But Mondragon had already placed the C-4 in a transparent evidence bag and was walking it over to a lead-lined cargo trunk the technicians hadn't hauled off yet. He carefully set it inside and locked the trunk, then ripped off his latex gloves, Vasquez standing next to him.

"Our killer left us a clue," Mondragon said. "She knew the *peritos* would be in a hurry to process the crime scene, so she slipped the C-4 just under the carpet."

"Or she couldn't risk carrying it across the bridge?"

"No, she could've easily tossed it in the river. She wanted us to find it. She's making a statement, rubbing our faces in it."

"That's your theory? That some female killer slices up a federal judge, then leaves behind leftover plastiqué to make us look bad?"

"She knew our procedures; that's all I'm saying. She wanted us to find this."

A purplish vein began to throb in Vasquez's neck. His face turned red and taut, his patience evaporating. "*God almighty*, Blas, it *was* a simple drug execution! The C-4 now makes it terrorist-related, and that means the army. Jesus H, what a cluster-fuck!" His voice pitched in frustration. "Goddamnit, this isn't that tough . . . just the cartels taking out some pain-in-the-ass judge, plain and simple. No conspiracy, no elaborate motives, no nothing, just another narco hit. The C-4 was supposed to go off to cover the murder, but it didn't. Why can't you just deal with it? And here's another flash, partner, we already look like shit on this one. We don't need anyone's help."

Mondragon pulled the handkerchief from his jacket and blew his nose. It was early evening and thousands of lights dotting the foothills began to flicker like low-hanging stars. Head down, he started to pack his rucksack.

"You're not gonna let this go, are you?" asked Vasquez.

Mondragon straightened, patting his pockets for his car keys. "What about La Línea?"

"Don't go down that road."

"Our secret organization of former policemen who do the heavy lifting for the Juárez Cartel—this couldn't be their work?"

"La Línea? Are you out of your mind? We write this up as La Línea and we'll both be hanging by our nuts from a lamppost."

"I'm just saying—"

"I don't give a shit what you're saying! Maybe you don't have family, but I do."

Mondragon relented. "Fine, a drug murder, pissed-off cartel bosses . . . write it up however you'd like."

"Thank you . . . thank you very much." A relieved Vasquez dropped an appreciative hand on his partner's shoulder. "There's a reason why they call it backup duty. The primary teams at the *Nueva Aurora* are on the hook for this, not us. You want a brick as a gift? I know someone who's in charge of the count."

Mondragon stared at what was left of the stacks of compressed dope and thoughtfully declined, figuring Vasquez's poker buddies would appreciate his gesture of goodwill.

Loosening his flak vest, Vasquez leaned in close. "Suit yourself. But if I hear any more crap about La Línea, I'm gonna toss your skinny ass off the Del Norte Bridge. We clear on that?"

Ignoring him, Mondragon fingered the outline of the silver charm swaddled in the evidence bag. He would messenger it over to an old classmate at the FBI forensics lab in El Paso for analysis and records review. If there was anything in their database, it would kick out. His gut told him there was more to this, but Hector was right. Why draw attention to oneself, especially on a case like this; much smarter to work outside the chain of command.

Half a kilometer away, a conga line of headlights snaked their way along a dirt road running parallel to the river. The S2 teams were about five minutes out. Mondragon twisted his stiff neck, smelling the thick, savory aroma of sizzling grease from the surrounding flat-roofed homes. He cinched his rucksack tight and scanned the neighborhood. From the rooftops a half-block away, white wisps of smoke wafted skyward from makeshift grills, the sweet smell of chorizo mingling with the more charred scent of charcoal. Basking in the aromas, he felt like a ghost: invisible, watching and waiting, sorting through the facts one by one. *But looking for what, for whom?*

Suddenly, a four-wheel-drive Toyota pickup with roll bars and state-of-the-art satellite gear, the signature sled of the Juárez Cartel, pulled up alongside the burnt-out hut, its hooded driver eyeing the stone-green F-250. Instinctively, Mondragon touched the silver charm.

The last remaining *escucha* climbed into the front passenger's seat, her expression so hard Mondragon felt a pit in the bottom of his stomach. She pointed her coral pink iPhone at him like a handgun. Mondragon turned his face to hide, and she laughed. The driver wheeled the Toyota in a counterclockwise circle, tearing off towards the river.

Relieved, Mondragon lifted his weathered face to the sky. Dark clouds had begun to mass over the horizon like an invading army. He hitched the rucksack over his left shoulder and listened to the distant bark of thunder, a drop of rain touching his cheek. Gazing at the menacing clouds, he wondered if his *asesina* was getting wet, too.

CHAPTER THIRTEEN

"How much longer is this going to take? My editor's screaming for two thousand words by tomorrow morning or he's going to replace me with an unpaid intern. A man can't write on an empty stomach." Diva-like, Andy Crowder sank deeper into the contemporary club chair, dangling a leg over the leather arm, his cell phone balanced precariously on his protruding stomach.

"You know, this drama queen routine of yours is really getting tiresome," chided attorney MaryAnn Taylor, not bothering to look up. "Just let me get this done, then we'll go for Chinese."

Crowder shrugged. He'd been shadowing her for so long he seemed like part of the furniture. Straightening her back, trying to improve her posture, Taylor's attention strayed from the sixty-two page summary on her desk that was due to her client by tomorrow afternoon, to her tinted double-paned window. Outside, it was a beautiful late afternoon, a warm Santa Ana stroking a row of elegant palm trees—

Enough, she scolded herself. *Get on with it.*

Turning to face her L-shaped desk, she tapped her wireless mic and started dictating. "My name is MaryAnn Taylor, senior counsel for Halverson, Moss, Kreune & Adams. Our firm has been retained by Physicians Liability Corporation of California to represent Dr. Ernest L. Girard and the Todd-Cohen Partnership d/b/a Hurston Neurological Institute in Claim Number CN17513-M14, Roberto Arévalo Martinez and Cynthia Lam Martinez versus the insured. Please allow this report to serve as an update in the above referenced matter."

Taylor was one of twelve senior partners in a Beverly Hills law firm that had been founded in the aftermath of the 1980 MGM Grand fire in Vegas. The original partners had been blessed with the macabre good fortune of representing a group of families whose loved ones had died of smoke inhalation, and the resulting litigation had been the firm's maiden voyage into the cutthroat world of high-stakes plaintiff work.

It had been a successful one.

As the practice thrived, the partners expanded into federal defense litigation, serving as co-counsel in 2015 for Hurston Neurological Institute in a nasty Stark Law case, Hurston's neurosurgeons being accused of self-referring patients to their wholly owned outpatient MRI unit. Taylor had fought tenaciously for the surgeons, negotiating a hefty but relatively painless fine and keeping the docs from being censured. That was the first time she had met Dr. Ernie Girard, and it was a match made in retainer heaven.

Blessed with a brilliant legal mind and an inexhaustible reservoir of stamina, Taylor had the two traits needed most to represent Girard and his ethically-challenged partners: first, a mega-dose of ambition, and second, the uncanny ability to juggle Hurston's endless legal foibles with the unshakable demeanor of a professional poker player. In the past month alone she had taken depositions in three medical malpractice cases, an IRS desk audit, a nasty paternity suit, and an embarrassing property settlement with an MTF stripper who went by the stage name of Hot Mess.

It was an exhausting, cynical gig with one upside—the money. Hurston's surgeons kept her in the low seven-figures, financing a ridiculously large alimony and an extravagant remodel of her second home in Rancho Mirage. Opening the first of six transcribed medical files, she arranged it neatly across her mahogany desk and cleared her throat. The firm used the latest speech-recognition software, which made her job easier, but the dictation was still going to be tedious. She tapped the mic again. "This medical malpractice case involves allegations of negligence, undue hardship, misrepresentation, and loss of consortium."

"Sounds like your ex," offered Crowder.

"Hush," she snapped, rewinding. "Plaintiff Roberto Martinez claims to have endured two unnecessary surgeries, causing significant pain and suffering and ongoing neurological deficiencies. Cynthia Martinez is suing for loss of society and companionship of her husband; plaintiffs are also seeking punitive damages. As you are aware, the co-defendant, Dr. Ernest L. Girard, had his medical privileges temporarily suspended by Santa Monica Memorial Hospital due to recreational drug use, and while we will argue that any information pertaining to Dr. Girard's suspension from and participation in multiple drug rehabilitation programs is irrelevant, plaintiffs have already obtained at least some of this information due to the attached letter mailed by Dr. Girard to his referring doctors, which describes in detail his addiction and eventual rehabilitation. New paragraph."

"You're representing the Antichrist, you know that, don't you?" Crowder had a hard time keeping still. He was self-medicating for ADHD.

But Taylor had had enough. She clicked off the mic and strolled across the plush twill carpet, standing within an inch of his face. "One more word out of you and we're done for the evening. No more quotes, no more background, nothing. You can write the rest of the article on your own."

Chastised, Crowder mimed a zippering motion along his lips.

"Good," she said, stepping back, and tapping the mic. "Consequently, we interviewed two of Girard's partners, Dr. Steven Todd and Dr. Aran Dvir, seeking any knowledge they might have about Dr. Girard's past drug abuse and his successful treatment programs. Their responses are noted below. New paragraph." Taylor grabbed the thickest of the gray medical files. With a big push from the federal government, the vast majority of physician practices had gone digital, but few of their IT systems were actually compatible, forcing Taylor to use hard copies for her confidential legal work.

"According to Mr. Martinez," she continued, "he saw Dr. Girard on referral from Dr. Hoyt Lindsey with a complaint of numbness in his right great toe. An MRI was ordered, which revealed a three-centimeter left sacral fluid collection with degeneration at L4-5 and L5-S1 vertebrae along with mild disc bulges in the spine. Dr. Girard explained to the plaintiff that he had a condition called 'Giant Tarlov nerve root cyst,' which was responsible for his numbness and back pain symptoms. The preferred course of treatment was to surgically install a shunt to allow the cyst to remain open and continually drain. Plaintiff reportedly asked Dr. Girard if there were any other options available, to which Dr. Girard allegedly replied, 'Only if you want to pick melons from a wheelchair for the rest of your life,' referring to the progressive nature of the plaintiff's condition and the fact that Mr. Martinez was an agricultural laborer. New paragraph."

Taylor paused to wipe her tortoiseshell bifocals. Her client, Girard, was the blue-blooded scion of a lettuce-growing clan in El Centro, California. Educated at the University of Denver and Yale School of Medicine, he had completed his neurosurgery residency at UCLA and had gone on to become an eminently successful spine surgeon. Treating Roberto Martinez had been a favor to his father, Winfred "Buster" Girard, who had pioneered the year-round cultivation of butter lettuce in southern California. Martinez had been one of Buster's foremen.

Taylor continued. "Mr. Martinez further claims that he was never told the procedure could cause severe nerve damage to his colon and bladder along with possible sexual dysfunction. He agreed to the surgery and expected to be back to work within five to six weeks. The surgery was performed, and post-operatively Mr. Martinez did poorly. He experienced numbness in his scrotum, penis, rectum, right leg, and foot. He also encountered routine bladder pain, constipation, difficulty urinating, and sexual dysfunction. While recuperating in the hospital, Dr. Girard advised Mr. Martinez that another cyst was probably present and recommended a second operation. Mr. Martinez was informed that the follow-up surgery had a success rate of about fifty percent."

"Unless your surgeon's on crack," Crowder added helpfully. "Then the odds go down considerably." Taylor spun, shooting him a look that made him flinch. "Sorry, my bad," he said, making another zipping motion across his mouth.

"New Paragraph. Eventually, Mr. Martinez sought another medical opinion and underwent surgery performed by Dr. Tobias Zuckerman at the Nancy Reagan Medical Center in Chino Hills. Mr. Martinez was informed that it took Dr. Zuckerman approximately four hours to remove the scar tissue and repair the damage done to his lumbar spine by Dr. Girard's previous surgery. Dr. Zuckerman also stated that when he approached the cyst it was 'totally virgin territory' and had never been operated on. Dr. Zuckerman identified the cyst and compressed all three nerve roots on the left side. A follow-up MRI ordered by Zuckerman showed no recurrent mass. When questioned by Cynthia Martinez as to how the cyst could've been missed during the first operation, Dr. Zuckerman told both plaintiffs that 'Roberto's surgery had been done while Ernie wasn't at his best.' When asked to elaborate, Zuckerman told the plaintiffs that 'Dr. Girard had been rung up by the Medical Board of California for recreational drug use' and advised them that they 'might want to hire a lawyer.'"

"No honor amongst thieves," opined Crowder.

This time, Taylor just smiled. Noting the time and date, she clicked off the mic and rummaged through her credenza until she found a honey-colored bottle of Johnnie Walker Blue Label Whisky wedged beneath loose files. She waved it at Crowder, who perked up immediately. "Now we're talking," he purred, watching as she poured two healthy measures in cut-crystal glasses, avoiding the stack of files piled high on her desk. Instead, she let her eyes wander to the corner window overlooking a vacant alley off Mulholland Drive. A few stories below a skinny hooker wearing a metallic black *"I Pimp for Jesus"* halter top was scavenging a Dumpster. An unsettling burst of panic leeched through Taylor's chest as she watched the child dig around in the trash, realizing she was about the same age as her daughter. "Andy, come here," she said, nodding towards the window. "Take a look at this."

Grunting, Crowder heaved himself out of the chair like a beached seal and shuffled over to the window. Wiping a stray curl from her cheek, Taylor remained transfixed by the youngster rummaging through the Dumpster until she emerged with a white paper bag from Pastry World. She tore it open, ripped off a corner from a half-eaten loaf of focaccia bread, and chewed several bites before tucking the bag inside her faux leather jacket and strutting back towards Sunset Boulevard.

Taylor's eyes followed the girl until she was out of sight. Her heart fluttered in her chest. Suddenly feeling melancholy, she walked over to her mini-refrigerator and retrieved a half-empty ice tray to add a couple cubes to her whisky. For no apparent reason, her eyes wandered upward along the wall to her Pepperdine law degree. Carefully she lifted it off its mounts and ran an index finger over the smooth polished glass, a wistful feeling clutching at her stomach. Fifteen years a successful attorney, full partnership after two, a beautiful, intelligent sixteen-year-old daughter—yet something felt missing. Work wasn't enough. She knew that—it never would be—yet her mind constantly drifted to her ex and his trophy wife and the new life they had built together.

MaryAnn was envious. And it was ridiculous to try to hide it.

She sank a large swallow of whisky and placed the diploma on her desk, then poured herself another shot of Johnnie Walker and shook the bottle at Crowder. His eyes lit up. "Par-tay on, girlfriend, I'm gonna sail right through this article."

Running a hand through her hair, Taylor gazed at her reflection in the window and wondered out loud, "Andy, do you really think it's all worth it?"

Fired up by the booze, Crowder had already started writing on his iPad. "Of course it is. Look at what you've accomplished . . . what you've done with your life—the money, the prestige, this office. Come on, girl, you're thinking too much. Where's that stonehearted closer we all know and love, the one who runs circles around the menfolk in this town."

But Taylor didn't answer. She took a sip of whisky and stared thoughtfully out the window, the soft lights along Sunset painting the swaying palms a subtle palette of colors. Her thoughts were interrupted by a distant speck of light climbing out of the clouds over LAX, reminding her of the jets she had tracked over La Guardia growing up in Queens, just another ambitious young girl trying not to seem tougher and smarter than her brothers. Her father had been her hero, slaving away in his tiny bodega, carving out a living for his family.

She took another pull of whisky and let the cool liquid burn her throat.

But for all his work, all that effort, what he got was shot and killed during a robbery when his sawed-off shotgun jammed on a pair of armed punks stealing a case of Pabst. Ever since then, MaryAnn had made sure that nothing ever jammed up in her life. Her maiden name was Cardenas. She had married young at Pepperdine, about as far away as one could get from Queens, taking her husband's last name before graduating. After the divorce, she had chiseled out an enviable career as a high-octane trial attorney and single mother, but tonight it just didn't feel like enough.

Crowder drained his second drink and was shaking his glass for more, but she put the bottle of Johnnie Walker back into the credenza and breathed in a lungful of filtered air.

Raising what was left in her tumbler, she offered a toast to her Jesus-loving hooker: "Sometimes, what happens in Hollywood really should just stay in the trash." Then she hit the Record button on her mic and picked up the next file. The night was young, and Dr. Ernie Girard and his wayward band of neurosurgeons had no shortage of legal troubles.

They would order in for Chinese.

CHAPTER FOURTEEN

"Will the applicants and counsel please take their seats." Juanita Reno looked up to make sure everyone did as she instructed. Oddly enough, she was the only committee member in attendance, as both Harold Chase and Dr. Ernie Girard had failed to show up for this morning's session.

"This Investigative Review Committee for the State of California Health Regulatory Board, Region Nine, is now in session. Since all the attendees have been duly sworn in, let's begin. Please state your names for the record."

"MaryAnn Taylor, committee's counsel."

"Jerry Anson for the appellant, Roberto Martinez."

"Thank you both. Ms. Taylor, you may begin."

Moving deliberately, Taylor unbuckled her black Kenneth Cole briefcase and removed several depositions, sorting them neatly beside her iPad. "Mr. Martinez, good morning," she said pleasantly. "After you first experienced numbness in your back, was there any other incidence of pain?"

Taylor figured this to be a routine investigative hearing—just get the facts entered into the record along with any expert testimony that Anson may have dug up. But more critically, she had managed to get her private client, Dr. Ernie Girard, the review committee's chairperson, recused from this case, safely tucking him away at the Crystal Horseshoe, where he was probably sharing lap dances with Chase, leaving Taylor to bust her tail trying to make sure any testimony regarding his drug addiction never made it into the review committee's transcript.

Her opponent, Anson, sat stoically across the hardwood table under a framed photograph of Governor Gavin C. Newsom. Nattily attired in what looked like a new two-piece Armani suit, Anson was seated between his anxious clients, Roberto and Cynthia Martinez, and for some reason Taylor thought the preening Texan looked quite satisfied with himself.

"Probably thinks he's got a winner," she muttered. "We'll see about that."

Humming to nobody in particular, Jerry Anson actually was quite pleased with his case. He was hunting big game this morning: Dr. Ernest L. Girard, neurosurgeon, civic pillar, and dope addict.Five days earlier, Anson had befriended a clerk at the Medical Board of California, who also happened to be a pinot noir aficionado. A meeting of minds took place, and the helpful clerk slipped him a copy of Girard's "confidential" stipulation for substance abuse, along with Dr. Ernie's aftercare plan and a printout of his latest drug test results. Three hundred bucks well spent, thought Anson, producing a smug grin.

Since Girard was chairperson of this committee, Anson was shooting for a complete reversal of his client's denial-of-care order *and* getting Dr. Ernie's drug history on the public record. To avoid California's limit on punitive damages, Anson had filed a multi-million dollar malpractice lawsuit in Las Vegas under the dubious logic that Hurston operated a satellite office in Summerlin. Eventually, the case would get tossed on a venue issue, but Anson wanted all the gory details to become public so he could kick-start settlement talks, killing two birds with one transcript, so to speak.

Nervously clenching and unclenching his fists, Roberto Martinez looked and felt uncomfortable. Having never sat in a formal courtroom setting, he fidgeted anxiously, his head on a constant swivel. He was a hard-working, amiable man in his mid-sixties, married to his wife Cynthia for twenty-seven years, the second marriage for both, Roberto after divorcing his first wife when she left him for an insurance adjuster from Encinitas, Cynthia after being widowed when her first husband was shot to death during a cocaine bust. The two had never had children together, but Cynthia had a daughter from her previous marriage, the young woman following in the footsteps of her deceased father, serving time in Chowchilla for methamphetamine trafficking.

From a legal standpoint, Roberto's denial-of-care appeal was straightforward. Despite his age, in June 2018 he'd found seasonal work at Eden Packing in San Pedro, his probationary pay fourteen bucks an hour, paid in cash off the books. But it was during the following harvest season that things began to look up.

Roberto was upgraded to lead packer and given a small raise. He performed well, was liked by everyone, and within three months was promoted to shift foreman at an annual salary of $61,500. To celebrate, the Martinez family had rented a small two-bedroom home in Torrance, where they lived quietly until Roberto began having back spasms.

His medical coverage was through *Golden State Plus*, the GavinAid behemoth that covered millions of Californians under the state's new single-payer system. Following his botched surgery, Roberto's multiple requests for ongoing treatment had been reviewed and denied by no less than three DHCS utilization review nurses.

"Was there any other incidence of pain, Mr. Martinez?" Taylor repeated her question even though she already knew the answer.

"Yes," he answered faintly.

Taylor leaned forward, tilting her left ear towards him. "Speak up, Mr. Martinez, we can't hear you."

Anson couldn't let that go. "Can we expect this to be counsel's tone for this morning?"

"I can't hear him, Jerry."

"Yes," Martinez answered in a loud, clear voice. "At first, the back pain came and went but then it started up my foot and leg."

"Your right leg?" asked Taylor.

"Yes, my right leg. When it got worse, I called my cousin who worked for Dr. Lindsey, a normal doctor."

"Do you mean a family practitioner?"

"Are you going to let him answer any of the questions on his own?" chimed in Anson caustically.

"A general practitioner," Martinez clarified. "That's what his office sign said."

"Thank you," Taylor smiled warmly. "Please, go on."

"My cousin made arrangements for me to see Dr. Lindsey at the Wellness Complex in Santa Monica, where he did a physical exam and ordered blood tests and an MRA."

"Do you possibly mean an M-R-I?" corrected Taylor.

"Yes, an MRI at Santa Monica Memorial, where they found the cyst."

"For the record . . ." Anson stood. "Dr. Hoyt Lindsey was the first physician to identify the cyst on my client's sacrum. He then referred Mr. Martinez to Dr.

Ernest L. Girard for evaluation and treatment, and it was Dr. Girard's impaired surgical skills that led to my client's debilitating complications."

This time it was Taylor's turn to look annoyed. "I'm sorry, Jerry, did I miss something? I didn't see any TV cameras this morning. I guess it's early."

"Get off it, MaryAnn. We all know why we're here today."

Reno rapped her gavel lightly. "Mind your tone, both of you. This is a state proceeding and I expect you both to show the proper decorum."

"Yes, Madame Chairperson," said Taylor. "But I'm still at a loss as to what Mr. Anson was referring to. I was hoping he might enlighten us as to why he thinks we're here this morning. I was under the impression that this was a scheduled medical appeal. Staff has identified unnecessary care being sought by the appellant, his client, and it's our mandate to protect California taxpayers from medical fraud and waste. But maybe Mr. Anson has a different viewpoint and can educate us on what we're missing?"

What followed were several uncomfortable seconds while Anson let the sarcasm pass. Gathering himself, he asked sharply, "Off the record?" Reno nodded. The court reporter stopped keying. "Clever, MaryAnn, but you know damn well what I'm talking about. You've refused our Requests for Production regarding Girard's drug use, and now you're trying to twist my client's lack of English into some kind of communication problem so your doped-up surgeon can skate on the malpractice case. That about sum it up for you, *counselor*?"

This time it was Taylor who nearly jumped out of her seat. "Doped-up?"

"Excuse me, narco-challenged."

"Is that what you're going to court with? Oh wait . . . my bad. You're not going to court, are you, Jerry? Not in Vegas anyway. Can't keep your venues straight—rookie mistake."

"How about trilingual?" suggested Anson.

Taylor looked at him, confused. "What in the world are you talking about?"

"Trilingual? A surgeon who speaks English, Spanish, and duck . . . quack, quack."

Reno pounded her gavel with authority. "That's enough, Mr. Anson. One more stunt like that and I'll excuse you both."

"Still off the record," growled Anson, staring a hole through the court reporter, who kept her fingers still. "This whole thing is a crock of shit. You should be ashamed of yourself, MaryAnn. Quit hiding behind a bunch of by-the-book nurses and put a legitimate settlement on the table, and let's get this man some help, for chrissakes."

This time it was Taylor's turn to pause as she inspected her notes. She let a few seconds pass. "Back on the record, Madame Chairperson?"

A relieved Reno agreed. She hated these harsh confrontations.

Taylor took a sip of mineral water. "Mr. Martinez, do you have a history of probable dysthymia or periods of depression?"

The entire room froze except for the court reporter's fingers, now flying.

"Don't answer that," snapped Anson. Martinez and his wife didn't budge. They had been well-coached.

"Mr. Martinez, did your mother suffer from bipolar disorder while you were growing up? Did your father abuse alcohol?"

Anson's face turned beet red. "And what does that have to do with anything?"

"As a twelve-year-old were you sexually abused by your priest in Tijuana? Have you ever sought mental health treatment? Have you or your wife ever used meth? Do you have a drinking problem?" Again, Taylor knew the answers to all these questions. She was just giving them a preview of her malpractice defense.

For his part, Anson could barely contain himself. His neck and forehead had turned blood red, his fists clenching. Batting his eyelids, he nearly shouted: "Unbelievable! What, are we sharing the crack pipe with our clients these days?"

"Mr. Anson!" Reno howled. "You are out of order, *sir.*"

Anson waved her off, spun on Taylor, who had calmly unbuckled her flapover briefcase and was shoving several loose files inside. "I'll expect your answers in writing by the close of business tomorrow," she said.

"Which will also include statements from Girard's partners that he's a sexual deviant," countered Anson. This time it was Taylor's turn to freeze. She nervously fingered her iPad.

Straightening his tie, regaining his composure, Anson touched Roberto Martinez on the shoulder, then pulled several documents from his own expensive eelskin briefcase and sorted through them slowly, theatrically, mining the moment. "Ah, here we all are," he drawled. "Dr. Steven Todd, Managing Partner of Hurston Neurological Institute and Dr. Girard's colleague, admits that he was aware of at least two drug-related incidents involving Girard, whom everyone at Hurston calls Doctor Ernie."

Taylor didn't budge. Neither Martinez said a word. The only noise in the room was the court reporter's fingers tap dancing across her keypad as Anson twisted the blade deeper. "According to Dr. Todd, his partner, Ernie Girard, is a talented spine surgeon who experiences sporadic lapses in judgment and often demonstrates erratic personal behavior. And while Dr. Todd admits that he has never seen Dr. Girard practice impaired, he does state that Girard has a substance abuse problem and a possible sexual addiction. Specifically, according to Dr. Todd, his partner enjoys drug-fueled carnal relations with both men and women, *simultaneously*." Anson paused, turning to the court reporter. "For the record, we were unable to discover any allegations of sexual misconduct filed against Dr. Ernest L. Girard in Los Angeles County, the State of California, or the State of Nevada, but records of his substance abuse and state-mandated rehabilitation requirements are available to the committee."

And we're not alleging the Defendant enjoys weird, drug-addled sex, your Honor. After all, this is California. Taylor could see how this was going to play out in court and, more importantly, the media. She tried to maintain her calm, seething that Dr. Todd couldn't keep his dime-store psychoanalysis to himself. She rubbed the back of her neck and took another sip of mineral water, wondering how much Anson really knew about Girard's latest tumble off the wagon.

Cynthia Martinez, on the other hand, had no such doubts. By nature she could go distrusting in a flash. It was a question of temperament, and of temper. She was a woman who took honesty very seriously, and right now she was livid that a rich, druggie neurosurgeon could practice so openly, while her daughter, Maria, had served time in Chowchilla for meth trafficking.

"*Cabrona puta*," she hissed through clenched teeth.

Taylor understood Spanish but refused to be baited. *Time to ratchet things up,* she told herself. "Mr. Martinez, you stated that following surgery your urinary function continued to be difficult? You also claimed to have problems with constipation? Is that correct, sir?"

Roberto Martinez looked to Anson, who nodded. Martinez's lips quivered as he spoke. "For a while I was able to have regular bowel movements with the help of prune juice and laxatives, but lately I've had to use enemas, and what do the doctors call it?" Martinez turned to his wife for help.

"Physical removal of impacted fecal matter." The words stuck like sandpaper to Cynthia Martinez's tongue. Furious, her thin voice dropped to a whisper. "They have to dig shit out of his rectum because of your skanky-assed doctor."

"Please, Mrs. Martinez," chimed in Taylor, "you're slandering a world-renowned surgeon."

Cynthia Martinez leaned over the table. "Perhaps you'd like to help out the next time Roberto has a bowel movement, *chica?*"

"Thanks, but I'll pass," answered Taylor, pulling another file from the stack beside her. "Mr. Martinez, in court filings you claim to have almost no sexual function following Dr. Girard's surgery, for which you are seeking payment for ongoing physical therapy and behavioral health treatments, not to mention civil damages. But according to your statements, sir, you're still able to get an erection and have slight feelings in the genital area. Now when you say an erection, sir, is that achieved with your wife's help or are you able to *get it up on your own*, so to speak? And what is the frequency of your sexual intercourse?"

Anson slammed his notebook on the table. "For the love of God, Madame Chairperson!"

Taylor pressed on: "Every other day, weekly, monthly? How often, Mr. Martinez? And before you answer, please remember that Mrs. Martinez has already given her deposition."

"Madame Chairperson, this has gone far enough." Anson stood, hands trembling.

But Roberto Martinez grabbed his lawyer's arm and gently pulled him down. Martinez's chin dropped to his chest, tears clouding his eyes. Deeply humiliated, he turned to his wife. "I'm sorry, *mi cariño*, I'm so sorry. But the woman lawyer's right, I'm no longer a man. I had the surgery, and I'm no longer a man for you." Martinez began to sob, his wife's eyes circling the room like a caged animal. As she comforted him, she looked drained, face livid, veins throbbing in her neck.

"That's gutter, MaryAnn, total gutter. I've seen more warmth at a carjacking." Increasingly irate, Anson latched his briefcase. Glowering at Taylor, his brown eyes flickered with payback. "Tell your malpractice carrier we're beyond settlement on this one, and make sure they know how pumped I am about frying this quack in court." He took a deep breath to calm himself, pushing a hand through his styled hair. "I got out of bed this morning with the crazy notion of getting this bogus denial overturned and having a real conversation about settling this case. But I gotta hand it to you, MaryAnn, this . . . this is inhumane even for you."

Taylor felt a twinge of guilt, but there was no middle ground, not when it came to Ernie Girard. The man demanded total ruthlessness, nothing less. "In that case," she announced tonelessly, "I petition this Review Committee to recommend to the Health Regulatory Board of the State of California to uphold its denial-of-care order for any further treatment for Roberto Martinez as related to the conditions described in his appeal. Additionally, we petition this Investigative Review Committee to strike any and all references to alleged drug use by Dr. Ernest Girard on the grounds that the proffered documents have not been substantiated by an independent third party. We only have the applicant's presentation of confidential peer review materials, which we have not had the chance to corroborate."

Reno considered the request for a minute before speaking. "I'm going to agree to the motion to uphold the denial-of-care order, but I'm going to allow the applicant's submission of Dr. Girard's substance abuse records—"

"That's completely inappropriate," Taylor rudely interrupted. "We haven't had the opportunity to verify these records, including how Mr. Anson obtained them."

"What are you accusing me of?" Anson asked feigning indignation.

"Where do I start?"

Reno cut them both off. "That's enough, you two. Ms. Taylor, you'll have five business days to review the accuracy and authenticity of these records—"

"This is ridiculous," Taylor interrupted again. "You wouldn't be remotely considering this if Dr. Girard was in attendance this morning."

"But he isn't now, *is he?*" Reno shot back. "And whose fault would that be?"

Silence answered her.

"Right," said Reno. "Both motions are moved as amended and seconded, all in favor?"

Since Reno was the only committee member in attendance, her vote was all it took. "The petitions pass, the denial-of-care order is upheld, and Dr. Girard's past history of substance abuse will be entered into the minutes. Counsel will be given the opportunity to complete evidentiary review during the next five business days and will be able to offer any changes or corrections to the minutes. I'm sorry, Mr. Martinez."

Cynthia Martinez exploded from her seat. "That's it? That's all we're getting out of this? No!" She shook free of Anson's hand. "I've been sitting here all morning listening to the two of you fight like a couple of *cabrónes* and no one is going to help my Roberto?"

"Cynthia," Anson interrupted, trying to console her.

"Get off me," she said, batting his hand away. "I need to know which one of you is going to take care of my Roberto? Huh, which one? Because I'm sick and tired of this *mierda*; he can't sleep, he can't walk. He can't even use the damn bathroom!"

For the third time Anson tugged lightly on her arm. "Cynthia, sit down. It's over."

"I said leave me *alone*." The anger welled up in her like a boiling tea kettle. Spinning towards the bench, she glared at Taylor. "What good is all this single-payer crap if nobody is going to help you when you're sick? Tell me, what good is it?" Embarrassed, Taylor didn't have an answer. The room had become deathly quiet. "Do you think this is fair? Do you think this is what the governor had in mind—this fake *puta* judge playing God, deciding who gets what and who doesn't?"

Having endured this awkward scene long enough, Reno pressed the red panic button beneath the table, and a pimply-faced law enforcement trainee emerged listlessly from the vending machine area. Circling Roberto and Cynthia Martinez, he retrieved Roberto's jacket from the back of his chair and escorted both of them to the documents table to sign out, the committee staffers averting their eyes as if they were witnessing an arrest. Only Andy Crowder stood and applauded.

"You bad, Five-O."

Walking slowly to the table, her head held high, Cynthia Martinez waited as the young officer handed Roberto's jacket to her. She took it, her hands trembling. The life she'd so painstakingly built seemed to be crumbling like so much dry clay. Unconsciously, she rubbed the Los Zetas tattoo on her left arm, reminding herself that she wasn't alone. Roberto's wet eyes smiled at her; he was so proud of her. He was always so proud of her. Soon, her pulse began to steady. She could feel the warmth returning, the old confidence coming back.

Her daughter would know what to do.

She was a clever woman and an even more cunning fixer. She would size up these worthless fools and make them pay. For the first time, a subtle grin curled across Cynthia's lips.

My Maria will make them pay.

CHAPTER FIFTEEN

From his stakeout position, Los Angeles County Sheriff's sergeant Charlie Rangel opened the shutter on his wide-angle lens, focusing his refurbished Nikon D5500 on the sliding screen door of a first-floor stucco apartment directly across the street from where he was seated. "Lute, take a look. Ain't that JuJu's boy, Devon? And get a load of them sweet-looking pants, my man's stylin' this morning. Ten bucks says they're the same ones he wore last month."

Rangel's suspect, a short, scraggly, wire-thin homeless man with eyes like saggy tea bags, had parked his shopping cart outside the screen door and was wiping his nose on the back of his sleeve. He looked around for several seconds, then walked in without knocking. Rangel's partner, Luther Hurt—Lute to anyone who knew him—trained his Steiner HX binoculars on the cart and with his free hand reached across the folding camp table and lifted a glazed twist from a box of Winchell's donuts.

The two Narcotics Bureau sergeants were running a stakeout from a third-floor studio in a dilapidated multi-use building that had been foreclosed on two months earlier. They'd been sitting there for four and a half hours, recording clients who wandered in and out of the stucco apartment.

"No way," Hurt mumbled, his mouth full. "JuJu ain't letting his boy out looking like that. Have Apodaca run last month's recon. Devon was all Rambo'ed-up, army surplus with pockets and shit running up and down the sides of his legs." Hurt activated a wireless lip mic curled over his left ear. "11:35 a.m., suspect

Anthony Devon Johnson aka Dinneylan Dog aka D-Dog has entered the premises at 1189 South Maryland Parkway, Apartment 18-B as in Bravo."

"Three names," whistled Rangel. "Ol' Devon's got himself three names. See, now that's our problem, big fella. Ol' bullshitters like you and me, we got just one name. But Devon down there, hell, he's got *three*. We're down two and we haven't even busted his sorry ass yet. How do you think JuJu keeps track of all them names? You think he's got one of them iWatches or something?"

"Charlie," Hurt grumbled, washing down the messy twist with a tepid cup of coffee. "How the hell am I supposed to know if JuJu's got a *goddamn* iWatch?"

"Whoa, ain't we the cranky bitch this morning."

"Give it a rest, will you. You're giving me a headache."

The cadaverous suspect retraced his steps out of the apartment and tossed a half-filled paper sack into his shopping cart, then slowly pushed the cart towards the north end of the alley. Hurt checked his wristwatch. "Looks like Devon's done shoppin'. Why don't we head on down there and see what goodies he'll be selling the local youth for lunch?" He pulled the lip mic closer to his mouth. "Visual contact was broken for approximately three minutes before the suspect exited the apartment at 11:38. My partner, Sergeant Charlie Rangel, has completed photo surveillance; please forward a copy set to Anticrime." Hurt switched off the mic and shoved the last of the glazed twist into his mouth. Rangel finished shooting his stills, then packed the camera. Both men watched as Devon pushed his shopping cart down the block and out of sight.

"I'll be baaack . . . ," Rangel mimicked, doing his best Terminator imitation.

Hurt nearly choked on his coffee. "Man that sucks. No really, that pukes. Don't ever . . . ever do that again, not Arnold, *ever*. You sound like some drag queen with a cock up its mouth."

"Whoa, whoa, whoa . . . not very LGBTQ, big man, didn't you get the email."

"You actually read that crap?"

"See, now that's what I'm talking about. That's exactly what I'm talking about—that smart-ass mouth of yours. Son, you done missed your calling."

"And what might that be?"

"Think about it. What would make your day?"

"You being transferred back to the AG's office."

"I was thinking law school, man. You could do it online."

"Law school, what the hell am I supposed to do at law school?"

"Dude, it'd be a cakewalk for a stud-dog like you. That quick wit of yours, all them fancy words you love using—talk about a slam dunk. Besides, what else you got going on other than busting old crackheads like Devon down there? Where's it written that Luther Hurt can't be one of them high-priced fancy lawyers?"

"On my mortgage papers . . . now shut up for a second, we got another visitor."

A four-door navy blue sedan crawled cautiously down a side alley and turned left, the driver slipping the Ford into an empty visitor's space next to the manager's office.

"Start unpacking the camera," said Hurt.

"Doing the dance, pards."

"We'll need front and rear shots of the vehicle and its plates."

Rangel pressed the lens against the sunscreen window, shooting several quick photos while Hurt called the vehicle in to their dispatcher. "Rick, I'm away from the car. I need you to run a plate for me: California tags, four, G as in Gordon, Nancy, Sam, three, eight, six . . . get back to me with an ID."

"Ever seen this guy before?" asked Rangel.

Hurt shook his head. "Must've been hookin' up someplace else."

Pudgy and self-conscious, the driver was a boyish-looking man in his mid-forties with thin reddish-brown hair cut long in front and wearing a sage green sport coat. His head was on a swivel, turning from side to side, looking increasingly anxious. He finished gnawing on a cuticle and climbed out of the Ford, smoothed his hair, then closed and locked the car door. Pausing to size up the decrepit apartment building, he pulled a wad of cash out of his front pants pocket and began counting it nervously.

"No, no, not yet, sweet pea," Rangel muttered helpfully. "Put that away."

"Keep rolling," prompted Hurt. "We'll need front and side shots and several facials as he enters the apartment." Stuffing the bills into his jacket, the driver wiped a bead of sweat from his chin, still avoiding eye contact with the screen door.

"Asshole's trippin'," said Rangel. "Dude must be running low. Twenty bucks says he's got no outstanding warrants, no parking tickets, nothing—a real-live Dudley from West Hollywood." The doughy suspect shuffled awkwardly through the screen door while Rangel rapidly snapped photos. The satellite phone next to Hurt buzzed. He picked it up and listened with a sour look. "You're kidding me.

Sure about that?" Hurt was put on hold. "Charlie, you're never gonna believe this. Our vehicle's registered to the California Department of Healthcare Services."

"Excellent . . . this is getting better by the minute."

"Dispatch just confirmed that Governor Gav is paying for this morning's smack haul. Man, is this gonna look good in tomorrow's *Times*. State employee jonesing on his lunch break, your tax dollars at work." Hurt grabbed a pen to write down the vehicle's registration number, then hung up. "It seems our hero is one of the best and brightest. Vehicle is assigned to the California Health Regulatory Board. They've got an office at Fourth and Hill just a mile from here."

"Probably the reason we haven't seen him around. I bet he's got his own source closer to home. Let's give him a couple more minutes, then we'll bust him for possession. Maybe he's carrying decent enough weight."

"Sounds good, but keep the camera out. Brass will want pictures of him leaving the apartment and getting into his car, the full chain of events. This guy looks like he can afford a real lawyer, not one of them newbie public defenders."

"He's back . . ." Rangel's camera followed the suspect out the sliding screen door and into his Ford. "Got him, let's go." This time he threw the Nikon into a vinyl case while Hurt locked the door behind them. The detectives trotted quickly down a filthy stairwell and ducked through an emergency exit into the late morning sun. Hurrying, Rangel leaped behind the wheel of their modified Caprice cruiser, Hurt riding shotgun. He slipped the vehicle two cars behind the suspect's sedan and for the next five minutes followed it downtown.

"Think he's heading back to the office for an early lunch," Rangel asked hopefully, "maybe something light?" The Ford turned into a restricted state parking lot, an electric security arm opening, then closing.

"And get lucky with you in the car?" replied Hurt. "That'll happen in my lifetime."

"Hey, I appreciate the love, big man. Remember to keep that big 'ol ass of yours down when we roll up on this guy. I'd hate to put a bullet in it."

Hurt smirked. "I'd be worried except I've seen you on the range. Just aim directly at my butt, I'll be safe."

Rangel found an empty parking space across the street, about thirty meters southeast of the suspect's vehicle. "Another twenty says he snorts right there in the front seat."

The suspect's head was barely visible. He appeared to be arranging lines on something flat in his lap. "Where's the Kevlar?" asked Hurt in a serious tone, his eyes never leaving the suspect.

"In the trunk."

"Ease on out real slow and grab the vests."

Rangel calmly opened the car door and turned his face away from the suspect. He walked the length of the Caprice, raised the trunk lid, and pulled out two dark Special Enforcement Bureau (SEB) flak-vests. Hurt called their position in to the dispatcher.

"Still enjoying lunch?" asked Rangel, sliding back into the car with the bulletproof vests. They each pulled one on and cinched the elastic shoulder straps.

"Hasn't budged. This could take awhile—or not. Wait . . . wait, there we go. That's it, let's move."

The sheriff officers leaped out of the car and covered the thirty meters in a dead sprint. Hurt approached the Ford on the driver's side where the window was open. The suspect was so immersed in his cocaine, he didn't see them coming until Hurt jerked open the front door and shoved his Smith & Wesson nine-millimeter into the man's astonished face. "Sheriff's officers! Get your motherfuckin' hands on the wheel, now!" shouted Hurt, his face inches from the suspect's. A rolled-up five-dollar bill was planted in the man's left nostril. The other nostril was pinched shut with a finger; a glossy *LA Vibe* magazine with three lines of cocaine rested neatly in his lap. "You deaf, asshole?" Hurt shouted again. "Hands on the wheel, *now!*"

"What? Wait a minute!" yelped the trembling suspect. "What on earth . . . what on earth are you doing? No, wait, wait . . . *wait, goddamnit!* This is some kind of mistake. This isn't mine . . . it's not mine. This is a joke, right? Who put you up to this?"

"Shut the fuck up!" ordered Hurt, his adrenaline pulsing sky-high.

The suspect straightened in his seat, trying to control his trembling. "Officers, this isn't what it looks like." All three men stared at the lines in his lap, the ridiculousness of his statement dawning on the bewildered suspect. His chin dropped to his chest, his arrogance melting with each breath.

Rangel looked at Hurt, winking. "You owe me twenty bucks."

Hurt leaned farther into the vehicle as a terrified look blanketed the suspect's soft face. His hands were shaking incessantly, his nose running like a faucet. "Okay, okay," he pleaded, "I'll come clean. I promise I won't do it again. I swear to God, just walk away and I'll dump it in the trash can right over there. We never met. With God as my witness, I won't do it again. I'll do rehab—the whole trip this time, all ninety days. You got my word on it. I swear on my mother's grave, just give me a break. That's all I'm asking."

Hurt carefully lifted the cocaine from the suspect's lap, mindful to keep his hands and arms inside the Ford so the evidence wouldn't blow away.

Rangel started reading him his Miranda rights. "You have the right to remain silent—"

"Wait—*wait, goddamnit*! It's just a few lines, a misdemeanor. What are you guys doing out here anyway? Busting eight balls in a state of California parking lot?"

Rangel finished reading him his Miranda rights. "Do you understand your rights as I've read them to you?" he asked impatiently.

"I'm not one of them—the filth who sold me this shit—but I'll give him up. I can do that. I will give you the guy who sold me this shit. I know how this works."

"Sorry, twinkie," replied Rangel. "We got quotas, and white snitches count double."

"Is that what this is all about—your goddamn quotas? Fuck, what a bunch of lowlife cretins."

"Lute, did he say what I just thought he said?"

"Let it go," Hurt said tightly. "Just pretend you learned a new word for the day."

"Hey, bitch," Rangel snarled. "I got a new word for you: sphincter, as in tight enough to open a fucking beer bottle."

"Oh, shit . . . *shit*! I'm sorry, officers. Shit, shit . . . shit!" The suspect covered his face with his hands, his entire body shaking. "I don't know what got into me. Come on, help me out here. It's just blow."

"Looks like enough weight for some serious time," said Rangel, easing him out of the car.

"*My job*!" The suspect's scream startled the sergeants. "I could lose my job! They can take my license away for drug use. *Oh my God,* I'm gonna lose my license! You two *puercos* are gonna cost me my job, my livelihood."

"Easy, cowboy, right about now I'd be thinking about a lawyer," advised Hurt, searching the suspect's pockets. He removed an expensive Ghurka wallet and pulled out a laminated State of California Identification Card along with a facilities access card. "Alright, Harold Allen Chase, we need an answer this time. Do you understand your rights as we've read them to you?"

"Damn right I do. I understand my rights!" Chase hollered. "Police brutality, somebody help me! Please, somebody help me! Police brutality! All lives matter, all lives matter!"

"Oh for fuck's sake," Hurt muttered, rolling his eyes. "Let's go, douchebag."

But Harold Chase planted both feet. "I'm not going anywhere. I know my rights."

A crowd had begun to gather outside the gated parking area, watching as Hurt Z-tied Chase, duck-walked him to the Caprice, and stuffed him in the back seat.

Rangel carefully poured the cocaine into a clear plastic evidence bag and checked the rest of the front seat. It was clean. Ambling over to the Caprice, he found Hurt on the radio to the station.

"We have in custody one male Caucasian named Harold Allen Chase, age forty-six," reported Hurt. "I need an impound tow at 824 Hill Street. Also send over a field investigation unit."

"Please repeat your location, sergeant," came back the voice over the radio.

Hurt was irritated by the request. "Parking lot at Hill and Eighth."

"Sergeant Hurt, was the arrest made on restricted state property?"

"That's affirmative."

"And the suspect is a state of California employee?"

"His ID says he's a physical therapist, but he's got state security clearance for something called the California Investigative Review Committee, Region Nine." There was an uncomfortable silence before the radio finally squawked back.

"There's going to be hell to pay on this one, Lute."

"I know," said Hurt, his voice grinding. "There always is."

CHAPTER SIXTEEN

"Ten times earnings after fees and expenses, Hurston's take pencils out to about $66 million."

Stephanie Simpson dropped a leather-bound copy of a prospectus onto Dr. Ernie Girard's desk then carefully set her Ray-Bans beside a porcelain vase full of freshly-cut roses. She poured herself a cup of single-origin Colombian brew into a bone china mug embossed with the Hurston Neurological Institute logo and delicately tested the coffee with the tip of her tongue.

At thirty-four, Simpson was the youngest partner in a Palm Springs mergers and acquisitions firm that had aspirations of becoming a major West Coast private equity player. For the past seven months she had been dragging Hurston Neurological kicking and screaming through the proposed sale of its practice to Deutsche Ärzte International, DAI, a German medical conglomerate, and for Stephanie it was like belly-crawling through broken glass. The latest crisis—a handful of senior partners getting cold feet—was not the first. She had been through the numbers countless times, and from her perspective the entire deal was a no-brainer. But unfortunately not everybody agreed, and right now all she could do was sip her brew and hope Girard could nurse this deal home.

Girard stood pensively in front of a huge cathedral window, savoring a spectacular view of the San Gabriel Mountains. He had quit listening several minutes ago and was admiring his trim waistline in the reflection off the polished beveled glass. He was AWOL from this morning's session of his Investigative Review Committee, opting instead for a liquid breakfast and several lap dances at the Crystal Horseshoe with Harold Chase. Only begrudgingly had he left the "Shoe" to take this meeting with Simpson, something he would never have dreamed of doing for anybody else, but he was enthralled with the woman to the point of obsession. Call it karma, call it irony, call it whatever you wanted, there were a dozen different psychological reasons for it, from an indifferent mother to sexual confusion to fear of commitment, and his overpriced shrink was having a field day, but Girard didn't give a shit. The woman was in his crankcase.

He smoothed his long wavy hair, noticing a few gray strands cropping up around the temples, then pivoted away from the window, sucking in his abdominals. Simpson was talking but he wasn't paying attention. Financial statements bored him to no end, and unless the deal had changed, as one of Hurston's founding partners he was in line to pocket over $9 million from the acquisition.

"Feel free to check the numbers," she suggested, a rare hint of anxiousness in her voice. "We used conservative growth estimates for patient volumes. Tax deferments were confirmed by your personal accountants." She nudged the prospectus towards him, her perfectly manicured nails barely touching the document. "It's all right there."

Girard tried to smile, a bead of perspiration working its way down the back of his neck and pooling between his shoulder blades. His breathing had become ragged, his pulse spiking like a teenager in heat. *What the hell's wrong with you?*

Attractive, urbane, remarkably savvy, Simpson was Ivy League smart and Wall Street tough, having earned her spurs as one of three female interns working the trading floor on the New York Stock Exchange, an unusual career move for a Harvard Law School graduate, but one that paid off handsomely when she joined a stuffy investment bank on Wall Street, where she spent two years in Lower Manhattan getting her blue-blood credentials in order. From there she'd accepted a partnership in a small startup M & A outfit in the financial hinterlands of Palm Springs and successfully played matchmaker to several physician-owned HMOs and a trio of major West Coast insurance carriers. She had met Girard trolling for clients at a New Age drug rehab "meetup" in La Jolla.

Losing patience, she took another sip of coffee, trying to keep her hands still. Her eyes had wandered to Dr. Ernie's ego wall, an elaborate montage featuring his Yale medical degree, his Mayo fellowship certificate, and a row of ornate plaques honoring Girard's various board directorships. There was also a signed 'thank you' photo from former governor Jerry Brown; several photos of Dr. Ernie with every

Vegas headliner worth his or her marquee; and a signed baseball bat from a former Los Angeles Angels outfielder whom Girard had performed a spinal decompression on.

"How many people know about this?" he finally asked, feeling the need to say something.

Simpson settled into a white leather tripod chair, crossing then uncrossing her tanned legs, looking magnetic in a charcoal-gray designer suit, silk blouse, and gray Ferragamo pumps.

"The entire deal, end zone to end zone?" she replied, somewhat perturbed.

"Yes, your complete due diligence, and not just the financials."

She flipped her silver blonde hair with a subtle flick of her right wrist, a nervous habit. "My partners, the tax analysts in Huntington Beach, a group of healthcare lobbyists we retained out of Chicago. They're former Obama people. They run a cute little boutique communications shop on Lake Shore Drive."

"Wonderful, I'm feeling better already."

"Okay, what? What's wrong? Why the holdup? Everyone's signed their confidentiality agreements. The Germans are waiting. Why isn't this happening?"

"Indulge me," Girard said bluntly.

A scowl creased her otherwise perfect, spa-pampered face. More frustrated by the second, she set down her coffee cup and enunciated slowly as if speaking to a dull child.

"Hurston's earnings are projected to grow at fifteen percent annually over the next five years—even with GavinAid falling apart. If we can get your compliance people to sign off on last year's financials, and the Germans are on board with those numbers, we can secure the initial down payment in thirty days. What I need—*soon, very soon*—is a green light from your partners. Why is this so hard to understand?"

Girard punched a red button on his phone console: "Katrina, no interruptions please." He released the button, got up, sauntered back to the window. "Nothing happens until our auditors pass the financials, so let's not get ahead of ourselves."

"Heaven forbid that."

Girard smirked into the window glass, amused at her impatience. From the reflection he saw her ease out of the tripod chair and walk around his desk. "Ernie, look at me," she demanded.

Girard didn't budge.

"*I said look at me.*"

With great reluctance he turned and faced her.

"We've got DAI's best-and-final offer on the table, and they're not going to tolerate a messy due diligence process. This needs to get done before Trump leaves office or DAI will walk. Everyone thought you could handle your partners. What seems to be the problem?"

Girard's fists balled into tight knots. Getting his partners this far had been like herding lemurs. "Politics, mind-numbing politics, the great and mighty Aran Dvir and that pious dick, Steven Todd, have grave philosophical problems with the whole deal, deep moral qualms." Girard mimicked his two senior partners. "Somehow the idea of making millions off the sale of our practice is morally inconsistent with Hurston's founding purpose of mission over money. It's all a pile of horseshit, but those two take three other partners with them."

"Fine, what can we do to move it along? I can line up a couple of consulting gigs with our pharma vendors, throw in a lectureship cruise. Will that help?"

"I appreciate the thought. But buying off partners with some half-assed consulting job or Love Boat seminar isn't going to get it done. Besides, the Medicare auditors eat that shit for breakfast, and I can't afford to go to jail over this."

Simpson stood to her full height, drilling him with a withering look. "IPO gold, that's what the *Journal* is calling it. The last gasp of our private healthcare system, the good ol' boys cashing out before the feds finally crack down and turn off the spigot. The Dems are driving towards single-payer and, trust me, that'll be the end of the good times." Her vivid blue eyes had a sort of maniacal gleam. "Southern Clinic in Savannah just cleared $100 million in an all-cash buyout from Regent Health. Their senior docs walked away with $16 million each, pre-tax. Imagine that, a bunch of no-name osteopaths raking in $100 million for a partially-insured book of business. It's like the housing bubble all over again."

Simpson's ferocity turned most men off, but for Girard it was an incredible turn on. He dabbed a drop of sweat off the right side of his face. "A tad melodramatic, don't you think, Steph. Nobody's curing cancer, we're just cashing in on the loyalty of our patients. Why do you investment bankers make it sound so grandiose? Does it help you sleep at night?"

"I sleep just fine, and *you* of all people should be lecturing on ethics. What would your colleagues say if they knew about your little kickback scheme with the plaintiff lawyers? All that cash you've been laundering through your airplane leasing company."

Girard's head spun, his eyes flashed. But Simpson's smug, expressionless gaze took the steam right out of him. Sulking, he shuffled closer to the window and slouched.

Instantly, Simpson knew she'd overplayed her hand and slid next to him, touching his forearm. "When it comes right down to it, none of this is really that complicated," she whispered, "Your average patient really doesn't want to believe it's big business. They'd much rather hang on to that quaint notion of their physicians serving the community. 'If you like your doctor, you can keep him,' remember that one? But we're running out of time, Ernie. We miss this deal and you'll be spending the rest of your career working trauma every fifth night."

Girard was staring at her reflection in the pane, fixing his wandering eyes on her perfect cleavage. "Lovely speech. Did you practice it in front of the mirror this morning?"

Embarrassed, she pulled back, grinding her teeth. "Just get me the *goddamn* deal, can you do that?" The severity in her tone caused him to flinch. "Sixty-six million dollars, that's more than enough to get you and what you call your career back on track."

"And you're doing this out of the goodness of your heart?"

"You know exactly why I'm doing this. I want to sip lattes in Aspen, scuba-dive in the Turks, make the season in London. And this deal gets me that much closer."

Aroused, Girard turned slightly away from her and closed his eyes, fantasizing about how good this was going to be. Screwing nurses and pharmacy reps were standard perks for any warm-blooded neurosurgeon but this woman, this analyst, was in a league all her own. He squared up to face her, his left hand easing up the side of her skirt, his surgically-trained fingers quivering. But when he started clumsily groping at her patterned hose, she slapped his hand away.

"For chrissakes, Ernie, how about we start thinking with big head for a change."

Startled, Girard looked back at her with a baffled expression. Like most neurosurgeons, he wasn't used to hearing the word no. She suppressed a smile as her eyes drifted downward to Girard's crotch, taking in his wilting manhood. There were a few seconds of embarrassing silence, her grin tightening somewhat before she pivoted, slid the Hurston prospectus into her calfskin folder, and poured herself a second cup of coffee. "What's left?" she asked, all business again.

"You tell me," sniffed Girard, swallowing through the spreading ache in his groin.

"Did you hear from the U.S. attorney? What's the word on your lawyer friends? What are the bloggers calling them, the SoCal Medical Mafia?"

Girard was having a difficult time taming his libido. Stalling, he turned to face the window again, smoothing the lapels on his tailored lab coat. He could feel her cold, hard stare boring a hole through the back of his head as she settled into the tripod chair. "The case is being handled by an assistant U.S. attorney named Munir," said Girard. "He heads a task force that investigates medical fraud and drug abuse. The word is he's tough, likes to see his face on TV, and that he'll probably be indicting Ralf Millette, the Ralfinator, as early as next week. Ralf is one of the richest plaintiff lawyers in LA. The man's been covering our asses for years. If he cooperates, this whole thing could unravel and I'd be pretty much screwed."

Simpson's entire body stiffened. This certainly wasn't the news she'd expected to hear. "Can you cut a deal?"

"First we need to know what Munir has got. Could be just another bureaucrat looking for an easy killshot. These guys never want to go to trial, especially with something as dicey as white-collar fraud. It's too complicated for juries, screws up their conviction rate. I've hired MaryAnn Taylor; she's a ballbuster. But the feds haven't called her yet."

"And you're sure they're not sandbagging your attorney . . . what's her name?"

"MaryAnn Taylor, and no, I'm not worried about the feds. They've got nothing. It's our internal audit that's bothering me. We've been . . . how should I say it, a tad aggressive with our billing practices, maybe a bit over the top."

"GavinAid or state employees?"

"State employees and a couple of Nevada HMOs. They're both demanding refunds. Plus our bean counters want to set aside an extra $5 million in reserves for any uncovered med-mal exposure beyond our current policy limits."

Simpson nearly laughed at that one. "Don't you mean *your* uncovered malpractice exposure? Four open cases if I'm not mistaken. And now that your drug history's been admitted into public record, you're ground zero for every ambulance chaser in the Southland."

"Thanks for the reminder, but I got it under control."

"Sounds like it. Who's handling the in-house audit? We certainly don't need any more surprises."

"Rory Armstead. It's just number crunching. He's got a few boy scouts down there, but there's nothing to worry about." Now that sex was off the table, Girard had grown weary of Simpson's interrogation. Squinting, he checked the appointment app on his smartphone. "If they run into any problems, Rory knows to call me. I chair Hurston's executive committee."

"And are we expecting problems?" Simpson had gotten up and was hovering over him. When he didn't answer, she squeezed his left arm. "*Ernie?*"

"There're always problems, Stephanie dear. We walk a fine line."

"Is that what you call it?—*a fine line?* How cavalier. Sixty-six million on the table and you're walking *a fine line.*"

"What can I say." He shrugged. "Life in the big leagues."

Unimpressed, she edged closer. "Well, Doctor, if there are any more problems—*fix them.* Or we're screwed. Do I make myself clear?" She didn't wait for his answer. "By the way, did you settle the Martinez case? I heard another spine surgeon testified that you operated on the wrong level and missed the cysts entirely."

His eyes jumped wide. "Who told you that?"

"It's not important. When's your next deposition?"

"In a week or two—*damn it*, Stephanie, where did you hear that information?"

She managed a wan smile as she adjusted her cross-banded blouse. "Answer my question about the Martinez case."

"I spent two hours yesterday handling damage control with my partners."

"*And?*"

"And it's not a problem."

"What does that mean, Ernie? Is it settled or not? This case can't go to a jury. You were stone-cold high in the operating room. Stuttgart won't tolerate that kind of publicity. Germans tend to frown on their neurosurgeons being dopers."

"MaryAnn said it was taken care of it. What else do you want from me?"

"And how does *MaryAnn* plan on taking care of it?"

"I don't know?—the usual drill. Dig up a few personal problems. Drag the plaintiffs through the mud, cut 'em up a bit. I didn't ask for a memo."

Simpson looked him squarely in the eyes and pulled his chin flush with hers. "Don't jam us up on this. Do you understand me? You barely-for-profits couldn't smell a hot deal if it slapped you in the face." Girard waved a hand in surrender, and she let go of his chin. "In the meantime, I'm moving ahead with the Germans. A final prospectus will be on your desk by the end of the week. If your auditors can guarantee the financials and your compliance people don't uncover anything out of the ordinary, DAI will wire the first payment within five business days, and we can put this thing to bed. All I need is a green light."

Simpson slid the calfskin folder into her briefcase, indicating their meeting was over. Pulling a gold key ring from the outside pocket of the briefcase, she strolled briskly across the cream-colored carpet, averting her eyes as Girard offered a limp handshake.

"Thirty days, Ernie," she ordained. "The offer goes off the table in one month. Try not to disappoint me." Appropriately dismissed, Girard gazed at her like a sad puppy, loathing his spinelessness as she sailed past him.

"Thirty days," she reminded him and slammed the door behind her. Girard stood motionless, arms at his side, looking down at his crotch.

Definitely, a bit deflated.

CHAPTER SEVENTEEN

"Where's Harold?" Dr. Ernie Girard seemed to be talking to himself.

The afternoon session of his Investigative Review Committee was running twenty minutes late, and Harold Chase hadn't made it back from lunch. When he didn't respond to his texts, Girard turned to Juanita Reno, who was not the least bit surprised that Chase had gone AWOL.

"I guess we'll go ahead without him," said Girard, a bit uneasy. Reno nodded her concurrence, and he scanned the gallery and began. "This committee is back in session. I'd like to remind the applicants that they're still under oath. I'm going to waive reading of the next case to get things moving along. Ms. Taylor, glad to see your familiar face with us this afternoon. No doubt we'd be lost without you."

MaryAnn Taylor gave Girard a confused, cryptic look. "Thank you, Doctor, wonderful to be here. Next applicant is Jaspal Ambani, Woodland Hills, Denial-Of-Care Order R-1-0-5-9 . . ."

"Yes, yes," Girard interrupted, "it's all right here. Cut to the chase, please."

"Left hip arthroplasty, denied. His records are up on your screen, the hard copies in front of you." Taylor gathered up her files and sat down.

Girard turned towards a slender, dignified seventy-one-year-old man with a shock of gray hair and deep-set brown eyes. Earlier he had entered the conference room with a pronounced limp. "Hip replacement, Mr. Ambani," Girard proclaimed in a tone laced with superior knowledge. "Pretty gnarly surgery, sir. You sure you're up for it?"

"Quite ready, your honor," Ambani replied nervously. "I can barely walk. My orthopedic surgeon, Dr. Modi, said I'm an excellent candidate for the hip replacement operation, but your nurses won't approve it. I don't understand why. I've done everything they've asked."

"It's a very expensive procedure, Mr. Ambani, and you're over the age of seventy. That puts you in what we call an 'added risk' category."

"What does that mean, your honor?"

"I'm not your honor, but what that means is, we automatically review all joint replacement surgeries for anyone seventy years or older. We're looking for possible complications, and I see that you're diabetic and have high blood pressure."

"Both are under control, your honor. I'm as healthy as a stallion. Is that the saying?"

Growing impatient, Girard turned to Taylor. "Ms. Taylor, could I impose upon one of your minions to produce a cost breakdown for hip replacement surgeries, aged seventy-plus?"

"I'm sure we can find something," she replied. "Jeremy?"

An alert, well-dressed twenty-something tapped several commands into his government-issue iPad, and a swirl of documents poured sleekly from a new deskjet printer. After reviewing the first and last pages, the analyst silently handed the stack to Taylor while Ambani and the rest of the crowd watched, impressed with the touch-of-a-finger display of their tax dollars at work.

"What are the median hospital costs for the surgery?" Girard asked.

"Costs or charges?" Taylor replied.

"Do I look like someone who's interested in markups? Just the costs, *please*."

"Between $36,000 and $40,000 per procedure."

"And the median cost for the hip implant itself?"

"Between $11,000 and $15,000 per case."

"So roughly a third of the total outlay is for a simple implant made in China? Don't you find that rather obscene?"

"Those are the numbers, Doctor." Taylor shrugged and sat down.

"Sir, if I may be heard?" From the back of the conference room a heavy-set businessman in a charcoal-gray suit stood and raised his right hand. "Bobby Lee Hawkins, assistant vice president, Cytogenic Corporation. Our company is the third largest manufacturer and distributor of orthopedic implant systems in the U.S., and for the record, it requires an average of thirteen years of scientific research and development, including FDA approval, for any of our implants to reach market. Our price represents the tremendous investment Cytogenic makes to assure each and every one of our products is safe and effective."

There was an uncomfortable silence while Girard glared at Hawkins as if he wanted to eviscerate him with a scalpel. "Why are you here, Bobby Lee? May I call you Bobby Lee?"

"Certainly, Doctor. One of my responsibilities is to monitor the judgments coming out of this review committee. As you're probably aware, Cytogenic offers a post-appeal support program for qualified patients whose surgeries have been denied."

"Post-appeal support," Girard repeated. "Is that like cash?"

"Legal assistance, sir."

Girard's face twisted into a bitter grimace as if he'd swallowed something particularly nasty. "What's the average markup on your hip implant?"

"That's proprietary data, sir."

"Of course it is," said Girard, rolling his eyes. "How much do you spend on government lobbying each year? A rough estimate will suffice."

"I'm not at liberty to say." The words rolled off Hawkins's lips like an effortless backhand.

"Are all your implants manufactured in China?"

"Bangladesh."

"Better yet—"

"Under stringent quality control, I might add." Hawkins was hitting all the right marks, but Girard wasn't buying any of it.

"Paying any more kickbacks to surgeons these days? Lucrative consulting deals, device royalties, foreign travel? I don't imagine to Bangladesh?"

"That's not the Cytogenic way. Besides, the feds have pretty much clamped down on all of that."

"And who says trickle-down government doesn't work? Thank you, Bobby Lee. I believe we're ready to rule."

Girard looked to Juanita Reno, who shrugged her shoulders as if to say, "It's your call."

"Very well, I'm going to overrule the denial-of-care order and allow Mr. Ambani to receive his hip replacement surgery." Girard paused for effect. "With the stipulation that his surgeon use a Cytogenic implant that Bobby Lee and his inbred cousins are going to provide at a discounted rate of say . . . $995? I like the sound of that, don't you, Bobby Lee? *Nine ninety-five.* Sort of like a used car salesman."

Hawkins' face turned slightly pale. "Yes, very man-of-the-street, sir. Unfortunately we're not in the discounting business. I've got shareholders to answer to."

"I understand . . . very important people, but I was thinking, wouldn't it be nice if you could make an exception just this once, sort of doing your part for healthcare reform, making single-payer great again. How about it, *Bobby Lee*, help us out here." Girard's voice dropped a decibel, letting Hawkins know he had a long memory and there would be other cases.

Swaying back and forth on his toes, Hawkins stared at his patent leather wingtips, biting hard on the inside of his cheek, his eyes staying glued to his glossy Cole Haans until there was nothing left to leech from them. He lifted his head and opened both palms. "Doctor, I stand before you a humbled man. I can't fathom what got into me. Of course we would be delighted to provide a discounted implant as part of our post-appeal program, *and* I thank you for allowing me to speak this afternoon. It's been very instructional."

"Duly noted, and the committee appreciates your generosity," replied Girard. "Mr. Ambani, it's your lucky day. You're getting a new hip, sir."

Ambani stood, bowing deeply in respect. "I am overwhelmed with gratitude, Doctor, and if ever I can be of service to you, it would be my greatest honor. Your wisdom is vast, and he who does kind deeds truly becomes rich."

Girard grinned laconically. "Obviously, you haven't met any of my ex-wives or their lawyers. Good luck with the surgery, sir. Next case, please."

CHAPTER EIGHTEEN

"How long was he detained?" Assistant U.S. Attorney Bipu Munir grimaced as he inspected the black flaky crust at the bottom of a very old coffee pot.

Sherri Austin, Lead Investigator for the Subcommittee on Oversight for the Committee on Energy and Commerce, U.S. House of Representatives, searched her copy of the arrest warrant. "Less than four hours," she answered, "long enough for him to lawyer-up and arrange a personal recognizance bond."

Munir's moist hands nearly smeared the hard copy report. A short, bandy-legged man with a three-day old beard and rosy brown eyes, his voice had a slight singsong quality that many of his adversaries often mistook for softness. "This is it? This is all we got after four hours of questioning? Who's his counsel anyway? I don't recognize the name."

"Local talent off the call list," said Austin, her clear green eyes rarely blinking. She was a former IRS attorney with an enviable conviction rate. From her tiny cubicle in the Rayburn House Office Building in Washington, DC, Austin's low-key style and dogged investigative skills had upended some of the cockiest white-collar criminals in the healthcare industry. Her specialty was unwinding complicated Medicare fraud cases, and on Capitol Hill she was viewed as a rising star.

"Fairly competent, though," she continued, "and pretty upset about the way we handled the whole thing. Managed to enlighten me on the numerous civil actions he'd be filing if Mr. Chase ended up with his pants around his ankles."

Munir threw caution to the wind and poured cold water into the plastic twelve-cup coffee maker. "It's a basic intimidation tactic. Did it work?"

She gave him a sly smile. "Bipu, you disappoint me. We introduced Chase to the dregs of last night's cage, quite a collection by the way. The magistrate's staff had the over-under at ten minutes before Chase started whining. I took the under. Rothstein, the senior public defender, laid the over. Said Chase had more moxie than we were giving him credit for."

"Who won?"

"Rothstein. After fifteen minutes the magistrate got worried about Chase getting love-rubbed by one of his cellmates, so they took him down to Interview Four."

The automatic coffee machine gurgled painfully, spurting a steam of hot java through a cacophony of hacking noises. Munir grabbed a Styrofoam cup, deftly slid the pot to one side, and slipped his cup under the spout, catching the first sprays of steaming liquid. They were in a small windowless booking area in the Alan Cranston Federal Annex in downtown Los Angeles, surrounded by eggshell-white walls, stained linoleum floors, and rows of harsh fluorescent lights reflecting brightly off sheet-metal tables with stainless-steel handcuff rings. The stench of disinfectant irritated Munir's sinuses. He sipped his coffee as he re-read the charges.

"Suspect's full name is Harold Allen Chase, Century City address, no previous arrests." Flipping through a few pages, his lips tightened. "And this is all we got? The arresting officers stated he was squealing like a Tea Partier in a whorehouse when they busted him."

Austin checked her smartphone. "Yeah, well, he was humiliated, that's for sure, and rambling on about his physical therapy license, but after an hour or so he got his act together and demanded to see a lawyer. By the way, are you getting any flak on this from downtown? I hear the guy's wife is high up in the California Secretary of State's office. It looks like our Harold's a death panel judge."

"*Death panel?* " Munir looked appalled. "What, are we riffing Sarah Palin these days?"

"What would you call it?"

"Chase is a member of one of the state's investigative review committees. The same committee chaired by Dr. Ernie Girard."

"Ahhh," Austin's eyes lit up. "I see where this is going. You're counting on Harold to roll over on the good doctor . . . bigger fish to fry. But I wouldn't go banking on his testimony too soon. The man may be a flake, but he's no pushover."

"See, now that's where we disagree. Harold Chase is up to his eyebrows in feces. He's been churning Girard's bogus back patients for the SoCal Medical Mafia for the last ten years, and I seriously doubt the man can handle a drug conviction."

"The what?"

"The SoCal Medical Mafia. Don't tell me you haven't heard of them? It's been all over social media and the networks. Started out as a loose group of local plaintiff lawyers and doctors referring auto accident victims to each other, then splitting the fees and jury awards, but the doctors got greedy and started feeding potential malpractice victims to their lawyer buddies. Then they persuaded the victims to undergo serious, sometimes needless surgeries, all to jack up the size of the personal-injury claims. Claims that should've been minor became major. Patients usually treated with pain management underwent complex spine-fusion surgeries, iffy joint replacements, etcetera."

"Did it work?"

"Yeah, too well. The docs would give false testimony when their patients sued and our hero, Dr. Ernie, was right in the middle of this cesspool. He's a spine guy. Got his start in the ER at Santa Monica Memorial fingering trauma victims for Medical Mafia attorneys, who then kicked him back a piece of the jury award or settlement."

"How much are we talking about?"

"Forensics figures about $14 million over the past nine years. He's been laundering it through an airplane leasing company in Mexico, calling it consulting expenses. That was until he gambled it all away or snorted it up his nose. The grand jury is considering indictments on conspiracy, mail fraud, money laundering, aiding and abetting, obstruction of justice, and witness tampering."

"Impressive. But how come this Medical Mafia couldn't protect Girard from his own malpractice problems?"

"Oh, they tried, but Girard's a real cowboy. Runs his practice like a Russian tractor factory. Knocks out 800 cases a year, plus he's got that nasty drug habit. Nobody can shield you on that."

"And you're counting on Chase to flip?"

"That's our play, and the real reason behind last night's little drama. We could've let Harold out on his own recognizance, but I wanted to make an impression. Like Girard, Chase is also a habitual drug user with a laundry list of upside-down real estate deals, tapped-out credit cards, and a mistress who likes baubles. Trust me—this guy can't take a bounce for cocaine possession."

"Fair enough, but he's not quite the puppy dog you think he is. Before lawyering-up, he said he could finger two staffers on his death panel for prescription drug kickbacks and over a dozen Medicare fraud cases. I'd like to have a go at him when you're done."

"Might be awhile. He's looking at felony weight possession." Munir gave the manila folder back to Austin and finished his coffee.

There was an odd silence while her eyes studied the linoleum floor. After a few seconds, she lifted her head. "Bipu, we need to talk about something, and you're not gonna like it."

"Then keep it to yourself."

"Sorry, no can do. You're getting help on this one, courtesy of our friend Congressman Aceves from California's 34th."

"Thanks, but tell the congressman we're good. Task Force has put in a huge amount of overtime and we got our dominoes all lined up. It's just a matter of time before Chase flips on Girard, and the rest of the Mafia will stumble over each other to cut a deal. I figure we're looking at a dozen indictments, easy."

"It's not that kind of help."

"What do you mean? What other kind is there?"

Austin straightened, peering at him with a flat, uncompromising expression. "Girard's airplane leasing company was flying monthly hauls into Juárez and laundering cash through a number of regional banks including the *Banco Comercial de Monterrey*. Some of the *Monterrey* money found its way into an ATF case that went sideways and was used to buy a load of M249 light machine guns bought illegally by the Cártel del Noreste. The Mexican attorney general's staff was helpful in tracking down the M249s, along with the cash used to buy them. We got a lot of cooperation from the AG's team in Mexico City, plus they kept their mouths shut, which in D.C. is a lot more important these days. Congressman Aceves decided to return the favor by offering one of the AG's special investigators a temporary liaison slot with your Task Force. They've got a related case going."

Munir's brown eyes widened to the size of almonds. "This is a joke, right?"

"Sorry. It's a done deal. In fact, your new tag-along is already here."

"Wait what? Sherri! What am I supposed to do with a Mexican cop in the middle of a major federal investigation? Does this guy know anything about our laws, our procedures, anything that might be marginally useful?"

"It's not my idea, Bipu. The Congressman wants it done and your deputy chief is trying to move up the departmental food chain. Health care is liquid-hot these days. Fighting medical corruption has become big game in the House and indicting a bunch of greedy LA surgeons is gonna generate a whole lot of headlines. Maybe get a few people re-elected. Plus, Mexico is front-and-center these days at the State Department. They're feeling bad about the way Trump cracked back on them."

"But why does it have to be the Mexican AG? They're more corrupt than the Colombians and they leak like a sieve. Would you trust 'em?"

Standing beneath a mustard yellow NO SMOKING sign, Austin tapped out a Newport and lit it, savoring that first breath of tobacco that addicts crave. She dropped her voice an octave. "I don't have to trust him. I just do what I'm told. Don't make this any harder than it has to be. Introduce him around, take him through his paces, let him make nice with the staff until the real work needs to be done, then cut him out. How hard can it be?"

"Do I have a say in any of this?"

She took another deep drag. "Sorry, another congressman wants to run for governor. Sound familiar? Get your office up to speed. Your new partner is waiting outside."

"Waiting where? Sherri wait—"

But Austin had snuffed out her cigarette and was retreating rapidly through a pair of automatic doors, waving airily. "Good luck," she offered in full stride, heading towards the parking lot. "My flight lands later tonight. Text me tomorrow and let me know how things turn out. *Ciao*."

Munir watched her exit through sliding bulletproof doors, feeling a caffeine-induced headache squatting in the back of his head. Buttoning his jacket, he cast his tired eyes around Central Booking, a three-story granite structure with recessed lighting and vertical slits for windows. The main entrance had a vaulted foyer with several built-in benches for visitors. Munir breathed in deep through his nostrils, tamping down his anger. *Let's get this over with*, he thought, and began threading his way past a line of drunks handcuffed to a stainless steel rail running the length of the hallway.

Near the circular front desk, Senior Investigator Blas Mondragon sat motionless, passively observing an endless parade of addicts and DUI suspects.

Gathering his rucksack, he stood as Munir approached and extended his right hand. "Blas Mondragon. I'm with the Assistant Attorney General's Office for the Investigation of Organized Crime."

Munir eyed him up and down. "That's quite a mouthful . . . the Office for the Investigation of Organized Crime. How's that going for you guys these days?"

"About as well as the wall is for you," Mondragon answered, returning the sarcasm.

Munir lifted an eyebrow, pausing before extending his hand. "Sorry, my bad, welcome to Los Angeles." He shook Mondragon's hand. "Good trip from Mexico City?"

"Actually, I'm based out of Juárez."

"Ah, Ciudad Juárez, helluva city. How's the Kentucky Club these days?"

"Hanging in there, the kids call it the Kentucky Bar. You know the city, Munir?"

Bipu noticed that Mondragon had pronounced his last name correctly. "Several years ago I spent three weeks in a counternarcotics training course at Fort Bliss."

"Assistant AG's staff was short-handed in Mexico City, so they farmed this one out to me. I'm part of a small investigative unit in Juárez, mostly drug-related homicides. Lately they've thrown in VIP protection since the narco-violence started ramping up again."

"Great, welcome to LA."

"Thanks, I just have to—"

"But I gotta tell you, your background could be a problem on this one. No offense, but we're working on a complicated white-collar case with several moving parts which will be defended by some very sharp, very nasty defense attorney pricks. I'm not sure how you fit into all of this. Again, no offense."

Mondragon's temper started to boil, but he made a deliberate effort to compose himself. "None taken. I'll do my best not to stumble around too much. But I got the file on this case, so why don't we make the best of it."

"*Like I said*, you haven't been read in on the facts of the case or the potential indictments. We're looking at possible fraud and racketeering charges on at least twelve potential suspects, a veritable who's-who of LA lawyers and doctors. I won't have time to babysit a visiting cop, and quite frankly it looks like they sent me the junior varsity."

Mondragon swallowed hard, his lower lip moving as he chewed it. Hitching his tattered rucksack over his left shoulder, his eyes froze on Munir like tiny dark voids. "No offense taken," he said in a strained voice. "But as long as we're being candid, the way you screwed up the arrest by waiting an hour before pressuring the therapist into talking and then losing him to his lawyer before you could lay the groundwork for a deal—very sloppy. But then, what do I know?"

This time it was Munir's throat that tightened. "Where the hell do you get off—"

"—and by now Chase has regrouped, and trust me, I know the type. He'll have drained whatever cash he's got squirreled away and hired a $750-an-hour criminal lawyer who'll soon be explaining to us how we won't be having any more holding-pen reunions with his client. And unless Chase cooperates, I'm guessing you really don't have much of a case. And if any of your investigators didn't follow proper procedures, the whole thing could get tossed at pre-trial."

Munir's eyes widened. "Our plan went down fine!" he lashed back defensively. "We're right where we need to be."

"Then it's all good," shrugged Mondragon. "Shall we?" Both men wedged their way through a pair of double doors. Behind them a row of homeless men were lined up for transfer to a new adult detention center. "Because that may be the last time we get a chance to talk to Harold Chase. I hope it was worth the circus."

Munir stopped dead in his tracks, spinning on Mondragon. "How about we save the good taxpayers of Mexico some money and I drive you back to LAX? I bet we can find a flight to Mexico City, my treat."

"Juárez," Mondragon corrected him.

Munir's fists bunched into knots. The two men stood face-to-face. "What hole did they dig you out of, *Mon-dra-gon*? And why am I getting the assistant AG's leftovers? This should've been big enough for Mexico City."

"Not everybody can be a superstar, Bipu. May I call you Bipu?" Mondragon didn't wait for an answer. "I got assigned to Juárez to open an anti-narcotics office in the middle of the first cartel drug war, kind of like holding back the ocean. But that's pretty mundane stuff for a high-flying assistant U.S. attorney."

"You didn't answer my question. Why are you here?"

Embarrassed, Mondragon hesitated an instant too long, Munir noticing his deserted gaze as they stood looking at each other. Finally, Mondragon spoke, his voice bitter. "Cocaine happened. Then the cartels happened. Then assault weapons by the truckloads happened, and judges and cops started dying on my doorstep. That's what happened, *Bipu*."

Munir caught a glint of brutality in the senior investigator's worn face. "The judge in Juárez, the one who was murdered with an M249 was he under your protection?"

There was another pained look on Mondragon's face as Munir hit home. His eyes looked downward. "The M249s were part of a gang diversion. They had nothing to do with the murder. The killer breached our security in the parking lot of a country club that was supposed to be airtight. Then kidnapped the judge, slit his throat, dumped the body at a pot house, and torched the building to scare off our snitches. The case is still under investigation. Our *peritos* think he used some kind of scalpel."

"And you were part of the judge's protection detail?"

Mondragon kept staring at his scuffed loafers. "Operation Safe Mexico. I was assigned primary back-up."

"*Operation Safe Mexico!*" Munir bellowed. "Are you fucking kidding me? This is how the assistant attorney general cleans up his messes? Some hump cuts the throat of a sitting federal judge while his security's out whacking off and he ships the loser to me. What happened to the rest of *Operation Safe Mexico*? Firing squad? Scrubbing toilets in Guadalajara?"

Mondragon pitched forward on the balls of his feet, swaying with each blow from Munir. He'd been down this road way too often for self-pity. Adjusting the straps on his rucksack, he straightened, his silence unnerving Munir, who was beginning to feel like a jackass.

The men began walking towards the electric doors, their silence lengthening with each stride. A sliver of light weaved its way through the double doors, which whisked open, and Mondragon and Munir stepped out into the circular driveway. A young attorney from Munir's office pulled up in an unmarked Chevrolet sedan, his crew-cut head barely visible through the tinted windows. Munir's eyes moved from the sedan to Mondragon. Reaching out, he grabbed the Mexican cop's left forearm. "Hey, I'm sorry about that. I was out of line. It's been a shitty morning, but what's done is done. You got any leads on the judge's killer other than the connection to the M249s?"

Mondragon paused. "It's a woman. I think I've met her. It was over a year ago in a hospital emergency room." Digging into the right front pocket of his faded jeans, he pulled out a small silver charm and tossed it to Munir. The assistant U.S. attorney caught it with his right hand.

"What's this?"

"Our *asesina* likes to leave a calling card. Unfortunately, she doesn't leave DNA. The FBI is running an MO check. I was hoping to find some sort of connection."

Munir gazed at the tiny silver charm. "What's this supposed to be?"

"An angel," Mondragon said, his voice barely a whisper. "Keep it. We've got two others."

CHAPTER NINETEEN

"Tell me again why I'm sitting here?" asked Dr. Ernie Girard, draped around a padded folding chair, sipping freshly squeezed papaya juice and looking like he wanted to disembowel someone.

It was going to be one of those mornings, lamented his attorney, MaryAnn Taylor.

The two were seated at a round pressboard table covered by a white linen tablecloth and positioned about as far as one could get from the podium in the High Tide Room at the Sea Cliff Resort & Spa. Four glossy hand-painted signs had been stationed around the brightly-lit room welcoming eighty-three shell-shocked attendees and their spouses to the Physicians Liability Corporation of California's (PLCC) Defendants Educational Retreat, PLCC being Girard's malpractice carrier.

"You were invited," Taylor answered patiently, "to help find constructive ways to cope with the emotional fallout of being sued and to understand the devastating effects it has on your family, staff, and colleagues." She was reading from the seminar brochure. "You'll learn hands-on techniques to help prepare you for your courtroom testimony—pay special attention to that one—and you will participate in mock depositions at the end of each session." She could hardly wait to see PLCC's cutthroat attorneys carve up Girard like a lab frog. That alone would be worth the price of the seminar.

"An invitation, you're sure that's what they sent me?" asked Girard skeptically.

"A thirty-day written notice of your required attendance might be a better description."

"Great. I'm wasting an entire Saturday because a handful of greedy patients want to empty my wallet. I thought we had tort reform in California."

"We do, but Proposition 64 increased the dollar limit on non-economic damages to $3.5 million if negligence can be proven, and that includes substance abuse. Since you've got four open med/mal cases, this training is deemed mandatory for a *habitual defendant*, which according to the terms of your policy you are. So you're going to sit there like a good soldier and pay attention. It's a wonder PLCC even covers you at all."

"I'm guessing the $4.8 million in group premiums Hurston pays each year has something to do with it."

"Welcome, everyone! Isn't it a great day to be alive?" A casually-dressed man in his mid-forties stood ramrod-straight at the podium, gazing back at his flock like an evangelical minister on crank, only with whiter teeth. "My name is Dr. Joshua Steinman, and I can't think of a better place I'd rather be than right here in this beautiful resort, helping you." Blessed with menthol-blue eyes and shoulder-length blonde hair, the Fabio-resembling Steinman had the prerequisite perma-tan and faux-Australian accent that were perfect for disarming Type-A physicians. "By training I'm a clinical psychologist specializing in post-traumatic stress disorders for high-achieving professionals. Over the years my clients have included physicians just like you who've been *petitioned* into this country's highly dysfunctional medical-legal abattoir. Today, it's my job to help you understand how this personal hardship can unleash a torrent of toxic behavioral problems. We'll be discussing practical ways to alleviate your stress, anxiety, and most important, let you know that you're not alone. But first, give yourselves a great big round of applause for being here this morning. Nobody knows how tough it is to get sued, and I'm just thankful we can all be together to share our feelings. Come on, give it up!"

"Get me out of here," Girard mumbled under his breath. But Taylor just smiled sweetly as the other attendees applauded warily.

But Steinman wasn't entirely off base. This seminar and the emotional crush of being sued was a sharp skewering of every highly-inflated ego in the room. Absorbing this morning's agenda with topics such as *Malpractice Metastasis, Maintaining Your Libido Post-Deposition,* and *Doctors Who Need Other Doctors* was enough to make you question why anyone would get into the profession. But fortunately this group was well protected. For the past twenty-one years, PLCC had an unblemished record for defending thousands of med/mal cases, having never lost a jury verdict. A critical part of that success was getting their "habitual defendants" through seminars like this one. The other part was its cadre of hard-nosed attorneys who would later demonstrate their considerable skills during mock depositions. It was all designed to buck up the doctors and their spouses for the humiliating ride that lay ahead, which could best be described as a witch's brew of denial, self-doubt, and all-out fury.

"Fantastic, absolutely fantastic . . . really beautiful, in my book you're all winners. What do you say, let's make this happen!" Steinman was a world-class cheerleader, hopping around the podium, adjusting his lip mic on the fly. He opened both palms to the group. "But before we begin, none of this happens without help, so how about a special thanks to our event sponsor, Cytogenic. First, for this wonderful breakfast they've laid out this morning." There was quiet applause. "And for the special noon luncheon . . . *and* later tonight our Graduation Cocktail Party which begins at six o'clock. Thank you, Bobby Lee. You're a true friend to all practitioners. I love you, man."

To more light applause, Bobby Lee Hawkins waved self-consciously. He was standing next to a glossy Cytogenic poster, and as Girard turned to catch his syrupy grin, the portly assistant vice president flashed the thumbs-up sign.

"Alright, how about we get this ball rolling?" Suddenly Steadman stopped, freezing in his tracks. Shaking his head, he closed and opened both eyes. "That was lame. No really, that was totally lame. That sounded like a plaintiff's lawyer." Muffled laughter. "*What do you say we beat this thing?* What do you say we take this lawsuit and stick it up somebody's keister and in the process turn our lives around. How about it?" He slid smoothly back behind the podium, looking like a Thoroughbred ready to race. "Yeah, you heard me! Let's make this the beginning of the next chapter in your new life. Let's take something that truly sucks and turn it on its head. But first," he held up his right index finger, "I want everyone to repeat after me: You have no right to judge me, you have no right—"

"Hello, Ernie, is my deal done yet?" Stephanie Simpson sidled into the seat next to Girard as he was taking a bite of his croissant. She looked almost edible in her Michael Kors cashmere sweater and skintight tube skirt. "We're running out of time and I need that vote."

"Nice to see you, too, Stephanie," said Girard, trying to mask his surprise. "And no, we haven't voted on the sale yet. By the way, how did you find me?"

"If there's a conference on med/mal defense, it's a good bet you're on the attendees list."

Girard eased forward in his chair, half-smiling. "Very funny. This is MaryAnn Taylor our corporate counsel. MaryAnn, Stephanie Simpson. She's handling the German deal."

Simpson extended her right hand. "Lawyer for these guys, must keep you hoppin'?"

"Probably not as lively as hustling private equity to non-qualified investors," sniped Taylor, not bothering to shake Simpson's hand. "I read the *Journal* article on Luca Manser and DAI. How does one go about finding neo-Nazi bottom feeders for clients these days? Is that a skill they teach you on Wall Street?"

Simpson gave her a wintry smile. "Coming from a lawyer whose clients could teach this conference, that's quite a statement. Still, it's a pleasure to meet you, but if you don't mind, I need to steal the good doctor for a few minutes."

". . . to fully understand the effects getting sued has on a physician," Steinman was in full bloom. "I embarked on a groundbreaking study—no, I think a better term might be *quest*—comparing posttraumatic stress disorder symptoms of returning Iraqi War vets with over 700 questionnaire responses I received from doctors, all over the U.S., who had been sued. And guess what? That's right . . . that's right, you know where this is going—*the results were remarkably similar.*"

PLCC was certainly getting its money's worth, thought Simpson, touching Girard's forearm. "Let's go outside. We need to talk."

"Shall I join you?" Taylor's response was purely instinctual, but Girard waved her off and followed Simpson through a creaking door into a hallway decorated in pastel-colored beach scenes. Nestled south of Los Angeles in Orange County, the Sea Cliff Resort had opened in 1987 as a beachfront spa for wealthy Angelenos. But after four owners and two leveraged buyouts, it was now controlled by a Peruvian mining magnate and had certainly seen better days.

Girard turned to face Simpson, drawing a deep breath before letting it out painfully. "What do you want, Stephanie? You know the partners don't meet until a week from Tuesday. So, no, I don't have an answer for you. Why are you here?"

"That's not good enough anymore. DAI needs some assurances. They got the financing lined up yesterday and the money boys are getting antsy. They need to know the timing on this deal is solid, and it's my job to assure them that you've got everything under control. Otherwise this whole thing could unravel."

"I don't know how many times I have to say this—there are no guarantees when it comes to my partners. They don't—"

"Shut up," she simmered, inching closer. Girard could smell her Fleur de Gardenia scent. "Look at me. I said, *Look at me*, Ernie. I need to know right now that we're good to go on this. You don't screw around with these people. They've got surveillance photos of you in Mexico."

Her words hit him like a punch to the stomach. "What are you talking about?"

"Your recent deposits, the money you've been laundering from your little Medical Mafia scam with the lawyers, they've got dates, teller video, copies of bank deposit slips, and they're willing to turn it over to the U.S. attorney, anonymously of course, unless you get with the program."

"But how—?"

"I don't know how and I don't care. All I know is they've got you in their pocket and they need two more surgeons to guarantee Hurston will vote the right way. And they're looking at you to provide those doctors before the next partners' meeting."

Girard's lips went dry, the taste of fear congealing in his mouth. He squeezed his eyes tight, his heartbeat phoning in loud and clear. Turning over his Juárez banking records could mean prison time. At a minimum he'd lose his medical license, and there was no way he could survive that. For several seconds, he couldn't move. He felt lightheaded, his own mind frozen with doubt. This was a new feeling for him—his life falling apart in slow motion with no clear indication of where the next blow might come from.

When he opened his eyes, Simpson was standing face-to-face with him, equally panicked. *Breathe*, he told himself, his skin tightening along his jaw. He was thankful none of his colleagues were around to see him decomposing like some first-year resident. He'd been working on the German deal for months, spending God knows how many hours trying to convince his weak-ass partners to pull the trigger, but they weren't there, not yet.

"Tick, tock, Ernie," Simpson said. "I didn't drive out here for the Shiatsu massage. We've got to pull something together fast."

But Girard refused to look her in the eye, his mind in overdrive, his heart slamming against his chest. Someone opened an exit door, and a wedge of sunshine slithered into the hallway. The proverbial light at the end of the tunnel, he mused, or a freight train headed right for my face? But then something fluttered in his gut, maybe nervousness, a measure of fear. Frustrated, he glared down the hallway, trying to zero in on what to do. Cutting a deal with the feds was looking more and more like the smart move, but it'd been smart moves that had gotten him into this mess in the first place. A thin line formed between his eyes, but it vanished a half-second later when he whispered to himself, "It's the money, idiot." It would always be the money. He wanted it, and by God he'd earned it! If he could just hold off the prosecutor long enough to get the DAI deal done, he could get his creditors off his back and stash a few million away in the Caymans. A ghost of a smile crept across his face.

If I'm goin' down it'll be with a boatload of cash in an offshore account and bonefishing on a fifty-five footer in the Out Islands.

"Drs. George Cook and Fred Benson are your guys," he said tonelessly. "Freddy's got two kids in college and Cook sells his used loafers on the Internet for extra cash. Both their votes can be bought for the right price."

"Alright, now you're talking. But where do we get the money? It's too late for me to tap my pharma sources and we gotta get this done ASAP." With a grinding moan, one of the conference room doors swung open, and Bobby Lee Hawkins shuffled out of the High Tide Room, frantically patting his suit jacket pockets for a pack of Camels. Pausing in the hallway beneath a murky lighthouse print, he looked around before making a beeline towards an exit, acknowledging Girard and Simpson with a nod of the head.

Girard grinned crookedly. "Stephanie, I think I see a way out." He flashed a cocky smirk, then glided up to the bewildered executive and slapped him on the back while holding the exit door open. "Bobby Lee, I think we have a few things we need to discuss."

CHAPTER TWENTY

"Good morning, Mr. Chase, thank you for coming. Make yourself comfortable while I introduce our team." Assistant U.S. Attorney Bipu Munir nodded towards several distinguished-looking attendees seated around his private conference table in downtown Los Angeles.

The curved boat-shaped table was the centerpiece of a spacious, well-appointed office expensively decorated in marblewood with sepia-toned prints of 1950's LA hung on two of the four paneled walls. "To my left," Munir indicated in a pleasant tone, "is Pamela Eisner with the State of California Licensure and Investigations Bureau. Next to her is Harry Adelstein, Special Agent for Organized Crime and Racketeering for the Office of the Attorney General, State of California, and seated beside him is Vanora Jackson, Executive Assistant for the Office of Compliance and Standards, Centers for Medicare & Medicaid Services. That handsome devil to her left is Manny Saenz. Manny is a lead agent with the Special Investigations Division for the Office of the Attorney General, State of California, and rounding out our joint task force is Brenda Snowden, Investigator for the Fraud Control Unit, Criminal Division for the California Health Regulatory Board, and Oscar Kreul, Senior Auditor for Program Investigations, IRS. Observing this morning is Senior Investigator Blas Mondragon from Mexico's Assistant Attorney General's Office."

"IRS?" asked a flippant Harold Chase, looking straight at Kreul, a hint of sarcasm in his voice. "Go easy on me. I voted for Trump."

There was a moment of uncomfortable silence, as nobody appreciated Chase's clumsy attempt at humor. Since it was his meeting, Munir cleared his throat and began. "Since everybody's here, why don't we get started. Mr. Chase, for the record you have waived your right to counsel and requested this meeting to offer information you say is relevant to your felony drug possession charge. Is that correct, sir?"

"That's right," Chase said brightly, turning his attention to Munir. "I definitely got some shit you folks oughta hear."

"Once again for the record, you've waived your right to counsel." Munir repeated for both hidden taping systems.

That brought a laconic shrug from Chase. "Yeah, I waive my right to a lawyer."

"Very good. You have representatives from three different branches of the federal government and senior officials from the state of California. So please," Munir threw open his arms, "tell us your story."

Harold Chase straightened in the leather chair, looking much more confident than he had any right to be. "I'm assuming all of you've heard of the SoCal Medical Mafia?" Chase paused as each head around the table nodded. "Good, then today's your lucky day because nine years ago I got in on the ground floor, and from the get-go Ralf had it all wired. Everyone was dialed in, from the patients to the surgeons to the therapists, even the plaintiff lawyers were on board. Then it all sort of blew up in our faces."

Munir felt a sharp thrill shooting down his spine. He studied Chase, trying to sort the truth from the usual bullshit that suspects peddle when they're bargaining for their freedom. There was an anxious silence as the physical therapist sipped his coffee, and Munir realized that the man was actually enjoying the attention. Since Munir chaired this task force on drug interdiction, the others had agreed to let him take Chase through his paces, and without a lawyer present, the complete transcript would read more like a magazine article than a confession. But for Munir the only thing that mattered was that it was legal, by the book, and that he would finally get a shot at indicting Dr. Ernie Girard.

"Ordinary fender bender," explained Chase, seemingly eager to please. Munir was constantly amazed at how suspects would suspend their right to counsel and open up like they were on some radio talk show. He assumed it was the need to share, or to be wanted, but somehow he'd figured Chase to be smarter than that. At each of his previous interrogations, the pudgy redhead had shown a certain amount of arrogance, even cockiness. At times he'd seemed nervous, but never intimidated, and there was a difference.

Munir needed to understand why.

"Bernadette Vigil, office manager for a pediatric cardiologist in Burbank." Chase had committed her name to memory. "Early thirties, decent looking, no criminal record, a hard worker—"

"Otherwise the perfect plaintiff," interrupted Munir.

"Bingo," said Chase, tapping his class ring on the hardwood table. "Bernadette was driving home from work on the 405 minding her own business when some moron clipped the rear bumper of her Honda Prelude, which propelled her into the SUV in front of her. No one was badly injured, the drivers exchanged information, and the whole thing would've been forgotten except Bernadette woke up the next morning with pain in her lower back. Not knowing what to do, she stopped by one of those doc-in-the-boxes and was told she'd have to pay cash for all her treatment costs upfront, since her auto accident could result in a lawsuit and her insurance might not cover it. Short on dough, Bernadette talked to her cardiologist boss, who said he'd try to help her out." Chase hesitated, inspecting the bottom of his white enamel cup. "Could I get some more coffee?"

As he had during their previous meetings, Oscar Kreul felt a pang of skepticism. *Could this coke-snorting dipshit really deliver the goods?* It was hard to imagine, yet here he was, gift-wrapped like some early birthday present.

Happily, Kreul lifted his right hand. "I got it. You take it black, right?"

At fifty-nine, Kreul was a veteran IRS investigator adept at putting suspects at ease no mattered how jacked-up the perps might be. Uncurling his lanky frame from the high-back executive chair, he bounded to an adjoining table where a pitcher of ice water and a thermos of coffee had been laid out. Turning, he asked matter-of-factly, "And how did you know her boss agreed to help her?"

Chase put his elbows on the table. "The Ralfinator."

"Pardon me?" Kreul feigned surprise. Although everybody in the room knew who the Ralfinator was, they wanted Chase to state his name for the record.

"Ralf Millette, the biggest, baddest plaintiff lawyer in LA," Chase said proudly. "The man is pure genius."

Kreul filled Chase's coffee cup and placed it in front of him. "A genius, no kidding?" he cooed. "Working at the IRS, we don't run into many of those. Anyone else for a refill?" Each of the task force members declined. They were more interested in letting Chase ramble.

"The next day," Chase continued—Munir was right, he enjoyed being the center of attention—"Bernadette gets a call from Ralf, who's gotten a text from her cardiologist boss. Ralf tells her he's in the business of handling auto accidents. That's how the process begins. Once the victim had been IDed, the Ralfinator would make the initial call, and within an hour he'd gotten her an appointment with Dr. Ernie Girard, which was nearly impossible since most of his patients had to wait weeks to see him. After examining her, Ernie referred her to me to start PT treatments. The whole process worked like clockwork because we never asked for money upfront. That was the trick. On her first visit to Ralf's office, Bernadette had signed a medical lien—that's also super critical—and that meant the victim would pay nothing unless she collected from a legal judgment or settlement. But if that happened, the person holding the lien, that would be Ralf, got paid first. Once the lien was secured, we'd run up the bill: physical therapy, cortisone injections, massage, aroma therapy, you name it."

"Sounds awfully clever," said Kreul. "What went wrong?"

Chase took a strained swallow of coffee. "Fucking Ernie Girard, that's what went wrong. The greedy shit gets into money trouble and starts operating on anything with a pulse." Chase closed both eyes, working his jaw.

Munir could see why Chase felt a certain level of animosity towards Girard. After all, the man had screwed up his gravy train, and hell hath no fury like a hustler who's been pimped.

But Chase managed to regain his composure. "Ernie was having his usual cash flow problems: drugs, gambling, another divorce—you know, rich people crap. So he started pushing Bernadette to have the surgery, said her pain would get worse without an operation, might as well get it done now. But Bernadette balked. Man, who wouldn't? It's nasty-assed surgery. Meanwhile, Ralf had filed a lawsuit against the driver who'd hit her, asking for a minimum of $250,000 in medical damages; non-medical to be determined later. What Ralf didn't know was that the driver turned out to be some organized crime investigator with the attorney general's office who was using his own *goddamn* car for government business."

Harry Adelstein, forty-three, could barely suppress a smile. His title, Special Agent for Organized Crime & Racketeering, gave him wide latitude to pursue any number of white collar crimes. It had been an incredible stroke of luck that a harmless fender bender—one that he had actually been at fault for—had unwound into a massive medical fraud case, earning him a spot on this task force. And as all of this was happening, GavinAid was gutting California's insurance industry. So

Harry, always the ambitious one, started eyeing a run at the state treasurer's job. His plan was to use his newly found seat on this task force to drop a few well-placed media leaks, leveraging the scandal into a sizeable bump in the early polls and earning him some seed money from the insurance industry.

"—which meant Ralf wouldn't be facing the usual ham-and-egg defense attorneys but a bunch of hard cases from the state of California," Chase lamented. "Basically, we were screwed."

"Would you like to take a break, Mr. Chase?" Munir asked warmly.

"No, I'm good."

"Once again, you understand you have the right to counsel," Munir reminded him.

Chase waved his left hand. "Thanks, but frankly I'm sick and tired of you lawyers. No offense." He looked around the table sheepishly. "I dumped my public defender. The guy was a complete nosepicker. I mean, who ever met an honest attorney."

No offense taken, thought Munir, *and if you ever do meet an "honest attorney," he or she wouldn't let you within a mile of us.*

"Please, continue," prompted Kreul.

"Well, almost immediately we were in deep *ca-ca*," said Chase. "Bernadette's case was assigned to an investigator in the attorney general's office, and very quickly he sensed something was out of whack. For a minor traffic accident, Bernadette had seen four doctors, a physical therapist, an acupuncturist, and a psychologist. Like I said, the SoCal Medical Mafia had girth. She had racked up more than $78,000 in medical bills, so the investigator got the bright idea to call one of his former colleagues who worked as a claims adjuster in the Santa Monica office of Safeco. He described the case and listed the medical providers involved, but before he could finish his buddy cut him off and asked if they were all tight with Millette. Just our luck, the boy scout investigator had stumbled into one of the sweetest insurance scams in LA history. Ralf and the docs were fingering innocent accident victims who'd agreed to be treated by Mafia providers, who would then convince them to undergo countless office visits and procedures—even needless surgeries—so they could inflate the size of the settlements. And the whole thing was cookin' like a wet dream until this government do-gooder gets off his lazy duff and works the case. What are the odds?"

As hard as he tried, the "do-gooder" in question couldn't help but clench his left fist in silent victory. Manny Saenz had served as a lead agent with the Special

Investigations Division for the Office of the Attorney General for fourteen years and when some blow-dried plaintiff lawyer with the self-appointed moniker "The Ralfinator" had filed a bogus $250,000 lawsuit against one of the state's own, well, he could expect the AG's full attention, and that's exactly what he got. What Saenz hadn't counted on was uncovering a scam that involved sixteen physicians and at least twenty other clinical professionals colluding on dozens of lawsuits that yielded tens of millions in settlements.

"Mr. Chase, could you describe for us specifically how the whole thing worked?" asked Saenz. "And I'm afraid we'll need all the juicy details." Like Kreul, Saenz had an easy way about him that encouraged suspects to relax and talk freely while pounding nails into their legal coffins.

Chase took another slow sip of coffee. "Specifics? Sure. How about lying under oath, coordinating testimony of expert witnesses, shielding one another from malpractice claims even for patients who had died, and stealing plaintiffs' settlement money with kickbacks disguised as contingency fees? That enough for you folks to drop my cocaine charges?"

The eight government officials sat in practiced silence for a moment before Munir finally spoke. "Mr. Chase, if what you've told us pans out we'll drop the cocaine charges. But Harold," Munir's eyebrows arched, "we'll need to hear everything. Every detail, and it better be good."

Relieved, Chase allowed himself a mangy, self-satisfied grin. "Oh, it'll be good alright, I guarantee it. See, I kept records: patient charts, x-rays, bills, everything. But the next time we get together I'd like you folks to bring my deal in writing, and do it up right because I'll have a lawyer with me, a good one." Chase's eyes brightened, his posture now ramrod straight. Looking around the table, he savored the surprised expressions on each of their faces. "Like I said, it needs to be in writing, all nice and tidy. All you've got right now is circumstantial, and that ain't gonna be good enough to convict these guys. They're too tough, even for you."

Chase paused. The room was deathly still. Outside, cell phones began to ring en masse.

Harold Chase was talking again, but Bipu Munir wasn't listening. Swallowing hard, feeling a surge of acid fluttering deep in his gut, he had just realized that this slimy physical therapist had played him. And that was going to be a problem.

CHAPTER TWENTY-ONE

"I looked pretty stupid at that Ambani appeal. And I'm not sure what was worse, being made a fool of or the fact that you enjoyed it so much," complained Bobby Lee Hawkins, slipping the pack of Camels into the inside pocket of his tailored suit. He had tapped out a cigarette and was now cupping his hands to light it. "Anything you want to say, Ernie, maybe like an apology?"

The two were standing in the parking lot of the Sea Cliff Resort, and Dr. Ernie Girard had several things he wanted to say, but they'd have to wait for another day. "Come to think of it," Girard replied brightly, further aggravating Hawkins, "I did enjoy myself immensely, but I do apologize, Bobby Lee. It's just that you make it so easy."

"Thanks," said Hawkins blowing a cloud of smoke over his left shoulder. "It's not enough that we bankroll your bogus medical directorships and non-existent clinical research, but now I have to be humiliated in public. And what were you doing giving some poor Paki cab driver a hip replacement on my dime?"

"It seemed like the right thing to do."

"A goddamned cab driver, for chrissakes, I had to take in the crotch for a camel jockey with a bad wheel."

"Bobby Lee, once again you're woefully misinformed. The patient's family is from Mumbai, and he's not your average taxi driver. He owns a Lyft franchise and has a union-protected taxi concession at LAX. It's just that some of us do our homework before these appeal meetings, one never knows when he might need a friend."

"Great. Being friends with you is gonna give me a heart attack."

"No, I'd say those Camels are your date with an early grave, and quit your bellyaching. Cytogenic netted over $1.1 million in profits off my surgeries last year, and that's as both wholesaler *and* distributor, so you didn't have to share a dime with the local sales group. Pretty decent cut, I'd say, especially off just one surgeon."

An odd disassociation descended on Hawkins, the same sensation he felt when he was about to get hit up for money. Taking another deep pull on his Camel, he donned a well-practiced look of disinterest. "Alright, what's it this time? I've only got ten minutes and I'd like to enjoy my cigarette for a few of those."

"Fresh funds—"

"Stop right there," Hawkins cut him off. "Our hands are tied right now and you know that. The justice department has practically set up shop at our headquarters in Crystal City. They're getting kind of picky these days about us paying device royalties to doctors who haven't actually invented anything. Crazy how that works."

Girard opened his mouth to say something but thought better of it, and instead offered Hawkins one of those "you're too stupid to live" looks while flicking a piece of dandruff off Bobby Lee's lapel. "This time it's not for me," he said calmly, maintaining control.

Hawkins raised both hands in surrender.

"I've got two partners with cash flow problems. They each have sizable patient volumes and would agree to use your implants. The hang-up is, I need your commitment by noon on Monday. We have a partners' meeting Tuesday night and I'm going to need to influence a few votes. Do you think you can handle that?"

"What are their names?"

"Dr. George Cook and Dr. Fred Benson.

"Specialties?"

"Cookie is a spine guy out of the University of Washington. He's well-trained. Did his fellowship in Portland, and he's built up quite a practice, knocks out 300 hospital surgeries a year and another 120 same-day procedures at our surgery center. He could help ramrod your minimally-invasive trials, maybe supervise the local research. Fred is an endovascular jock. You're gonna have to work with me on this one, show some creativity. Maybe you could hook him up with one of your stroke programs in the Valley. He's got nice academic credentials. How many vascular research projects is your subsidiary sponsoring right now?"

"Eight."

"Any of them peer reviewed?"

"Three . . . two more in the pipeline."

"There you go. Twelve grand a month as your new research medical director. Let's get a contract worked up."

Hawkins took a step backwards, along with another deep drag on his cigarette. He held the smoke, then exhaled slowly. "What's in it for us?"

"Excuse me?"

"Oh, I'm sure your guys will play ball, but I'm going to need a little bit more on this one. Some guarantees." He blew another cloud of smoke, but this time it was into Girard's face. He was enjoying having the upper hand for a change. Girard was up to something, and Hawkins made a mental note to call Dr. Steven Todd, one of Girard's partners, to find out exactly what was going on.

Hawkins snuffed out his cigarette. "Got any idea, Ernie, how many knee and hip replacements come before your GavinAid committee each month . . . any idea at all?"

Girard cast his eyes about the parking lot. "Why would I know something like that?"

"How about spine cases that require hardware, what do you think, how many?"

Girard sighed. Centering his attention on Hawkins, he tried to bore a hole through the cocky salesman with his eyes, but could feel the sands shifting beneath his feet. There was a time when this soft, middle-aged mouth-breather wouldn't even look him in the eye. Somewhere along the way, Bobby Lee had grown a pair. "Fine," Girard said almost to himself. "You obviously have some numbers you'd like to share, so please, go ahead. But for the love of God, quit jerkin' me around. We've got to get moving on this."

But Hawkins would have none of it. He wasn't in a hurry and met Girard's anxious glare with a sly grin. "Relax, Ernie, it's just that some of us like to do our homework before sponsoring a malpractice seminar for habitual defendants. One never knows when one might need a friend."

Girard felt a sudden surge of acid clawing at the back of his throat. "Touché, fucktard."

"On the average, nineteen knee replacements, twelve hip, and twenty-one spine procedures come before your committee each month," Hawkins recited in a flat even voice. "So we've got a lot invested in your little death panel, and we'd like to see a few more of those denials get overturned."

Girard wasn't amused. He had a pathological hatred for everything this dumpy salesman stood for, but right now he was screwed and he knew it. "Fine, you get Cookie's consultancy agreement and Fred's medical directorship put together by Monday at noon, and I'll start overturning half of the committee's spine cases and joint replacement denials."

Hawkins felt euphoric. It was not every day he got one over on a prima donna like Ernie Girard. "See, now that wasn't so hard, was it?" he gloated as a piece of trash blew across the parking lot. Seething, Girard turned, tracking the burger wrapper as it twisted and danced in the morning breeze, thinking how apropos it was to his life at the moment. Hawkins thrust his right hand forward, a callous smirk lifting the edges of his mouth. "Then I believe we have a deal."

Disgusted with himself, Girard stared at Hawkins's freshly manicured nails and his shiny LSU class ring and refused to budge. Looking up, he watched the food wrapper sail away. Finally, after a few uncomfortable seconds, he reached out and squeezed the salesman's clammy hand like a vice grip, grinning as Hawkins winced. When Bobby Lee tried to pull his hand away, Girard wouldn't let it go. "We have a deal," Girard whispered, tightening his grip, "and I don't ever want to see your worthless face in my committee chambers again."

CHAPTER TWENTY-TWO

Just south of State Route 1, east of Malibu Bluffs Park, overseeing spectacular coastline views from Santa Monica to Queen's Necklace and Point Dume, the elegant enclave of Malibu Colony was one of the first areas inhabited after this gorgeous stretch of beach was opened to the public in 1929.

Since then its understated elegance had become home to a handful of California's lucky one-percenters, along with a growing number of hedge fund felons, Russian oligarchs, and Chinese expats. But behind one guarded security gate, a single estate in particular stood out.

Almost eighty years old, its elegant Cape Cod-style house was partially surrounded by a two-meter-high privacy hedge that encased a three-bedroom guesthouse, an infinity-edge pool, and a sand-and-grass backyard that stretched lazily for an unheard of fifty meters. For obvious reasons it was considered one of the Colony's crown jewels. What visitors didn't see tucked behind the giant wildrye and hummingbird sage and pink bougainvillea was a state-of-the-art German Xenyum surveillance system staffed round-the-clock by three teams of former *Kommando Spezialkräfte*, KSK, special-forces commandos.

At ten minutes after nine o'clock in the evening, still watching MSNBC, its owner, Luca Manser, swallowed his third tumbler of Bushmills before jabbing at a hidden button under his antique credenza. The button activated a modified single-line intercom. "Sandy, tell Mr. Eberstein he'll have to wait a few more minutes. I need to take this call."

Manser was sitting at a Pueblo writing desk that nicely complemented the Navajo pottery and Papago pictorial baskets adorning the study's polished granite walls. On this night, Oscar Peterson bent a solo in the background; other evenings it was Miles Davis. When the pearl-and-black DSS 4450 console lit up, he answered it curtly. "Stephanie, lovely to hear from you. Where are you calling from?" He listened to her answer. "Not good enough. Disconnect immediately and use your encrypted cell phone. Yes, off you go." Manser shook his head and waited. The console lit up again. He punched Connect, then lifted the receiver to his right ear.

A counter-encryption package had been installed four years earlier and was updated every month. The study was also swept daily for listening devices, and the estate itself relied on a solar-powered system with two backup SAB diesel generators. German engineered, of course.

"Did he say why?" Manser asked into the receiver. More silence. At his feet a long-haired cat purred, nestled on a 1914 Kashan rug. "Fine, that won't be a problem. Text me the medical directorship agreements and the cost figures and, Stephanie, do it before the rest of his partners find out." The cat rolled onto its back, swatting at air. "And tell Dr. Girard he'll have to find another lawyer. This is a federal case now. Ms. Taylor can buy a ticket like everyone else."

Manser hung up. Another phone line flashed. He leaned forward and pressed the intercom button. "Mr. Eberstein is still waiting," the woman's voice calmly reminded him.

"Fine, tell him to come in and have a seat. I'll be right out. And when Ms. Simpson calls back, put her through."

"Yes, sir."

The hinges on the brass-and-oak front door squealed noisily as if in pain.

Dieter Eberstein, Manser's CFO, stood dripping in the hallway, having just ducked through the evening showers. His hands were buried deep in the pockets of his soft kangaroo leather overcoat and his shoulders were hunched, befitting a man with the weight of the world on him. He unbuttoned his coat as he nervously walked down the foyer into the newly renovated anteroom, where he took a seat on an empty divan. A horsehair-stuffed chair sat opposite him and behind it a plaster cast of a frieze from the Parthenon in Athens. The rest of the room was filled with renderings of medieval German cathedrals and a set of chrome and stainless steel Barcelona chairs by Mies van der Rohe, along with familiar works of Matisse, Monet, and Francis Bacon.

Despite the soundproofing, Eberstein could hear Manser's booming voice through the six-panel pine door to what he liked to call his American Indian room.

"Listen to me. I said use the off-shore accounts . . . I don't care. I said *I don't care!*" Manser barked into the phone receiver. "Just get the funds ready for transfer in an hour. Yes, one hour. *No, goddamnit!* Nobody does a thing until I say so. Get back to me when the transfer is ready." He jabbed the disconnect button and stood, inspecting his reflection in the window before opening the door. "Good to see you, Dieter. Come in. How are you holding up?"

Eberstein stood and entered cautiously. The arrest of Harold Chase, followed by the therapist's decision to become a federal witness against Dr. Ernie Girard, was weighing heavily on the CFO's mind. "Come, come, have a seat," Manser offered. "Would you like a drink? You look like you could use one." Manser took a final puff of his Davidoff then snuffed it in an onyx-lined ashtray. He went to the crystal decanter and poured Eberstein a healthy measure of whiskey, refilling his own. Above his desk hung a diploma from NYU; to its right, a silver-framed medical degree from the *Universitat Dusseldorf.* Few people knew that Dr. Luca Manser had never actually practiced medicine. He had gone straight from medical school to the prestigious London Consulting Group in Cambridge, serving as an expert in clinical informatics. Then in short order he had risen from associate director to partner to senior member of the firm's executive committee. There were conflicting accounts of what had happened next, but it was clear that the firm flourished under his leadership. But after a few years, the London Group's executive committee became increasingly disenchanted with his far-right German politics, and in 2005, after he'd lost his bid for the Bundestag, they accepted his resignation and he became chief medical officer and executive vice president of Ambulatory Surgical Hospitals of America (ASHA) in Los Angeles.

During his time at ASHA, Manser developed a detailed understanding of the byzantine nature of the U.S. healthcare system, knowledge he would later use to launch *Deutsche Ärzte International,* DAI, which got its start with the purchase of six decrepit nursing homes in Bavaria and their eventual conversion into upscale private hospitals. From there DAI grew spectacularly, expanding first into the U.K., then Costa Rica, Cyprus, and finally the U.S.

Today it owned or operated twenty-four hospitals.

"For heaven's sake, Dieter, quit gawking like some confused tourist and sit down. By the way, thanks for the heads-up on our long-lost Mr. Chase. I was stuck in a briefing with our lawyers about the refinancing project."

Eberstein took a seat, surreptitiously massaging a thin white envelope—his buyout demands—in his left front pants pocket, making sure it was still there. His tired eyes avoided the older man, focusing instead on a secure facsimile machine scrolling noisily in the corner. The laser fax was pumping out black-and-white close-ups of Harold Chase entering a downtown building in Los Angeles, followed by headshots of eight different federal and state of California law enforcement professionals arriving at roughly the same time. Manser watched his CFO's reaction. "He's rolling over like a well-trained spaniel."

Eberstein's eyes stayed fixed on the fax machine. Shifting his aching legs, he forced himself to focus on the situation at hand. If he didn't concentrate, his painfully-crafted career could be washed away like grains of Malibu sand at high tide. This was fast becoming his worst nightmare.

"Well, Dieter, I've got to hand it to you," Manser said tightly. "I can't imagine anyone screwing this up any worse than you have . . . but a *goddamn* physical therapist caught in a cocaine bust!" Manser's face turned beet red. To settle his hands, he shuffled faxes. "Tell me, where on earth do you find these incompetent cretins?"

Eberstein didn't say a word; his bloodshot eyes stayed silently glued to the faxes. He had caught the 9:20 Lufthansa flight from Frankfurt to LAX, then driven straight to the estate to try to salvage what was left of his teetering career. Sadly, it wasn't off to a good start.

Immediately after his release from jail, Harold Chase had texted Ernie Girard demanding $200,000 to hire a top-flight Hollywood criminal lawyer. Up to his neck in his own gambling debts, Girard had panicked and called Stephanie Simpson, describing in great detail Chase's arrest and his involvement with the SoCal Medical Mafia. Girard had also told Simpson about Chase's cache of clinical records that could tie the whole thing back to him. Simpson had then called Eberstein at DAI's Stuttgart office in full meltdown mode.

"Maybe Girard can cut a plea deal?" offered Eberstein, his voice tightening.

Manser raised his hand. "And give up whom? He's their target: a high-profile neurosurgeon who's been fingering potential malpractice patients, falsifying medical records, and engaging in massive billing fraud. No, Dieter, I'm afraid we can't let our Mr. Chase testify. Our whole deal could unravel."

Eberstein's back straightened. A splotch of sweat dampened the front of his cotton twill dress shirt. He blinked furiously to clear his head.

"How quickly can you contact the cartel?" asked Manser.

"Within twenty-four hours. But do you think that's wise?"

Manser froze, slowly turning. "Yes," he said bitterly, his temper rising. "Yes, Dieter, I think it's entirely *fuckin' wise*, given how you've shitted the bed so thoroughly on this one! So could you please get onto the cartel and make certain they receive a recent photo of Chase."

Eberstein looked down at his black moccasins, embarrassed. "I'll make sure they get one," he said. "What about Simpson?"

Manser leaned back in his chair, a bright surveillance lamp bleeding across the Navajo pottery as a security guard holding back a tethered German shepherd passed outside the bulletproof windowpane. "Don't worry about Stephanie. I'll take care of her. Just get ahold of the *comandante* and get his woman hitter up here ASAP. Use one of the disposable cell phones in the office next door and, Dieter, try not to screw this up."

Relieved, Eberstein wiped a drop of sweat from his forehead, his pulse palpitating.

He was still in the game.

CHAPTER TWENTY-THREE

Stretched across a hemp-rope hammock, a Red Stripe baseball cap and a pair of Oakley Echelons shading her eyes, Angel aimed her spotting scope at a three-story villa directly across the tranquil bay. Her hammock was hanging outside Casita 9 in the lush Carato Bay Resort on the North Sound of Virgin Gorda in the British Virgin Islands. Her target, Manuel Rodriguez, the head of the Knights Templar Cartel, was navigating a 150-horsepower Bradley 30 powerboat around Gun Island, pointing out recent home improvements to two of his four bodyguards.

Angel lifted her Echelons and scribbled a few more notes on a cocktail napkin.

Rodriguez, his wife, twin daughters, and four-year-old son visited the North Sound every April for the annual Spring Regatta. Having received a tip from her client, Angel had been surveilling their private villa for the past four days. She had entered the country under a legitimate Costa Rican passport as Valeria Ferrier. To maintain her cover, she had been dutifully performing the arduous tasks of lounging tourist: sunbathing, snorkeling, ocean kayaking, and attending several gluttonous sunset cocktail receptions. By 3:50 p.m. on day five, she watched the last piece of her puzzle fall neatly into place.

Rodriguez's lanky house servant wore a lavender-blue Carato Bay golf shirt with barley-colored cargo pants and tan dock shoes. With the exception of the bodyguards, he was the only person on duty from 11:00 a.m. until dinner, and as Angel tracked him through her scope, she began to detect a very specific routine.

Every day at exactly 3:30 the servant would sneak out of the villa's delivery entrance, prop the door open with a small volcanic rock, then make his way down a rutted path that ran parallel to a massive outcrop of boulders Rodriguez had laid as a tidal break. Pulling a lid of Colombian red from his shirt pocket, the slender thirty-something would settle on a clump of dried kelp that had washed up from the beach and light up. It was his afternoon break and he took it religiously, smoking exactly one joint before following the same path back up to the delivery door.

This time, though, he ran into a slight problem.

Standing outside the metal door, arms at his side, he saw that his rock had slid a few centimeters to the left, allowing the door to shut. Frantic, the servant tried the knob but it was locked. Looking around in panic for a second, he saw no one, so he made a cardinal mistake and pressed 0-3-1-7 into the security key pad. An instant later the door clicked open, and Angel's face broke into a wide, satisfied grin. She had found her way into the villa. Pouring a celebratory shot of Arundel rum, she unconsciously rubbed the silver angel medallion dangling round her neck. After a minute, she flung her legs off the hammock, reached down and pulled a metal wastebasket to her, and struck a match, lighting the dark blue cotton-polyester cover of Valeria Ferrier's passport.

Watching the gilded letters of the Costa Rican coat of arms wilt under the flame, she tossed the passport into the waste basket and made sure it burned completely. During the next few days it was critical that local records still showed Ms. Ferrier to be on the island. Angel had entered the British Virgin Islands through the West End Ferry Terminal in Tortola, purposely booking herself on the 6:00 a.m. ferry from Red Hook so she could blend in with the morning workers commuting from the U.S. Virgin Islands, the West End Terminal being the most lightly-guarded of the BVI stations. Customs had been predictably cursory— Ferrier's passport had been swiped and stamped and an official note of her entry logged into the computer records of the BVI.

Once outside the terminal, Angel had intentionally avoided the local van drivers and hiked five hundred meters along a two-lane highway until it curved out of sight from the terminal. Checking both ways, after letting a rusted Mercedes-Benz van pass, she had peeled off the shorts and top covering her bathing suit, stuffed them into a waterproof duffel, and tied the duffel round her left ankle. She dove headfirst into the breaking tide and breaststroked a kilometer out into the ocean, her head bobbing just above the cresting waves, her eyes trained on Frenchman's Cay as she angled towards a black-and-white 240 Sundancer yacht that she had spotted from the ferry as they'd approached Tortola.

Swimming up beside the yacht, she gripped one of the grab handles on a silver dinghy attached to the Sundance, and with her free hand tossed her duffel into the dinghy's hull. Then she cut the double-stranded rope that tied the dinghy to the bow of the Sundance and swam silently beside the small raft, letting it drift for several minutes away from the yacht before climbing in and starting its two-stroke engine.

Fortunately the swells had been calm and she had been able to put some distance between herself and the Sundance. As she approached a private club south of the West End Terminal, she changed into a modest block sport skirt and dry-fit top and pulled a second Costa Rican passport in the name of Elena Espriella from her duffel. It was still early in the morning, and a few of the yacht club members were having breakfast. The terminal being between ferries made it that much easier to slip unnoticed between a forty-six-foot Sunliner and an Ocean Yacht Sportfish.

Once she'd docked, Angel tied a loose, sloppy knot to make certain the dinghy would soon be floating unattended in the nearby swell, and trundled up the boat ramp, flashing her passport at the customs officer. This temporary entry point near the terminal had been set up to accommodate the arriving yacht crowd and wasn't equipped with facial recognition technology. The helpful guard had set aside his newspaper, dutifully entered the passport name and number into his laptop computer, and handed the passport back to Angel.

For a second time she entered the British Virgin Islands under a new name. And with any luck it would be the same name she'd be using when she left the country a week later.

•　　　•　　　•

Angel's teeth were rattling from the cold, but she felt the warmth returning to her joints.

The soft, lightweight neoprene skinsuit wasn't quite everything the scuba shop owner had claimed, but after an hour of fighting pitch-black swells, Angel was lying flat on her stomach, hiding under a lip of sifted white sand. She had hand-crawled over a low slope along the beach, pausing to inspect the shore, searching for motion sensors. Given the closeness of the slope to the lifting tides, she figured the beach to be clean, but still scanned every centimeter through her infrared goggles, spotting only seashells.

Until now.

Meant to look like a string of landscape ornaments, a row of passive infrared outdoor sensors with adjustable sensitivity and immune to radio frequency jamming had been laid S-shaped along a raked sweep of sand a few meters above high tide. Angel tossed her turbo fins into a clump of dried kelp, lifted a pair of Number 10 Bard-Parker scalpels from her lockout pocket, and balanced each in a hand. Earlier she'd added extra adhesive tape to the handles. They felt perfect.

Taking a deep breath, she steadied herself, eyes roving across the shoreline, following the sensors along the sweep; there was not a soul in sight. With the evening waves crashing against the sand, she flexed her knees and centered her weight on the balls of her feet, then began counting backwards from ten. At "four" her hamstrings tensed, and with a smooth rolling motion she cannoned past the nearest sensor, which reacted immediately.

The noise was deafening. Angel sprinted several more meters, threw her body flat against a massive coconut palm and waited.

The villa's delivery entrance was just a few meters to her left. Within seconds she heard a pronounced click as the bulletproof door opened, then closed, followed by loud swearing as one of Rodriguez's security guards appeared carrying a nine-millimeter Uzi submachine gun. The ex-*Fuerzas Especiales* commando was still in good physical shape, but had grown complacent working the private sector; his tactical response was severely lacking as he wandered several steps from the door without properly assessing the situation. He was rewarded with a scalpel blade across his carotid artery, followed by a callused hand that smothered his shrill keening.

He bled out in the lush white sand.

Moving swiftly, Angel entered the security code, pausing as the bolts clicked open.

Stepping inside the villa, she heard a disinterested voice ask, "Was it a heron or another one of those cocksucking flamingoes the missus brought back from St. Thomas?"

Another former Mexican special forces commando, his back to the door, was inspecting a shelf of half-empty liquor bottles. He'd expected his colleague to report back with another false alarm triggered by one of Rodriguez's imported birds. The first scalpel entered through his vocal fold, the second slashing left to right severing his laryngopharynx.

He died silently, clutching an open bottle of Hennessy Cognac.

Two down, two to go. The guards worked in pairs, two on, two off. The alarm would have woken the off-duty pair, who'd be responding once their colleagues didn't call in.

Angel raced barefoot up the cypress-wood stairs to the second floor. On her right she spotted a wide hallway leading to a pair of bedrooms for the children and a separate guest room.

Having identified each of the rooms from her surveillance, she stopped at the entry of the hallway and counted backwards from five, praying none of the children stepped out of their rooms.

She was rewarded with silence.

Perfect, no collateral damage.

She climbed the staircase, barely touching every other step, and arrived on the third floor with the master bedroom on her left. Through a partially-opened window in the middle of the hallway, she heard voices coming from outside. The two relief guards were working their way along the gravel path from the separate servants' quarters, their vulgar profanities directed at the island's overstocked supply of exotic birds. Angel figured she had about sixty seconds. She opened an enormously wide bedroom door. Her first reaction was one of utter amazement at the depth of snoring coming from the huge canopy bed where Rodriguez's wife slept soundly. Angel crouched, her eyes circling the room. A light went off and the bathroom door opened. Angel was standing face-to-face with an astonished Manuel Rodriguez, who barely managed a muffled grunt before the *asesina* covered the distance between them and slammed both stainless-steel scalpels into the drug lord's throat, leaving him coughing up gouts of blood.

Angel jerked the blades from Rodriguez's neck. The *jefe* staggered backwards into the bathroom, crashing loudly into a marble vanity and dragging several toiletries onto the tile floor. Suddenly, like a splash of freezing water, a hysterical scream pierced Angel's consciousness. It was a long, howling shriek that seemed to energize the villa. Angel spun towards the bed. It was the eyes she would always remember: sable-black, unholy wide like a hyena's. Rodriguez's wife sat straight up in her bed and screeched again, which roused Angel to her senses.

The cypress floor was slick on her bare feet as she covered the stairs two at a time. When she hit the bottom level, she crashed through the storage room door and hurdled the sprawled corpse of the second security guard before bursting out the unlatched delivery door.

As she sprinted down the hidden path, she heard the crackle of small-arms fire. Several rounds smacked the palm tree above her head. She ducked under its spiky fronds and veered off the path, hoping to confuse her shooters.

The outdoor lights kicked on. Angel raced up the sharp slope, her feet pushing hard into the sand, her arms and legs pumping rhythmically. The smell of cordite singed her nostrils. Suddenly a palm tree beside her sprouted holes, another round—*zwip*—and bark splintered above her shoulder. She cut deeper into the brush, tearing towards the crown of a hill. At high tide, she figured she had about three meters of depth to work with if she could throw her body far enough off the edge of the highest rock into the swirling ocean. For the past two nights she'd been scouting the break of the waves using her scope. She was confident the tide was deep enough. Well, mostly confident.

With the subtle whiz of tracers slicing through the thick mangroves, her adrenaline kicked in, and she opened her stride. She saw the edge of the rock face right before she leapt, and with all her strength slung her body into the pounding breakers, another round hissing into the waves below her.

The cold water hit her like a slap to the face. Within seconds she penetrated the pounding surf, pulling hard, using her sinewy arms and shoulders to drag herself deeper into the ocean. Slugs ripped the water so fast she could see columns of compressed air streaking past her torso. A flood lamp tracked above her. With her lungs screaming, she kept pulling deeper underwater, stroking to the south edge of a rocky outcrop, then surfacing to catch her breath. As she looked back at the windward side of the compound, backlit like a prison, the sporadic gunfire was broken only by howling screams from the third floor. Tracer rounds streaked across the evening sky like deadly fireflies. Keeping her head low in the water, Angel breaststroked atop the waves for the next hour, swimming back to the empty beach where she had staged tonight's hit.

Once on land, she gathered her gear from under the scrabble of an agave-like Century plant and crawled cautiously on her hands and knees until she found the sandy hiking trail that led back to the Carato Bay Resort. From there, Valeria Ferrier, the guest at Carato Bay, had reservations for an early morning ferry to Elbow Creek. The ferry would be crowded. No one would remember the woman or where she'd gotten off, and the trail would die there. No cabs, no ridesharing, no airline reservations. There would be no record of Valeria Ferrier ever leaving the BVI.

Staying low in the brush, Angel quietly stuffed her wetsuit into the canvas duffel and stripped down to a pair of nylon board shorts and a blue-and-gold Corona T-shirt. She buried the duffel in a pre-dug hole beneath one of the poles holding up the deck of the vacant casita next to Number 9, then pulled out her passport in the name of Elena Espriella from the back zip pocket of her trunks. Following the only road out of Carato Bay, she eventually hailed a delivery van headed to a convenience store in Spanish Town near the Taddy Bay Airport.

As the van got closer, Angel made sure she hadn't been followed then thanked the driver, got out, and walked the remaining half kilometer to the tiny terminal. Twelve hours earlier she had used the Espriella passport and a credit card in the same name to book a flight to Los Angeles via San Juan, Puerto Rico. It had been a long time since she'd been home.

Even better, it seemed the Zetas had a new job for her.

PART THREE

CHAPTER TWENTY-FOUR

"Any reaction from last week's meeting?" asked Senior Investigator Blas Mondragon, helping helped himself to a Perrier Lemon. Assistant U.S. Attorney Bipu Munir didn't bother to look up from his bow-front desk, rolling his neck in a half circle, trying to work out a kink.

Following the task force meeting the other members had waited patiently for Harold Chase to be escorted out of the building, then left one by one, Munir reassuring each of them the investigation was still on track. But his words had sounded hollow, and his eyes were met with a great deal of unease. As ordered, Mondragon had sat silent through the entire meeting, impressed with Chase's sandbagging performance.

"I bet he had a sit-down with his lawyer within twenty minutes of our meeting. Probably ran him through our entire questioning step-by-step, which turned out to be nothing more than a pile of hearsay from an accused drug user. Looks like you're back to square one."

All he got was a non-committal grunt from Munir, who was lost in thought behind his desk. Still somewhat shell-shocked from Chase's demand for a lawyer, Munir had hoped to use the cocaine bust to bludgeon the pasty-faced physical therapist into testifying against Ernie Girard and the SoCal Medical Mafia. Now his entire legal strategy was circling the drain. Even a hack lawyer would be smart enough to limit Chase's involvement from here on in.

Not exactly what Munir had intended.

"Let's put a tail on him," suggested Mondragon. "He's an addict; he'll use again."

"We don't have the manpower. Besides, it'll look like harassment."

"I could do it, arm's-length. You'll have complete deniability . . . no harm, no foul."

This time Munir looked up, face full of fatigue. He leaned forward, clasping his hands, his eyes searing a hole through Mondragon. It was late morning and warm sunlight filled the office, tinting the walls a soft pumpkin shade. The burnt-nut aroma of freshly-ground espresso drifted from the reception area. Munir uncoiled his hands and anxiously tapped an engraved fountain pen on his leather blotter, taking long deep breaths to compose himself, his eyes never leaving Mondragon. Finally he stood, enunciating slowly. "Not in a million years. I don't care if Chase's goofy red hair catches on fire at Grauman's, you will not be within a mile of the man. Do I make myself clear?"

"I was just saying, I could observe from a—"

"Wait, I'm sorry, did I stutter? I don't think I stuttered. What part of 'you will not be within a mile of the man' did you not get? Shall I repeat it *en español?*"

"No. Thanks, I got it."

"Good, and let me remind you that you don't have any jurisdiction in this country. You are a visiting law enforcement guest, and if I catch you anywhere near Harold Chase, I'll turn you over to ICE for the quickest deportation ride in the history of the United States government, and I'll get bonus points from our president for doing so. Now I need you to look me in the eyes and tell me you understand what I've just told you . . . completely."

"Yes, but—"

"—but nothing. You can attend the follow-up meeting when Chase shows up with his lawyer and, again, you'll not utter a word. Not a single, solitary word."

"It's all hearsay evidence. You won't get a conviction with any of it."

"And that would be *my* problem. Just focus on helping the FBI run down an ID on your killer so we can extradite her back to Mexico, and even better—send you home with her."

"Her name is Maria Gomez."

Munir sat back down, tapping the pen again, feeling his blood pressure rise. "Okay, I'll bite. Who the hell is Maria Gomez?"

"The FBI reran the silver charms through their latest extraction equipment at Quantico and found microscopic traces of DNA on one of them. They matched it to a Maria Gomez. She's in your system because she served three years in Chowchilla for meth trafficking before getting released."

"I thought your techs couldn't find any identifiable DNA off the original crime scene forensics."

"They couldn't. But your DNA analyzers and sequencing equipment are much more sophisticated than ours. *Gracias*, by the way."

"*De nada*, our U.S. tax dollars at work. How long did you say the suspect was in Chowchilla?"

Mondragon scanned his dog-eared notepad. "March 2012 through February 2015, did the whole ride, no parole. Then she just walked out and disappeared."

"FBI have any ideas?"

"They figured she skipped across the border, went native. They also think she might've run into gang trouble in prison. Her jacket listed one of her cellmates as a former courier for the Gulf Cartel. Do you remember pre-9/11 when a group of Mexican Army Special Forces operators were recruited by the Gulf Cartel to serve as the cartel's military wing? They called themselves Los Zetas."

Munir shrugged. "Vaguely, but it's been almost twenty years. I thought most of them were dead or imprisoned by your military years ago."

"I checked the records on Gomez's cellmates during her incarceration. For ten months in 2013 her bunkmate was Camila Reynosa, *La Mula*, an original *mensajera* for the Los Zetas in Chihuahua City. When Reynosa got out in November, 2014, she hooked up with her old crew hauling meth for nine months until she got shot dead in an ambush in downtown Juárez. I'm thinking Gomez got out of prison and looked up Reynosa before she died."

"Makes sense, but how are you going to find her?"

"Gomez's parents still live in Torrance. I thought I might pay them a visit, start there."

Appalled, Munir's eyes flared again, his blood pressure spiraling. "Not in your wildest dreams," he nearly shouted, grinding his molars. "Not in this life, not in the next one or the one after that!"

Mondragon flipped his notebook closed: "You sure?"

"Never been more sure in my life. The last thing I need is you out there roaming the streets of LA. Got that?"

"Loud and clear, *jefe*." But Mondragon's mind was already three steps ahead. "Wouldn't dream of disobeying you."

"Good, now get out of my office."

CHAPTER TWENTY-FIVE

"I don't know how you can expect a person to be a functioning member of society if she's dragging her leg around like a stump. It seems almost medieval to me." Dr. Ernie Girard lifted a trim eyebrow as he spoke. "Motion to overturn staff's denial-of-care order. Do I have a second?"

"I'll second that motion."

"Thank you, Harold," said Girard. "All in favor?"

Both Girard and Harold Chase, out on bail, raised their hands. The third committee member, Juanita Reno, shook her head no. "That's the fifteenth out of eighteen cases this week," she complained. "Might as well have the UR nurses call in sick if we're going to overturn every one of their denials."

"Maybe we'd be better off if a few of them did," chirped Girard. "A few less UR nurses wouldn't be the end of the world. It might add some balance to this tribunal."

Rubbing her forehead, Reno turned to the court reporter. "Let's go off the record."

That was the cue for fifty-eight-year-old Suzuë Takashi, the happy applicant, to flash an enthusiastic thumbs-up at Girard and Chase and hobble towards her family at the back of the room, her scheduled knee replacement surgery back on track again. Reno watched her leave. After a moment she turned to MaryAnn Taylor, the committee's counsel. "MaryAnn, I'd like to go into executive session. Would you please excuse the staff? And we won't be needing you for the rest of the evening either."

Sensing a chill among the members, the investigative review committee employees quickly packed up their belongings, grabbed whatever coat or jacket they had brought, and hurried out of the conference room. What few guests remained also got the hint, except for Andy Crowder, who was rocking back and forth in his chair, oblivious to the exodus, tapping nonstop on his iPad. "That means you too, Mr. Crowder," ordered Reno.

Crowder barely looked up.

"Mr. Crowder." Reno's voice elevated.

This time Crowder lifted his head and gazed at her, confused. "But this was just starting to get good," he whined. For a few seconds the two eyed each other, until Reno gave a slight nod to two security guards, who stepped out from the vending machine area and escorted Crowder out of the conference room, his shrill voice echoing off the walls. "No touching. Get your hands off me, you pissant Neanderthals. Whatever happened to transparency, Juanita, the public's right to know . . . had to call in the goons, your own personal bunch of Fuhrmans!"

"Rather Gestapo-ish, Juanita," said Girard, making no effort to hide his sarcasm. "I didn't think you had it in you." She put a finger to her nose, indicating silence as the guards closed both doors. Girard leaned back in his Naugahyde chair, sighing heavily as if he had better things to do, which in a few hours he did. His partners were meeting in Bel Air to decide if Hurston was going to accept DAI's offer to buy out their practice.

Beside him, Harold Chase was fidgeting like a child with ADHD. Running a hand through his thin red hair, he sipped what smelled like gin from a Pasadena Rogues coffee mug. His physical therapy practices had just signed on to become the official rehab provider for the city's new Arena football team. Girard kept eyeing his wristwatch, anxiously tapping his fingers on the conference table. He had no idea what Reno was up to. She had never done anything like this before, but whatever was going on she wasn't in a hurry, scrolling silently through her smartphone.

"Surfing for porn?" Chase asked. "I'd be careful—the IT pukes can access your account. I learned that the hard way when I tried to order a cashmere beanie. They sent me a—"

"Shut up, Harold," Reno bristled. "I don't know what the two of you are up to, but I don't like it."

Girard edged up in his chair. "Is there something you'd like to get of your chest, Juanita?"

"Yes, as a matter of fact there is, *Ernie*. The number of overturned spine and orthopedic denials this past week has more than doubled from the two previous months combined. Either our nurses and case managers have mysteriously lost their skills, or the two of you have decided to make a conscious effort to flip these denials. I'm betting on the latter. But what I can't figure out is why? Somehow I'm guessing kickbacks. It's always about the money, isn't it, Ernie? "

Girard ran a fingertip across his temple, squinting. "That's quite an indictment, Juanita, and I think I speak for Hal when I say that we're both hurt." Girard did his best to look wounded. "I don't have the foggiest as to what you think we're up to. We're just trying to exercise our best medical judgment and keep an open mind on each and every case. But lately your nurses have become awfully sloppy and, quite frankly, way too big for their britches when it comes to assessing care options—"

"Stop right there," Reno cut him off. "It's just like you to twist this into some kind of doctor-nurse thing. Nobody's questioning your medical—"

"Ah, but you are," interrupted Girard, raising his right palm. He wasn't about to be browbeaten by her. Leaning forward, he dropped his voice a decibel. "I believe you quite emphatically accused Harold and me of being on the take. That's a libelous statement."

"Not if it's true," Reno corrected.

"Then present us with your evidence," demanded Girard leaning back in his chair.

There was a studied silence while Reno simmered: she should have known Girard would stonewall, point the finger elsewhere, politicize the issue. She also realized that she hadn't come prepared. She should've culled through the medical records and prepared some pertinent statistics to make her point. *Well, water under the bridge*, she told herself.

Girard was studying her, looking victorious. Finally he said, "We're all frustrated that single-payer hasn't lived up to our expectations, and we know what a big player your union was in getting GavinAid passed. But now that the whole program is at risk, your nurses seem to be ratcheting things up, kicking a few more patients to the curb. Did someone from Sacramento reach out to you?"

Reno felt like throwing a file folder at him. Glowering, she wrestled to say something, but instead shuffled through a few documents, gathering herself. She realized this wasn't going as planned, and she could feel Girard's eyes on her. "Do you have any real proof of these wild accusations?" he asked. "Any facts or complaints questioning our medical judgment, or is this just posturing, fake news."

Reno didn't respond. She felt the heat in her chest expanding. Pivoting from Girard, zeroing in on Chase, she froze him with her glare. "And where do you fit into all of this? Just the bagman again, legal fees starting to mount up?"

Chase flinched, eyes flitting about the empty room like a frightened doe. He was about to say something when Girard cut him off. "You still haven't told us what we're being accused of, Juanita. And I'd like to remind you that while you feel safe here in private session, if you make any of your unsubstantiated accusations in public, even some your off-the-record blogs to your social media pals, I will sue the holy fuck out of you. Now, is there anything else you'd like to discuss? If not, I've got a meeting to attend."

But before Reno could answer, a security guard stuck his head through the door. "Doctor Girard, we've gotten several phone calls from your office. They said their texts weren't getting through. They need you in the ER at Santa Monica Memorial, immediately. They've got a child with head trauma. And someone named Rory Armstead has also been trying to contact you. He says it's important."

"Did Armstead say anything else?" Girard stood, pulling on his suit jacket.

"GavinAid problems," answered the guard with a shrug. "He said you'd know what that meant." But Girard didn't. Feeling sick to his stomach, he thumbed Armstead's number into his cell phone while hustling down the aisle, not bothering to finish the meeting.

"We're not done yet, Ernie!" shouted Reno.

Girard approached the ridiculously large cast iron doors and paused, turning to face her with a deep sigh of frustration. "Yes, Juanita, you are. We're adjourned," he replied, holding her eyes. "And remember what I said about any unsubstantiated rumors. You don't want my attorneys mucking around in your life. They'd carve you up like a holiday turkey."

Frustrated, Reno barked, "I'm watching you, Ernie! I've called the DHCS auditors. You're toast."

But Dr. Ernie Girard was already out the door.

CHAPTER TWENTY-SIX

Driving north on Cabrillo Avenue, Blas Mondragon turned left onto West Carson Street and cruised slowly past a high school, hoping the address he had for Roberto and Cynthia Martinez was accurate. It was the last one listed in Maria Gomez's jacket before she was processed out of Chowchilla.

Gomez's prison records had shown only ten visits during her entire three-year hitch, all from her mother. The records also showed an unremarkable prisoner who did her time under the radar—no fights, no gang activity, and no attempts to rehabilitate herself into a new profession.

Once released, she simply disappeared into the wind.

The bungalow he was after had a large red-and-blue FOR RENT sign staked at the front of its postcard-size lawn. A neatly trimmed half-meter-high hedge encased the house, whose fiber cement siding was painted a soft vanilla white. Mondragon parked his rental SUV a block away so he could watch the couple working diligently in the yard. Both were in their sixties, and were arranging furniture and bric-a-brac for what looked like a garage sale. He assumed this was Roberto and Cynthia Martinez, and immediately noticed how Mr. Martinez, while game, couldn't help his wife with any of the heavy lifting. Every so often he had to sit in an overstuffed recliner chair and lean forward, rubbing his lower back. Just the opposite, Cynthia Martinez was a petite dynamo, darting in and out of the house, bustling around the yard, arranging cooking supplies on a thin blanket before wiping off an old George Foreman grill. The only time she slowed was to stack an ancient set of hardback Encyclopedia Britannica in alphabetical order atop a chipped wooden dresser. At five foot four, she had cocoa colored skin, a slim figure, and looked stressed but dignified. Her long brunette hair was tied back, no nonsense. She was the one in charge.

Having seen enough, Mondragon dismissed his original plan of impersonating a DEA agent and decided the truth would be the better option. Besides, he wasn't expecting much. He just needed to know if either Martinez had been in contact with their daughter, and if so, Blas would have to find a way to review their phone records without Bipu Munir finding out.

He unfastened his seat belt and looked up and down the street, spotting a distant neighbor mowing his lawn. He eased out of the Ford Escape, locked the doors, and walked casually towards the rented bungalow. "Good afternoon," he offered pleasantly from a distance, standing outside the hedge, his arms hanging motionless from his shoulders.

At the side of the house he spotted a small tabletop fountain made of decorative driftwood, along with a copper basin and rustic earthenware spread across the small yard. Both Cynthia and Roberto turned, looking him over without offering anything. "My name is Blas Mondragon. I'm a senior investigator with the Office of the Assistant Attorney General of Mexico. I'd like to ask you a few questions about your daughter, Maria."

Mondragon didn't wait for their response. Instead he pushed his way through the gate and followed a slender flagstone path across the yard before halting and flipping open a leather booklet. Inside was a laminated identity card with an old photo of a much younger Mondragon.

Cynthia took the booklet and studied the card carefully before handing it back to him. "Maria is my daughter from a previous marriage," she said. "We haven't seen her in years. Besides, she's done her time. What do you want with her?"

On the drive over, Mondragon had thought through each of his questions, but since he was working from a nearly empty file in a city he had no familiarity with—under the threat of deportation if he got caught—he didn't have much room to maneuver. Making it tougher, Cynthia Martinez didn't appear to be intimidated by his law enforcement credentials.

"Your daughter is wanted as a person of interest in the murder of a federal judge in Juárez," Mondragon explained, keeping his voice level. "She's a fugitive and she's in over her head. I'd like to help out." That brought a disbelieving smirk from Cynthia, the corner of her mouth lifting into a half-smile that contained zero empathy, only contempt, for Mondragon.

"Since when have the *federales* ever been interested in helping out anyone other than themselves?" she asked scornfully.

"Good point," replied Mondragon, "but she's working for people who could get her killed. Either by the FES or the state police or by one of the rival cartels who were paying off the judge she murdered. I got Maria's name off a DNA trace from an FBI file. If I can find it, her enemies can too, and killing a federal judge earns one a great many enemies. I think she could use a few friends."

"Maria can take care of herself," Cynthia countered, the other corner of her lip pulling back in a sly sneer. "She's managed to avoid you so far. Maybe she's just smarter than you?"

Mondragon shuffled forward, casually assessing everything around him. "That wouldn't be much of a stretch, ma'am," he confided, working his way past Roberto, halting just outside the front screen door and looking in. "In fact, I bet my boss would probably agree with you. He often wonders how I ever got the job in the first place." Seeing nothing inside, Mondragon took a couple steps backwards and continued circling the items for sale on the freshly-cut Bermuda lawn, pausing to run a finger along the spine of one of the encyclopedias.

"Pity you have to sell these. They're classics, aren't they?"

Cynthia stepped between Mondragon and her collection of reference books. "My entire family learned English from these books," she said defiantly, "so they're worth more than just money to us. But because of my husband's surgeries we need the cash. So if you're finished, we'd like you to leave. Maria is doing fine without your help. In fact, she's never been better."

Mondragon's eyebrows arched as he ran a hand across a hickory wood rocking chair. "I thought you said you hadn't seen her in years?"

Flustered, Cynthia pivoted and started back towards the front door, covering her mouth with her hand. Mondragon didn't say a word. He didn't have to. He listened to the gurgling noise of the fountain and the neighbor's power mower down the street. He hadn't gotten a single solid answer, but sometimes the slip-ups are most useful.

Deep bass from a car stereo pulsated. A vintage Chevrolet Impala low-rider cruised by. Cynthia's shoulders lifted and she hesitated near the door. "You'll never find her, señor, not if she doesn't want to be found. But one never knows; she just might find you." After a lengthy silence, she closed the screen door, leaving Mondragon standing next to her husband.

But Blas knew that once inside, she would call her daughter, and that's exactly what she did. Pressing ten digits on her cell phone, Cynthia waited. A strange voice came back, a cutout. She recounted the last few minutes, including a full description of Mondragon, knowing that her daughter would want to know who the *federales* had sent. Mother and daughter shared everything, but for the first time in memory she couldn't hide her worry.

Fingering the Immaculate Mary rosary beads tied around her wrist, Cynthia's eyes tracked Mondragon as he walked away. She knew she couldn't afford to lose Maria, not again. The last time had nearly killed her.

•   •   •

Mondragon had re-parked his Ford Escape under a magnificent Cyprus tree three hundred meters south-southeast of the Martinez's rented bungalow, slightly hidden around a curve in the traffic circle. He settled in and waited. He had a hunch. By four o'clock a black two-door Fiat passed by the Martinez home three times before parking directly in front of it.

That didn't take long, he thought, tracking the driver through a pair of Bushnell binoculars he had "borrowed" from one of Munir's staff investigators.

When the driver's-side door opened, he immediately recognized the same smooth-faced woman and her flat vacant eyes from the ER over a year ago. Maria Gomez, nicknamed Angel, unlatched the front gate and wandered comfortably among the secondhand items spread across the yard, stopping to handle a few of the curios, calmly inspecting each. She spent a few extra moments with a slim, tattered hardback book. Cynthia Martinez spotted her and came bounding out the screen door, hugging her warmly, mother and daughter happy to see each other.

Mondragon put the binoculars in his lap, shut his eyes, and inhaled the rich aroma of bougainvillea growing pell-mell about the neighborhood. The beauty of Southern California never ceased to amaze him. A tiny web of wrinkles appeared at the edges of his dark eyes as a satisfied smile crept across his face.

He had found his suspect.

CHAPTER TWENTY-SEVEN

Eight-year-old Marcus Robinson gazed fuzzily at the seal-blue monitor, its constant beeping reminding him of why he should have worn his seat belt like his grandmother had told him to.

A welter of tubes and IVs were connected to his body, and when he tried to lift his head an arrow of pain shot down his neck, causing him to yelp. The ER nurse pivoted and touched his cheek, her face taking on a stern look. "Lay still," she said, "I'm almost done."

Restless, Marcus cocked his head to one side, but the warmth of her hand calmed him.

A sliver of fluorescent light sliced through the curtains. The hospital emergency bay was the standard Level III setup: multiple bays with state-of-the-art monitoring equipment, an IV transport hovering near a 700-pound rolling trauma stretcher with upright side rails, a defibrillator, and a red-drawer medication cart. Outside, a horseshoe-shaped nurses' unit fronted the bays, a handful of emergency room employees moving effortlessly between them.

Having arrived without any ID, Marcus had mumbled his name to a paramedic and was immediately rolled into one of the bays, where he had been given a mobile CT scan and hooked up to several of the monitors. He lifted his head again, attempting to smile, wide-mouthed. It was the best he could do. Everything else hurt. The trauma nurse gently touched his arm.

"Hello, young man," she said pleasantly. "Do you know where you are?"

There was a pregnant, awkward silence while Marcus stared at her. His tongue felt like pumice. Gargling roughly, he tried to clear the blood and saliva from his throat, but after a few uncomfortable attempts he licked his lips and shook his head "sort of."

"Marcus, you're in the emergency room at the hospital. You've been in a car accident and have a concussion. We need to check you out, observe your vitals." She eyed an ECG readout. It was normal. But her patient looked drained, except for his eyes which were bright enough to light up a room. Studying her face, Marcus seemed to be weighing what he saw before he closed his eyes and listened to the quiet whisper of oxygen moving in and out. After a few seconds, the nurse turned away and called through the curtain. "Has Dr. Girard answered his page yet?"

Marcus couldn't hear the response.

But the nurse, Janette Patterson, did, and clenched her jaw.

Her ER was almost full tonight: a tibia fracture in Bay 6, an early stage OD in the observation unit, a couple of drunks sleeping it off, and a badly injured skateboarder. The assigned traumatologist had been MIA for the last forty-five minutes, probably upstairs earning a few extra bucks rounding for his off-duty colleagues. Multi-tasking was the euphemism passed around the nurses' station, but that didn't make it right. Incensed, Patterson listened to the drunk next door heave into a plastic container. She felt like screaming.

But that won't help, will it, she told herself. Her patient had endured serious head trauma, possible intracranial damage that required an immediate neuro consult. But so far no one could track down the neurosurgeon on call, Dr. Ernie Girard. She gave Marcus a weary smile, and for a soft moment he looked back, confused. Her thoughts were interrupted by another shrill beep. One of his IV bags was running low.

Patterson removed it and started a new one, wiping a bead of sweat off her forehead. She adjusted the overhead lamp, tapped several keys on the bedside laptop, and waited.

Marcus' eyes opened wider, concentrating on the tip of her nose.

Although she was standing directly beside him, his pupils had tightened to the point where he could hardly see her. Patterson brushed one of the leads off his cheek and a neuromuscular monitor reacted. Lifting his bandaged head with one hand, she kept an eye on the arrhythmia display. His swollen lips curled into a strained grimace. His breathing had become sporadic, both lungs emptying then filling in rapid cadence. She checked the flow of one of his IV bags, the seconds ticking away in her head. Something was wrong. Her anger bubbled up and she squeezed her eyes shut, badly wanting to slap someone.

Opening her eyes, she took a breath, released it, then double-checked her patient's heart rate and ventricular tachycardia. Both were stable, no signs of desaturation or cardiac arrest. His oxygen levels were fine, but she could hear low rasping sounds as saliva settled in his throat.

"Hang in there, you're going to be alright," she whispered, more to herself than to Marcus.

The din from the arrhythmia indicator caused her heartbeat to skip. "What now?" she breathed. Resetting the monitor, she adjusted the pulse oximeter and rechecked his blood gases.

Not great, but she'd seen worse.

Feeling more in control, she started a peripheral IV line to get an infusion pump going. She glanced at her watch. It had been almost ninety minutes since the child had arrived. He had been dropped off as part of a "twofer"—his ambulance already carrying a passenger when its crew decided to double down and respond to a collision near Euclid Park—the driver beating two other "buses" to the crash scene.

There was another clatter; someone singing outside the ER bay. Patterson snuck a peek through the curtains at the nurses' station. "Could you please call Dr. Jurani and tell him I need him down here STAT," she ordered the aide. "And tell him this patient hasn't been seen in over an hour."

The wire-thin aide assumed a flat, puzzled look. He was a tall, lithesome twenty-something sporting aqua-blue cornrows. "Sorry, the doc's busy upstairs. But I'll let him know you need him."

"Do that," snapped Patterson, "and while you're at it, tell him *right now*."

Forcing down the anger, she tapped the touchscreen. Each digital wave was holding within its prescribed range, no signs of nausea, hypertension, or even rapid heartbeat. She gripped Marcus' left wrist. His pulse was weakening. Her fingers gracefully engulfed his hand. "Stay strong, it's gonna be fine. We're hunting down a neurosurgeon. He should be here any moment."

•   •   •

Except the one they were looking for was sitting in the Santa Monica Memorial physicians parking lot yelling into his hands-free Bluetooth, his Porsche Cayman GT4 wedged between a charcoal-colored BMW 640i and a Fuji White Land Rover Range Rover.

"*What?* What do you mean they quit paying us?" Dr. Ernie Girard shouted into his phone. "That's gotta be illegal."

"Not if you're the state of California," countered Rory Armstead, Hurston's Director for Audit and Compliance, on the other end. "They've implemented a sixty-day freeze on all accounts payable." Armstead had been huddled in his office for the last hour, fielding panicky phone calls from cash-strapped neurosurgeons. "Somebody in Sacramento finally worked up the courage to admit the program is failing. GavinAid is officially tapped out, broke, no more *dinero*. The state is gonna be issuing hard-copy chits they'll redeem when things stabilize. I'm assuming that's code for a federal bailout. They've also called in a couple of private insurers to work through their payables and figure out how much is owed and to whom."

"*Christ-on-a-fucking-horse*, what a goddamn nightmare! Can you believe this shit? The state's printing chits like some two-bit banana republic! This is fucking worse than Obamacare. Did they give you a timeframe?"

"No, and I don't know what to tell you either. Months, probably less than a year, but it's gonna take time and they'll need federal money. The good news is that the congressional Dems aren't going to let single-payer fail. My contact in Sacramento says that the governor and both U.S. Senators have reached out to Washington. They're hoping for a bridge loan to cover the cash flow problems—"

"From this administration? Don't hold your breath. How much does the state of California owe us?"

"Slightly less than twenty million. Most of it's over ninety days. It'll be up to twenty-five mill by the end of next month. I've started calling our bankers. We're going to need some type of short-term financing."

"*Unbelievable* . . . fucking unbelievable. The Germans hear about this?"

"Probably. Governor's going to make the official announcement later tonight after the network news cycle."

"Alright, at least that gives us a window."

"Yeah, if you want to get sued," warned Armstead. "And I ain't gonna be any part of that."

"Dickless gnome! How about you grow a pair and see if you can't get this fucking deal done. Does that work for you?"

"Not if it gets me sued, Chiefy. It ain't worth the trouble."

"Fine, what about our malpractice reserves? The accountants said they wanted more?"

"An additional five million. It's in their audit notes. They want us to add an extra five mil to our legal reserves account. Nobody has any faith you can defend your lawsuits, and the Germans aren't gonna be on the hook for the verdicts either."

"Lovely. This is getting better by the second. What about tonight's vote?"

"Still scheduled, but you'd better get here soon. Where are you anyway?"

"Hospital parking lot. Memorial's got a kid with a possible subdural hematoma. I can't get out of it. Can you postpone the vote for a few hours?"

"Iffy, but I'll try. The Germans want an answer tonight. They've got their financing approved and they're ready to go—oh, and call Simpson. She's been speed dialing me like a bobcat on crack. The woman's in pure meltdown mode."

"Leave it alone. I'll call Stephanie and calm her down. But I want you to tell Arnie to delay that vote. I'll get there as soon as I can."

"10-4, but you'd better hurry."

Girard disconnected and jumped out of the Porsche, swearing under his breath. He checked his wristwatch; not enough time. Pulse throbbing, the anger ready to explode inside his head, he scanned the parking lot, his neck and shoulders rigid with stress, and for the next few seconds watched the last of the flickering sun reflect off the blades on the single-engine evac copter, glazing the hospital rooftop in metallic silver. To the west, menacing rainclouds massed over the ocean, covering the sky with bruises. This was his worst nightmare: the first and only thing he had ever been afraid of—failure.

He stood for what seemed like an eternity, his mind churning through his problems, letting his thoughts form and reform, feeling his way along. Oddly, it felt reinforcing—his refusal to cave in—but right now it took every ounce of effort to fight back the doubt and think. Somebody was hollering at him, the sound barely audible over the traffic noise, but he didn't budge. An idea was taking shape, a glimmer of strategy that could easily translate into an endgame.

A sly smile traced his lips, followed by a surge of adrenaline.

Suddenly, he was all motion.

Striding through the ER entrance, he barked at an EMT to follow him, his pace and stature screaming confidence, every neuron firing. He crashed through the ER doors into the nurses' station. The aqua-haired aide pointed to Bay Four, and Girard snatched the stethoscope from around his neck and flung open the curtains. He had to get this done quickly. Patch up the kid and get back to his practice, turn this thing around. The clock was ticking.

He knew his life depended on it.

CHAPTER TWENTY-EIGHT

Blas Mondragon uncurled his cramped legs, his back propped against the red Dumpster.

He was covered in a moldy canvas jacket, his clothes and hair slightly disheveled, his eyes bloodshot from squinting. Stubble had sprouted in patches along his neck and chin. He pressed his eyelids shut, his face feeling pinched. Despite the unseasonable chill, a thin ribbon of sweat trickled down his chin as he readjusted his sore hips against the smelly Dumpster.

Along the street, a diesel bus cruised past, rainwater trailing from its tailpipe. As it sped up to beat a yellow traffic light, Mondragon's eyes swung across the street to a garish patio home sitting catty-corner from him. From his observation point he had open sight lines on a two-block perimeter and could see everything coming or going into the neighborhood.

The front entry area of the eclectic-looking home had circular fluorescent lighting, assorted plastic palms, and a fuzzy-wire lamp that made it look like some low-end drag club rather than the walk-in whorehouse that it was. Creeping across its tile roof, a tangle of spiky bougainvillea partially covered a whitewashed cinder block wall. Through his waterproof spotting scope, Mondragon could barely make out the home's antiquated security system, a hodgepodge of homemade wireless pads and motion activated sensors. Nothing he couldn't handle.

He slipped the stolen scope into his jacket pocket and blew on his hands, cursing LA's late winter weather. Since Bipu Munir had frozen him out of the investigation, he had taken it upon himself to tail his suspect, Maria Gomez, after recognizing her at her parent's home. And it hadn't been easy. The former convict had obviously had some sort of counter-surveillance training, doubling back frequently through crowded malls, ducking in and out of service exits, doing stop-and-turns in parking lots, not subtle but effective, forcing Mondragon to follow from a distance until Gomez was satisfied she was clean. The suspect had then jumped onto the Rosa Park Freeway, veered off at South Western Avenue, and cruised through Olympic Park before easing into an empty driveway two blocks south of the garish whorehouse.

After two pass-bys on foot, she had decided it was safe and had entered the patio home through the front door. Mondragon had parked his rental Ford Escape northwest of Gomez's Fiat, pulled the knee-length army surplus jacket over a forest green hoodie, both purchased at a Santa Monica thrift shop, and settled into his spot beside the Dumpster.

For the next few minutes the muffled sound of LA traffic splashed through the evening shower. Barely visible under the blue halogens, the cars' watery shadows wormed their way along the wet asphalt, a river of brake lights blurring through the showers. A strong gust blew across West Pico, the wind and rain mixing with the faint smell of car exhaust causing Mondragon's eyes to water as he blew warmth into his hands.

Across the street a flimsy curtain parted. Mondragon covered his spotting scope with his right palm and watched a petite prostitute do her thing, her tiny body clearly visible in the high dim light. As the girl's silky brunette hair washed back and forth across her face, her motion, a smooth rhythm rising and falling like a striped Sunfish bobbing lazily in the Pacific, almost felt cathartic.

Jesus Christ, get your head out of your ass. Focus, damn it!

Feeling guilty, Mondragon lifted himself onto his toes and was thinking about circling the block to get a better position inside the backyard, when a black-and-white Los Angeles Police Department cruiser roared onto Pico, sirens blaring, its headlights sliding over his body. He crouched deeper, hunching his shoulders into the tattered jacket and pulling the grimy hood over his head. As the cruiser passed, Blas tilted his head downwards. Nothing here, just another homeless man on a dreary soggy night, and the cruiser continued down the street. A wet breeze dampened his face.

"It never rains in California," Blas muttered to himself, blowing on his fingers. "Tell me about it."

CHAPTER TWENTY-NINE

I just need some information, that's all." Angel's voice was quiet, soothing. "He's one of your regulars. His name is Harold Chase. Can you give me any idea when he might be back, who he sees?" Once she had received the order from the cartel to eliminate Chase, Angel had bribed the therapist's bail bondsman for his cell phone number and a cartel contact had traced several calls to this whorehouse over the past couple of months. Slightly confused, a young prostitute fidgeted at the edge of her bed, pulling on a sheer blue robe while nervously raking a handful of hair with her peacock-green fingernails.

"Place sucks, doesn't it," she said, more a statement than a question. She slid off the metal-framed bed and strolled to a mini-bar, wiping a streak of dust off the fake armoire. The bedroom had a tired nautical look, overdone in seascapes and rattan chairs and table lights made from washed-up shells. "I'm getting out in a week," she said, admiring herself in a full-length mirror. "My roommate's brother runs an escort service in North Scottsdale, says I can clear thirty-five hundred a night, easy." She twisted open a Jim Beam miniature and offered it to Angel. The *asesina* waved her off. "You alright?" the prostitute asked. "You don't look so hot. I got some weed in the cabinet, Seattle Blue."

"Thank you, but I'm good," said Angel, giving her a passionless smile.

"Suit yourself." The prostitute pivoted towards the mirror as Angel's gaze drifted to the bedroom door. The locks were hardware store issue; neither would require much finesse. The younger woman opened a curved wooden drawer beside the closet and pulled out a vinyl cigarette-making kit along with a cellophane bag full of pot. She rolled a joint, flicked a cyber yellow lighter, and dragged twice, giggling like the nineteen-year-old she was. With her back to Angel, she kept staring at herself in the mirror, loosening her robe, offering Angel a hit. "Come on, fire up, it's on the house."

Angel cast the girl a sideways look then pushed herself off the bed and in a smooth, practiced motion glided across the tiny room and grabbed the young woman's right biceps. "I asked you a simple question and I was hoping to get a simple answer. Have you ever seen this man? His name is Harold Chase. He's a customer." Angel's eyes were cold. Thinking better of it, she stepped back, loosened her grip, and opened both palms. "Come on, help me out here. Then I'll get out of your hair, promise."

"Grab her like that again and they'll be hauling you out in a body bag." The stern voice turned out to be that of a rail-thin teenager who'd strayed into the bedroom. Offering her best fentanyl-induced grin, she was pointing a Beretta M9 semiautomatic at Angel's stomach, flicking a blond curl out of her pale blue eyes. She took a half-step closer. Angel could see that her tanned face was swollen and covered with heavy pancake makeup. She had slipped into the room through the adjoining door. The *asesina* cursed herself for not throwing the deadbolt inside.

"How about we try this again?" asked the blonde. "Five hundred cash for the whole hour and if we get any more of that Mexican tough-bitch shit, we're gonna have a problem."

Angel's face went completely blank, her lips tense. She stood motionless.

"I'll take that as a yes," said the blonde. "Put the cash on the bed, and no freaky shit this time."

Angel tilted her head in a manner that indicated she understood, took a step to her left, and reached into her waterproof jacket hanging from one of the bedposts. She fished out a slender calfskin wallet, removed several one hundred dollar bills, and tossed them on the comforter. "You give frequent flyer miles?" she asked flippantly, trying to lighten the mood.

"Yeah, right," said the blonde, setting her Beretta on the nightstand, eyes frozen on the cash. Smiling, she lifted her one-piece chemise and pulled it teasingly over her head. She was taller than most, her five-foot-nine-inch frame carrying the wispy body of a frequent drug user. She also had a sharp nose, delicate cheekbones, and perfectly straight white teeth. She slid out of her Spandex G-string, draped it nonchalantly over the bedpost, and turned to face Angel, stark naked. "Tell you what, you get your head on straight and I'll let you in on a secret."

Angel looked attentive for the first time. "Sounds interesting. Okay, I'm game."

"You got any idea who you're partying with tonight?"

Aroused, Angel eyed the young blonde. "Playmate of the Year?" she answered facetiously.

The blonde took a sip of her partner's Jim Beam, then touched the tip of Angel's nose with her finger. "Just tell me what you want."

"I thought you said something about a secret."

"It's nothing, really, no big deal."

"No . . . I'd like to hear it. Come on."

"It's just that some people know who I am, that's all."

"You one of those strippers that Trump boned?"

She jerked her hand back, covering herself, embarrassed. "Fuck off, twat." There was something angry in her eyes, resentful. Angel immediately realized she'd made a mistake and reached out, softly touching the blonde's cheek, this time choosing her words more carefully.

"Sorry, my bad, but I'm in a hurry. Can you help me out? This man's a regular." She tossed two color photos of Harold Chase onto the bed. "Any idea when he might be coming back?"

Still pissed, the blonde snatched her thong off the bedpost. "Get out, now."

"Come on, lighten up," said Angel, scrambling across the bed. She grabbed the blonde by the forearm. "We're not done yet."

But the girl jerked her arm away. "Fuck off."

"Hey, I said I'm sorry," Angel apologized. "Nobody said anything about fashion models or starlets or whoever you are. It's just a party, remember. What's your problem?"

"Read my lips," said the blonde. The muscles around her jaw flexed. "Get the fuck out, *now!*"

But Angel was no longer listening. She started counting out four hundred dollar bills from her wad. From behind the flimsy bedroom door she heard the clump-clump of a man's heavy gait, followed by the scuffle of the front door opening, then closing. "Girls, it's just money," she said, adding another hundred dollar bill. "Is this guy coming over anytime soon or not?"

But the blonde wouldn't budge. "What are you, a cop? Because we don't dime-out."

"Do I look like a cop?"

"We ain't snitches either," said the blonde. "That don't play well around here. A girl can get slapped upside the head for talkin' to cops."

Angel stared into the blonde's bloodshot eyes. "Fine," she relented, "you win. Can I at least get that drink?"

The blonde's shoulders sagged as she wandered to mini-bar. She poured another Jim Beam into a smudged snifter glass. "You know what? I think I've got a headache."

Angel slid another hundred dollar bill behind the blonde's left ear. "But I'm not quite ready to go home yet. Help me out here." The blonde's tired eyes brightened as she grabbed the bill, then quickly snatched the rest of the cash off the bed and stuffed it into a suede crossbody bag sitting beside the Beretta on the nightstand.

"I swear," Angel said sincerely, "I'm totally clueless as to who you are. I don't even know your name." She smiled subtly, her eyes magical, her voice low and warm. The blonde softened, leaving her chemise on the bed. "Jasmine," she answered, "and this is Mistence."

"Jasmine what?"

"Just Jasmine around here."

Angel moved closer to her. "Well, Jasmine, I believe I was promised a party."

"I'll go freshen up," said Mistence, strolling into the bathroom and shutting the door.

Angel swirled her Jim Beam like it was top-shelf cognac. Pulling a chair over, she sat beside Jasmine and handed her the drink. The teenager drained it, careful not to dribble, then propped both legs on Angel's right knee and, without a word, eased her body onto the killer's lap, straddling her crotch. Angel had earlier surveyed the musty bedroom, noting every piece of furniture, every window and two-way mirror, impressed that the owner had bothered with a closed-circuit camera—an ancient Magnavox rotating noisily in the hallway. Angel reached behind Jasmine's head and gently wrapped her right arm around the teenager's neck, keeping her elbow sharply flexed. Then she began compressing both forearms and biceps against the girl's carotid arteries.

Terrified, Jasmine tried to scream, dropping her snifter as Angel's grip tightened, vice-like. Within seconds Jasmine's head began to droop. Leaning forward, Angel gently set her unconscious body on the thin carpet and had barely looked up when the bathroom door opened.

Mistence stepped out, adjusting her robe. When she saw Jasmine on the floor, she lunged for the Beretta, but Angel was too quick. She tossed Mistence face-down on the bed, pinning her arms behind her as she dropped both knees into her back. Holding the girl's head and shoulders down, Angel quickly bound the prostitute's wrists together with her leather belt, then ripped out a lamp cord, tied it around Mistence's ankles, and stuffed a cotton handkerchief in her mouth.

The teenager's muffled screams would be nothing out of the ordinary. In fact, a few clients might enjoy it. Bending her knees, Angel deadlifted Mistence and set her half-naked body in the bathroom tub. Then she returned to the bedroom and retrieved Jasmine, laying her beside her friend in the tub. Satisfied, she gazed benignly at the two young prostitutes before returning to the bedroom.

The digital clock above the armoire read 6:45. Angel retrieved a pack of Pall Malls from her jacket and sat tiredly on the bed, crossing her legs. She'd have to wait for Harold Chase. This was his regular night. His cell phone records showed a total of seven calls to the whorehouse, five occurring on Tuesdays. Angel rubbed her eyes and pulled a cigarette from the pack. Using Mistence's Bic disposable, she lit up the Red 100. It was a bit surreal, she thought, staring at the dusty seashells, the shitty bed, the soulless room—two girls stacked in a tub. Most of her hits made so little difference, and she was always surprised at how easily she took to it, especially when it was one of the cartel *gamberros*. She rationalized it as taking out the trash, human disposal. All her victims were grade-A pigs, deserving whatever fate she dealt them. There was never any need for remorse or doubt. But in the bathtub were two young women, girls really, and this time it was different. Angel knew she couldn't kill them. There was no way she could carry that weight.

Stubbing out the cigarette, she lifted her chest and stretched, scanning the room. She knew she had to wipe down every hard surface she had touched, so she grabbed a towel from the bathroom—both girls were still silent—and started wiping down everything, failing to notice the flickering light hidden inside the overhead flush mount lamp. The LED bulb was connected to a mini-wireless alarm that was triggered to go off silently every sixty minutes unless one of the girls hit the remote override. It was a common safety feature for many of the whorehouses.

One that Angel missed until it was too late.

CHAPTER THIRTY

An LAPD squad car cruised to a halt in front of the patio home and two police officers got out.

The oldest was Latino, mid-forties, medium-build, with black hair and a slight limp from a torn meniscus that had never healed properly. But he still moved with the self-assured swagger of a veteran street cop, a Benelli M4 tactical shotgun in his right hand the great equalizer. His crew-cut partner was thirtyish, built like an ex-football player, and strapping an old-school .45-caliber Kimber Classic with a Ruger LCR revolver tucked in a backup holster on his right ankle. They had been working together for three years. As they approached the front door, neither seemed to be in a hurry, silent homeowner alarms being the bane of their profession.

Crouching low, Blas Mondragon tried to fade into the shadows, pulling his overcoat over the top of his head as the two cops stood in front of the patio home. The last thing he needed was to be questioned by LAPD. The front door of the whorehouse was locked. The younger cop shook the knob, and that's when Mondragon heard a slight concussive sound like steam whistling through a kettle. It was an entry alarm, but neither officer seemed concerned. The younger cop pounded hard on the door but got no answer. Annoyed, he stood beneath the portico, not sure of what to do next, when a sudden piercing scream came from inside the house. He drew his Kimber and planted both feet, tightening his hamstrings. Nodding to his partner, he drove forward, smashing a shoulder into the right inswing of the door. Once, then twice. Finally on the third try the doorjamb exploded.

His partner, shotgun up, slipped inside ahead of him, the younger cop following right behind. Both officers cleared the front area, then separated. The younger one picked his way down the main hallway, clearing rooms until he saw Jasmine's paneled door partially open.

Entering carefully, glancing into the tiny bathroom, he spotted a groggy body sprawled in the tub next to another girl, who'd managed to spit out her gag out and was screaming at the top of her lungs: "Help us! Fucking help us! She's here . . . she's still here!" On his bonephone, the officer said something to his partner. Then leading with the barrel of his Kimber, he moved cautiously through the bedroom door, visually clearing the room. He had taken a couple steps into the bedroom when an empty Jim Beam miniature rolled across the floor. Glancing at it, the cop turned. Angel slid out from inside the closet and drove her palm into the man's trachea, staggering him backwards.

Like a cage fighter, she followed quickly with a hammer fist to the right side of the cop's jaw, dislocating his mandible. Then planting her left foot, using all her momentum, she threw a crippling kick into his right knee, staving in his patella and dropping him like a sack of flour.

The young officer bellowed like a wounded animal. Angel pressed her body flat against the wall, snatched Jasmine's Beretta off the nightstand, and pointed it at Mistence.

"Not a word," she warned as she waited for the second officer to cross the threshold.

It didn't take long.

The barrel of the combat shotgun poked through the doorway as the other cop called out to his partner. His eyes froze on the younger man moaning, gripping his knee. That was all she needed. Angel grabbed the barrel of the Benelli with her left hand, took a half step forward, and brought the Beretta down hard on the bridge of his nose, shattering his nasal septum. There was an explosion of blood as the veteran cop hesitated before lunging at Angel, who drove him backwards with a headbutt, then tripped his ankles, sending him sprawling sideways to the floor.

Mistence howled, a desperate, keening wail. Angel felt it more than she heard it. Sensing movement, she spun counterclockwise and saw the younger cop gathering himself off the floor and reaching for the Ruger in his ankle holster.

Moving like a wraith, Angel closed to within a meter and slammed the Beretta across his jaw, sending a single incisor flying out of his mouth. But she hadn't gotten enough torque in her blow, and somehow he managed to stay on his feet. The cop centered himself, blood streaming down his face. Then with a bestial roar he launched himself at Angel, crushing her against a bedroom wall, driving the breath from her lungs.

Both crumpled, but Angel had the wherewithal to disengage and flatten herself against the armoire, her breath coming in shallow spurts. The muscular cop had tumbled to the right of the bed. He regained his balance and was bringing up the Kimber, but he was an instant too slow, the grip of the Beretta catching him flush on the left temple and pitching him face-first onto the bed, unconscious.

Nearly vomiting, Angel twisted her head to one side and dropped to both knees, feeling a stabbing pain circling her lower neck. She winced as the ache shot down her collarbone like a sledgehammer, her eyelids growing heavy, her stomach cramping. She was probably concussed. Shoving a hand behind her neck for support, she touched the deep bruise on the back of her shoulder while her eyes roamed across the bedroom. Both cops were down, neither moving.

Good. That would buy her a few minutes, which was critical since her timing had to be perfect. She couldn't make her move until the first responders arrived.

Pulling herself up, she slouched against the wall and stared at the mess.

Bad luck with the girls, she admitted. They could've made it so much easier. Best laid plans, she thought, but she would adjust on the fly, improvise, overcome. A rush of air escaped her lungs. Her expression grew strained, anxious. She was still angry over the senseless assaults when she noticed that the rain had stopped.

Almost time.

Within a few seconds she heard sirens, and rotating beacons flashed outside the bedroom window. Screeching tires slammed to a halt, followed by footsteps and urgent voices.

Angel dropped into a tight crouch as she draped a red brocade bedspread over her body.

Out the window the radio traffic grew louder.

Then she heard it—a hiss, like a rattlesnake.

She curled tight, keeping her head down. Suddenly the entire bedroom filled with bright, jarring orbs of light and deafening noise. Angel huddled low, staying motionless, deprived of orientation. But LAPD backup had arrived precisely on time. Given the heightened level of violence that was pervasive throughout Los

Angeles, the police had long ago added M84 stun grenades, or flashbangs, to their beefed-up street crimes arsenal. One of those stun grenades had rolled up to the bedroom door, and the fierce explosion had sent splinters flying in all directions.

Angel tossed aside the bedspread, crouched beneath the bedroom's only window, her back flat against the wall, and counted backwards from ten. She felt something warm dripping down the side of her face, pain hammering her temples. For a fleeting moment, she thought she might collapse. But she had sized up the window, and with a tight, violent kick, she knocked out the screen and tumbled headfirst into a thick hedge, the smoke and teargas covering her escape.

Huddled in the damp soil, she steadied herself, waiting for a specific moment.

When she heard the ambulance sirens, she wiped a trickle of blood off her jaw, brushed the dirt and hedge trimmings off her clothes, and buttoned her jacket. Then, without a flicker of hesitation, she began walking down the sidewalk in the opposite direction of the whorehouse as responding police cruisers wheeled past her.

•   •   •

From underneath his hoodie, Blas Mondragon admired the fireworks. LAPD certainly knew how to throw a party: 12-gauge Mossberg shotguns, flashbangs, plenty of busted windows, and one massively shattered doorway. Impressive. What was left of the barred front door and its funky lighting had been obliterated.

Within seconds of the backup team entering the house, a blinding flash, accompanied by a 170-decibel roar that could be heard from blocks around, caused Mondragon to flinch. Sitting up on his heels, he watched Maria Gomez kick out a bedroom window screen, slide a leg over the sill, and scan the yard. With ice in her veins, she pulled her slender torso up and out the window and tumbled into the thick hedge that surrounded the house. Then she waited patiently for the first responders to arrive. Once the backup cops and private ambulance crew had entered the whorehouse, she buttoned her jacket and began walking brazenly away in the opposite direction, her head turning as an LAPD cruiser came screeching around a corner.

Cat-like, Mondragon circled the Dumpster, keeping it between him and the arriving first responders. Then he began tailing Gomez as she walked towards her Fiat, pulling his hoodie tight, keeping as far back as he could. Shuffling awkwardly like a drunk, he stopped every block or so to inspect a trash can. It was obvious

Gomez was on high alert: crisscrossing streets, doubling back, stealing a newspaper from one of the yards and pausing under a fanning tree, pretending to cover her head with a damp section.

But Mondragon kept his distance. He gritted his teeth, his entire body shivering, looked up at the dark sky and blew on his hands for warmth.

It was going to be a long night, he thought, a very long night.

CHAPTER THIRTY-ONE

"Please tell me you found a neurosurgeon," begged Dr. Alex Kalekas, poking his bald head through the flimsy curtains, looking nervous. Usually unflappable, Kalekas was a well-regarded hospitalist, but tonight he had agreed to serve as backup to the ER's scheduled traumatologist, and that had turned out to be a mistake. After two hours of prime-time trauma, Kalekas knew he was in over his head.

"Hardly, but it was nice of you to stop by." Janette Patterson's simmering sarcasm carried above the monitors. She had gathered Marcus Robinson's bloody clothes and bundled them into a red canvas bag marked Hazardous. "Possible head trauma, maybe a subdural hematoma," she said, catching him up. "One of the private ambulances brought him in about an hour and a half ago. We called Girard, but nobody's answering. Tried his PA, but he's tied up at another hospital, said Girard was in some type of committee meeting. We finally got ahold of his service and they assured us that he's on his way." Her smartphone vibrated and she checked the message. "Brandi just got a text from the shift supervisor. Girard is in the doctors' lot. He said to keep the patient stable until he gets there."

"Works for me," said Kalekas, visibly relieved. "Watch and wait until the cavalry arrives."

But Patterson wasn't having any of it; she barely controlled her anger. "Doctor, this patient has been waiting on a neurosurgeon for over ninety minutes.

I've paged the traumatologist three times, but nobody seems to be able to find him. Is Dr. Jurani sleeping it off somewhere?"

"In the ortho casting room, snoozing like a newborn baby. Poor guy just came off a thirty-six hour shift."

"And you've been rounding for him upstairs?"

"Clinical multi-tasking—"

"Bullshit," she seethed.

Kalekas stiffened, rubbing his bald scalp. "It's Janette, right? Listen, Janette, things have a way of working themselves out if you don't ask too many questions . . . okay?"

"I'm sure they do, but this patient's condition isn't working itself out, so why don't you do something about it, *okay?*"

Kalekas took one look at Marcus Robinson's vital signs and reluctantly nodded. He pulled on a pair of latex gloves, pressed a metal floor pedal that activated the overhead voice recorder, and began dictating. "Time is 19:09, Dr. Alex Kalekas attending for Dr. Jurani who's in consult. Patient is experiencing sporadic seizures due to possible neurotrauma." Kalekas' gray eyes homed in on a milky CT scan. "Linear fracture to the right temporal with a lacerated artery causing an inflated epidural hematoma; staff has attempted to contact the neurosurgeon-on-call for possible emergency craniotomy, but there's been no response until a few minutes ago when the house supervisor advised that Dr. Girard is on the premises, ETA unknown. We were instructed to continue stabilizing the patient, but his condition appears to be deteriorating." There was silence at both ends of the exam table as long blisters of blood dribbled across Marcus's lips. "Alright, let's get a depressor in his mouth. I don't want him swallowing his tongue. Any sign of Girard, yet?"

But before Patterson could answer, the ECG alarm reacted. "Blood pressure's sixty over palp, too low for the monitors," she called out.

"Okay, we can't wait for Girard," said Kalekas, casting a sideways glance at Patterson. "Call Five South. I saw Jeffrey Cohen up there an hour ago cruising for patients. Tell the staff to find him and let him know we need a neurosurgeon, STAT. *Move, people,* faster is better."

Still surrounded by an ocean of white, Marcus Robinson opened his eyes and kept them focused on Patterson. "Give me a smile," she whispered. "Everything's going to be alright."

He lifted his swollen head until his face was inches from hers, a thin trail of blood seeping down the left side of his jaw. "Where's my grandma?"

"Upstairs in ICU," Patterson replied. "You'll see her soon enough."

His pupils were acting up. "Is she okay?"

"She's a strong woman, just like her grandson."

Marcus batted his eyes, smiling. Patterson touched his hand, then turned to the medication cart just as the respiratory monitor squealed a nauseating pitch. When she spun back towards Marcus, a stream of reddish-brown vomit sprayed across her scrubs. Several monitors activated, but before she could do anything the bay curtains flared open.

"Obviously, I can't leave you sugar-tits alone for a second." Dr. Ernie Girard blew through the curtains dressed in green surgical scrubs with someone else's stethoscope wrapped around his neck. He brusquely elbowed Kalekas aside. "Somebody, anybody, start talking to me." There were a few seconds of silence as Girard checked Marcus's pupils. They were pale as glass, the skin around his cheeks dry and papery. The neurosurgeon cocked his head to one side, his expression searing a hole through Kalekas. "Where the fuck is Jurani?"

Dropping his eyes, Kalekas wisely avoided the question and started briefing. "Patient is approximately eight years old; involved in a high-speed auto accident; presented with unknown trauma to the head and neck. We've ordered a CT scan. I saw a possible—"

Girard cut him short when the bedside telemetry reacted again. "Shit, we've got a possible bleeder. In less than two nanoseconds I'm taking this patient upstairs for an emergency craniotomy. Call Jurani—*I don't care where the hell he is*—and have him meet me in the OR. Doctor Kalekas, give me a hand here." Girard tromped on Kalekas' left foot as they manhandled the rolling stretcher towards the elevator. "Nurse, mark him out at 19:12 and call the OR. Tell them we're on our way." But as Girard pushed the stretcher through the curtains towards the elevator, something caught his eye and he stopped dead in his tracks. Voices were firing at him from all directions, but he stood over the boy's face, finally realizing who it was. "My God," he murmured.

Marcus's eyelids batted open. "Hey, Doc, how's it hangin'?"

Girard regained his composure. "Obviously better than you, son. I hope you didn't get any blood on that new hoodie of yours. I spent half an hour online shopping for it."

"Natch, dog," Marcus grinned droopily. "It's still at home."

"Good boy. Now let's get you upstairs to surgery." With Kalekas behind him, they pushed the stretcher into the elevator. Girard's cell phone vibrated. Pulling it from his scrubs, he checked the message. It was from Stephanie Simpson: *Call me ASAP.*

Kalekas heard Girard mutter "unbelievable" as the elevator doors closed.

CHAPTER THIRTY-TWO

"While you were in the air, we got a few updates on our situation," explained Luca Manser, sipping whiskey as he paced his study. He paused near a magnificent Fragonard. A gray domestic longhair cat rolled over on its back, purring at the sight of Manser's cap-toe oxfords.

A few feet away, with both hands in his pants pockets, Dieter Eberstein rocked rhythmically back and forth on his heels, wishing he had accepted Manser's earlier offer of a Scotch. Having been airborne for eleven hours on a flight from Heathrow to LAX—he'd been putting the final pieces of the financing together in London—followed by another two hours navigating Los Angeles's mind-numbing traffic, he was groggy and jet-lagged. The security around the Malibu compound didn't help either, the outward display of weaponry causing his pulse rate to spike.

"In the chaos of breaching the patio home, LAPD lost Angel," said Manser, scrolling through texts. "Somehow she slipped out a bedroom window while their backup team almost blew the house apart. But she did manage to disable two police officers before leaving. Both are in the hospital, one with a broken jaw, the other concussed. And you'll love this—it seems the house is owned by a shell company whose sole shareholder is Ernest L. Girard, M.D. Now the cops want to talk to Girard."

"How good is your source?" asked Eberstein, feeling the need to say something.

"Letter perfect. The police are quite pissed off that two of their own got worked over pretty good by a woman. They put out an all-points bulletin on Angel, and my source tells me the hookers gave them a pretty solid description."

Eberstein felt ill. "That doesn't sound too promising, but I imagine a professional like her has a bailout plan?"

"Whatever, the woman's on her own now, arm's-length, and I doubt Girard will hold up either. LAPD probably has enough to threaten criminal prosecution."

But Eberstein wasn't listening. He wiped a dab of moisture from his brow. A dreary rain had lingered sinc early evening. Cold and damp, the brooding darkness matched his mood. "Anything else from the after-action reports?"

"Just what I've told you," said Manser still scanning his smartphone.

"What about fingerprints . . . DNA?"

"In a whorehouse?—they've got more sets than the DMV. Fortunately, it appears Angel was smart enough to keep her hands off the windows and doorknobs. Plenty of DNA though, but it'll take 'em weeks to sort that out."

"Any video surveillance?"

"Nothing usable. It seems she kept her face hidden from the hallway cameras." Manser paused to gaze at his reflection in an ornate full-length mirror. Dutch-made and handcrafted with inlaid silver aspen leaves, the mirror had been bought at an estate auction in Rotterdam because his girlfriend at the time had liked it. A bit too overwrought for his tastes, but it filled the room and as he stared at his reflection, he was surprised to see how exhausted he looked, his long honey-colored mane falling unchecked to his shoulders, his eyes bloodshot. But he also saw something else staring back: doubt, hesitation, the look of indecision. Something of the prey, he thought, rather than the hunter. Well, we'll have to change that. His smartphone buzzed again. "Chase just got picked up by some federal prosecutor named Munir. They're questioning him as we speak. I think it's pretty fair to assume that good ol' Harold is giving up the SoCal Medical Mafia."

"What's their next move?"

"Standard federal procedure would be to charge Girard, but they'll probably wait until they can convene a grand jury and get their ducks in order." Blood was now pumping through Manser's temples. He lifted a rough Gauloise from a Russian gilt cloisonné case and stuck it between his lips, but didn't light up. "We've got to put some air between us and Girard, and quickly. Did you hear about the announcement out of Sacramento?"

"No, I've been on a jet all day."

"The governor's scheduled a press conference later tonight so he can tell the whole world that his single-payer program is in deep shit and that he's suspending payments to all providers for the next ninety days. They'll get chits instead, which are supposed to be redeemable at a later date. But he won't say when."

Eberstein's shoulders sagged. "Wow, okay . . . well that's that. I'll tell Simpson to revoke our offer to Hurston. They were scheduled to vote on it tonight, but this will shut—"

"Oh, for crying out loud, Dieter, don't be such a fuckwit. Of course we're moving ahead with the deal. GavinAid's failure will put a dagger in California's single-payer experiment. There won't be a politician within a mile of that Dumpster fire. Have you seen the latest after-hours trading on the for-profit insurance companies? Their stocks are skyrocketing. Private medicine is back, my friend, and we're about to own one of the largest neurosurgery practices in the Southland. I've already talked to Simpson, told her you'd get her a new offer within the hour—one that's much lower now that GavinAid has crapped out. I also need you to get on a conference call with our acquisition team in Stuttgart. I want a revised estimate on how much Hurston has in receivables, especially those sitting with the state, and I want a timeframe on how long it will take to get them paid. The feds will posture, but they're going to have to step in with a bailout. Nobody's going to let California's hospitals and doctors slide into the Pacific."

"What about Girard?"

"The state prosecutors won't move until the feds have leveraged him with what Chase gives them. They'll probably charge Girard with conspiracy, but he'll have a few days before they drop the hammer, and the locals won't do anything until the feds are finished with him. Either way, he's done practicing medicine. Maybe we can help speed things along? Find an encrypted server and email this Munir fellow everything we've got on Girard's latest trip to Mexico, and send a copy to the IRS. Should make for some interesting reading. They'll be on his doorstep before he sees a dime from the sale of his practice. In the meantime, let's get the process rolling on recruiting his replacement. How hard can it be to find a neurosurgeon who wants to live and work in Bel Air?" Manser rapidly scrolled through several photos, tapped on a color shot and showed it to Eberstein. "My source at the LAPD just texted this one—real beaut, huh? Catches just the right light."

It was a close-up of the prostitute Jasmine in a holding cell. Eberstein glanced at the photo and felt a surge of acid churning through his gut. He reached into his shirt pocket and tore off an antacid, chewing it slowly. With his other hand, he loosened the button on his shirt collar and rubbed his temples. For the first time he heard Korean K-pop sifting from a room next door. Manser must be entertaining a young guest?

"Nice," the CEO muttered, perusing another text from his police source. "The feds just sealed Harold Chase's files. That was to be expected. Hell, every coke dealer in Santa Monica had him on speed dial. I bet his prints are all over the whorehouse. And now you can bet they'll squeeze him hard for Girard and the rest of the SoCal Medical Mafia, and probably what he knows about the hookers. The man's in deep caca." Manser ground the unlit Gauloise in a fused glass ashtray, then pulled back the royal-blue curtains that kept the world at bay. Two security guards patrolled a gravel sweep that meandered north towards the beach, a pair of German shepherds straining at their leashes. "Come here," he ordered. Eberstein got up and stood next to him, warm air from a gas fireplace pawing at their legs. "Tell me what you see out there?"

Lights were everywhere. From beyond the scrub oak, muted security lamps lined the crushed stone path that circled the estate. Eberstein heard a deep bass rumble cutting through the evening sky, the *whump whump* of a giant helicopter's rotors, its running lights twinkling. The lit markings showed LAPD insignias as the copter pulled around in a tight circle, its swirling blades slicing through the clouds like butter. Watching the guards canvass the grounds, Eberstein was beginning to understand just how tense this evening was about to become. Not with the usual business of buying and selling a physician practice, but with every scheme Luca Manser could muster to protect himself from being linked to a cartel assassin who was now on the lam.

"You want to know what I see?" asked Manser. "I see the entire command structure of LAPD on high alert because two of their own got the shit kicked out of them by someone who knew what she was doing. The same person who also assaulted two young women and LAPD can't fade that type of publicity. They *won't* fade that type of publicity. They'll go old-school on her if they catch her, no Miranda, no calling-in, just a beating, maybe a bullet." Manser's thick neck twitched. "And they won't give a shit that she's a woman."

Outside the arc lights surrounding the infinity-edge pool sparkled in the thin mist. The direction of the breeze shifted subtly, bringing with it the fresh scent of wet scrub pine nested against a razor-wire fence. Heavily-armed security guards, former German *Kommando Spezialkräfte*, KSK, Special-Forces from Berlin, patrolled the entrance north of the main guesthouse, not bothering to conceal their Heckler & Koch MP5 submachine guns, a couple of older hands carrying contraband AK-47s with banana clips. Strolling past the window, one of the guards squinted through the tinted glass, and Eberstein felt a vague sense of uneasiness settling over him. "You said they didn't get a visual of Angel when she was in the building?" he asked.

"There was a surveillance camera in the hallway outside the bedroom door, but it was barely operable. It caught the back of her head walking down the hallway to a room. That's it."

"Tape get released yet to the media?"

"No. The crime lab is cleaning it up, but they've released a sketch. "

"And your source inside LAPD is sure of this?"

"One hundred percent."

"Then we'd better get busy." Eberstein punched several numbers into his own cellular phone, waited a few seconds, then pressed several more. "Get the team together," he said curtly into the phone. "I want a VSAT conference call in twenty minutes."

Manser was standing motionless in front of the Fragonard, rubbing his eyes, inhaling the stale overheated air warming the room. He loosened his own shirt collar, his eyes pinned to his cell phone. "They're not wasting any time," he announced. "Subpoena was sworn out ten minutes ago. I imagine they're waiting for Girard at both his home and office."

"I can get the new numbers to Simpson in about an hour. She can have the revised offer to Hurston a few minutes after that. I imagine they'll stew a bit, but given their cash flow problems, any stragglers shouldn't be too tough to convince. Should we contact the cartel about Angel?"

"Hell no!" lashed Manser. "Once we get this deal done, we're finished with those savages. I want everything burned, all the texts, records, everything."

Eberstein paused. A loud rattling noise reverberated from outside the window. The motion sensors had abruptly reacted to a heavy cloudburst and gusts that whipped through the scrub oaks. Straight ahead the silhouette of the compound's edge stood out like a grim prison, the color and thickness of steel wool backlit by swirling security lights. In the shadows, at the stone base of the guesthouse, a pair of security guards patrolled in night gear. Eberstein could see the reflections from their pump-action repeater shotguns as headlights rose up. To the southeast the road continued for fifty meters, then bent right, approaching then pulling away from the guesthouse. He watched a pair of armored SUVs come and go, the LAPD helicopter still sweeping out over the ocean, its taillights winking then fading.

A night to remember, Eberstein thought as he grabbed his overcoat and left.

CHAPTER THIRTY-THREE

"Team Leader, this is Command. Give me an update, Lute. "

The harsh voice whistling in Sergeant Luther Hurt's right eardrum was obscured by a thin rupture of the endolymphatic and perilymphatic chambers in his inner ear causing fluids in both chambers to mix, short-circuiting his hearing. To compensate, Hurt wore a flesh-colored miniature receiver that looked like a hearing aid and magnified radio traffic coming in from his lieutenant, who was commanding a squad of Los Angeles County Sheriff's Department, LASD, Emergency Operations officers from a Forward Command Post, FCP, on the rooftop of a nearby art gallery. Their "target" was a few blocks off Persian Square in LA's Westwood area.

The once thriving neighborhood was a patchwork of empty storefronts and overpriced office spaces scattered among the more affluent retail shops that surrounded UCLA. It was a perfect location for tonight's practice drill.

"Talk to me, Lute," the lieutenant's voice commanded in Hurt's earbud.

"Nothing to report," Hurt answered tightly, "other than it's goddamn wet out here. Suspect hasn't come our way."

"You're sure of that?"

"Yes . . . positive."

"Alright, we've screwed around long enough. Time to saddle up. You'll breach in sixty seconds. Wait for my call."

Hurt held up all five fingers to his eight-man counterterrorist team, carefully leaning his aching back against the boarded-up "Iranian ice house." He had no intention of waiting for his lieutenant's call. This entire drill had devolved into one giant cluster-fuck with the FCP gung-ho about rolling out its latest toy in bad weather, a militarized Typhoon K Hexacopter that required five LASD technicians to deploy on the gallery roof. *Five!* They looked like a bunch of pimply-faced college rejects playing video games and mainlining Dew and Skittles. In a live-fire situation involving real terrorists, getting five techies to the scene in rainy LA traffic would take a couple of hours at least.

His team had finished positioning a pair of 400-watt wobble lights around the back entrance of the ice house. Pressing the barrel of his sawed-off shotgun against the doorjamb, in marked contrast to the ripped young commandos behind him, Hurt, age 42, was short, compact, with a thick torso and bulging stomach. His weathered face stretched into a long, sloping forehead that led to a receding hairline dotted with curly iron-gray hair. But there was more to the man than fading physical prowess. Hurt had once been a veteran street deputy with a quiet sense of strength, both mental and physical. Not much had changed over the years.

Flicking aside a persistent drip of water, he muttered, "To hell with it," and pulled a few extra shotgun shells from his vest pocket. There was a moment of stillness before he clenched his right fist. "On my count . . . four . . . three . . . two . . ."

"Wait!" ordered one of his team members. His Warlock had suddenly activated. The Warlock was used to jam radio frequencies employed to detonate IEDs, Improvised Explosive Devices. "I got one, sergeant," the commando radioed. "Two meters to your left near the roll-off trash container, an explosive device buried beneath a pile of garbage bags."

"Two more outside the hinges of the door," reported a sniper in Hurt's earbud. The shooter was using an infrared rifle scope designed to pick up targets at 600 meters. He'd caught telltale wires on the window next to the front door of the ice house. Hurt pulled the tiny receiver from his ear and waited for the Warlock to work its magic. "Gentlemen, are we clear?" he asked into his lip mic.

"Good to go, boss," responded the sniper.

Two operators moved forward and set a radio-controlled explosive. The pair stepped back, looking at Hurt. He nodded. A heart-stopping roar thundered through the chilly night. But Hurt barely heard it, just a chorus of guttural vibrations echoing inside his "good" cochlea as his eight operators scrambled past the roll-off trash container and through the ragged opening in the ice house created by the charge of plastiqué. Before they had breached the cage, Hurt had warned his team not to assume the frame would give just because of dry rot. "Test the locks first . . . and heads up for any secondary homemades," he'd advised.

Sadly, his warning proved prophetic.

Suddenly, three of the eight commandos came somersaulting out in a hail of damp wood fragments. *Whoa, the techno dinks went all out on that one*, admired Hurt. He'd have to let Ben know his crew had a future as bomb makers. In a real live-fire situation, Hurt's incursion team would be down three operators, giving the terrorists on the opposite side of the door that much better odds. Plus, the sight of blood created emotion—the wrong kind: fear, anger, rage.

Exactly what the terrorists wanted.

"I've got Triviers," shouted Hurt. He dropped to one knee, cradling his sawed-off Merkel, and lifted one of the "wounded" operators by his tactical vest. The young deputy sheriff was covered in metallic red paint. Hurt dragged him to the lip of a gutter. "Command, we've encountered multiple IEDs and I've got three down, five inside," Hurt reported into the lip mic. "I need medics, STAT." He continued to follow protocol, which required evacuating the wounded before calling in backup. Meanwhile, the neighbors observing the drill from nearby buildings remained fascinated as another faux explosive lit up the dreary night, disgorging wafts of black smoke from the shattered crawl space that led into a three-story warehouse.

The security alarm was still blaring when what was left of Hurt's team entered the red-brick basement. Making their way swiftly to the target area, a spacious storeroom in the back of a loading dock, they began clearing the area with purpose, ignoring rows of brand-new radial tires stacked high against the water-stained walls and moving in a coordinated manner, smashing their way through an interior hollow core door that led to a second storeroom packed with dozens of mannequins and cardboard boxes full of women's lingerie. Each box had been marked with the quantity and date in Farsi so the seller could ship directly to Tehran for payment in euros.

The entire haul had been confiscated from a Sunni drug trafficker with diplomatic immunity operating out of the Iranian consulate. And while they couldn't hold the trafficker, they could confiscate his stash until the Iranians admitted ownership and coughed up the full amount for duties and taxes, which wasn't going to happen in this lifetime.

"Sergeant, you're gonna want to see this!" shouted one of the officers. He was standing over a huge cast-iron cistern that funneled precious rainwater through pipes from the roof. Carefully lifting the circular steel lid, Hurt shone a bright Maglite on several strands of torn fabric. He circled the beam twice and saw nothing but pitch blackness. Swearing softly, he radioed. "Premise has been breached. Our suspects have packed off. Secure the crime scene, note the time, this drill is now concluded."

Their "terrorist" cell—in real life, three hyperactive probationary cadets—had slipped out of the cistern and crawled on all fours through fetid sewers before climbing up and out through a manhole near the Ronald Reagan UCLA Medical Center along Le Conte Avenue. Hurt figured there would be hell to pay for the team in charge of perimeter security, but that was somebody else's problem. He retraced his steps out of the warehouse and reached the pavement just in time to see a KCAL 9 News van arrive. Apparently even a disaster drill is worthy of late-night news coverage. Hurt covered his head from the rain and slipped between a pair of SUVs, pretending not to hear the reporter's frantic shouting. He glanced left, then right, before hurrying across the traffic, making sure to keep the parked vehicles between him and the van before disappearing into an underground parking garage, the deafening bursts from nearby sirens rattling off the garage's dank cement walls.

Confident his team had passed its portion of the drill, Hurt unlocked the front door of his black 2011 Mercedes E320 and put both hands in the small of his back, stretching. He was wet and tired, having been up since six that morning. He unstrapped his tactical vest and tossed it into the back seat, then reached for a pack of Chesterfields on the dashboard and tapped one out.

For a few seconds he gazed at the thin white cigarette, feeling guilty about his latest failure to quit, then shrugged it off and lit up. Closing his eyes, inhaling deeply, he thought about a cold beer and the Liga MX *fútbol* replay streaming on ESPN and was about to turn the ignition when his personal satellite phone buzzed.

"Sorry, closed for the evening, call back some other time," he whispered.

Stubborn, willful, and utterly contemptuous of modern technology, Hurt let the phone buzz for several seconds while pulling a few more drags on his Chesterfield, trying to unwind.

But the phone refused to cooperate.

"Who the hell could this be," he grunted, angrily flipping a two-volt switch beneath the steering column. The security latch to the glove compartment released and he pulled out an encrypted satphone—used so the public couldn't monitor LASD channels—and glowered at it like he might crush it under his left rear tire.

But that wasn't possible because it had been assigned to him personally, so he entered his access code and waited for the Receive light to flash green. Then he tapped in his personal ID code and held the phone to his good ear.

"Luther? Hey, Lute, is that you, big fella?" The muddled voice on the other end was a familiar one.

Hurt turned up the volume. "What do you want, Charlie?"

"How'd the drill go?" asked his partner.

"Minor disaster, but thankfully it's over."

"Sorry to hear that. Hey, we just got a call from the feds."

Hurt felt a fingertip burn. Startled, he snubbed out his cigarette in the ashtray. "What do they want?"

"For us to go sit on some neurosurgeon at Santa Monica Memorial until they can get their people over there . . . his name is Dr. Ernie Girard. Right now he's in emergency surgery. We're supposed to wait there until he finishes."

"Sounds like some limp-ass dog and pony show to me. Why can't LAPD handle it? I'm fried, man. I've been up since six."

"This came directly from the U.S. attorney's office. They don't want LAPD involved because Girard owned a whorehouse where there was an incident this evening. LAPD nearly leveled the place. Two of their officers got sent to the hospital with their faces kicked in by some chick. Feds think LAPD is too jacked up right now and might do Girard some harm. U.S. attorney doesn't want the locals screwing up a big case he's got goin' against the doctor."

Hurt tossed the Chesterfield out the window and rubbed his hands over his weary eyes, whispering, "Fuck me."

There was silence at the other end of the radio. "Was that an offer, big boy? Sorry, but you're not my type. You don't cuddle enough."

"Oh, for the love of . . . one of these days, Charlie, I'm gonna put a bullet in your nut sack."

More silence. "And you suck at pillow talk, too. I'll be there in twenty minutes."

CHAPTER THIRTY-FOUR

"Luca, what on earth are you doing? Those are *my* fees you're giving away!" Stephanie Simpson bobbed through the solid pine door connecting Luca Manser's study to his American Indian Room, a syrupy, cotton-candy K-pop tune wafting behind her.

Manser's face twisted into a sour, dyspeptic look. "Dear Lord, what is that noise?"

"The new NCT Dream. The kids can't get enough of it. It's trending on Spotify."

"I didn't understand a word you just said."

"My point exactly—a girl's gotta stay relevant. Nobody wants to become an old fossil." Winking, she congaed over to his hand-carved desk and swayed beside him. "This band is ridiculously hot in Europe and on both coasts in the U.S. We have a client in New York who's trying to bundle them into a massive new label, go after the Asian markets." She leaned forward, peeking over his shoulder, a steady patter of rain drumming on the windowpane behind them. "So I'm just supposed to sit tight and wait for Dieter to call with your latest offer?"

"That's about it. And expect a much lower bid given GavinAid's impending meltdown. To our wondrous good luck, it appears to be bargain basement day on neurosurgeons. Pity that Dieter doesn't know how close you really are. He could just walk the offer over."

After his meeting with Manser, Dieter Eberstein had taken up shop in the lavish guest house hidden behind a thick boxwood hedge twenty meters east of the main house. He was busy preparing the revised offer for Hurston Neurological.

Swinging her body to the sugary boy band beat, humming softly, Simpson obsessively checked her cell phone every few seconds. "Looks like Hurston's partners have pushed back their meeting by an hour," she reported, scrolling through texts. "They're waiting on Girard. He's in emergency surgery."

Manser turned. "Do they have a quorum without him?"

She texted Rory Armstead, who was sitting in on the meeting. His answer came back almost immediately. "Yes, all the owners are there except Girard."

"Excellent. Given the impending fallout from GavinAid, I'm sure Armstead can explain the new financial realities to his doctors, draw 'em a picture so to speak."

But Simpson was barely listening, flowing to the latest NCT track. "No doubt," she said breezily. "The man's a bit of a straight arrow, but he's sharp when it comes to numbers. I don't imagine it'll be too tough explaining how the practice is gonna start hemorrhaging cash like an open wound and how no bank in its right mind would touch 'em with a ten-foot pole. I wouldn't be surprised if the vote was unanimous."

"Perfect. When you talk to Dieter, tell him we can use the cash we're saving on the new discounted price to prop up the practice until we can flip it with our other hospitals to—"

"Luca!" she screeched. "You're not listening to me. Those are my fees you're chopping to bits." The boy band faded, the moment lost. "I've got partners to answer to."

"And what if I decide to use your firm on the Regent deal? Three hospitals and Hurston for $1.1 billion. Would that interest your *partners*? Or would they rather quibble over eight percent of $70 million versus the same cut on $1.1 billion?"

A peppy new track kicked in, the beat simple, hypnotic. Simpson's mood brightened. Shimmying again, her blue eyes blazing away, she thumbed out a text to her senior partner: "Good news, one deal countered and a huge new one in the pipeline." It would be the firm's biggest deal ever, and she would be lead rainmaker on it. "Let's see how the boys like that," she muttered, admiring herself in Manser's inlaid silver mirror. Her cell phone trilled. Caller ID showed Dieter Eberstein. She opened the short text, raised an eyebrow, then tapped back her response. The new bid was considerably lower, but there was wiggle room. Armstead would have to find the right number and deliver his docs.

My God, this could actually work.

A fresh salvo of raindrops splattered against the windowpane. Harbor lights strobed against the surging tides. Adrenaline pumped through Simpson's veins like electric current.

The rush of the deal, she thought. It was better than sex.

Dreamily, she waved at Manser, lost in her music, the tunes upbeat, carefree. He shook a bottle of Glenfiddich, offering, but she refused. Nothing but espresso tonight. She had to keep a clear mind and strong nerves. They were almost home.

God bless GavinAid.

•　　　•　　　•

Angel certainly didn't feel like dancing. The rain had started up again.

Soaking wet, she paused under a coast live oak, pretending to cover her head with a sopping newspaper stolen from a nearby yard. Her black Fiat was about fifty meters south, and she had been strolling around an empty high school and its surrounding neighborhood for the last two hours, her eyes sweeping everything.

The neighborhood felt safe. There were very few pedestrians out in the rain. No CCTV or static cameras, just rows of tiny lawns encased in thick hedges with the occasional palm tree or two. More importantly, no one appeared interested in her. She spotted a few lights on in the widows, but there was no rustling of curtains, no sense of being watched.

Moving to stay warm, she approached the Fiat, ducking slightly as an LAPD squad car rounded the corner and zipped past her. It was perhaps at that point, with the sirens wailing, that she made her decision. She was quite sure the two prostitutes had given the police a detailed description of her, including the fact that she was looking for Harold Chase—who was probably swarming with LAPD now. She was also quite certain that it wouldn't take long for the investigators to realize that she was a professional, the way she'd manhandled their colleagues. So she had a choice—either keep hunting for Chase or get out of the country?

An LAPD crime scene van splashed through the intersection, followed by a blue-and-white TV satellite news truck. Angel watched both vehicles turn left and head in the direction of the whorehouse. Others wouldn't be far behind.

Time to move . . . right now.

She unlocked the driver's side door and crawled into the front seat of the Fiat as a burst of rain slapped against the windshield. As she ran her left hand beneath the driver's seat, her fingers touched the sleeve of a turtleneck sweater wrapped around a small leather "run" bag. She pulled out the bag and unfolded the sweater. Then she kicked off her suede shoes, stripped off her red tannin cowl neck, and stretched the Shetland wool sweater over her head. Reaching under the passenger's seat, she pulled out a pair of denim jeans wrapped tight in a reversible T-buckle belt. She lifted up her back and buttocks and twisted out of her damp malin pants, then squeezed into the jeans and cinched the belt. Next, a thin wallet full of Mexican pesos and a VISA card went from the run bag into her right front pocket, the name on the credit card matching a false U.S. passport that was also in the bag. Dressed, she lifted her head above the steering wheel and let her eyes sweep the block. It was clean. Sifting through the pockets of her wet clothes, she removed a wad of fifties and for a brief moment toyed with the idea of driving straight south; she could be in Tijuana in four hours, from there a bus ride to Ascensión. But the thought was crass, panicky, so she pushed it out of her head. If she wanted to get home to Duque and Cheché and the safe house in Juárez, it would be the long hard route through LAX, Puerto Vallarta, and an endless bus ride north through Durango and Chihuahua, losing herself in the crowds, checking her back every step of the way.

The final touch was a gray nylon windbreaker and a Red Stripe baseball cap. Sitting up straight, she inspected herself in the rearview mirror: Not perfect, but acceptable. She twisted the ignition and the engine turned over smoothly. Cautiously she nosed the Fiat into traffic, taking a moment to let her eyes adjust, wipers flicking rainwater back and forth.

The neighborhood passed slowly as she searched for an on-ramp to the freeway. Her mind wandered to her cats. She hoped Cheché's original owner—the bookish young teenager who had returned from Janos to study at the Loretto Academy in El Paso—was enjoying the condo and not letting her spoiled felines run roughshod over the place.

The thought brought a smile to her face, her sense of defeat starting to evaporate. The task ahead took on a complexity that kick-started the hypervigilance she had come to depend on, even crave. *Just follow your training and avoid mistakes,* she reminded herself. *With good tradecraft you'll have four, maybe five days.*

After that, the cartel will come after you.

CHAPTER THIRTY-FIVE

Dr. Ernie Girard was standing beside Marcus Robinson in the ICU. He tugged off his scrub cap and tossed it into a trash receptacle. It was nearly ten o'clock in the evening and Marcus lay partially reclined, catheters and drips circling under his coverlets, a nurse rehanging an IV bag.

Surgery had been quick and not overly complicated. Once Girard had found the exact location of the bleed, he had drilled a small hole in Marcus's skull and drained the hematoma. Given the boy's age and good health, he would recover quickly which was a relief.

As he scrolled through his text messages, all twenty-one of them, the muscles around Girard's jaw clenched and his blood pressure percolated. The Hurston partners' meeting had been over for an hour and his panicky colleagues had voted unanimously to sell the practice to DAI for $59 million. "Bastard krauts," he grumbled, "took us to the cleaners." But his partners were running scared, the GavinAid meltdown striking the fear of God into them. The Germans had simply been shrewd enough to take advantage. *Still, what's done is done,* Girard told himself, *just try to make the best of it.* His share would pencil out to about $8.5 million, which would cover a multitude of sins.

One of the monitors abruptly reacted and an ICU nurse slid past him to reset it. To concentrate his mind, Girard reread his most recent text from Rory Armstead indicating that the final documents would be signed and notarized in the next hour, but leaving no mention as to why his signature wouldn't be needed.

That's odd, he thought. Standing beside Marcus, he felt a flutter of panic in his gut.

The critical care nurse finished checking Marcus's bag and Girard gave her a dog-tired look, noticing a slight tremor in his right hand. His pulse was racing, his heart skipping a beat every fifteen seconds or so, its rhythm irregular. Dehydrated. He suddenly wondered why there were no congratulations texts from his partners.

He thumbed a message to Aran Dvir, but got no response. The same thing happened when he tried three other partners. *Something's not right.* He texted Stephanie Simpson, but it bounced back as undeliverable. Scanning his own list of messages, he spotted a recent text from Juanita Reno: "LAPD picked up Harold Chase. He is being questioned about an assault on two police officers." Girard stood motionless, eyes wide, face twitching.

If Chase rolled over, he was totally screwed.

"There you are. I heard surgery went well. How's the boy holding up?" Dr. Vihaan Jurani strolled cockily into the room and pulled up Marcus's medical records on the bedside laptop. Seething, Girard kept his eyes straight ahead. "Good of you to make it, Vihaan," he acknowledged, his tone sharp. "Say, I could use your help on something."

"Sure," offered the thirty-three-year-old Jurani, tapping in an order. "What's up?"

Jurani inched closer to the LED lights, his head almost touching the patient lift. He had a lean sculpted look, almost ascetic, if not for his heightened level of wariness. The young physician had a reputation as a talented trauma doc, but his love of money and a pile of medical school debt had turned him into the house hustler, racking up shift after shift even if it meant working seventy-two hours straight.

Girard spent a moment inspecting Marcus's vital signs. "Here's my problem, Vihaan," he began, turning to face Jurani, a cold fire in his eyes. "I need one very good reason why I shouldn't report you to the medical staff. This child was admitted to your ER over three and a half hours ago and this is the first time you've laid eyes on him. Does that in any way sound like acceptable medical practice to you?"

Jurani offered a nervous grin but kept scanning Marcus's electronic records, feigning interest. "Come on, Ernie, Kalekas had it covered—"

"Fuck Kalekas! He's up to his eyeballs in shit for lying on the medical record. So I wouldn't put a whole lot of stock in him having your back—so, *again*, give me one good reason why I shouldn't report you."

"Are you serious . . . really? Because that's rich coming from you given the way you respond to our calls. We're lucky if we ever get to talk to you the way your PA triages every text we send. It's a joke."

Girard didn't flinch. "But we're not talking about me . . . are we?"

"Maybe we should be," Jurani threatened.

A shimmer of arrogance appeared on Girard's face. "Vihaan, if you think you've got the horses for that, be my guest. But you're the primary intake physician tonight, so how big a woody do you think administration is gonna get if they find out their ER was uncovered for three hours? This hospital could lose its license, and I'd damn sure not count on Kalekas to cover your ass. He's got his own medical staff privileges to worry about."

For a considerable time neither spoke. Jurani apparently realized he had a serious problem and backed off, deflated, shoulders slumping. His worried eyes skittered across the ICU floor. He let a couple more seconds pass before looking at Marcus. "I'm glad he's doing okay," he said quietly. "And there's no need to bring medical staff into this. I was sleeping one off in the ortho casting room. I'd worked back-to-backs plus my own shift so I could spend a week in Kauai with my brother-in-law next month. He's wrangled a tee time on Ocean Course at Hokuala. It's taken me four months to work a date into my schedule. So how about a break this time, Ernie. Let it go."

"Once again, *why?*—Give me one good reason, and golfing doesn't cut it."

Jurani hesitated, tapping his class ring on an oxygen tank. "Okay, how about two sheriff's sergeants are waiting downstairs in the main lobby. They want to talk to you. The night supervisor told me she was putting them off until you finished surgery."

Girard froze, staring at Jurani. "Did they say what they wanted?"

"They weren't very outgoing. Rather pissed that the night supervisor wouldn't let 'em upstairs to the ICU waiting lounge. What kind of trouble are you in, Ernie?"

But Girard wasn't listening. His adrenalin was cycling too fast, his hands visibly shaking. He took a deep breath, exhaled, a cold sweat working its way down the small of his back. "How long have they been downstairs?"

"Less than an hour. The supervisor said she'd let them know when you were finished."

Marcus Robinson started to squirm. An ICU nurse hovered nearby, pretending to be busy. She checked his IV bags as Girard's smartphone buzzed. Caller ID said it was MaryAnn Taylor.

"Talk to me," Girard growled. And she did for several minutes while his eyes screwed tight, his jaw clenching again. "They've still got Harold?" he asked, his body sagging from the tension. "I see. Well, that doesn't sound very promising. I'll have to call you back in a few minutes."

What Taylor had described was two LAPD detectives showing up at Hurston's Bel Air office wanting to interrogate Girard about his ownership of an illicit whorehouse that had been raided earlier that evening. In addition, an assistant U.S. attorney had called wanting to question Dr. Ernie about conspiracy charges concerning his involvement with the SoCal Medical Mafia, and there was a notice from his malpractice carrier, Physicians Liability Corporation of California, cancelling his policy effective immediately.

And there was more.

Having been informed about each of these debacles, his practice partners had voted to expel him from the group, no doubt trying to cut him out of the DAI deal, and Taylor had received a call from an IRS agent demanding a sit-down with Girard to discuss anonymous charges of unreported cash being laundered through a pair of Mexican banks.

Girard gazed down at his cell phone, the tiny hairs on the back of his neck bristling. He closed his eyes for a split second and felt a sudden tilt deep inside. Psychiatrists call it denial, or disassociation, a sense of detachment from oneself, and a lesser person might've buckled under this avalanche of shit. But Dr. Ernie Girard was a true force of nature—a man who made his own weather. He rotated his neck, clearing his mind. Despite everything that had been dumped on him, a plan was taking shape, gaining weight and momentum.

He entered a final note in Marcus's electronic medical records and gently clasped the boy's left hand. "Son, can you hear me?" Marcus's grip tightened. "Your grandmother will be discharged tomorrow morning. She'll be up here to look after you, so I want you to try and relax and get some sleep. I've got to go." Girard turned to Jurani. "I need you to make sure they don't discharge him early. Four days should be more than enough time—and help his grandma line up some home health care. Do that, Vihaan, and we'll call it even."

Jurani nodded. "Thanks. I won't let them send him home without my signature."

"Fair enough," said Girard, running a restive eye over Marcus. Swirling at the edges of his mind were what to do next and in what order. He punched in the number for Rory Armstead's private cell phone, his focus sharpening. The accountant answered on the third buzz. Girard chose his words carefully. "Hello, Rory. Quite a night you folks have had. It's my understanding that my gutless partners took a vote without my presence this evening." Girard listened while Armstead explained what had happened. He shut his eyes, feeling a tourniquet closing around his chest, squeezing each breath. He sucked in a gulp of air, controlling his temper. "Which of my Judas-assed partners made that motion?"

Armstead gave him a name and Girard swore under his breath. "Bastard, I should've seen that one coming. Prick's got the hand-eye coordination of a J-1 chiropractor. Would any of them like to speak to me face-to-face?" Armstead responded vaguely while Girard fingered the gold Saint Christopher's medal around his neck. A nurse stuck her head into the room and Jurani gave her a sharp look. She retreated quickly. "No . . . no need to wrestle any of them to the phone," sneered Girard. "But, Rory, I want you to listen to me very carefully. I have a proposal to make, and you're gonna have to keep my spineless ex-partners in the conference room for another hour so they can hear me out. What? Don't bullshit me. I know they're still there signing papers. I just need them to listen to my proposal. They can either hear what I have to say, or I'll file an injunction on the DAI deal and tie it up in court for years. And we both know Hurston can't handle the blowback to its cash flow. Do you have a pen?—well get one, and yes, I'm dead serious. I'll call you back in forty-five minutes. Just keep those fucksacks in the room. Oh, and Rory, I want to know exactly how much liquidity Hurston has down to the last penny. Including that secret slush fund you've been hiding off the books." There were a few seconds of silence. "You didn't think I could read a balance sheet, did you? Come on, Rory, you're better than that. I'll you call back in forty-five minutes. Have the cash amount ready for me by then." Girard pressed End.

He tamped down an adrenaline rush as a wave of light-headedness washed over him. The ICU seemed almost noiseless, just the occasional beep from a monitor. Jurani was standing perfectly still, mouth agape. Marcus's brown eyes had widened, a tiny smirk inching its way across his lips. "You bad, dog," the child whispered.

Girard stepped closer to him. "I've got some good news," he said playfully. "We took a peek inside your skull and there's actually a brain in there after all."

Marcus's smile stretched across his entire face. "That'll make grandma proud. She always said I had no sense."

Girard nodded. "Marcus, it might be a while before we see each other again, but I'm going to send you a package. Open it with your grandmother and be smart about it and, son, make something of your life. Will you do that for me?"

Marcus's large eyes fixed on Girard's. "No problem, but what's up? Where are you going?"

Girard fixed him with a mirthless grin. "A vacation, Marcus . . . a very long vacation."

CHAPTER THIRTY-SIX

Great pillars of clouds hung thick over LAX as a black-and-white LAPD Eurocopter peeled off in a wide arc towards the 405, its searchlights pinwheeling. It was nearly midnight, and Angel was worried that the Eurocopter might be tailing her. But that was the paranoia talking. If the cops really did have a bead on her, they would be swarming with squad cars by now.

She nursed her way down West Century Boulevard, passing block after block of airport hotels, fast food restaurants, and boxy office buildings. Even at this hour traffic was stop-and-go, the lights never quite synchronized. Nearing one of the chain hotels, she pulled off into an empty space outside a covered self-parking garage and turned off her headlights. Sitting silent for a few minutes, pretending to check her cell phone, she made a quick visual of the front of the hotel, her eyes zeroing in on an off-duty shuttle bus. It was nothing out of the ordinary, so she restarted the Fiat and looped around the half-circle entryway and back onto West Century Boulevard, U-turning into an all-night Taco Bell across the street.

Again she killed the engine and sat fussing with her phone, scanning her rear and side view mirrors. Her objective was simple: throw off any surveillance but don't make it look intentional. A jet roared overhead. The rain had abruptly stopped, ocean breezes gently whipping the palm trees in the parking lot. She twisted the Fiat's defrost to high and waited.

Now confident she wasn't being tailed, she circled wide of the Taco Bell drive-through and re-crossed West Century back into the hotel lot, cautiously navigating her way past the main entrance. She eased the Fiat to the front of the self-parking security arm. As she waited for the machine to disgorge a ticket, engine idling, her eyes darted back and forth to the mirrors. Spotting nothing unusual, she accelerated up the ramp to the fourth floor and pulled into a tight space between a GMC Sierra 1500 pickup and a pine green Ford Expedition.

She killed the engine, pulled out her cotton handkerchief, and began wiping down the Fiat's interior, paying special attention to the steering wheel and ignition area. Satisfied, she grabbed her run bag, locked the car door, and stepped out of the Fiat. Pausing, she bent her knees and stooped towards the pavement as if she had dropped something. It took less than ten seconds to locate both fisheye security cameras: two static 720p models with night-vision LED tucked under low-hanging vents in opposite corners of the ceiling. Pulling the bill of her Red Stripe cap lower over her forehead, she pivoted away from the nearest camera and quickly wiped down the door handle. With her face angled downward, she began walking towards a bank of elevators. Fortunately, several of the security lamps inside the garage had been busted out, and her features were blurred by shadows. Standing in front of the elevators, staring at her shoes, she pressed the button for the lobby and waited.

At this time of night, probably only one or two of the elevators were running, but she had no intention of getting on either. The vast majority of public parking garage elevators had security cameras mounted inside the cabs. Lifting her heels up-and-down like a woman in a hurry, she counted to three then abruptly crashed through the Exit door and hustled down a concrete staircase that smelled of disinfectant and weed. On the second floor, her car keys and parking ticket went into a locked trash container. She stuffed her baseball cap into the run bag, zipped the windbreaker up to her chin, and paused on the first floor to inspect her reflection off a glassed poster advertising the hotel's spa package.

Given the night she'd had, all-in-all not too bad, she thought, smoothing her jet-black hair. She decided to loosen the zipper on the jacket to let more of her turtleneck show, then ran her hands down the legs of her jeans, checking for water stains. They were clean.

She popped the security bar and the heavy metal door sprang open. She stepped out into a pair of smoked glass globes: security cameras covering the elevator bank.

Shit . . . nothing you can do about it, keep moving.

She strode into the lobby. On her right was an empty Starbucks kiosk next to a car rental booth. Near the front entrance a bored valet lounged behind the concierge desk, his face stuck in his cell phone. Twenty meters away on the opposite side of the lobby was a granite-top reception area flanked by two glass display cases flogging expensive sunglasses and jeweled wristwatches. Behind the reception desk stood a rail-thin employee, his cheeks flecked with acne, checking in an elderly Japanese couple.

Angel nodded to both guests as they rolled their Proteca luggage past her on their way to the elevators. Taking a few quick strides towards the reception area, she stood by the granite counter and politely asked, "Do you have a business center? I must've left my cell phone upstairs in my room."

The youngish twenty-something was dressed in a gold-and-black jacket and pressed slacks and instinctively pushed his square-framed hipster glasses up onto his nose before pointing to a small alcove next to the closed gift shop. Angel spotted two laptop computers. Both looked like fifteen-inch Dells, probably used for email and boarding passes.

She thanked the agent, relaxed a bit, then threaded her way past a sprawling gas fire pit, newspapers and lifestyle magazines flung about its flagstone base. She almost tripped over an empty luggage cart before sliding into a seat in front of the keyboard. The laptop was a Dell Inspiron 7000, and it took her less than five minutes to book a mid-morning Delta flight directly into Puerto Vallarta from LAX, buying a round-trip ticket using her VISA card, even though she had no intention of using the return segment. Purchasing a one-way ticket less than twenty-fours before departure almost guaranteed being flagged by Homeland Security, something she would rather avoid.

Now her problem was where to stay for the next eight hours. Checking into the hotel even with her false ID was out of the question. The skinny dweeb at the front desk would certainly remember her face and clothing. So it was time to improvise.

Fortunately, luck was with her.

When the hotel's electronic front doors whooshed open, a damp wind feathered Angel's hair. As she pushed the strands out of her face, a thickset man in his late thirties breezed through the hotel's front entrance with a mild look of disappointment on his face. He was alone, and Angel easily tagged him as a visiting businessman. Not overly dressed in dark khakis and gray sport coat, he had trim curly brown hair and a deliberate economy of movement that marked him as a former athlete of some kind. But there was something else: a certain vibe, a sort of desperation, along with a pair of eager brown eyes that seemed to be searching too hard, too restlessly. A night on Sunset Boulevard not all it was cracked up to be? wondered Angel.

Surveying the lobby, the businessman decided on a seat near the fire pit, where he perused a copy of last week's *LA Vibe*. The stern face of Governor Gavin Newsom glared from its cover under the bold headline *Single-Payer: The Rise and Fall of the Gavinator*. Andy Crowder's byline was near the bottom of the cover. As Angel studied the skittish businessman and caught a glimpse of naughtiness in his wandering eyes, an idea came to her.

She memorized her airline confirmation number, cleared the computer's browsing history, then switched seats to the opposite laptop, idly surfing the *New York Times* and *Washington Post,* waiting for the desk agent to abandon his post. When the youngster finally got up to carry a FedEx package to the back, Angel checked the valet—still engrossed in his cell phone—and drifted over to the fire pit, letting slip a catty remark about Governor Newsom's handsome profile. The businessman looked up with a cautious smile, probably wary of the come-ons from the Sunset hustlers working the streets, but there it was, that intimate look of hope: warm and relaxed, almost a relief. Sensing an opportunity, she sidled next to him and saucily noted a slight flaw in the Governor's necktie. The businessmen's eyes blinked owlishly. She made another off-handed joke then seconds pooled into minutes as they talked, both pretending to be interested in the article on Newsom. Finally, Angel proposed a nightcap.

Her new friend accepted.

Audacity works wonders, she reminded herself, suggesting the businessman lead the way.

As she trailed him, she noted the desk agent hadn't returned from the back room and the valet was still thumbing his cell phone. A sly smirk worked its way across her face as the businessman guided her towards a neon *Dos Equis* sign, a sense of relief flooding her body.

She wouldn't be sleeping in the cold after all.

●   ●   ●

But it looked as if Senior Investigator Blas Mondragon might be.

He had found a parking spot behind an off-duty airport shuttle van that gave him a direct view of the hotel's front entrance and an open sightline to the garage exit from the Ford Escape's rearview mirror. It was decision time. He had been sitting outside the hotel for twenty minutes, having tailed his suspect, Maria Gomez, across a goodly portion of West Los Angeles to this high-rise hotel near LAX. Even though Gomez seemed to be in a hurry, her tradecraft had been precise, her driving technique first-rate. Using well-schooled anti-surveillance maneuvers and constant snap checks, she had forced Mondragon to keep his distance. But Blas had managed to stay undetected, and right now his prey was either huddled inside her black Fiat somewhere in the parking garage or in the hotel.

Somehow, Mondragon doubted Gomez had hunkered down in the garage. Far too much foot traffic, plus there were surveillance cameras on every floor. And she would definitely feel trapped. No, he was fairly certain his *asesina* had taken a room inside the hotel somewhere or burrowed into a utility closet or empty conference room. Instinctively, he patted his right pectoral where his Beretta automatic was usually holstered under his armpit. But the gun was locked in a safe at home in Juárez, replaced by a nagging sense of vulnerability.

For the first time that evening, a thin layer of marine fog had crept in from the ocean, muting the bright lights along West Century Boulevard. Not the omen he was looking for. The dull ache in his head had turned into a steady throb that was spreading behind his eyes. His fingers curled tight around the steering wheel. He was running out of time. He checked both his side and rearview mirrors, eyeballing the front of the garage—there was no movement. Directly behind him was the automatic ticket booth. Parked in an adjacent driveway sat a yellow-and-red plumber's van, a Honda Ridgeline, and a silver Kia Soul. The night shift, he assumed. He opened the SUV door, locked it, and immediately felt a cold shiver spread up and down his body.

Having tossed the hoodie and Army surplus jacket into the Escape's back seat, he was wearing only a threadbare houndstooth sport coat and corduroy slacks. A helicopter came in low over the power lines, circling the block before veering off towards the ocean, the laconic thrum of its rotors eventually lost in the mist. The evening traffic was thinning, but Mondragon could still hear the revving of car engines as they downshifted, tires hissing on wet asphalt.

"Snap out of it," he muttered under his breath, making a deliberate effort to shake himself. This intense feeling of isolation had morphed into a dark melancholy that seemed to linger over him like a thick, black cloud. Worse, he couldn't shake the edgy feeling that he had gotten too far out on his own: no backup, no jurisdiction, not even a weapon, for chrissakes.

Blinking twice, he put a hand behind his neck and twisted his head from side to side, working out the soreness. Above him the wind blew a light skim of mist across a web of power lines. Mondragon watched the gleaming wires sway back and forth, his consciousness oscillating in time with their rhythm. His thoughts had begun to drift to his home, his poetry, the job. But they seemed to soothe him, the anxiety beginning to dissipate, the remoteness fading. Gazing up at the night sky, a silky half-moon had snuck in through the clouds. His eyes tracked it and he thought of how many times he had counted the stars at home. A wet breeze touched his face; he caught himself. *Stay focused, it's almost over.* If he could keep his wits about him for just a few more hours, this would be over one way or another.

He smoothed his rumpled sport coat, rubbed both hands together for warmth. A street lamp near the Taco Bell suddenly flickered off, darkening his corner of the parking lot.

An omen? he wondered, rearranging his badge and ID wallet so they could be lifted out in an instant. Or maybe he was just getting soft?

He smiled to himself, whispering a prayer to Saint Jude, patron saint of lost causes, because this was starting to feel like one.

CHAPTER THIRTY-SEVEN

Ernie Girard spoke quietly on his cell phone. His tone was warm, his mind working through logistics with the caller. After agreeing on a pickup time, he thanked the man and ended the call, then turned to Dr. Vihaan Jurani. "Please tell me you have a swipe card to the back stairwell?"

Jurani nodded. "Follow me." He escorted Girard out of the ICU and down the hallway to a barred metal door. He flashed an orange RFID key card across the frame-mounted reader, the lock clicked, and Jurani pressed the bar. "Comes out on the first floor at the rear of the gift shop. Here, you might need this to get out." He handed Girard the swipe card. "Leave it under my right rear tire when you're done. Mine's the red 4Runner parked in the CEO's spot near the front entrance. Space is never used."

"Sounds about right," said Girard. "Thanks, and make sure the kid doesn't get discharged early."

"Done. Where are you headed?"

Girard paused at the question, a shadow from an overhead fluorescent light sliding across his face. "Somewhere quiet," he said, propping the door open with his foot. "I need to get lost for a while."

●　　　　●　　　　●

Luther Hurt tossed the month-old magazine onto an armless two-seat bench and glowered at his wristwatch, feeling as if he might pull it off and throw it against the wall. "When did the supervisor say Girard would be finished?"

"Over an hour ago," answered his partner, Charlie Rangel. "The bastard's avoiding us. He knows he's in deep shit, and he's hiding upstairs like some rich jagoff waiting for his lawyer."

"What about his car?"

"You mean the Porsche Cayman in the doctor's lot? Got any idea how much fun I had booting that mother? Better than sex."

"Funny, that's what your wife says too."

Rangel laughed. "Nice. I was gonna grab you some coffee since there's a cappuccino machine in the cafeteria, but now I'm rethinking that."

Hurt checked his watch, again. "Christ, the feds really owe us for this one."

"Yeah, but what can you do. You want a coffee or not?"

"Sure, fine . . . thanks."

As Rangel pushed away from his sled-base chair, the exit door next to the gift shop cracked open an inch and Ernie Girard spotted the two sheriff's officers in the waiting area. He eased the metal door shut, leaned against the painted cement wall, and waited. His ride would be here any minute and he had to get past those officers. Thinking for a moment, he lifted his cell phone from the inside pocket of his lab coat and punched in the number for the evening supervisor. "Daliyah, it's Dr. Girard. The kid's resting fine in the ICU, and I'm done rounding for the night. Could you send the sheriff's officers up to the doctors lounge? I'll be there in a couple of minutes, and tell them I don't have all night." He ended the call and cracked the door open. Within seconds one of the officer's cell phones buzzed. The sergeant listened for a moment, then rang off and went searching for his partner in the cafeteria.

Girard buttoned his lab coat and walked quietly out the stairwell door and through the main entrance, hesitating near the valet parking stand.

Several cars back, the bright rooftop Taxi sign atop a green and white Toyota Corolla flashed twice before pulling past the valet stand and coasting up to Girard. The driver rolled down the passenger-side window. "Good evening, Doctor, miserable weather. Need a lift?"

"How's the new hip, Mr. Ambani?" asked Girard, sliding into the front seat.

"A treasure, Doctor. My life has changed dramatically. I can now wrestle with my grandchildren, walk miles with the wife, even play golf at the club that tried to blackball me once. I owe it all to you, sir."

"Nonsense, it was the right decision. I was glad to help . . . and thank you for coming."

"As you would say, 'Nonsense,' it's my honor. Where are we going tonight—LAX?"

"No, I'm afraid that some people I'd like to avoid might be watching that airport. Do you feel like a late-night drive, Jaspal?"

"At this hour, the freeways are ours."

"Then how about we set sail for Orange County airport?"

"Ah, John Wayne, the Duke. Going on a vacation, sir?"

"Caribbean. Orange County to DFW to Fort Lauderdale. From there we'll keep my final destination our secret. It's probably a long shot, but the cops or the feds may eventually want to talk to you, and as far as you're concerned you dumped me off at the Orange County airport and have no idea where I was headed. Is that too much to ask?"

"Again, nonsense, but I think we'll consider ourselves even, if that's agreeable with you?"

"Fair enough, the ledger's clean. Would you mind stopping next to that red 4Runner on the left? I need to leave something under one of the tires."

"Certainly," said Ambani, edging the cab next to the Toyota parked in front of a 24-by-18-inch scarlet sign warning *Hospital Administration Only-Violators Will Be Towed.* Girard hustled out of the cab and tucked the card key under Jurani's right rear tire, then wedged his own cell phone under the left front tire. Anyone trying to track the phone's GPS would show him at the hospital, right up until the phone got crushed.

He jumped back in the cab and buckled his seat belt. "John Wayne Airport, Mr. Ambani, but first a pit stop. It wouldn't be a road trip without Gatorade, a bag of corn nuts, and a burner phone or two."

"Whatever you say, Doctor," Ambani smirked. "I'm starting to feel young again."

•　　　•　　　•

"Where the hell is he?" demanded Luther Hurt, his voice rising.

He and Rangel were standing side-by-side, directing their frustration at the evening supervisor, a tall, willowy woman in her early fifties from Nairobi, with strong cheekbones, short toffee colored hair, and intelligent blue-gray eyes. Fourteen years of working the 11:00 p.m. to 7:00 a.m. shift meant she had seen and heard everything and wasn't about to be intimidated by either sergeant. She took a short step to her left, closed the door to the doctor's lounge, and turned to square up both sergeants. "I am *not* Dr. Girard's keeper. He called earlier and said he'd be up here in a few minutes. Said he'd just finished rounding and that his patient was resting in the ICU. He also said that he didn't have all night to chat with you two. Other than that, I don't know what to say. Now if you'll excuse me?"

"Could you call him again?" asked Rangel impatiently.

The supervisor shrugged, a prolonged, disinterested shrug before tapping Girard's number into her cell phone and waiting. There was no answer. Trying to be helpful, she called the ICU and the ER clerk, and finally the late-night valet at the front entrance.

"He did?" she repeated. "How long ago?" The supervisor covered the cell phone with her hand. "One of the kids working the valet stand said Girard left ten minutes ago in a green-and-white taxi."

"Goddamnit!" snarled Hurt. "Did he get a cab number or license plate?"

The supervisor repeated the question into the cell phone and listened to the answer, then shook her head "no."

"Crap," vented Rangel, "crap, crap, crap! The bastard had the supervisor call us up here so he could take a bounce out the front door. And he was smart to avoid the doctor's lot because he knew we'd be watching it, pretty savvy for a quack."

The longtime supervisor recoiled at the use of the q-word. "If there's nothing else, I've work to do," she said.

Hurt and Rangel looked at each other. Deprived of a next move, both nodded, but the supervisor didn't leave immediately, hanging back to eavesdrop on what kind of trouble Dr. Ernie had gotten himself into this time.

"Green and white means it's independent," said Hurt, "so there's no central dispatch we can call. Great, this is just great. He's got at least twelve minutes on us. Charlie, contact LAPD and have them put out an all-points bulletin on Girard.

He's in a cab, not a rideshare, so there's got to be a record somewhere, and get onto the lieutenant. We'll need a warrant to track his cell phones."

Rangel pulled out his smartphone. "Will do." He turned to the evening supervisor. "Hey, sorry about the attitude earlier, it's been a helluva day. Thanks for your help, and if Girard calls or returns to the hospital could you contact us immediately?" He gave her a business card. The supervisor looked at it while trying to hide a fleeting sparkle in her eyes.

"Somehow," she said under her breath, fingering the card. "I'm thinking that's not going to happen anytime soon."

•   •   •

And it wouldn't.

Heading south on the 405, with traffic flowing smoothly, Jaspal Ambani was chugging tangerine Gatorade, hip-hop music pounding on the radio. The cab smelled of corn nuts. His estimated time of arrival was slightly over an hour, which suited Dr. Ernie Girard just fine. He had a new prepaid flip phone pinned to his right ear.

"How much did you say?" Girard fired back into the black AT&T LG B470. Rory Armstead, who was on the other end of the line and seated at the head of a conference table full of anxious neurosurgeons, repeated the number. "You're sure about that, Rory? That's it?" pressed Girard. "A little over $6.2 mil . . . that's all Hurston has on hand?"

Armstead assured him that the $6.2 million was the entire amount Hurston Neurological had in its checking and sweep accounts at Inglewood National Bank. "Fine," Girard continued, "then this is how it's gonna work. I'm going to text you my resignation letter effective immediately, and I'll sign over all my partnership shares the minute I receive confirmation that the entire $6.2 million has been wired to this account number." Girard recited several numbers. "Given that you bastards owe me almost $8.5 million from my share of the DAI sale, I'd say you're getting off pretty easy."

A few minutes passed while Armstead spoke with the assembled surgeons. Ambani's head was bobbing to Young Thug. Armstead finally came back on the line; the neurosurgeons had agreed to transfer the money. Girard's skull fell back against the headrest, his fists clenched in victory. It wasn't a fortune, but it was enough. Added to his liquidated retirement account and some funds he'd stuffed offshore for a rainy day, he had enough to buy his yacht and spend the rest of his life bonefishing the Caribbean while dodging anybody who might come looking for him. It wasn't perfect, but it was damn good.

"How long before you can transfer the funds?" he asked, barely suppressing a booyah. He listened to the answer. "That'll work. Let's get this done." He abruptly ended the call, flipped the AT&T throwaway onto the carpeted floor, stomped on it several times until it shattered, then tossed the pieces out the window.

Grinning from ear-to-ear, Jaspal Ambani turned up the radio and tapped lightly on the steering wheel as he navigated his way along the fast-moving 405, Drake thumping away.

"Good news, Doctor?"

"The best, Jaspal," said Girard relieved. "The very best. Now let's get to Irvine."

CHAPTER THIRTY-EIGHT

The automatic doors opened with a soft swish. Blas Mondragon cruised through the front entrance of the hotel lobby, sneaking a quick glance to his left at the night valet, who didn't bother looking up from his cell phone.

Standing behind a long granite-topped reception area, a bored desk agent in a pair of designer eyeglasses greeted him halfheartedly before returning to his folios. Mondragon didn't see anyone else in the lobby. "Excuse me," he said. "Are you in charge tonight?"

The desk agent looked up, mildly surprised by the question. "Randy Whitmore. How can I help you, sir?"

Mondragon jacked up his posture, making a show of hitching back his shoulders. His right hand cast about his coat pockets before briskly flashing his ID across Whitmore's face. "Blas Mondragon, LAPD Airport Security Division. You're the shift supervisor?"

Whitmore looked at him dumbfounded. "I guess so," he answered warily, "until eight o'clock. But we have a manager on call if you'd rather speak to her?"

Mondragon put his ID away, knowing full well he didn't want to speak to a night manager. "No, you'll do, Randy. I'm looking for a Hispanic female in her late thirties, slender, attractive. She would have checked in during the last hour or so."

Whitmore's limpid blue eyes became more alert. "Sorry, I just came on about an hour and a half ago. The only guests I've registered were a Japanese couple, and they were both over seventy."

"What about other visitors? I'm sure you have a lounge."

"Around the corner. It's open until 2:00 a.m. Knock yourself out."

Mondragon thanked him. His eyes made a brief clockwise circuit of the lobby, homing in on a neon *Dos Equis* sign. The valet's attention had switched to a copy of the *Los Angeles Times* while Whitmore had returned to his checkout folios. Mondragon decided to give the lounge a try. At least if Gomez wasn't in there, he could get a beer before staking out the dank parking garage.

•   •   •

A shimmer of irritation flashed across Angel's face.

The new arrival's demeanor was all wrong, too attentive, watchful. His eyes had skimmed the empty lounge with its faux-Mondrian murals and pine tables and soft leather chairs, trying not to seem too interested. But she could feel his stare, and a voice in the back of her head started to howl. The man took a stool at the curved ironwood bar, using the reflection off a *Modelo Especial* mirror to monitor Angel and her businessman friend.

Something isn't right. Doubt began to seep into Angel's mind. The stranger's appearance: his scuffed shoes, frayed sport coat, posture, age, the empty eyes—it was all wrong.

The tiny hairs on the nape of her neck bristled. She risked another look, carefully studying him. No way was he LAPD. They would have blown in with a team of SWAT all Ramboed up. Ditto the feds with their black-windbreakered FBI thugs. And ICE? ICE would've simply snatched her up, flex-cuffed her ass, and dumped her across the border.

Who then?

Angel's "date" had the annoying habit of tapping his fingers on the table, talking nonstop, and loudly slurping his cocktail. The man's babbling was giving her a headache. The only way to get him to stop was to suggest they finish their drinks upstairs.

Predictably, it worked. As she stood, she flashed a final look at the stranger then followed her date past the hostess stand and out of the lounge, walking straight towards a bank of elevators. She refused to look over her shoulder to see if they were being followed.

The stranger caught the elevator just as the doors were closing, apologetically standing next to the businessman, who was oblivious to anything but Angel's cleavage and wouldn't stop talking, rambling on about an important meeting he had rescheduled so they could spend the morning together. She smiled mechanically, staring at the stranger, an instinct coming into play. There was something familiar about his mannerisms: the poised slouch, the practiced apathy, the restrained intensity that radiated off him like a beacon. She knew cops like this one in Colombia and Mexico: true believers, men who clamped down on their suspects like rabid dogs, never letting go. *"¿Qué piso quieres?"* she asked in Spanish.

The stranger looked up, appreciating the attempt but in a quiet manner said, "Sorry, I don't speak Spanish."

Angel nodded, clarifying, "What floor?"

"Nine, please," the stranger replied.

But before she could press the number, the randy businessman leaned across and swiped his key card for eleven, the concierge floor, then pressed nine.

"Puta-moron," Angel mumbled under her breath. Her idiot date had unmindfully given the stranger their floor number. The stranger gave Angel an arid smile, causing her to fix both eyes on the marble Crema Marfil tile, where they stayed until the elevator stopped with a jolt, the door easing open. *"Tenga una buena noché,* she offered, searching for a reaction.

But the stranger just shook his head, patting his pant pocket, searching for his key card.

He stepped out and the doors closed quietly behind him.

•   •   •

Blas Mondragon slid out of the elevator, muttering "good evening," and waited for the doors to shut. He hurried down the hallway, pushed through the stairwell doors, and sprinted up two flights of stairs, praying that security was lax on the concierge floor.

He was rewarded with an unlocked stairwell door and peeked out, catching the eager businessman swiping his key card to Room 1108 and ushering Gomez inside.

Mondragon waited for the room door to close, then scanned the ceiling, easily identifying the fisheye security cameras, wondering if the VIP lounge was staffed at this late hour. If it was, and he couldn't produce a room card, he was screwed.

He strode briskly down the hallway, still patting his pant pockets as if he was searching for something. Luck was with him as he strolled past the newly-refurbished VIP area, a former workout room redone with ultra-hip Scandinavian furnishings, high-backed stainless steel chairs, and an open kitchen. Thankfully it was empty, only an overenthusiastic sportscaster screeching from a massive flat-screen television mounted above the sandstone countertop.

Mondragon opened the French-door refrigerator and helped himself to a can of tonic water. He took a seat on one of the steel chairs where he could keep an eye on the elevators in case his suspect decided to bolt. He knew he had piqued Gomez's radar; she had immediately tagged him as someone who didn't belong, probably wondering how he'd gotten past the desk agent. He eased off the chair, walked over to the flat-screen, and turned down the volume. He needed to think. Obviously Gomez was staying close to LAX to catch a plane and if she got on a jet before he could detain her, she might as well be on the other side of the world. Since Bipu Munir had confiscated his passport and specifically ordered him not to tail anyone, calling LAPD was out of the question. It seemed his options were few and lousy.

Frustrated, he wandered over to a large picture window, opened the cordless roller blinds and gazed out at the shimmering panorama of one of the world's busiest airports.

The rainclouds had moved on as a large jet from the Airbus A340 family approached from the northwest off the ocean. Mondragon's eyes were drawn to its sleek fuselage, the color of tarnished silver, as it landed smoothly, taxiing for several minutes before passing under the gaze of the Theme Building, its iconic arches lighting up like some imaginary spaceship. Draining his tonic, he turned away from the window and across the hallway spotted a beige three-shelf housekeeping cart parked beside a large utility closet, a roll of toilet paper peeking out from under the cart's cover. Mondragon studied the cart, looking but not seeing, when an idea popped into his head. *Why not?*

Tossing the empty tonic can into the trash receptacle, he checked the hallway—this late nobody was around—buttoned his sport coat, walked across to the utility closet, and tested the doorknob. It was unlocked. Taking one final look around, he twisted the knob, slipped inside, and flipped on the lights. On his left, hanging from a snap-lock grip near a dustpan, he saw exactly what he needed.

CHAPTER THIRTY-NINE

A shroud of guilt smothered her body.

Stopping at the white leather divan, Angel retrieved her wrinkled jeans and pulled on her turtleneck sweater. Filtered sunlight sifted through the mesh curtains. Anxious, she hunted for her shoes; the airport hotel suite giving off a sterile, soulless vibe that she just wanted to get away from. Lifting up a leg of the divan, she peeked underneath. Nothing.

Damn, why can't I just find my shoes and get out of here.

She looked under the matching sofa, again nothing. In the center of the room, four tubular steel chairs gathered around a glass coffee table holding a half-empty bottle of room service tequila. A raindrop chandelier centered the space with two doors leading off the living room. In the room on the left was the businessman, Phillip, taking a shower. Angel buttoned her jeans, still searching the living room, and out of the corner of her eye spotted her shoes under Phillip's pants.

Gotcha.

"You're leaving now?" Phillip's shrill voice startled her. She hadn't heard him coming out of the bathroom. The stocky businessman stood barefoot near the bedroom door, a thick towel wrapped around his paunchy waist, a patch of curly black hair twisting in a sternal pattern across the center of his breastbone. "I can't believe this. You're leaving? Sneaking off like some hooker? I thought we were going to spend the morning together. I cleared my schedule until noon. We talked about this on the elevator." His voice pitched higher with each sentence, jangled by betrayal.

Angel dropped her eyes. Trying to avoid a scene, she inched past the coffee table and slipped into a gap directly beneath the chandelier that gave a crisp illusion of space and angle. "Listen, I'm sorry," she said, "but I gotta get going. My shift starts in an hour. Maybe we could—"

"*But we talked about this!*" Phillip's face reddened. "We were gonna hang out together, get some breakfast. I trusted you!"

Angel kept gazing at the floor. She was losing control of the situation.

"I didn't say anything about hanging out . . . you heard what you wanted to hear in the elevator. But I've gotta get to work before my shift starts. I'll call you later."

Phillip blinked like he'd been slapped. "Right . . . you'll call me later. Sounds like you're blowing me off." His lower lip quivered. He was decomposing fast. "We were supposed to spend the morning together, get to know one another . . . you promised."

Hearing the word "promised," Angel knew things were definitely getting away from her.

There was a knock on the door across the hallway: "Maintenance, we got a water leak. I need to check your bathroom. Anybody there?" No answer. A key card passed across the lock and the door hinges squeaked loudly. "Hotel maintenance," the voice repeated loudly, "anybody in here?"

Sliding closer to Phillip, Angel touched his forearm. She had to shut this down. "Maybe you're right," she confessed. "I guess I could call in sick. Work can wait." She pulled off her sweater and casually tossed it on the divan.

Relieved, Phillip's shoulders sagged, the stress draining from his body. Embarrassed by his cloying behavior, he made a half-hearted attempt at amends. "I appreciate it, I really do. What do you do for a living? I don't think you ever told me."

That's because you were so busy talking about yourself, thought Angel. "Does it really matter?" she answered. "Or are we just making conversation."

"I guess not," said Phillip, a smarmy grin plastering his doughy face. He let his towel drop. The *asesina* took him by the wrist and pulled him close. "Wait," said Phillip, gently pushing her away. He tiptoed around the glass table and snatched the bottle of tequila. "A little pick-me-up for later."

Angel grabbed both tumblers and brushed a glass against Phillip's hairy chest. "Why wait?"

"I don't suppose there are any more lime wedges?"

Angel found a couple of desiccated slices on a gold-tone service tray, poured them both shots and squeezed what she could out of the wedges into Phillip's drink. She toasted, "*Salud.*" The glasses clinked.

A drink would be fine, she figured, might even calm down this horny pud. The digital clock above the gas fireplace blinked 7:45 a.m. She had plenty of time to get to the terminal. Phillip touched his tumbler to her cheek. "You're magnificent," he whispered, using an index finger to trace the square bandage covering a tattoo on Angel's right triceps. "What happened here—jealous lover?"

"Gunshot wound," she teased, "but it's healing nicely."

The answer excited Phillip. Facing each other, they finished their drinks and he pulled her tight against his body, tenderly kissing her right nipple. He cupped the back of her neck and playfully bit her left earlobe. She felt his lips brush against the side of her head.

"Why don't we get rid of these?" suggested Phillip, slipping a thumb inside the elastic of her panties. But she eased backwards, slowly spun Phillip towards the bedroom, and followed closely behind. As they crossed the door header, she closed the gap, clasped her hands, and slammed them hard between his shoulder blades. Then she hooked his ankles with her foot and sent him sprawling face-first to the carpet. On top of him in an instant, she wrapped her right arm around Phillip's neck, biceps pressing against one side, forearm pushing against the other, and firmly shoved his head forward, squeezing.

Phillip's legs kicked wildly, slamming a foot into the coffee table and sending the tequila bottle smashing into the glass top. Shifting her torso for leverage, Angel kept both arms locked, careful not suffocate him, tightening her hold until she felt his body go limp.

After several seconds, she released him.

Gathering herself, she scrambled over to the divan, ripped out the cord from a bronze floor lamp, and lashed Phillip's hands behind his back. Using his leather belt, she wrapped it around the businessman's ankles and tied them together. Then she snatched a ribbed terry towel from the ice bucket and stuffed it into his mouth. Satisfied, she dragged the listless body into the bathroom and dumped him next to the toilet. Her face felt flushed. She forced out a shaky breath, making herself focus.

She stood in front of a backlit vanity mirror. The woman staring back looked deathly tired. She grabbed an embroidered towel from a polished glass shelf, peeled off her clothes, and turned on the shower. On the counter was Phillip's toiletry bag. She rummaged through it and removed a toothbrush and small tube of toothpaste. She then stepped into the walk-in shower and let the warm water soothe her tense body. She could barely keep her eyes open as she replayed every move in her mind, making certain there was no exposure. By the time she'd toweled off, she had just enough leeway to wipe down the room and get to the airport. She tossed the towel on the floor and again poked through Phillip's toiletries. She used his hairbrush, added a splash of cologne, and pulled on her jeans and sweater. Looking over the suite, she picked up Phillip's khaki slacks that were wadded up on the floor and searched the pockets. Out came a Lexus smart key. From another pocket, a cowhide wallet embellished with tonal spike studs. She opened the wallet and removed $263, an AMEX Black Card, and a bank debit card. She kept the cash and stuffed the cards and wallet between the seat cushions in the divan.

Having made a mental note of everything she had touched, she used the damp bathroom towel to wipe down every fixture and piece of furniture. It would take over twenty minutes, but she was thorough. When she was done she dropped the towel into the shower and turned the tap to full blast. Then, using the TV remote, she found the Bloomberg channel on the wall-mounted plasma Samsung in the bedroom and pressed the volume to its highest level. When Phillip woke up, it would be difficult to hear his muffled cries above the din of the television.

Turning to inspect herself one last time in the mirror, she eyed a few flecks of silver in the temples of her jet-black hair. Someone knocked at the door.

Angel froze, her legs almost liquefying.

The knocking came again, two firm raps vibrating the flimsy door. "Excuse me, maintenance. I apologize, but we have a plumbing problem. Is anybody in?"

CHAPTER FORTY

Bipu Munir was beside himself as he paced his downtown office, snarling into a desk phone, switching back and forth from conference call to field update as it became increasingly clear that Dr. Ernie Girard was in the wind.

"Nothing?" he pleaded into the hands-free speakerphone, its backlit LCD screen showing three other calls waiting.

"Nothing on CCTV, no hits on his credit cards, nothing off the cell phones. It's like he's vanished," answered Sergeant Luther Hurt. "We got a warrant to track both cell phones and traced one to the hospital; the other is at his home. He's not using either one of them."

Munir put his hand behind his neck, massaging it, turning his head from side to side. He squeezed his eyes shut, trying to keep control of himself. It was almost eight o'clock in the morning. He'd been called out of bed three hours earlier when the search for Girard had come up empty. Girard's sidekick, Harold Chase, had spent three hours last night in an interrogation room with Munir's investigators, who had let Chase know in no uncertain terms that a contract was out on him and a killer was running loose. If he didn't cooperate they would release him with no police protection.

No hero, Chase conferred with his lawyer and cut a deal in less than a minute. He'd then spent the next hour unburdening himself like a confessed sinner, detailing the entire scam—the award-splitting between SoCal Medical Mafia attorneys and its doctors; Ralf Millette's role in the entire scheme; the bogus consulting company used to launder the Mafia's money through Mexico; even where all the hard-copy records were stashed—at a self-storage warehouse in Burbank; finally, a very precise description of his and Girard's ongoing efforts to overturn certain care denials appealed before their investigative review committee.

"LAPD got anything?" asked Munir.

"Squatta-natta, sorry."

Munir's head began to throb. He rested his forehead in his hands, eyes pressed into his palms, acid churning away in his gut. Odds were Girard would eventually pop up and get hauled in, but the dull ache in the top of his skull left him with a nagging worry that this asshole surgeon might have the means and wherewithal to run.

"Did you get the Typhoons up?" he asked.

"Both Hexacopters are up and surveilling," responded Hurt. "One is circling near LAX, scanning all the incoming streets, the 405 and 105. The other is over Beverly Hills tracking the canyon roads around Girard's home."

"Who's with Command?"

"My partner, Charlie Rangel. He's babysitting the candy-asses. If any of them spot something, Charlie will call on your private line."

"Okay . . . I guess that about covers it. Keep me apprised."

"Try and relax, he'll turn up. They always do."

"I hope you're right," said Munir, feeling a cold sweat in the small of his back. "We need him to make a mistake."

•　　　•　　　•

But that wasn't going to happen.

Having stopped at a Target in Irvine near John Wayne Airport, Jaspal Ambani had parked his cab under a low-hanging palm tree and was sipping Gatorade while Ernie Girard worked through several international phone calls on the GSM unlocked cell phone and SIM card he had bought at a Best Buy. Girard was bouncing money from Nassau to Singapore to Nevis and finally back to George Town in the Cayman Islands. The transactions would cost him a small fortune in fees, but the money was safe and difficult to trace, and there would be several more transfers to avoid the feds. His stash would be there waiting for him when it was time.

Next, he left Ambani in the cab, walked into the Target, and picked out a long-sleeve Guayabera shirt, a pair of PacSun swim trunks, a three-pack of boxer briefs, two floral short-sleeved shirts, a pair of linen slacks and a nylon duffel bag. A Miami Dolphins baseball cap and a pair of mirrored sunglasses completed the cash purchase, and within twenty minutes he was back in the cab checking his wristwatch. It was two-and-a-half hours until his flight from Orange County to DFW. He had used his upgraded airline status to reserve a round trip ticket that he would pay for in cash with no intention of using the return flight. But more importantly, it was only five minutes until Turtle Rock Savings & Loan, sitting at the opposite side of the parking lot, would open its doors.

Five years earlier, Girard had bought a fifteen-unit apartment complex on Irvine Center Drive, at the time noticing the nondescript Turtle Rock S&L squeezed between a twenty-four-hour tanning salon and the Hui Yin Massage Parlor. Thinking it might be wise to keep a wad within easy reach—but not too close to his home or office—Girard had taken out a ten-inch by ten-inch by twenty-four-inch safe deposit box at Turtle Rock and stuffed his passport, a sleeve of Krugerrands, four rolls of cash ($5,000 per roll), and his first wife's diamond engagement ring—the one she had thrown at him during their divorce proceedings—into the box.

Ambani crunched the last of the corn nuts, then fired up the Corolla's four-cylinder engine, waiting patiently as Girard tore off the tags on his new purchases. Dr. Ernie jammed everything into the duffel except for the Guayabera shirt, the baseball cap, and the mirrored Ray-Bans. Those he put on with his scrub bottoms.

"Time to check in for your flight?" asked Ambani, polishing off the Gatorade.

"Just one more stop and then we'll hit the airport. And Jaspal, thank you again. You've been a great help."

"My pleasure, Doctor. I must say, it's certainly been a learning experience. Would it be possible to drop you a line wherever you get settled?"

"It would, but it might be awhile. Some pretty nasty characters are gonna be out looking for me, so I'll have to keep moving for the next few months. But when I get a chance, I'll text you a cell phone number. It'll probably be a disposable, so use it quickly."

"Sounds like a plan. I'll look forward to it . . . where to next?"

"Just across this lot. Park in front of that gelato shop. I don't want the bank security cameras catching your plate numbers."

Ambani did as instructed, dropping Girard off in front of the Five Star Gelato Shoppe just beyond the range of Turtle Rock's external security cameras. Killing the engine, he watched the doctor enter through the S&L's revolving glass doors just as the clerk was unlocking them.

Since he was first in line, the trip to the security deposit box was brief and painless, and Girard waved off the clerk's offer of a private cubicle. He emptied the contents into his duffel, relocked the box, then walked briskly out of the S&L, tossing the safe deposit key into a Dumpster near the Five Star. "Good to go?" asked Ambani, chuckling at his lingo, thinking he sounded like a wheelman.

"Oh, most definitely good to go," Girard assured him, slipping his passport into the front pocket of his loose-fitting Guayabera shirt before rolling the gold and cash inside his new swim trunks. He brought the wedding ring up to the bright sunshine, inspecting it.

It sparkled brilliantly: a five-carat cushion-cut diamond bought nineteen years ago with his first quarterly bonus check. Humming to himself, he took one final look at the ring, then grabbed Ambani's left hand and pressed it firmly into his palm.

"Keep it for cab fare. Maybe it'll bring you better luck."

Ambani was silent for a moment, a rascally grin coiling across his lips. He tucked the ring into his shirt pocket and shifted the cab into gear. "I think it's time to go fishing, Doctor."

Girard nodded, gazing out the car window, his eyes resting on the retreating parking lot. "I believe that's the smartest thing I've heard all morning."

CHAPTER FORTY-ONE

"Maintenance, anybody in there? Hello? I've got a plumbing leak on the floor. *Hola?*"

The knocking was rapid, staccato. Angel cracked the suite door open, the chain catching.

"Sorry, maintenance. I just need to check your bathroom. It'll only take a few minutes."

"Could you come back later? My husband's asleep," Angel lied. "Maybe an hour or so." She heard the door close, but the inside lock didn't catch for some reason. "I said come back in an—"

But Blas Mondragon was moving fast.

He rammed his shoulder into the doorframe, snapping the safety chain and drilling his suspect with a flying tackle that sent her staggering across the coffee table towards the divan.

Stunned, Maria Gomez, aka Angel, immediately regained her senses and rolled to her left, centering her weight on the balls of her feet before firing an open palm at Mondragon's Adam's apple.

Barely sidestepping the blow, Mondragon lunged straight at the woman, but a crisp left jab hammered his ribs. He gasped and dropped to both knees, nauseated from the blow. In the back of his mind he knew this was his only chance, so he rolled onto his side, scissor kicking his legs, trying to hook Angel's feet. But he was out of shape, out of practice, and out of strength. The woman was younger and more athletic and easily kicked away his feet. But Blas was blessed with a feral toughness born of years on the streets, and quickly regained his feet, throwing a looping roundhouse that glanced off Angel's right ear. He tried to follow it with an upward knee to her stomach, but the agile woman was simply better in tight.

Striking back with a close-fisted blow, she caught Mondragon square on the chin, blurring his vision. She then pounced on him like an animal, hitting him with a two-handed pincer chop to the temples, dropping him a second time to his knees. Blood pounded in his ears. But before he could move, she slipped nimbly behind him and grasped his head in a vice-like half nelson, sliding it lower into a sleeper hold, tightening her grip. Mondragon reached back with both hands, flailing wildly, trying to grab a fistful of hair.

But gradually, listlessly, he began to lose consciousness.

Fading slowly, he heard a shower running and the muffled cries of someone in the bathroom. A tiny tic trembled at the edges of his mouth as he tried to drag air into his lungs, his chest convulsing, eyelids growing heavy. Squeezing them tight, he conjured up images of his grandmother. He heard himself produce a strangled, gurgling noise in the back of his throat, the sort of noise one makes when one is suffocating.

Then came darkness.

•   •   •

"Shit," Angel muttered, releasing her grip. She listened for stray noises in the hallway, then leaned against the divan, breathing heavily, her awareness oscillating in time with her respiration. The shower was still running, Phillip sobbing through his gag. She stared at her attacker, recognizing him from the lounge and elevator. Tough old bastard, she thought, gaining her feet. She glanced embarrassingly around the suite.

The room looked like a tornado had hit it; the wiry stranger had fought like a badger. She ran a hand down her neck, feeling a deep bruise stretching across her trapezius muscle. Her entire chest ached from being slammed by his shoulder tackle. She looked at her hands. They were shaking from adrenaline. She calmed the spasms and let her head loll backwards, but her stomach was cramping, panic beginning to flare in her mind. There was no time to clean up the mess. Her flight to Puerto Vallarta was set to leave in two hours. She had to get moving.

She brushed her hair and adjusted the turtleneck sweater. For an instant, she thought of killing both men, but that would only trigger a manhunt and certainly an alert at LAX.

Better to let hotel personnel find them. They could spend the morning listening to Phillip whine about getting robbed by a woman he'd picked him up in the hotel lounge. But it wouldn't take much to connect her to him, and she was certain the hotel lobby had security cameras. Still, it would take hours to sort it all out and by then she would be in Vallarta.

She finished straightening herself and inspected her face one last time in the mirror. She made sure her passport was tucked into the back pocket of her jeans, then in pain shuffled over to the bar sink and drank water from the spigot. Taking one last look around, she sucked in a deep breath, smoothed her clothes, whispering, "Now or never," and opened the suite door.

Hallway light streamed in as the pleasant smell of fresh pastries wafted from the continental breakfast being served in the VIP lounge. Voices began to filter from the elevators, accompanied by a surge of television noise. The door next to her opened and a tired looking guest retrieved his *Wall Street Journal*. Angel's stomach calmed. All around her an ordinary day had started. She took another deep breath, then confidently stepped into the hallway and closed the door behind her. She slipped a Do Not Disturb sign over the door handle, stole a newspaper from across the hallway, and stuffed it into the splintered jamb to hide the damage.

She would have about as long as it took for the real housekeeping staff to knock on her door. But that would be long enough. It was time to go home.

EPILOGUE

At dusk, Dr. Ernie Girard kicked off his sandals and let his toes dangle in the surf. The tide was rising, the ripples tickling his feet. Even after a year on the water he never got tired of the sound of the ocean: the gentle break of the waves, his new fifty-six-foot motoryacht bobbing sedately in its slip. He had waited until late afternoon to visit the island's only branch of EuroCredit, catching a helpful manager who had walked him through his transactions just before the staff began to shut down their computers.

That being done, he had returned to the marina to celebrate.

Loud, boisterous voices echoed along the water's edge. Girard turned to see a herd of locals from a nearby condominium complex making their daily pilgrimage to the pier to pay homage to the island's picturesque sunset. The late afternoon winds had calmed and the boardwalk was filled with foot traffic. Long queues at the outdoor bars stretched around the patios as tourists in lurid shorts and cutoff T-shirts enjoyed happy hour. Ninety minutes earlier, Girard's money had been transferred into six different banks, bouncing from a branch in Zürich to numbered accounts in Panama, the Caymans, Dominica, Costa Rica, Nevis, and the Bahamas. All hard to trace, but easy to get to. It had been the last piece of a very elaborate puzzle, and now it was just a matter of sailing to each to collect his money.

Something he had plenty of time for.

His only other duty for the day had been to secure a FedEx envelope and pay for a three-day delivery to the States. A polite desk clerk in the lobby of the

Colonial had been more than accommodating; the envelope contained a certified check on the balance of what was left in an account for a limited liability corporation he'd hidden from his second wife at a small credit union in Malibu. Two days earlier it had taken several phone calls and three different confirmations, but he'd finally managed to get the funds transferred from California to the EuroCredit branch from which the certified check was drawn.

He looked out over the vast, seemingly endless horizon. The distant waters speckled in a kaleidoscope of colors—burnt orange, sienna, ultramarine. The striking sunset wasn't letting anybody down and as the waves broke below him, Girard's eyes skimmed the blue-gray surf, a contented smile working its way across his lips. He was thinking about the LLC money and where it was headed, and how it would be put to much better use than his ex-wife's latest casita remodel. He gently kicked the seawater circling his toes.

The thought made him happy.

•   •   •

Angel pressed Send on her encrypted laptop and gently pushed back from her desk.

Standing, she stretched her arms above her head and turned to the kitchen. Cheché was watching her every move and started towards the pantry behind her. Duque climbed down from the windowsill and followed. It was almost midnight and the neighborhood was quiet. A full moon reflected off a gigantic dome, painted with dazzling mosaics of the sun, directly across the street. Listening out an open window, she heard voices that grew softly louder. Below her, to her right, she heard whispers—two lovers frolicking on their balcony, their muted sighs punctuated by moans of pleasure. Knowing she shouldn't, Angel eavesdropped, taking in as much as possible before quietly shutting the window, both cats rubbing against her ankles.

She stood silent for a moment, staring at the flickering lights of Juárez, envious of the lovers. The cartel had forgiven her for returning home without permission, more out of necessity than anything. Professionals with her skills were hard to come by since so many of the *sicarios* had been killed or imprisoned. Plus, her reputation had skyrocketed since the Ramirez hit, so it was easier to forgive and forget and promote her to *Director de Seguridad*, a new job that meant a bump in pay, along with a guarded villa in one of the new gated *fraccionamientos* north of

Chihuahua City and a handsome updated townhome in the Cuauhtémoc neighborhood in Mexico City. But despite her new-found largesse, Angel had chosen to live in her small condo near the Campestre with Duque and Cheché, relying on complete anonymity for security. And for the past year it had worked. But tonight, staring out at the lights, somehow it all felt empty, lonely.

Shaking herself, she decided that early tomorrow morning she would cross into El Paso and make the drive to Mesilla near Las Cruces. She would spend the morning at the plaza—she loved its shops and galleries—and maybe even stop for a bowl of menudo. If there was time, she would also pay a visit to the Zuhl Library on the campus of New Mexico State. In the past, she had used a fake NMSU faculty ID to access their computer archives. The *comandante* had several new digital scams he was excited about. Angel could to do some online research.

She would also call her mother. It had been a while. There was a bench outside the library near a sculpture, the grounds encased in high desert flora, the area quiet, secure. She was surprised at how much she missed her mother. She had nobody to talk to, to share her life with.

Cheché purred again.

Angel leaned down and stroked the top of her head. She arched her back as Angel turned the kitchen lights off. Duque joined them, wide-eyed. She paused to admire the stars twinkling in the vast darkness, trying to imagine what a different life would be like, one with a normal family, a normal job.

But Angel knew that wasn't going to happen. This was the life she had made for herself. It would always be just the three of them.

That part would never change.

•   •   •

The day after Angel made these plans, Blas Mondragon passed a rack of student discount booklets on Mesquite Street and lifted the lid, snatching one. He thumbed through the pages, searching for a reasonable rental apartment, preferably something cheap and without a rowdy undergrad for a roommate. Blas had nine months left on his curriculum, and what was left of his savings was starting to evaporate.

Having returned to his alma mater, New Mexico State University (once an Aggie, always an Aggie), he was studying for a Master of Criminal Justice degree, and the meager stipend he earned from his teaching assistantship barely covered his monthly expenses. What he badly needed was a new place to live, but passing Lenny's, a vanilla chai latte called to him, so he pushed through the front doors of the roasting house and ordered, scoring an empty table outside.

The early afternoon sunshine felt warm and cozy and he pulled the Sunday edition of the *Las Cruces Sun-News* from his backpack and skimmed its headlines. His eyes were immediately drawn to a story at the bottom of the front page describing a tourist getting mugged in a motel room off Interstate 25 in Doña Ana. Leaning back in his chair, a stillborn grin on his lips, he sipped his latte, and after a few seconds the memories came flooding back.

It was thirteen months ago: he'd been barely conscious in a hotel suite near LAX, a bulky, slightly-crazed businessman screaming at the top of his lungs at a hotel security guard. He was claiming Mondragon had stolen his cash and credit cards. The unarmed guard had immediately radioed LAPD, who fortunately took their time getting there, giving the flaky businessman—whose name was Phillip— the opportunity to regain his composure and realize that Mondragon wasn't in tandem with the wayward lover who'd robbed him. She had been a trained cartel assassin, and the pissed-off Phillip had no idea how lucky he really was.

When the cops finally arrived, they searched Mondragon and finding he had no wallet, cash, or credit cards, had radioed a Lyft to drive him back to his motel in Brentwood.

Bipu Munir had called within the hour, his irate voice rising so loudly that Mondragon could hear him a few feet away from his cell phone. Mondragon's visit to the States was officially over. On the ICE flight back to El Paso and in the converted school bus ride across the border into Anapra, he'd had plenty of time to think, to take stock of his life. Even with the new president making all the right noises from Los Pinos, honest police work would never be more than a dangerous calling. With border relations between the two countries starting to improve, an acquaintance at the DEA had told him that the FBI was looking for bilingual consultants with practical knowledge of Mexican law enforcement.

He suggested Mondragon consider a new career in border criminology.

Mondragon bit.

Receiving admission to the Masters program at New Mexico State, he was pleased to discover that the rigors of academic life suited him perfectly: the collegial atmosphere, the daily challenging of his mind, everything but the Spartan existence. He flipped through the Sports Section, got up to get a refill, and abruptly froze in his tracks.

It couldn't be.

Mondragon stared blankly at the attractive woman sitting at a table inside Lenny 's and felt his throat constrict, the thud of uneasy recognition belting hard against his chest. The *asesina* hadn't changed much during the past year. The same taut physique still obvious under her short-sleeved chambray shirt and stretch commuter pants, the same easy mannerisms, the same habit of scanning the room every few minutes. And she seemed to meld easily into the college milieu. Quietly nursing her espresso, reading her *New York Times*, so unremarkable it caused Mondragon to flinch. Two peas in a pod, he mused. Two professionals blending into their surroundings like chameleons, pretenders who didn't warrant a second look.

Then something unusual happened.

Nothing.

Blas Mondragon did absolutely nothing.

No panic, no sense of guilt, no desire to rush in and fix the situation. It wasn't his problem anymore. She had bested him; he'd changed careers. Good riddance.

He drained his chai, tossed a dollar into the plastic tip bucket, and stuffed his newspaper in the outer pocket of his backpack.

Exiting the roastery, thankful for his new life—one without *narcotraficantes*, corrupt cops, and blasé politicians—he felt a slight spring in his step as he floated along the sidewalk, a spread of salmon-colored bougainvillea cresting along a stucco wall to his left, a newly-planted Eldarica pine guarding the entrance to the campus on his right. His mind wandered to his late grandmother. *She would be proud of me,* he told himself, *of that I'm certain.*

But she would also want him to find a cheaper apartment.

•   •   •

"GavinAid Lives" was the headline splashed across the front page of the *San Francisco Chronicle*. After thirteen months, a reorganized *Golden State Plus* had finally begun to repay its contracted hospitals, physicians, and other caregivers, albeit at rates that were far below what they used to receive for their Medicare and Medicaid patients. But after a year of crippling cash flows, none of the providers were complaining.

True to form, the Trump administration had refused to consider a federal bailout, the president tweeting "California's LIBERAL granola-eating medicos won't get a dime! NO TARP for greedy hospitals and doctors. Time to SECEDE!!" The new incoming administration was equally hand-tied, having run on the promise to only review GavinAid and make recommendations to Congress. So it was up to California's congressional delegation, led by Speaker Nancy Pelosi and with the help of Governor Gavin Newsom, to bring immense pressure on the U.S. banking industry to provide low-interest bridge loans to the state's hospitals, doctors, and nursing homes so they could stay afloat.

And it had worked.

The year also bought enough time for "Gavin's Angels" to squeeze out any excessive use of medical services and for the hiring of hundreds of billing specialists to troubleshoot *Golden State Plus's* inept office practices. Eventually it all began to work, but the debacle was not without its costs. While the rest of the nation watched California's medical communities struggle—covered ad nauseam by the television networks, cable pundits, and social media bloggers—any federal or state plan championing the implementation of a single-payer system was shuffled to the political backburner. In fact, the industry went in the exact opposite direction. Corporate consolidations reached new, dangerous levels of "too big to fail" and part of that merger mania swallowed up Deutsche Ärzte International, DAI.

After acquiring Hurston Neurological Institute, Luca Manser bundled the practice with three of his rehab hospitals and sold the tranche to Regents Expanded Care based in Las Vegas. Four months later, Regents was bought out by Tertiary Care Hospitals of America, TCHA, a national for-profit chain headquartered in Nashville. After absorbing Regents, TCHA decided it wanted to expand into the European market and with Stephanie Simpson shepherding negotiations, DAI agreed to be acquired by TCHA for $2.6 billion with Dieter Eberstein being named CFO of the new parent corporation.

But for Luca Manser, it was time to call it a career.

Taking his $974 million payout, he retired to a leafy, gated community in the Gellért Hill neighborhood overlooking Budapest, assuming a staff role as chief moneyman and lead ideologue to Viktor Orbán, the nationalist Prime Minister of Hungary. But Manser lasted only five months in his new position, collapsing and dying from a coronary embolism he incurred during a skinhead brawl at a neo-Nazi celebration in Munich.

As for Governor Newsom, he finished his first term with his head held high. California once again led the nation in job growth, but the single-payer calamity was all people could talk about and his once promising political career was permanently derailed. But making the most of his situation, he decided to take his newfound knowledge of healthcare administration and become the president and chief executive officer for the largest hospital and insurance company in the world: Amazon Blue Cross/Blue Shield.

•   •   •

It was almost noon when Esther Robinson thanked the FedEx delivery woman and closed the door to her apartment. It wasn't often she received an overnight package, and this one had an originating address from a country she didn't recognize.

She split the seal on the FedEx, folded it open, and shook out a fine white linen envelope addressed to her grandson Marcus. Scribbled across the large square flap was a message: "Make sure he uses it for college."

Esther's fingers trembled as she carefully opened the envelope and stared at a certified check for $187,063 made out to Marcus Allen Robinson. She took a half-step backwards, catching herself on the arm of the sofa, her eyes frozen on the check. Her breath went tight before she could relax enough to let it out slowly, a huge smile widening across her face.

"Marcus, get in here!" she yelled towards the kitchen. "Grandma has something special to show you."

NOTE FROM THE PUBLISHER

Word-of-mouth is crucial for any author to succeed. If you enjoyed *Asesina*, please leave a review online—anywhere you are able. Even if it's just a sentence or two. It would make all the difference and would be very much appreciated.

Thanks!
Black Rose Writing

ABOUT THE AUTHOR

Craig Keffeler is the author of *Asesina* and a former healthcare executive with more than thirty years of experience. He is currently working on his next novel. To learn more visit him at craigkeffeler.com.

Thank you so much for reading one of our **Thrillers**.

If you enjoyed our book, please check out our recommended for your next great read!

The Tracker by John Hunt

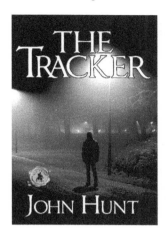

"A dark thriller that draws the reader in." –*Morning Bulletin*

"I never want to hear mention of bolt-cutters, a live rat and a bucket in the same sentence again. EVER." –*Ginger Nuts of Horror*

View other Black Rose Writing titles at www.blackrosewriting.com/books and use promo code **PRINT** to receive a **20% discount** when purchasing.

CPSIA information can be obtained
at www.ICGtesting.com
Printed in the USA
FSHW010613150220

9 781684 334841